Joan Jonker was born and bred in Liverpool. She is a tireless campaigner for the charity-run organisation Victims of Violence and she lives in Southport with her son. She has two sons and two grandsons.

Also by Joan Jonker

When One Door Closes
Man Of The House
Home Is Where The Heart Is
Stay In Your Own Back Yard
Last Tram To Lime Street
Sweet Rosie O'Grady
The Pride Of Polly Perkins
Sadie Was A Lady

Walking My
Baby Back Home

Joan Jonker

HEADLINE

First published in 1998
by HEADLINE BOOK PUBLISHING

Firt published in paperback in 1998
by HEADLINE BOOK PUBLISHING

10 9 8 7 6 5 4 3 2 1

ISBN 0 7472 5853 8

Typeset by CBS, Felixstowe, Suffolk

Printed and bound in Great Britain by
Clays Ltd, St Ives plc

HEADLINE BOOK PUBLISHING
A division of Hodder Headline PLC
338 Euston Road
London NW1 3BH

My gratitude to Lorna and Bunny,
who have never faltered in their support
and loyalty to Victims of Violence.
Without their commitment the charity would
not have survived its twenty-two years.

A friendly greeting from Joan

Let me introduce you to Dot Baker, and her two children, Katy and Colin. Stubborn as a mule is Dot, but full of warmth and humour. And meet her friends and neighbours, who will fill your hearts with laughter. An accident brings a stranger into their lives. John Kershaw is a well-to-do man who wears expensive tailored suits and talks with a plum in his mouth. As Dot says, 'Even his ruddy poker is posh!' These characters have become my friends, I hope they become yours. Except for the baddies, of course, but they'll get their comeuppance . . .

Chapter One

Dot Baker shivered as she hurried down Edith Road, her thin coat no protection from the bitterly cold wind. She'd been late getting out of work and was worried because she wouldn't be home for the kids coming in from school. No fire lit for them to warm themselves in front of, no smell of dinner cooking on the stove. Still, it wasn't often she was asked to work late so they wouldn't mind just this once. And it meant a few extra coppers in her wage packet next week which would go towards having Colin's shoes soled.

As soon as she turned the key in the lock, Dot could hear her son and daughter talking, and when she stepped into the tiny hall she could hear the crackle of wood. She hoped it was Katy lighting the fire because she was very sensible for a thirteen-year-old, but eleven-year-old Colin was different. A real boy, who would do anything his mates dared him to. He had no sense of danger and she wouldn't trust him with a box of matches.

'Ye're late tonight, Mam.' Katy was kneeling in front of the hearth and she turned her head to smile at her mother. She was holding a poker through the bars of the grate, lifting the sticks of firewood to let the draught in to fan the flames. 'I'd have started the dinner but I didn't know what we were havin'.'

'I don't know meself what we're having, sunshine. I wasn't expectin' to work late or I'd have peeled the spuds last night.'

Colin sidled up to her. 'Can we have chips from the chippy, Mam?'

Dot slipped her coat off and threw it on the couch. 'You and yer flamin' chippy! We can't afford to be forkin' out to buy chips, we're not made of money.'

'Ah, go on, Mam, just this once,' he coaxed. 'Three

1

pennyworth of chip and scallops between the three of us.'

Dot's husband had died ten years ago, in 1924, of pneumonia – a young man of twenty-eight. They'd had four blissfully happy years together in their little house in the Orrel area of Liverpool before fate stepped in and took him from her. She still missed him so much, and every time she looked at her son it was like a knife turning in her heart. He was the image of the father he couldn't even remember – the same jet-black hair, hazel eyes and lopsided grin, even the way he held his head and walked with a slight swagger. All constant reminders and the reason she found it hard to refuse Colin anything. 'Oh, all right, just this once,' she conceded.

'Yer shouldn't ask when yer know me mam's struggling as it is,' Katy said, hands flat on the floor to push herself up. 'It's cheaper to make a pan of chips than go to the chippy.'

Colin grinned. 'I'm glad you're not me mam, we'd never get anythin'.'

'I wouldn't be so soft with yer, that's a dead cert.'

Dot sighed. 'That's enough, I'm too tired and hungry to listen to you two squabbling.' She reached for her coat and took a purse from the pocket. 'Here's a threepenny bit, son. Run all the way an' I'll have a pot of tea brewed by the time yer get back.'

When the door closed on him, Katy shook her head. 'Ye're spoiling him, Mam. He's got to learn that he can't have everythin' he wants.'

'I know, sunshine, but I feel sorry for him. All the other kids in the street have dads that can take them to the park for a game of football, buy them comics and give them pocket money for the Saturday matinée. Colin's missing all those things.'

'He's not the only one suffering, Mam! I can't have anything I want, and look at yerself – out working at the British Enka every day except Sunday, and then yer've the housework to do. Our Colin should be made to pull his weight. He's eleven years old, not a baby.'

'He's not a bad lad, Katy, don't be hard on him. At least he doesn't bring trouble to the door like some lads do.'

'I know he's not a bad lad, Mam, I love the bones of him.

But he's got to learn to grow up – you can't carry him for ever.'

'Let's leave it for now, sunshine, I'm too tired to argue. I'll stick the kettle on an' butter some bread for when he gets back.'

'I'll see to that, Mam, you sit down and rest yer legs. The fire's caught now, so take yer shoes off and warm yer feet.' Katy picked up her mother's coat and hung it on a hook behind the door. 'We'll eat the chips out of the newspaper, eh? They always taste nicer.'

Dot smiled at her daughter. What she'd do without her she didn't know. Katy could do the housework as well as herself, and the washing and ironing. And when it came to shopping she could spot a bargain as quick as someone twice her age. The local shopkeepers knew better than to try and fob Katy Baker off with a rotten cabbage or a stale loaf. 'Ye're a good girl, sunshine. I'd be lost without yer, I really would.'

Katy giggled. She was a pretty girl, very like her mother. They were both slim, had the same thick auburn hair, turned-up noses and perfect white teeth. But while Dot's eyes were hazel, her daughter's were a vivid blue. 'Flattery will get yer nowhere, Mam, except for a cup of tea and a buttie. Yer'll have to settle for that.'

She had reached the door of the tiny kitchen when they heard shouting coming through the wall of the house next door. It was a man's voice, loud and angry. 'He's at it again, Mam. Why is he always shouting at her?'

'He's just a bad 'un, Katy, a real bully. How Mary ever came to marry him I'll never know. She's just the opposite, quiet and pleasant.'

'They haven't been married long, have they?'

'They got married just before they moved here, four years ago. Mary's only twenty-six now, and the queer feller's twenty-eight. He looks older because he spends every night in the pub knockin' the beer back. Yer can tell he's a boozer by the colour of his face and the beer belly he's got hangin' over his trousers.' Dot kicked off her shoes and wiggled her toes in front of the fire. 'That's probably what he's shoutin' for now. He's after money for the pub and she's got none.'

3

Katy filled the kettle and lit the gas ring. 'How many rounds of bread shall I cut?'

'Two rounds each should do. We can always cut more if we need it.'

The roar from next door brought Katy from the kitchen. 'Mam, does he hit Mary?'

Dot gazed into the flames for a moment, wondering whether it was fair to worry her daughter. But she'd be leaving school at Christmas, entering the world of the grown-ups. Perhaps it would be better to prepare her for that world, rather than let her think life was all sunshine and roses. 'Have you ever noticed that sometimes we don't see Mary for days on end?' she said quietly. 'Or that she uses the entry when it's dark to get to the corner shop for her messages? Well, those are the times she's covered in bruises after the bold lad has given her a good hiding.'

Katy looked horrified. 'But that's not fair! There's nothing of Mary – she's as thin as a rake, she couldn't stick up for herself! Why would he want to hurt her?'

'I gave up trying to figure Tom Campbell out a long time ago, my duck. He's got a good wife in Mary, I don't know what more he wants. She keeps the house spotlessly clean and feeds him well, considerin' the little money he gives her. In fact, that's why she's so thin – she starves herself to feed him.'

'Hasn't anybody said anythin' to him, tried to stop him?'

Dot's laugh was hollow. 'Apart from us, and the O'Connors on the other side of them, nobody knows. He's as nice as pie to everyone, butter wouldn't melt in his mouth. He's an angel outside the house and a devil inside. And what makes him tick, only the devil himself knows.' There was a rap on the window and Dot hastily slipped on her shoes. 'That's Colin, don't mention next door in front of him. Yer know what he's like for repeating things, and Mary would die of shame if the whole street knew her business.'

'It's her horrible husband that should die of shame, not Mary,' Katy said as she went to open the door. And as she stood aside to let her brother pass, she muttered under her breath, 'If he was my husband I'd hit him with the poker. I'll

4

never let any man knock me around.'

Colin breezed in, his cheeks whipped to a rosy red by the wind. 'That feller next door's not half givin' the pay-out. He's got a right cob on over something.'

'It doesn't take much to start him off, son, he's a bad-tempered bugger if ever there was one.' Dot took the steaming parcel from him and the smell of chips set her mouth watering. 'You can have yours on a plate if yer like, but me and Katy are eating ours from the paper.'

'Yeah, me too! I asked the man to put plenty of salt and vinegar on an' he did, he put lashings on.' Colin licked his lips. 'Yer can't beat chips from the chippy. They always taste better than the ones made at home.'

The fire was crackling merrily now, making the room look more cosy. 'Push the couch nearer the fire, son, might as well make ourselves comfortable.' Dot set the parcel on the table and after opening the newspaper she tore it into three and shared the chips and scallops out evenly. 'Dig in, kids, while they're still hot.'

'I got the cane in school today.' Colin's voice was matter-of-fact. As well it might be, since getting the cane was nothing unusual.

Dot's hand paused on its way to her mouth. 'What did yer get it for this time?'

'I wasn't the only one – half the class got it.' The lad grinned when he pulled out a chip that was about six inches long. 'Look at the size of this, Mam, it's a whopper.'

'Colin, I asked yer what yer got the cane for. It's nothin' to be proud of, yer know.'

'It wasn't my fault, it was a stupid lesson! Even you couldn't have done it, Mam, or our Katy.' Colin put that bit in for spite. His sister was always in the top three of her class while he had never been higher than sixth from bottom. 'It was a music lesson and Mr Jarvis told us to draw eight lines across a piece of paper. I did that all right, it was easy. Then he told us to put one of those musical notes on each line, and we had to make a tune out of it. I thought he was havin' us on at first, it was that far-fetched. I mean, fancy expectin' us to be able to make a tune! Me mates were all the same, they just sat lookin' at the piece of paper, not a clue what he was on about.' Colin tore at the newspaper to make sure he hadn't missed any chips before screwing it into a ball and throwing it on the fire. 'Then Mr Jarvis came around, rapped us all on the knuckles with a ruler and told us to get stuck in.'

'I don't believe that!' Katy looked at her mother and winked. 'Mr Jarvis wouldn't tell yer to get stuck in.'

'No, he didn't use those words.' The boy's eyes were full of mischief as he sprang to his feet and plucked the poker from the brass companion set. 'This is what he said. "You, boy, don't sit staring into space, get those notes down".' He had his teacher's nasal voice off to a T, and his stance. Even his lips were set in a straight line and his eyelids were blinking fifteen to the dozen, both familiar features of Mr Jarvis.

Dot and Katy were doubled over with laughter. 'If the poor man could see yer now, it would be ten strokes of the cane across yer backside.' Dot wiped her eyes. 'And yer'd deserve every one of them, yer little monkey.'

'Go on, finish the tale,' Katy urged. 'What happened?'

Colin put the poker back on the companion set. 'We had to hum the tune we'd made up.' Once again, his eyes danced with mischief. 'He started off with the clever clogs, you know, like David Conway and Peter Flynn. Yer might know they'd do well – both of them are too clever for their own good. They'd managed to make a tune up and Mr Jarvis was delighted with them. He'd praised them to high heaven, said they were a credit to the class and would make somethin' of themselves when they grew up. They were sittin' there with silly smiles on their gobs and I felt like clouting them one.'

'Don't be going all around the world, son,' Dot said. 'How did you get on?'

'I wouldn't ask if I were you, Mam, 'cos yer won't like it.'

'I'm askin', Colin, so spit it out.'

'I did the notes all right, they're easy. All yer do is draw a line down, put a little egg shape on the bottom and fill it in with black pencil. And I made eight of 'em, like Mr Jarvis said. The only trouble was, I put them all on the same line and when he asked me to hum the tune, I had to hum the same eight notes. He wasn't very happy about that.'

'I can't say I blame him,' his sister giggled. 'It must be like trying to flog a dead horse teaching the likes of you.'

'Oh, yer ain't heard nothing yet, Sis, the fun was only just startin'.' Colin's high, boyish laughter filled the room. 'Yer know Spud Murphy who sits next to me – well, he hadn't got a clue either, so he copied me. And Danny, next to him, copied him. Half the class had done what I did, that's why half the class got the cane.'

'I don't know what I'm laughin' at,' Dot said, wiping her eyes. 'I've got an idiot for a son and I'm sittin' here laughing me ruddy head off.'

'I was goin' to tell yer not to worry, Mam, 'cos it's not catching,' Katy put in, 'but I could be wrong in our Colin's case if half the class have caught it off him.'

'Oh, very funny.' Colin put a thumb in each ear, wiggled his fingers, rolled his eyes and stuck out his tongue. 'If I'm such an idiot, yer wouldn't trust me to put the kettle on for a cuppa, would yer?'

'I'll do it.' Dot rose to her feet and ruffled her son's hair. 'You two have a game of Ludo or Snakes and Ladders, pass the time away before bed.'

'Can I have the oven shelf in me bed, Mam, to warm it up?' Colin wheedled. 'I was freezin' last night, I couldn't get warm. It's all right for you two, yer can snuggle up together.'

'Take it up now, then, and by the time yer go to bed it'll be lovely and warm. But don't forget to wrap that piece of old sheet around it or the bedclothes will be filthy.' Dot rubbed her arms briskly when she walked into the kitchen, it was like ice. It was only October, the bad weather had come early this year. They were in for a long winter.

After Colin had gone to bed, mother and daughter curled up on the couch, their feet tucked under them. They both looked forward to this hour on their own, when the house was still and they could relax and talk about their day in work or at school. The fire was dying down and Katy asked, 'Shall I put a few cobs of coal on, Mam?'

'No, sunshine, we'll have to take it easy with the coal.' Dot didn't hide anything from her daughter, although she sometimes worried she was making her old before her time. But she had to have someone to confide in and Katy was sensible and understanding. 'I was thinking I'd be able to have Colin's shoes repaired with me bit of overtime money, but if the cold weather keeps up I'll have to ask the coalman to drop me an extra bag of coal in, otherwise we'll freeze to death with the draughts in this house.'

'I've only got two more months at school, Mam, then I'll be working. Yer won't be so hard up for money then. I know I won't be earning much, but every little helps, doesn't it?'

'Whatever you bring in will be a godsend, sunshine, believe me. A few extra shillings a week will make all the difference.' Dot gazed around the room which was exactly as it had been when her Ted died. Not a thing had been renewed, not even the wallpaper, because she'd never had the money. Her wages were spoken for before she even got them. Every Saturday she put the rent money away without fail. If they had nothing else they would have a roof over their heads. And coppers for the gas were put on a shelf in the kitchen alongside a two-bob piece to pay for a bag of coal. The little she had left over had to keep them in food and clothes, and both were in short supply. Nearly all her neighbours lived on tick from the corner shop, but although she'd been forced into it on a few occasions, Dot was dead against going into debt. If you couldn't pay one week, you certainly couldn't pay double the next.

'The teacher was talkin' to us today about when we leave school, Mam, an' she asked us where we'd like to work an' if we had any ambitions.'

Dot forgot her troubles to smile at her daughter. 'Oh, aye! Did yer tell her yer had ambitions to become a film star?'

'You can laugh, Mam, but Miss Ferguson certainly didn't think it was funny when Bella Knight told her that.'

'Go 'way! She didn't, did she? I was only kiddin', I honestly didn't think anyone would be daft enough to say that to a teacher.'

'She did.' Katy swung her legs off the couch and stood in front of her mother. 'Imagine I'm Bella Knight and I've got blonde hair in a plait that reaches to me backside. And now Miss Ferguson has asked if we have any ambitions.' Katy straightened her face and pouted her lips before sticking her hand in the air. '"Please Miss, my dad says I'm beautiful enough to be a film star".'

Dot gasped. 'What did the teacher say?'

'It took her a couple of minutes to quieten the class down, as all the girls were in stitches. Then she said, "Humility is a virtue, Bella, vanity is a sin. When you go home, tell your parents what I said. Now, has anyone got a sensible answer for me?".'

'There's somethin' wrong with that girl, there must be! Has she got all her marbles?'

'She's like a big soft baby, Mam.' Katy curled herself up on the couch again. 'Her mam and dad spoil her rotten. She's only got to say she wants something and they get it for her.'

'They're making a rod for their own backs, if yer ask me. The parents must have more money than sense.'

'She's got two older brothers workin', so there's three wages going into the house. Bella gets a new dress practically every week, and they don't come from a stall at Great Homer Street market, either.'

Dot patted her daughter's hand. It grieved her that she couldn't give her children the things other kids had. 'Even if she was dressed like a princess, sunshine, she wouldn't hold a candle to you.'

'Oh, I don't mind, Mam. I'm not jealous of Bella – in fact, I wouldn't change places with her for a big clock. She's nothing but a snob, bragging all the time. It's no wonder she hasn't got one friend; none of the girls like her.'

'And what do you want to do when yer leave school? Any ideas?'

'I've given it plenty of thought, Mam, but it's more a case of what job I can get, never mind what I'd like. I could try Vernon's at Linacre Lane, they take school-leavers on and it's only five minutes' walk. But they work all day Saturday, right through until nine o'clock, and if I got a job there it would mean our Colin being on his own until you got in.'

'It would also mean yer'd never have a Saturday night out, sunshine, and Saturday's the best night for young ones. It's pay-day for everyone, and when yer get yerself a boyfriend he wouldn't be very happy if he couldn't take yer out on the one night he's sure to have a few bob in his pocket.'

Katy blushed. 'It'll be a long time before I get meself a boyfriend.'

'Don't you kid yerself! Yer'll have the boys running after yer, you take my word for it. And, Katy, get as much as yer can out of life while ye're young, sunshine.'

'I'll only be fourteen, Mam! That's too young to be thinkin' of boyfriends.'

There was a catch in Dot's voice when she said, softly, 'I was only fourteen when I met your dad. It was a few years before we started courting seriously, but I knew from the minute I laid eyes on him that he was the one I wanted to spend the rest of me life with.' She closed her eyes and a lone tear trickled down the side of her nose. 'It wasn't to be, but the ten years I knew him were the happiest of my life. Your father was a good man, Katy, and I worshipped the ground he walked on.'

Katy's young face was anxious. 'Don't upset yourself, Mam. You have all those happy years to look back on, which is more than a lot of women have. Look at poor Mary, next door. She won't have many happy memories of her husband, will she?'

'I can tell yer this much, my love – if my Ted were alive he wouldn't sit here listening to a woman being knocked around. He'd be in there like a shot, and it would be the queer feller nursing bruises, not Mary.'

Katy shivered. 'I'm gettin' cold now, Mam. Shall we go to bed and snuggle up?'

'Hang on, I'll put the flat iron on the gas stove for a few minutes. If we stick it at the bottom of the bed while we're getting undressed, it'll be warm for our feet.'

'Mam, ye're going to spoil me, like Bella's mum does.'

Dot put her arms around her daughter and hugged her tight. 'No one could spoil you, Katy Baker, ye're unspoilable.'

Katy rapped on the brass knocker and smiled when her friend's mother answered the door. 'Is your Doreen ready, Mrs Mason?'

'She won't be two ticks, girl, she's just nipped down the

yard to the lavvy.' The Masons lived a few doors up from the Bakers, and Doreen had been Katy's friend since the day they'd started school together. Betty Mason was a big woman, with a huge bosom and stomach, a round, fat, happy face, and a ready smile. 'It's this bleedin' cold weather, Katy. It's got us all runnin' down the yard every few minutes. My feller said this mornin' that it was a toss-up which I had less control over, me mouth or me bladder.' Her bosom and stomach shook as her raucous laugh echoed in the almost deserted street of two-up two-down terraced houses. 'He's a real caution, is my feller. Yer never know what he's goin' to come out with next. A laugh a minute, he is.'

'Mam, can I get past or we'll be late for school.' Doreen squeezed by into the street. She was the same build as Katy, but she had fair hair and blue eyes. And where Katy had a slightly turned-up nose, Doreen's was long and thin. 'Come on, if we don't get a move on we'll miss the bell and that means being kept back tonight to do lines.'

'Give them a good excuse an' they won't keep yer back.' Every ounce of fat on the huge body wobbled with mirth. Betty thought up what she was going to say next. 'Tell the miserable buggers that yer mam went into labour an' yer couldn't leave her.'

'Mam!' Doreen was mortified. 'Come on, Katy, before she comes out with any more of her pearls of wisdom.'

Katy was grinning as she was pulled along by her arm. 'Ta-ra, Mrs Mason, see yer tonight.' She loved Doreen's mam; she was so cuddly and warm, always happy and always ready to do a good turn.

They reached the end of Edith Road and a boy who had been lounging against the wall came towards them. 'Ye're late this morning, I thought I might have missed yer.'

'Yer should have gone on, Billy,' Katy scolded. 'Yer shouldn't have waited for us.'

'Nah, I don't mind waitin' for yer. If we run we'll make the gates before the bell goes.' Billy Harlow lived a few streets away and neither of the girls could remember how, when or why he'd taken to waiting for them so he could walk to school with them. It wasn't that he'd ever been one for playing with

11

girls, he was a real boy. He was the leader of the gang of local boys who liked nothing better than to play footie or marbles, and when he was younger he always had patches on his short grey trousers where he'd torn them climbing trees or sliding down the railway embankment.

The three ran all the way to the school and sighed with relief to find the gates were still open. The girls turned into the playground of the girls' school while Billy ran on to the boys' playground. 'I'll wait for yer tonight,' he called, 'but if you're out first you wait for me.'

'Well, hurry out,' Katy called back, ''cos I've got to get home for our Colin.'

Doreen slipped her arm through Katy's. 'Not long to go now before we won't ever have to worry about being late and missing the bell.'

'No, we'll have other things to worry about, like clocking in at work on time. At least in school they only give yer lines or the cane if ye're late, but in work they stop yer pay.'

'I'm getting excited, are you, Katy? Just think, they'll be giving us a wage packet every week. Me mam said if I buy me own clothes I can have more pocket money, but if I want her to buy them I'm only getting one or two shillings, dependin' on how much wage I get.'

They were walking down the corridor, jostled by other children rushing to be at their desk before the priest arrived for morning prayers. 'I'm goin' to give me mam as much as I can,' Katy said, 'at least until she can straighten herself out. She's been living from hand to mouth for as long as I can remember, and she never buys anythin' for herself. If she had nice clothes, my mam would be really pretty.'

'Come on,' Doreen whispered, rushing ahead. 'Here's Father Kelly and yer know what a tyrant he can be.'

When school was over for the day, Billy was waiting outside for them. He was a well-made lad, with sandy hair and hazel eyes, and he was head and shoulders over other boys his age. Some of his class-mates sniggered and gave him sidelong glances as he stood waiting outside the girls' entrance, but no one dared say anything because Billy Harlow was noted for being able to take care of himself.

'What are you goin' to do when yer leave school, Billy?' Doreen asked. 'Have yer made up yer mind what yer want to be?'

'I'd like to go to sea, but me mam said she'd have me hide first.' His voice was breaking and it moved from a high note to a deep growl. 'She wants me to be a plumber, like me dad, 'cos she said there's always work for plumbers. So me dad's goin' to see if he can get me in as an apprentice.'

Katy chuckled. 'At least yer'll be workin' with water, even if yer can't sail on it.'

'I will go to sea when I'm older, and me mam can't stop me. I want to see somethin' of the world before I settle down an' get married.'

'Huh, you'll be lucky!' Doreen grinned. 'Who'd have you?'

Billy grinned back. 'They say there's a fool born every minute, Dot, so there's bound to be someone daft enough to have me.'

Katy had stopped listening; she was watching the familiar figure ahead of them. It was Mary Campbell, scurrying along with a basket over her arm, her head bent and her eyes on the ground. Mary was ten years younger than her mam, but she looked ten years older in the dowdy black coat that almost reached the ground. 'Billy, has your dad ever hit yer mam?' she asked suddenly.

Billy looked puzzled for a moment, then he let his head drop back and he roared with laughter. 'Katy, yer've seen the size of my mam! Me dad wouldn't stand an earthly with her! He wouldn't want to hit her anyway, 'cos they get on great together, but if he was ever daft enough to try, she'd flatten him with one belt.' The very idea had Billy's imagination running wild. 'In fact, she wouldn't need to give him a clout, she'd just have to blow on him an' he'd be down for the count.'

'That's a funny question to ask, Katy,' Doreen said. 'What brought it on?'

'Nothing really.' Katy shrugged her shoulders. 'It was just that I heard of a woman bein' knocked around by her husband and I wondered if it was a common thing.'

'Not in our house, it's not,' Billy said. 'And it wouldn't be anywhere if I was around. No man should lay a finger on his

13

wife, and I wouldn't stand by and let it happen.'

'In that case I'll marry you, Billy,' Katy chuckled. 'And I'll remind yer of those words every time yer lift yer hand . . . even if it's only to scratch yer head.'

Billy squared his shoulders and threw out his chest. 'Did yer hear that, Doreen? Yer see, I told her there was a fool born every minute.'

'Hey, Billy Harlow!' Katy gave a good impression of being indignant. 'Don't you be callin' me a fool or I'll clock yer one.'

'Oh, ye're not a fool, Katy, not when yer've said yer'll marry me. It proves how sensible yer are and what very good taste in men yer have.'

'Well, I'll have to take me taste with me now, 'cos I've got to go an' see to our Colin. Come on, Doreen, it's all right for you, yer've nowt to worry about.'

'I'll see yer in the mornin', then,' Billy said, 'and I'll walk to school with yer.'

'Yeah, OK, Billy,' the girls chorused. 'Ta-ra for now.'

Chapter Two

'D'yer feel like walking down to Edwards' shop with us, Katy?' Doreen looked up at her friend who had opened the door to her. 'Me mam wants me to get her a quarter of their home-made walnut toffee.'

'We've just finished our tea, I'm helpin' me mam wash the dishes.' Katy held the door open. 'Yer can come in and wait, if yer like.'

'Yeah, OK, as long as it's only a few minutes.' Doreen slipped past her friend and waited until she'd closed the door. 'Me mam said she just fancied some, her mouth was watering at the thought, so I was to run like the clappers.'

Colin looked up from the borrowed comic he was reading. 'My mouth would water at the thought of walnut toffee, too. Except I won't be gettin' any.' He gave Doreen a cheeky wink. 'Mind you, in a couple of weeks I'll be quids in when our kid starts work. She's bound to give me pocket money.'

'Hey, you!' Katy wagged a finger at him. 'I'm not bound to do anything! If yer give a hand around the house and make yerself useful, I might just think about it. So it's up to you, my dear brother. If yer want money then yer've got to earn it.'

Dot popped her head around the door. 'Hello, Doreen, I thought it was your voice. On a message for yer mam, are yer?'

'Only to the sweetshop in Hawthorne Road . . . me mam loves their home-made toffee. I've asked Katy to come with me for company.'

'She'll be glad to get out for a while, won't yer, sunshine? Go on, get yer coat, I'll finish the dishes.'

Katy reached up to take her coat from the hook behind the door. 'Our Colin said he'll dry the dishes for yer, Mam.'

'Yer what? I never said no such thing!'

'Oh, my mistake,' Katy said as she slipped her arms into her coat. 'I could have sworn yer said yer were goin' to help around the house to earn some pocket money.'

Colin threw her a look of disgust as he closed the comic and pushed it down the side of his chair. 'That's blackmail, that is.'

'No, not blackmail, just business. If yer like Mrs Edwards' home-made toffee so much, then earn yerself the money to buy some.' Katy jerked her head towards the door. 'Come on, Doreen, or we'll have yer mam after us.' She turned to look at her brother. 'Life's hard when ye're growing up, Colin, but the sooner yer learn that money doesn't grow on trees, the easier yer'll make it for yerself.'

Dot winked at her son. 'Come on, sunshine, never let it be said yer can't dry dishes.'

Katy was pulling the front door behind her when she heard her brother say, 'Oh, all right, I'll dry the blinkin' dishes, but don't blame me if I break something.'

'You break any of me dishes, son, an' I'll break yer flippin' neck.'

Katy grinned as she banged the door. 'My brother's in for a rude awakening when I start work. He won't know what's hit him coming home to no fire, and no dinner on the go. But he's got to grow up sometime. He's capable enough, it's just that me mam's spoilt him so much he doesn't think he should do anything.'

The streets were deserted; it was too cold to be out of doors if you didn't have to be. Katy shivered as she linked her friend's arm and they moved closer for warmth. 'Only ten days, Doreen, then we'll be out looking for a job. We won't be kids any more, we'll be young ladies.'

'I can't wait. Just think, I can choose me own clothes without havin' to wear what me mam buys for me.'

'I think your mam's got good taste, yer always look nice.'

Doreen pulled a face. 'Nah, I'd rather buy me own.' She pushed open the door of the sweetshop and gave a sigh of pleasure. 'Ooh, it's lovely and warm in here.'

Molly Edwards was behind the counter and she smiled at

the girls. 'Ye're me first customers in ten minutes. We had a mad rush before, with the men calling in on their way home from work for their ciggies and the *Echo*, then it went dead. My feller's in the back having his dinner while he's got the chance, then it's my turn for a break. Anyway, what can I do for yer?'

'Just a quarter of walnut toffee, Mrs Edwards, and me mam said will yer break it up small 'cos although she's got a big mouth, it would have to be as big as the Mersey Tunnel to get some of your pieces of toffee in it.'

Molly gave a hearty laugh. 'I can just imagine your mam saying that. She's got an answer for everything, has Betty Mason.' She reached into the glass display counter and took out a tray of toffee and a small steel hammer. 'I suppose she told yer to make sure I gave her some with walnuts, as well, did she?'

Doreen nodded. 'I wasn't going to say anything about that. One complaint is enough, never mind two.'

'Oh, pay no mind to that, girl, yer mam's bark is worse than her bite.' Molly expertly broke the slab of toffee. 'Don't say I said it, but yer mam is all talk and no action.'

'If I told her that, I'd have to duck quick – she'd flatten me.'

Molly weighed the toffee then put it in a small white paper bag. As she was handing it over the counter to Doreen, she smiled at Katy. 'I was talkin' to yer mam before, when she came in for some matches. She told me yer were leaving school next week.'

'Yeah, isn't it great!' Katy's face beamed. 'In two weeks' time I hope to be working.'

'Any idea what yer want to do?'

'I don't mind, although I don't really fancy factory work. But if that's all I can get then I'll have to grin and bear it. I was goin' to try Vernon's but me mam put me off with the Saturday late nights. I'll try The British Enka or Johnson's Dye Works.'

Molly thanked Doreen as she took the twopence and threw it in the till. Then she glanced back at Katy. 'Have yer thought about shopwork?'

17

'No, nobody's mentioned shopwork.'

'D'yer think yer'd like it?'

'Mmm, I don't really know.' Katy frowned in concentration. 'I like people, so I'd enjoy that side of it. But it would depend upon what sort of a shop it was, I suppose.'

Molly raised her brows. 'What about this one?'

Katy gasped. 'Are yer pulling me leg?' Without waiting for an answer, she went on, 'Yer are, I know yer are.'

'I haven't got the energy to pull anyone's leg, Katy, and that's why we need a junior shop assistant. Me and Mr Edwards are worn out. Don't forget he's got to open at six every morning for the men going to work, they're our best customers. And look at the time now, and we're still open. Me feet are killing me and me backache's chronic.'

Katy could feel her excitement rise. She'd take a job in this shop like a shot. It was nice and clean and so colourful with all the jars of sweets on shelves behind the counter and the glass display of toffee and chocolates. And besides the cigarettes, newspapers and comics, they sold odd things like babies' dummies and Beecham's Powders. 'I'd love to work here, but I don't know whether I'd be any good or not.'

'I wouldn't be asking yer if I thought yer couldn't do it, girl. But we could only pay yer seven and six a week.'

Katy's mouth opened as wide as her eyes. 'But that's as much as I'd get anywhere! In fact, some places only pay six bob to school-leavers.'

'Yes, but anywhere else yer'd have set hours, yer wouldn't here. We wouldn't expect yer to turn up at six in the morning – me and Jim would see to that. But we would want yer to work until seven on some nights. Yer'd get time off for it, we're not looking for slave labour.'

'Ooh, I'd love it, Mrs Edwards, I really would.'

'Well, ask yer mam when yer get home and yer can let me know tomorrow. I can't see her objectin', but better ask anyway.'

Doreen was seething with jealousy. 'I'll take the job, Mrs Edwards, and I don't have to ask me mam because I know she'd say it's up to me.'

Molly would have preferred to have asked Katy when she

was on her own, but she was seldom seen without her friend. And when it came to choosing one of the two, there'd been no competition. Katy had a ready smile, was always pleasant and far more mature for her age than Doreen. Oh, she was a nice enough girl, but inclined to be sullen and pull faces when things didn't go her way. You couldn't have that in a shop, it would lose you customers.

'I've asked Katy now, girl, I can't un-ask her,' she said diplomatically, 'so let's wait and see what her mam has to say about it, eh?'

'I'll call in tomorrow night and let yer know, Mrs Edwards. And thanks, I do appreciate yer asking me.' Katy spoke calmly but she was fuming inside. And as soon as they were out of the shop she turned on her friend. 'You were quick off the mark, weren't yer? I think yer had a flamin' cheek!'

'Well, I'm after a job the same as you.'

'That doesn't give yer the right to try and pinch one off me! If it had been you Mrs Edwards asked, I wouldn't have dreamed of trying to snatch it from under yer nose.'

'Oh no, little Miss Goody Two-Shoes, you never do nothin' wrong, do yer?' Doreen's lips quivered with temper. 'Well, yer can keep yer rotten job, I don't want it.'

'Oh, don't you worry, I *am* keeping it.' The friends were no longer linking arms and their bodies were well apart. This was the first real row they'd ever had and Katy was upset. She didn't want to fall out with Doreen but she certainly wasn't going to give in to her. She needed a job more than her friend did, and if push came to shove she'd fight her for it. Seven and six a week would make all the difference to her mam, especially with Christmas coming the week after she left school.

Not a word was spoken after that until they came to Katy's house. 'I'll give yer a knock in the morning.'

'Please yerself.' Doreen tossed her head and kept on walking. 'I can find me own way to school.'

Katy stood watching her friend's retreating back for a few seconds before sighing and turning to go indoors. Then she heard her name being called and saw the woman from next door but one standing on the step beckoning to her.

'Do yer want me, Mrs O'Connor?'

'Sure I'll not keep yer a minute, me darlin'.'

Katy was impatient to get home and tell her mother about the job, and also about what Doreen had done. But the soft Irish accent was one that she couldn't refuse. It had fascinated her since she was old enough to understand that there was something different about the way the O'Connors spoke. As a toddler she'd found it difficult to make out what they were saying, only knowing that she liked the soft lilt and the smiles that went with it. Maggie and her husband, Paddy, had come to Liverpool fifteen years ago as a newly married couple and had been delighted with the small house in Edith Road. They were good neighbours, didn't bother anybody, were always willing to help.

Katy put a smile on her face and walked back to where Maggie was standing with her arms folded across her thin body. 'Did yer want something, Mrs O'Connor?'

'If yer mammy could spare a few minutes, me darlin', sure I'd be grateful. I'm mindful that she's been workin' all day, and she'll be tired, but I'd not keep her more than a few minutes, so I wouldn't.'

'If it's a message yer want, Mrs O'Connor, I could get it for yer.'

'No, it's not a message, Katy me darlin'. Sure don't I have all the time in the world to get me own shopping in, with me man out working all the hours God sends? No, child, it's just a few words I'd like with yer mammy, that's all.'

'Well, you go in out of the cold, Mrs O'Connor, and I'll tell me mam to give yer a knock on the window.' Katy wondered how long it would take to tell her mother the surprising news. She wanted to do it now, while the excitement was at its height. 'It might be fifteen minutes but she will come.'

'Thank you, Katy, and may the good Lord shower you with His blessings.'

As soon as she got home, Katy passed on the message. 'I wonder what on earth she could want?' Dot grumbled. She was sitting in front of the fire and didn't feel like moving. 'I've just got meself all warm and comfortable.'

'I told her yer wouldn't be there right away, so yer don't

have to jump up. Wait until yer hear my news, Mam, yer won't half get a surprise.'

'I hope it's a pleasant surprise, sunshine, I could certainly do with one. I've been sittin' here trying to work out in me head how we're going to manage over Christmas, and believe me the prospect looks bleak. I've been putting a few coppers away each week in the butcher's and the greengrocer's, so we won't starve. But there's no way I can run to presents.'

'Mam, will yer stop yer worrying and listen to me?' Katy took a deep breath and announced: 'I've got meself a job.'

Dot huffed. Her daughter goes out with a pal for a quarter of toffee and comes back with a job. Some hope! 'I'm in no mood for fun and games, sunshine,' she said firmly.

'Mrs Edwards has asked me to go and work in the shop, Mam,' Katy said excitedly. 'I wouldn't pull yer leg over something like that. She said I was to ask you first, then let her know tomorrow.'

Dot studied her daughter's face for several long seconds before uncurling her legs and leaping from the couch. 'It's true! Oh, you clever girl, it's true!' She held Katy close and rocked her from side to side as she had done when she was a toddler and had fallen over and hurt herself. 'Aren't you lucky? I am so happy for yer, sunshine, and proud of yer as well. Fancy that, now, not left school yet and got a job already.'

'If Doreen had had anything to do with it, I wouldn't have got the job.' Katy slipped from her mother's arms and looked to where her brother was viewing the scene with more than a little interest. 'If you repeat any word of what I'm going to say, Colin, I'll not only never speak to yer again, I'll never, ever give yer any pocket money.'

In the boy's mind he was picturing Edwards' shop with all those sweets and comics. Surely his sister had landed the best job in the whole world. And he certainly wasn't going to be stupid enough to jeopardise his chances of gaining from it. 'Cross my heart and hope to die, Sis, I promise I won't breathe a word.'

Katy told them both of the little episode with Doreen. 'I couldn't believe me ears, Mam, honest. She actually asked Mrs Edwards to give her the job instead of me.'

21

'The hard-faced little madam! I've a good mind to go down there now and tell her mam, the selfish, cheeky so-and-so. And she's supposed to be yer friend! With friends like her, sunshine, yer don't need enemies.'

'No, Mam, just leave it. If Doreen's funny with me in the morning then I won't bother with her no more. But perhaps she was just a bit jealous and she'll have got over it after she's had a night's sleep.'

'Yeah, she's not worth worryin' about.' Dot pulled on her daughter's arm. 'Sit next to me and tell me all about yer new job.'

'I don't know anything, Mam, because she told me to see whether you approved first. And she wouldn't tell me her business in front of Doreen, anyway.' Katy's lips stretched into a wide smile. 'The only thing I know about the job is how much wages I'll be getting. Guess how much, Mam?'

Dot wagged her head from side to side. 'They say shop-workers aren't on good pay, so I'd guess about six bob a week. But with it being on the doorstep yer'd have no fares to pay out and that's a big consideration.'

Katy's heart was so full of pride and satisfaction she thought it would burst. She struck up a pose, nose in the air and hands on hips. And in a haughty voice she said slowly and calmly, 'Six shillings, indeed! I'll have you know that I've been offered seven shillings and sixpence, if you don't mind.'

Dot and her son spoke simultaneously. 'Go 'way!'

Katy nodded, happy with the surprised looks. 'Seven whole shillings and seven whole pennies. Not bad, eh, for a beginner?'

'Not bad? It's bloody marvellous!' Tears came to Dot's eyes. 'Yer've done very well, sunshine, and I'm so proud of yer. Mind you, it's only what yer deserve.'

Crafty Colin had his mind to business. 'I dried the dishes for me mam, Katy, an' I didn't break one. If I do them every night, and I get the messages in, will yer give me tuppence a week pocket money?'

Dot tutted. 'For heaven's sake, son, give the girl a chance, will yer?'

'No, let him be, Mam,' Katy said benevolently. 'We might as well get it sorted out now. If you and me are at work all day, we'll need Colin to pull his weight. If he washes the dishes, makes the beds and tidies around before he goes to school every morning, and gets any shopping we need on his way home, then he deserves to be paid for it. So I'm prepared to give him threepence a week pocket money if he agrees to the terms of his employment.'

Dot grinned at her son who was looking remarkably cheerful. 'If yer add raking the fire out, and setting it ready for one of us to light, I'll give him another threepence.'

Colin was over the moon. For sixpence a week he'd scrub the house from top to bottom. He could buy his favourite comic instead of borrowing it, get a bag of ollies together so he could lick some of the bigger boys, and buy sweets with what was left. 'I agree to the terms of me employment, and can I start me job tomorrow?'

Katy chuckled. He was a crafty article. 'I don't leave school until the end of next week, then I've got to work a week in hand. So yer won't be getting any money for a few weeks. But if yer start learning right away, yer'll be really good at yer job by the time the first pay-day comes along.'

The boy's face fell. 'I might have known there'd be a catch in it. Here was me thinkin' I could buy meself some comics for Christmas.'

'Don't be selfish, Colin,' Katy said sharply when she saw a hurt look cross her mother's face. 'There's others in the house beside you, and none of us will be getting anything. It's worse for me mam, she's got all the worry of finding the money for food. So try thinkin' of someone except yerself for a change.'

'This is the last Christmas we'll be skint, son.' Dot felt heartily sorry for him. He was only a child, really, and all children expected a present off Father Christmas. 'With Katy startin' work, things will look up, you just wait and see.'

'Hey, Mam, don't forget Mrs O'Connor.' Katy rolled her eyes. 'I said fifteen minutes an' it's been longer than that.'

'Yeah, I'd better make an effort, it's not often Maggie asks for anything. It can't be important or she'd have been knocking on me window before now.' Dot went to collect her coat. It wasn't fit weather to go out without one, even if it was only two houses away. 'That was smashing news yer had for me, sunshine. It hasn't half cheered me up.'

'So yer don't mind me working in the shop?'

'Mind? I'm over the ruddy moon! Yer can tell Molly I said that when yer see her. Now I'd better scarper, but I won't be long.'

Maggie opened the door immediately to Dot. 'I'm sorry to bring yer out on a cold night like this, me darlin', but sure if I don't talk to someone I'll go out of me mind, and that's the truth of it. My Paddy said I should steer clear, mind me own business, but I'd not rest easy if I just sat back and did nothing.'

'Is Paddy in?'

'That he is, me darlin'. Isn't himself sitting in front of a roaring fire toasting his feet? Come away in, and see the man for yerself.' Maggie led the way into the living room. 'It's Mrs Baker, Paddy. Would yer not be moving yer feet to let her see the fire?'

While Maggie was small and thin with dark hair and deep blue eyes, her husband was just the opposite. He was about six foot two with muscles that strained the seams of his shirt. His hands were the size of ham shanks, huge and rough from the shovels and picks he used in his work. He had a mop of blond hair, pale blue eyes and a handsome, weatherbeaten face. He pushed his chair back and stood up when he saw Dot. 'Come in, Mrs Baker, it's a pleasure to see yer, so it is.'

Dot was fond of the O'Connors, they were so warm and friendly. She often thought how sad it was they had never had any children because they would make lovely parents. Maggie said it was God's will, but Dot knew it was a constant heartache for them. 'Get back in that chair, Paddy. There's no need to stand on ceremony with me – we've known each other too long.'

Maggie plumped a cushion on the couch. 'Sit yerself down, me darlin', and take the weight off yer feet. I know yer must be cursing me for bringin' yer out when yerself has been working all day, but it's worried sick I am about that poor lass next door.'

'Has he been at it again? I haven't heard anything – not tonight, anyway.'

24

'It was before yer came home from work. I'd been doin' a bit of washing and had the back door open to let some of the steam out, when I heard them. Mary must have gone down the yard to fill the coal bucket and from what I heard, didn't the queer feller himself follow her. He was cursing and swearing at the top of his voice, so he was, ranting and raving like a lunatic. It wasn't that I wanted to listen, but sure it's deaf yer'd have to be not to hear him when he takes off. I was about to close the door so I wouldn't have to listen to the foul language, when I heard a loud smack and a cry of pain from Mary. Then the poor soul must have dropped the coal bucket because there was an almighty crash.'

Dot was tutting and shaking her head in anger. 'One of these days someone will swing for that man.' She turned to Maggie's husband. 'I'm sorry, Paddy, it's an insult to you to call him a man. I was goin' to say he was more like a wild animal, but then I'd be insulting the ruddy animals. At least they look after their own.'

'Sure, I was beside meself, so I was,' Maggie said. 'I felt like goin' around there with me brush and giving the divil a damn good hiding. But the size of me to him, what chance would I have? So I stood behind the door blessing meself and praying to the good Lord to put a stop to the poor woman's agony.'

'What I can't understand is why Mary doesn't tell her family. She's got parents living in Walton, and she's got married brothers. If they knew what was goin' on they'd flay the living daylights out of me laddo. But she won't tell them! When I asked her why, she said she didn't want to worry them. Apparently they didn't want her to marry him in the first place. They warned her he was no good.'

'So that's the reason she doesn't have many visitors.' Paddy nodded as though a query had been answered. 'She did tell me wife once that she came from quite a big family, so she did, and we wondered why they never came to see her.'

'It's one of the mysteries of the world to me,' Maggie said. 'Two young people, only married a few years, sure they should still be acting like sweethearts, and that's the truth of it. I'll not lay any of the blame at Mary's door – she's as quiet and as meek as a lamb. It's himself that's at fault. He must have been born with the divil inside him.'

Dot sighed. 'It's no good approaching him, he'd give yer a go-along sooner than look at yer. All I can do is have a word with Mary – try to get her to see the sense of telling her family so they can sort him out. If she doesn't do somethin' about it, he'll end up killing her one of these days.'

'I'd not like yer to go away thinkin' I'm a coward, Mrs Baker,' Paddy said. 'Sure, I could pick the man up with one hand and break his neck. But as I've told me wife, we're strangers in this country and I'd not like the police coming to me door.'

'I don't think ye're a coward, Paddy, anything but. And I understand how yer feel and agree with yer. That apology for a human being next door – he's not worth getting into trouble for.' Dot gave him a wide smile. 'Now I've got a bone to pick with yer, Paddy O'Connor. Isn't it about time yer called me by me first name? We're all about the same age, but yer make me feel as old as the hills, calling me Mrs Baker all the time.'

'Sure, I'll do that, Dot, and it's meself that'll be honoured.'

Betty Mason opened the door to Katy and her eyes widened in surprise. 'She's gone, girl. She said yer were goin' to be late so she'd go on without yer.'

'OK, Mrs Mason, thanks.'

'Ay, hang on a minute,' Betty said as Katy went to walk away. 'What's goin' on between you two? Our Doreen had a right gob on her last night and it hadn't improved much this morning. She nearly bit me head off when I asked what was wrong, so I left her to get on with it. If she wants to be miserable, that's her look-out.' She leaned against the doorframe and folded her arms, which disappeared beneath the mountainous bosom. 'Have you two had a fallin'-out?'

'Not really.' Katy didn't want to give too much away. 'Last night Mrs Edwards offered me a job in the shop and I think Doreen felt a bit left out. She'll get over it before the day's out, you'll see.'

'I'm glad yer got the job, Katy, it'll help yer mam no end.

Don't take no notice of me daughter. If the silly cow wants to sulk then leave her to it.'

Katy smiled. 'I'll do that, Mrs Mason, but I'll have to run for it now or I'll be late for school. Ta-ra then.'

'Ta-ra, girl, an' I'm real glad for yer,' Betty shouted after her. 'The first thing yer learn when yer start in that shop is how I like me walnut toffee in small pieces, and with plenty of walnuts in, d'ye hear?'

Katy turned and waved. 'I'll measure each piece and count the walnuts.'

When she turned the corner of the street and saw Billy Harlow waiting for her, Katy showed her surprise. 'I didn't expect you, I thought yer'd have gone on with Doreen.'

'Nah, I told her I'd wait for yer.' Billy fell into step beside her. 'She mumbled somethin' about yer being late. I couldn't make out what she was saying so I told her to go on.'

'We had a tiff last night and she's got a cob on.' Katy glanced sideways as they hurried along. She wasn't going to make matters worse between herself and Doreen by telling people what had really happened, but she had to tell him the news that had kept her awake half the night. 'Billy, I've got a job!'

'Go 'way.' His footsteps faltered and he did a little skip to get back into step before asking, 'Where's the job?'

'Edwards', the sweetshop.' They were by the girls' entrance now and as she turned into the gates, Katy said, 'I'll tell yer about it tonight.'

Billy's grin covered his face. 'I'll wait for yer and walk yer home.'

'I won't be walking, Billy, I'll be legging it hell for leather. As soon as I've got the fire lit and given our Colin a buttie to keep him going until me mam comes in, I'll be off down to the shop to get some more details off Mrs Edwards. You know, like when does she want me to start, what me hours will be and do I need an overall. There's stacks of questions running round in me head but I'm that excited I can't think straight.'

'Yer'd better think straight in case Father Kelly picks on yer to answer a question out of the Catechism. Otherwise yer might get kept back to do lines.' Billy saw his teacher standing ready to close the gates. 'I'm off, I'll see yer later.'

Doreen passed her friend in the corridor and looked through her, no sign of recognition on her face. Oh well, thought Katy, if that's the way she wants it, then that's the way she'll get it.

When she got home Katy was met by a very smug-looking Colin. He'd cleaned the grate out and laid the fire ready for lighting. And he'd set the table ready for their dinner. 'Oh, you lovely boy, I could eat yer.' She gave him a hug and a big smile. 'I can see ye're going to be a big help to me and our mam.'

'Just remember when ye're in the money, Sis, that I knew yer when yer had nowt.'

Katy ruffled his hair. 'Will yer be all right for half an hour while I run down to Edwards'? I want to make sure I've got the job otherwise I won't sleep tonight.'

'Ah, ay, but put a match to the fire before yer go, it's flippin' freezing in here.'

'OK, and I'll wait until it's caught, but don't you dare fiddle with it when I'm out.'

Fifteen minutes later, filled with trepidation, Katy pushed open the door of the shop where she hoped she was going to spend her working days. There were quite a few customers in and she stood at the back, not wanting to trouble Mrs Edwards when she was busy. But the shopkeeper flashed her a smile and jerked her head. 'Come round the counter, girl, and get the feel of it.'

Sensing all eyes on her, and shaking with nerves, Katy lifted the hinged part of the counter and passed through before lowering it carefully. She knew several of the customers and returned their smiles. 'Oh, aye, what's all this then, Katy Baker?' This was from Mrs Williams who lived in the same street. 'A blue-eyed favourite, are yer?'

Molly Edwards tutted. 'Ye're a nosy bugger, Rita Williams. But for yer information, I'm hoping Katy is coming to work here when she leaves school next week.'

Katy plucked up the courage to say, 'I am if the offer's still open.'

Molly smiled her pleasure. 'Then yer can start feeling yer

way around, girl. Anyone just wanting an *Echo*, Katy will serve yer.'

Jim Edwards came through from the back room and winked at Katy. 'Welcome aboard, girl. It's a change to see a pretty face behind the counter.'

'Well, you cheeky bugger!' Molly handed over a bag of Dolly Mixtures and held out her hand for a halfpenny. 'Did yer hear that?' Her eyes moved from customer to customer. 'She hasn't even started yet an' he's making a pass at her!'

'I wouldn't entertain havin' a pretty young girl workin' in the shop.' Rita Williams pursed her lips and nodded knowingly. 'Yer'd never know a minute's peace if yer left them alone together. What you need is someone with an ugly mug.'

Molly spluttered, 'Are yer applying for the job, Rita?'

When Katy joined in the laughter that followed, her nerves disappeared completely. She'd love working here, she just knew she would.

'I'll take over now, Molly.' Jim took the jar of sweets from his wife's hands. 'You and Katy sit in the back and sort out yer business in peace.'

'Yer'll have to excuse this place,' Molly said, hastily moving boxes to free a chair for Katy to sit on. 'We've got a lot of extra stock with it being Christmas. There's over a hundred customers in the Christmas Club and next week is goin' to be murder trying to make their orders up.'

'I can come after school every day and give yer a hand,' Katy said eagerly. 'I pick things up easy – it won't take me long to get used to where everything is.'

'Oh, that would be a big help, girl. Me and Jim will be run off our feet in the shop, never mind making orders up.' Molly rested her chin on her hand and studied Katy for a second. 'Was yer mam all right about yer taking the job?'

'She was as pleased as Punch, Mrs Edwards, she really was. And I'm so happy and excited I can't wait to start.'

'Would she let yer come for a few hours after school, and maybe work Saturday for us? We'd pay yer for it, of course.'

Katy's eyes sparkled. 'Oh, yes! Me mam would be glad of the few extra coppers. She has a struggle every week, but I don't have to tell you that, yer've known us long enough.'

'I have a lot of respect for your mam, Katy. She hasn't had an easy time. She's done a good job bringing you and Colin up without a man behind her, and I take me hat off to her.'

'She's the best mother in the world, Mrs Edwards, and I love her to bits.'

'And she adores you and the boy.' Molly had always had a soft spot for this girl. Even though her shoes were down-at-heel and her clothes patched and darned, she always had a smile on her face. 'There's not much to tell you about the shop – yer can only learn that from experience. The hours are forty-eight a week, and we'll work out the times to suit all of us. You don't have to work a week in hand, yer'll be paid every Saturday for the week's work yer've just done.'

This was the best news yet and had Katy sitting ramrod straight. 'I don't have to work a week in hand?'

Molly shook her head. 'No, girl, no week in hand. We're only a small shop and when yer get paid it'll be for work yer've already done. If yer don't work, yer don't get paid, it's as easy as that.'

Katy sighed with pleasure. 'I'm glad I'll have a few bob to give me mam. Even two bob would make such a difference to her.'

'You do the work, girl, and we'll give yer the money. And, Katy, I think we're all goin' to get on like a house on fire.' Molly grinned. 'Just don't run off with my feller, that's all I ask.'

While Katy was being given news that pleased and excited her, Doreen wasn't faring so well. As soon as she'd got in from school her mother had collared her and sat her down at the table. 'Have yer made it up with Katy?'

Doreen's fair hair fanned her face when she shook her head. 'It's not up to me to make it up, she's the one what started it. She told me I had a flaming cheek, and I'm not lettin' her get away with that!'

'I was in the sweetshop today,' Betty's voice was deceptively calm, 'and I mentioned to Molly about Katy getting the job. In a roundabout way, I got the story of what really happened. And I'll tell yer this, if I'd have been Katy I'd have done more

30

than tell yer yer had a flamin' cheek, I'd have clocked yer one. Of all the dirty tricks to pull on a friend, that one takes some beating, believe me.'

'I don't know what all the fuss is about. There was a job goin' and I asked for it! Where's the harm in that?' Doreen's face was defiant. 'Yer want me to get a job, don't yer?'

'Don't you pull that face on me, my girl, or use that tone of voice. Of course I want yer to get a job, but not at the expense of someone who's been yer mate since yer were babies. If you can't see what yer did was a lousy trick, then I'm probably wasting me breath talking to yer, but for me own sake I've got to get it off me chest.' Betty took a deep breath to calm her frustration. 'Over the years, when you've been gettin' new dresses and fancy shoes, Katy has had to make do with cast-offs. But never once has she moaned or complained, because she loves her mam and understands she can't afford the sort of gear you were gettin'. I can't count the number of times I've heard her telling yer how nice yer looked, but never once have I heard you paying her a compliment. Even when she's offered a job with the chance to earn a few bob to buy herself the things you take for granted, ye're not happy for her, are yer? Oh no, yer try and steal it from her! Well, if ye're wondering why Molly offered the job to Katy and not to you, just stand up and take a good look at yerself in the mirror. Ye're my daughter, but ye're selfish through and through. The best thing that's ever happened to yer was having Katy Baker for a friend. She was a good friend to you, but you were never a friend to her. Falling out with her is your loss, not hers.'

Betty pushed the chair back and stood up. She smoothed down the front of her wrap-around pinny as she eyed her daughter. 'Carry on the way yer are, Doreen, and ye're in for a lonely life.'

31

Chapter Three

'Things *are* looking up, aren't they, sunshine?' Dot drained her teacup, careful to keep her lips on the side of the cup that wasn't chipped at the rim. New crockery was way down the list of things they needed, but it would be heaven to have a cup and saucer that matched, still had its handle intact and was minus chips and cracks. 'It seems yer've landed on yer feet with the Edwards. They sound like good employers.'

'They're awful nice, Mam, so friendly and easy to get on with. And fancy them lettin' me serve some customers – not many would do that. I only sold papers, but they let me take the money and put it in the till. I was terrified at first, then I began to enjoy meself. A couple of our neighbours were in and they pulled me leg a bit, but it was all in good fun and we didn't half have a laugh.' Katy passed a slice of bread over to Colin. 'Can you eat this? I'm full up with all the excitement.'

Dot laughed. 'Have yer ever known yer brother to refuse anything that he can put in his mouth? Old seven bellies, that's him.'

'Don't upset him, Mam, for heaven's sake – it's Be Nice to Colin time.' Katy put her arm across her brother's shoulders. 'If I go to the shop after school, will you do the same as yer did today? Set the fire and the table, and run to the shops if necessary?'

Colin narrowed his eyes. 'Will I be on for the threepence yer promised me?'

'I don't know how much I'll be gettin' meself, but I did promise, so yeah, I'll give yer the money. But don't ever come the old soldier, Colin, and say yer didn't do this, that or the other 'cos yer didn't feel well. No work, no pay.'

'He'll keep to his word, won't yer, son?' Dot smiled across

the table. 'He knows which side his bread's buttered on. In a couple of weeks we'll all feel the benefit of the extra money coming in. Life will be much easier.'

'Mam, I've been thinking.' Katy pushed her plate to one side so she could rest her elbows on the table. 'If you've got enough to pay for the food over Christmas, can the few bob I earn be spent on Christmassy things? Just a few streamers and some tinsel to brighten the place up.'

'It's your money, sunshine, so you can do what yer like with it.'

'No, Mam, it's not my money, it's *our* money. All these years you've had to go out to work to keep me and Colin. Now I'll be able to pay my whack towards the housekeeping, and when Colin starts work he can do the same. But just this once, for Christmas, can't we go mad and buy things that are not really needed, but will brighten the house up?'

There was a trace of sadness in Dot's smile. 'Yeah, go on, you go ahead and brighten the place up. We might have empty purses, but our tummies and our hearts will be full and the house will be cheerful . . . what more can we ask for?' She glanced at the clock. 'What time does the queer feller next door go out every night, d'yer know? I want to have a word with Mary and I'm not going when he's in.'

'Around eight o'clock, I think,' Katy said. 'I've never really taken much notice, but it's roughly the same time every night.'

'I'll get these dishes done first, then I can sit and have a warm while I'm waiting. You keep yer eye out for him passing the window, Colin, there's a good boy.'

Katy gave her mother a hand with the dishes, then they pulled the old dolly tub out to put some clothes in to steep overnight. 'I won't be able to do these for yer tomorrow after school, Mam, 'cos I'll be going straight to the shop. But I can show our Colin how to use the dolly peg in the morning, and he can have a go. He won't do it properly, yer can't expect that, but at least he'll get the worst of the dirt out.'

'No, yer need to use plenty of elbow grease when yer use the dolly peg and he wouldn't understand that 'cos he's never had to do it. Yer can't put an old head on young shoulders, sunshine, it wouldn't be fair to try.' Dot picked a dirty shirt off the floor and held it out. 'This has been sewn that many times it won't take much more. The material's so thin now it wouldn't stand a needle and thread.'

'Never mind, Mam. After the holidays yer can buy him a new one.'

At that moment Colin poked his head around the door. 'Mam, he's just gone past.'

'OK, son, I'm just waiting for the pans to boil to fill the tub, then I'll slip next door.'

Dot waited after knocking at the door but there was no sound. She knew Mary was in because the woman never went over the door at night. So when there was no answer to her second knock, either, she lifted the letter box and shouted through, 'Mary, it's Dot. Will yer open the flippin' door before I freeze to death?'

After a few seconds the door slowly opened several inches, just enough for Mary's forehead to be seen. 'What is it, Dot?'

'I wanted to have a word with yer, that's all. It seems ages since you an' me had a really good natter.'

'Could yer make it another time, Dot, I'm busy right now.'

'No, Mary. Now I've made the effort to get off me backside, leave a nice warm fire just to see yer, I'm not comin' back another time.' Dot kept her tone light. 'Yer haven't got a fancy man in there, by any chance, have yer?'

'I don't feel very well, Dot. Make it another night, please.'

Dot put her hand on the door and pushed it open. 'If I have to stand here all night, love, I'm not leaving until I've had a word with yer. So before I turn into a bloody icicle, move aside and let me pass.' She stepped into the hall, giving her neighbour no option but to move back and let her in. 'I hope yer've got a good fire going, Mary. I'm frozen right through to me flippin' marrow. Goose-pimples all over, I am.'

Mary closed the door and shuffled along the hall in a pair of well-worn slippers. 'I've just put a few cobs on the fire, they'll burn up in no time.' Her shoulders drooping, she led the way into the living room. Just inside, she turned, a hand covering the left side of her face. 'I walked into a door in the dark and gave meself a black eye.'

Dot reached over and pulled her hand gently away. 'Oh, my God!' Mary's eye, and the top part of her cheek, was black and blue, and so swollen the whole side of her face was disfigured. 'He did that to you?'

'I told yer, I walked into a door!' There were tears in the other woman's eyes. 'It was me own fault for not lookin' where I was going.'

'Come off it, Mary, I wasn't born yesterday. Yer never got that by walking into a door, I'd stake me life on it.' Dot took hold of her elbow and led her to a chair. 'Sit down, sunshine, and then I can park me carcass as well.' She waited until her neighbour was seated then chose a chair facing her. 'What did he hit yer for this time? And don't try and give me some cock-and-bull story, Mary, 'cos yer make a bloody awful liar.'

Her head bowed, Mary picked nervously at her nails. 'I said somethin' that upset him, but he didn't mean to hit me, it was just in the heat of the moment. He said he was sorry afterwards.'

'Will yer stop making excuses for him and stop ruddy well blaming yerself every time he gives yer a go-along? You are married to one bad-tempered, evil bully, an' it's about time yer put a stop to it.' Dot huffed. 'He was sorry afterwards, ey? Yeah, I'll bet he was. So sorry he went down to the pub to drown his sorrows. I'll tell yer what, Mary, if he'd have done that to me he'd have been sorry all right. I'd have taken the bloody poker to him.'

'I haven't got the energy to fight back, Dot, I'm no match for him. You're right, he is a bad-tempered bully and I rue the day I ever married him. I should have listened to me mam and dad, they could see through him from the first day they met him. But I was too stupid to listen to them, I thought I knew better. Now I've got to live with my mistake for the rest of me life and there's times I wish I was dead.' She burst into racking sobs.

'In the name of God, Mary, that's no way for a young woman of twenty-six to talk. If yer hate yer life so much, then do something to change it! I know ye're no match for him, but yer've got brothers. Ask them to sort him out – at least put the frighteners on him.'

When Mary lifted her head, Dot's heart went out to her. One eye was completely closed with the angry bruises and swelling, and the other was blurred with tears. She'd been such a pretty woman when she'd first come to live in the street, with a nice slim figure, her mousy-coloured hair always well groomed, velvety brown eyes and a ready smile. The woman facing Dot now bore no resemblance to that person. She was painfully thin, her hair was straggly, her clothes dowdy and she had the air of someone who had given up on life. When she spoke her voice was thick with emotion. 'He's taken everything away from me – me self-respect, me confidence and me peace of mind. But I still have some pride, and I'll not ask my family for help. I married Tom against their wishes, I made me own bed and now I must lie on it.'

'So yer carry on being a punch-bag for a man who isn't fit to wipe yer shoes on? Yer've just said yer've still got some pride left, but yer can't have, Mary, because if yer did yer wouldn't stand for what he's doing to yer. While ye're prepared to take it, he'll keep dishing it out, and what sort of a future is that?'

'I'm expecting a baby.' Mary's voice was so low Dot had to strain to catch what she was saying. 'I went to the doctor's yesterday morning and he examined me. For the first time in years, I thought the future looked rosy. I was daft enough to think Tom would be pleased, that having a baby would change him.' Her laugh was bitter. 'How wrong I was. He flew into such a rage he frightened me. He was shouting at the top of his voice, poking me in the chest and his eyes were nearly popping out of his head. It was my fault I was pregnant, I was a stupid bitch and he didn't want no brat in this house.'

Dot was beside herself with anger. 'The more I hear of this man, the more convinced I am that he's not right in the head. He gets you in the family way, blames you for being a stupid bitch, and calls his own unborn baby a brat! He wants putting in a strait-jacket and locking up in an asylum for the insane. D'yer know, there's folk a lot more sane than he is, in the blinkin' mad-house.'

'I was so happy when I came out of the doctor's yesterday, I even walked with a spring in me step. I've always wanted a baby, and I thought it would be the making of Tom, that he'd be proud at the thought of becoming a father. Like the stupid bitch he says I am, I even had visions of him putting his arms around me and kissing me.' Mary fingered a piece of loose thread hanging from the sleeve of her cardi. 'Me happiness was short-lived, he saw to that. Now I'm sorry I'm expectin', 'cos how can I bring a baby into the world when I know what sort of a life it'll have?'

'I give up!' Dot snorted. 'I can't find words bad enough to describe what I think of him. Yer tell him ye're carrying a baby, his own flesh and blood, and he belts yer one! Honest to God, this is one time I wish I was a man. I'd give him the hiding of his life.'

'I knew he was going to hit me, I can always tell, so I picked up the coal bucket and ran into the yard. I thought he might calm down a bit if I left him to think it over, but he followed me and this,' she tenderly fingered her bruised face, 'is what I got for me pains.'

'I'm not goin' to tell yer no lies, Mary, there's no point. I knew what had happened because Maggie O'Connor heard it all. She's not a gossip-monger, as yer well know, but she told me because she was worried about yer. She'd have been a damn sight more worried if she'd known he was belting yer because yer were pregnant.'

The sigh that came from Mary was one of despair. 'I never thought I'd end up like this, never in a million years. When I was young I used to be full of life, out dancing every night and I had my pick of dozens of boys. If only I'd married one of them, how different things would have been. But no, I met Tom Campbell and he swept me off me feet with his sweet-talk and his promises of married bliss. Like a fool I fell for it, and for a few weeks it was bliss. Then, when it was too late, I found out the hard way what he was really like, and why. He told me his father used to beat his mother regularly. Apparently he taught Tom that the only way to keep a woman in her place was to rule her with a rod of iron and to belt her if she ever stepped out of line. And Tom didn't take his mother's side. He looked up to his father, you see – thought he was a real man.' Mary's next sigh came from her heart. 'I think we'd been married about a month when he first hit me, and he's done it regularly ever since.'

'Well, it's got to stop right now,' Dot said, putting her foot down. 'Yer haven't only got yerself to think about, there's an innocent baby growin' inside yer that yer've got to protect. If the queer feller is allowed to keep on belting yer every time he feels like it, yer could end up having a miscarriage and I'm sure yer don't want that.'

'Oh no, I want this baby!' Mary looked horrified. 'It would be someone of me own that I could love and cherish. But you don't know how evil my husband can be. He said he didn't want a brat in this house and believe me, Dot, he's cruel enough to beat me to a pulp if it would get rid of the baby. And nothing I could say or do would stop him.'

'Pack up and go back to yer mam, Mary, that's my advice to yer. Pocket yer pride and go back home, where yer'll be cared for by people who love yer. And the baby would be safe from harm.'

'It wouldn't be as easy as yer make it sound, Dot. Oh, me family would welcome me with open arms and they'd look after me and the baby. But Tom knows where they live and he'd be around there like a shot, banging on the door and shouting his head off. He'd bring shame to me mam's house, and I'll not put her through that.' Mary gazed into the flames as they danced around the glowing coals, spurting and cracking. 'No, I'll have to stay here and make the best of it.'

'I think yer want yer bumps feeling, Mary, and that's being honest. But if that's the way yer want it, there's nowt I can do about it. But I want yer to promise me that if he ever goes to hit yer again, yer'll give a knock on our wall and I'll come in. I can't see him touching yer in front of a neighbour who might tell everyone in the street what sort of a man he is. He wouldn't want his cronies in the pub to know he beats his wife, and her in the family way. He'd have to slink down the street, not swagger the way he does now, and he'd have to find another watering hole.'

'I won't burden you with me troubles, Dot, but I'm glad yer came tonight because I feel better just for talking to yer. I won't let him hurt me baby, I'll promise yer that.'

'Well, if things get out of hand, yer know what to do. If I'm not in, shout for Maggie – she'll come running. Don't for God's sake try and cope on yer own if yer see he's in one of his moods or yer'll end up being sorry.' Dot stretched her arms over her head and yawned. 'I'm all in, it'll be an early night for me. It must be old age creepin' up on me, Mary. I can't stand the pace like I used to.'

'I should think yer would be tired, working every day and the house and kids to see to. Yer've got enough problems of yer own without worrying about me.'

'What are neighbours for, sunshine, if it's not to help one another? And we're not only neighbours, we're mates, aren't we? And yer've got a good mate living on the other side of yer, too. Maggie would be a good friend to yer if yer'd let her. Don't be so bloody stubborn, Mary, yer might be glad of Maggie's help before ye're much older. Neither of yer go out much during the day, so why don't yer invite her in for a cup of tea? It would do yer the world of good to mix with people, buck yer up no end.'

'Look at the state of this place, Dot, it's not fit to invite anyone into. Tommy hasn't any pride in his home, he won't even give me the money so I could paper it.'

'Don't be makin' excuses, Mary, my house is a damn sight worse than this. I can't even remember what the pattern on the wallpaper was, it's faded so much.' Dot stood up and smiled down into the disfigured face. 'Still, I've got me daughter starting work soon and after I've bought some decent clothes for all of us, I'm going to have a bash at decorating the living room. I've never done it before, but there's a first time for everything.'

Mary stood up and followed Dot down the hall. 'Thanks for coming. It's a change to have someone to talk to and get things off me chest.'

Dot stepped into the street and pulled her coat around her. 'I think it's cold enough for snow but I hope I'm wrong. The soles on the only pair of shoes I've got are paper thin – they wouldn't stand up to trudging through snow.' She shivered and put her hands up the sleeves of her coat. 'Yer know where I am if yer want me, now don't forget.'

Miss Clements raised her head from the books she was marking and rapped the end of her pencil on the desk. 'Letty Kennedy and Nita Williams, will you stop talking and get on with your work! If you were as good at stretching your minds as you are at stretching your mouths, perhaps your arithmetic book would be full of ticks instead of crosses. Now get on with it, and if I have to tell you again you'll be kept back in detention.'

Both girls answered, 'Yes, Miss,' and before bending their heads over their books they rolled their eyes at each other and pulled faces. Next week couldn't come quick enough for them. The teacher's eyes lighted on Katy Baker. The girl was deep in concentration as she applied herself to the additions, subtractions and multiplications set out in her book. She was a good pupil, was Katy, diligent, clever, polite and forever pleasant. She'd miss her when she left. 'Katy, would you come to my desk for a moment, please?'

Katy laid her pen down by the inkwell, and full of apprehension made her way to the front of the class. 'Yes, Miss Clements?'

'I believe you have a job to go to, Katy.'

'Yes, Miss, in the sweetshop in Hawthorne Road. I'm very lucky and really looking forward to it.'

'I'm very pleased for you and I know you'll do well. You've been an excellent pupil, Katy, one of the best I've ever had. I bet your mother's proud of you, isn't she?'

'Oh yes, Miss, she's over the moon. With my wages coming in she won't have to scrimp and scrape every week.'

'When do you start?'

'I could start right away, 'cos the shop's very busy with Christmas so near. But with us not breaking up until next Friday, I won't be able to start proper until after the holiday. I'm going every night after school to give Mr and Mrs Edwards a hand, though, and I'm glad about that because it means I'll be able to give me mam a few bob to help her out.'

Miss Clements studied her face for a few seconds before saying, 'You can go back to your desk now, dear.'

It was as the girls were filing back into the classroom after the playtime period was over, that Miss Clements again called Katy to her desk. 'Miss Boswell would like to see you in her office, Katy. Would you go along now, please?'

Her tummy beginning to knot with fear, Katy asked, 'I haven't done anything wrong, have I, Miss?'

'Not at all, dear. There's no need to be afraid. Miss Boswell will explain to you.'

Katy wasn't comforted by the teacher's words as she walked down the now-deserted corridor. The headmistress was a very strict woman whose very glance could send shivers down your spine. Being called to her office wasn't something you looked forward to because it usually meant you were in trouble. But although Katy racked her brains, she couldn't think of anything she'd done that would give rise to this. So it was with mixed feelings that she knocked on the office door.

'Come.'

The tone in which that one word was spoken was enough to set the girl's nerves on edge as she pushed open the door. 'You wanted to see me, Miss Boswell?'

'Ah, Katy Baker. Come in, child.' Miss Boswell looked like a typical headmistress. Her iron-grey hair was combed straight back and plaited in a bun to rest on the nape of her neck. Her clothes were tailored and mannish, and her face, even in repose, looked stern. She peered over the top of her pince-nez glasses to where Katy was hovering just inside the door. 'Come in, my dear, and sit down.'

Katy perched on the edge of the chair facing the headmistress across the desk. She was clasping and unclasping her hands, convinced by now that she was in for a ticking-off. To think she'd gone right through her school life without ever being sent to this office for being naughty, and now here she was, with just one week to go.

Miss Boswell straightened the pile of papers in front of her before pushing them to one side. 'Miss Clements was telling me you had a job to go to, Katy.'

'Yes, Miss Boswell. It's in a sweetshop near where I live.'

'Miss Clements also told me that your future employers would like you to start as soon as possible with their busiest period of the year ahead, is that true?'

Katy's sigh of relief was audible. So she wasn't here for a ticking-off, thank goodness. 'Yes, Miss, but they understand I can't start until I leave school.'

Miss Boswell's features relaxed and a faint smile crossed her face. Miss Clements had told her of the girl's home circumstances, but she wasn't going to embarrass the child by repeating what she'd heard. 'From the day you started school, Katy, you've been an exemplary pupil. If all the girls were as hard-working as you, how much easier the life of a teacher would be. Because you have worked so hard, and because there is little you will gain by staying on the extra week, I have decided that, if you wish, you can finish here tomorrow. I will have your reference ready for you before you leave.'

Katy was stunned. 'Oh, Miss!'

'Would that suit you, Katy?'

The girl screwed up her eyes to stop the tears, but one managed to escape to roll down her cheek. 'Oh yes, Miss. And thank you, Miss.'

Catherine Boswell wasn't as hard-hearted as she made out, but she'd found out long ago that if the children thought you were weak, you lost the battle to control them. But there were times, such as now, when her heart melted. 'I wish you luck in your job, Katy, and your new employers are very fortunate to find someone of your calibre. Now you may go back to your class while I get on writing out these references.'

Katy stood up. There was so much she wanted to say, but knew if the words came, so would the tears. 'Thank you, Miss Boswell.'

The headmistress dismissed her with a smile and a nod of the head. 'Close the door on your way out.'

Billy Harlow had trouble keeping up with Katy that night. She ran as though she had wings on her heels. 'Are yer really leavin' tomorrow?' he panted. 'For sure?'

'Yes for really, and yes for sure.' Katy's smile wouldn't stretch any wider. 'Miss Clements told the class that because I had a job to go to, the Education Officer had agreed to my leaving a week early.'

'What did Doreen have to say? I bet she was dead jealous.'

'Me and Doreen are still not speaking so I don't know what she thinks. I don't care, either, Billy, 'cos she's like a big soft kid.' Katy came to a halt and bent double to take a deep breath. When she straightened up her deep blue eyes were dancing. 'I'm so happy and excited I feel like jumping in the air and shouting out loud.'

'I bet yer mam will get a surprise.'

'I can't wait to tell her.' Katy took to her heels again, eager to get to the shop to pass on her good news. 'I've been workin' it out in me head, and I'll have at least ten bob to give to her before Christmas.' They were passing Billy's house now, but Katy didn't slow down. 'I'll see yer tomorrow, Billy.'

'I might see yer later if me dad wants ciggies.'

Katy heard his voice and waved, but his words didn't sink in. Her head and her heart were so full she thought they'd burst. But when she got to the shop she knew she'd have to keep her news until later because there were quite a few customers in, including two women from her street. And the last thing she wanted was the neighbours knowing before she'd had time to tell her mam. Particularly these two, Rita Williams and Dolly Armstrong; they were the biggest gossips going.

'Come on, girl, get behind the counter and roll yer sleeves up,' Molly grinned. 'This lot don't like being kept waiting, they think I've got a dozen pair of hands.'

Katy threw her coat in the stockroom and then asked the small crowd, 'Who's next?'

'I am,' said Rita Williams.

'No, ye're not,' Dolly Armstrong said with strong emphasis. 'I was here before you.'

'You were not!'

'Oh, yes I bloody-well was!'

'Well, bugger me.' Rita by now was red in the face. 'You lying mare, Dolly Armstrong.'

The other folded her arms and her chin jutted out. 'If I'm a mare, Rita Williams, then you're a lying cow.'

'A cow! A bleedin' cow!' Rita pushed her sleeves up ready for action. 'I'll give yer cow, yer bleedin' mare.'

In the stockroom, Jim Edwards heard the raised voices and dropped the box he was emptying, while Molly left the customer she was serving to move down the counter to where Katy was standing. And as one, the remaining customers backed away from the feuding couple before the battle commenced. Not one person left the shop, mind, they wouldn't miss this bit of excitement for the world.

The two women were squaring up to each other when the shop filled with laughter. All eyes turned to Katy, whose head was thrown back and her rich clear laughter ricocheted from wall to wall. Caught off-balance, Dolly and Rita looked at each other and shrugged their shoulders. 'Can yer tell me what the hell yer find so funny?' Dolly asked. 'I didn't hear no one crack a joke.'

'I think you two are dead funny.' Katy wiped the tears away with the back of her hand. No one was going to be allowed to spoil her day. 'I can't imagine what a horse and a cow are doing in a sweetshop. We stock most things, but not hay.'

It started with a low titter, then grew to full-blown laughter. And it put a stop to Dolly and Rita's fight – after all, how could you have a serious punch-up when everyone was laughing their heads off? And if they didn't join in, people would say they were miserable cows, or mares, or even something worse.

'I'll solve the problem for yer,' Katy said when calm was restored. 'I'll serve both of yer at the same time – how about that?'

'Suits me, girl,' Dolly said. 'How about you, Reet?'

'It's OK by me.' Rita grinned sheepishly at Katy. 'Yer've got more sense than the pair of us put together.'

Katy took great care to make sure Dolly's quarter of wine gums and box of matches were laid on the counter at exactly the same time as Rita's ten Woodbines and the *Echo*. She held out both hands to take the money, went to the till and came back with a halfpenny in one palm and a penny in the other. 'There yer are, yer can't fall out with that service, can yer?' She was grinning widely. 'Mind you, yer deserved it for giving us all a laugh. I'm going to enjoy working here if all the customers are comics, like you two.'

Dolly bent her elbow and said to Rita, 'Stick yer leg in, girl.'

Arm in arm the two women walked towards the door. 'It was funny, wasn't it, Dolly?'

'Yeah, I quite enjoyed it.' They stepped into the street and as Dolly turned to pull the door behind them, those left in the shop heard her say, 'Mind you, I didn't think it was funny at the time, not when yer called me a lying mare.'

'What about you callin' me a cow? I mean . . .' The rest of the words were lost as the door closed on them.

'Oh dear, oh dear, oh dear.' Jim Edwards held his head in his hands as he shook with laughter. 'They'll be at loggerheads before they get halfway up the street.'

'I don't think I've ever seen anything so funny.' Molly sniffed up. 'Yer did well there, Katy, my love. Brilliant, yer were.'

The few customers still in the shop agreed. 'Yer handled that like an old-timer, queen,' said one, while another piped up with, 'Yer took the wind out of their sails, right enough.'

'I wasn't going to let them fight in this shop,' Katy told them. 'If they must fight, let them do it in the street.'

Molly looked at her husband and chuckled. 'You and me must be getting old, love. There'd have been bedlam here, with us flapping, trying to separate them, when all it took was a laugh from a fourteen-year-old. I can hardly credit it. It seems our new assistant will be able to teach us a thing or two.'

Katy beamed. 'Would yer like yer first lesson on Monday?'

'Yer mean Monday week, sweetheart.'

'No, I mean *this* Monday.' Oh, how Katy was savouring these words. 'The headmistress is letting me leave school tomorrow because I've got a job to go to.'

Molly's eyes lit up. She put her arms around the girl and hugged her tight. 'I'm so glad, love, because me and Jim are up to our neck in it. An extra pair of hands will make all the difference. I had a feeling in me bones that you were going to be lucky for us, and I was right.' She looked to her husband. 'I said that, didn't I, Jim?'

'Yes, yer did, love.' It was a long time since a smile had stayed so long on Jim Edwards' face. 'And we're not only

46

getting an extra pair of hands, we're getting a referee to sort out the troublemakers. But perhaps I shouldn't say that, or Katy will be asking for double pay. Better not praise her too highly – she might start getting ideas.'

Chapter Four

Katy went to work on the Saturday morning feeling very grown-up. Even though she was wearing her gymslip under her coat, and knee-length school socks, her head kept telling her she was now a working girl going out to earn a living. The weather was miserable, bitterly cold with a hint of snow in the air, but everything in her little world was bright. Her mother had been delighted she was leaving school and starting work the week before Christmas, and her joyful exclamations were still ringing in Katy's ears. As for Colin – well, what he was going to do with his sixpence a week pocket money was nobody's business.

As she pushed open the shop door and heard the bell tinkle, Katy was thinking that at last the Baker family were going to be able to afford, perhaps not luxuries, but a decent standard of living.

As soon as she got behind the counter, though, there was no time for dreaming of the nice things to come. She was rushed off her feet with what seemed a never-ending stream of customers. Molly was working with her while Jim stayed in the stockroom making up the lists of Christmas orders. Most of the sweet jars had the price on them so Katy didn't have to bother Molly very often to ask for help. She was quick with her hands and nimble on her feet, and she never forgot her mother's advice to keep a smile on her face.

It was one o'clock when Jim came through to say it was time for her dinner-break. 'There's a meat pie out there for yer, love, and I've made a pot of tea. I'll give Molly a hand until yer come back, then she can have a break.'

Katy wasn't sorry to sit down and rest her feet and mind. It was all go behind that counter, but she'd really enjoyed it and told herself she was very lucky to have a job where you could have a laugh and a joke while you worked. And weighing the sweets out was a novelty, although it had taken her a while to gauge how many she should pour on to the scale. She'd given everyone in the shop a laugh when a little girl asked for two ounces of Dolly Mixtures and the fingers on the scale had spun around to half a pound when she'd been too heavy-handed with the jar.

Katy popped the last piece of the meat pie into her mouth and wiped the back of her hand across her mouth. She wouldn't mention the Dolly Mixtures at home, she decided while sipping her tea, at least not in front of Colin. She'd never hear the end of it if he knew, and the whole street would have heard by the next day. She'd wait until they were in bed to tell her mother and they could have a good laugh under the cover of the sheet.

The afternoon was just as busy as the morning, but there were two incidents which had Katy's infectious laugh ringing out. The first was when Doreen's mother came in and Molly went to serve her. Betty had shaken her head with determination. 'It's not that I don't like yer, Molly, but I want to show Katy how I like me walnut toffee.' She delved in her pocket and brought out a tape measure. 'Yer see this, girl? Well, that's an inch that way, and an inch this way. I don't want any pieces bigger than that. And in each piece, I want to see some walnut.'

'You can sod off, Betty Mason,' Molly laughed. 'Ye're not asking for much, are yer?'

Katy could see Betty's mountainous bosom quivering and knew she was having a good laugh inside. But the big woman kept her face straight. 'Listen to me, Molly Edwards, if I go to T.J. Hughes and ask for a yard of material, then it's dead on a yard I'll get. So what's the difference in me coming here and asking for an inch of toffee, six times over?'

Molly was ready for her. 'You win, Betty, I'll just get a pair of scissors and yer can cut yerself six squares of toffee. You know exactly what yer want so it's best all round if yer do it yerself.'

Katy wanted to tell her boss that nobody ever got the better of Betty Mason, but she decided silence would serve her better. She watched the big woman pocket the tape measure before rubbing her chubby hands together, a gloating smile on her face. 'Now ye're talking, girl. Pass me that bloody tray of toffee and the hammer.'

Molly's mouth gaped. 'I can't let yer do that! I was only kiddin', I didn't think yer'd take me serious. Other people buy that toffee, yer know, and they wouldn't be very happy if they knew you'd had yer ruddy mitts all over it.'

'What about me? I'm expected to eat it after *you've* had yer mitts all over it! At least I know where my hands have been; only God knows where yours get to.'

Molly's mouth gaped wider. 'Well, the bloomin' cheek of you! Are yer suggesting that me hands aren't clean?'

'I'm not sayin' nothing, girl, except when I passed the window the other day yer were standin' there picking yer nose. That was after yer'd given yer head a good scratch.'

Molly burst out laughing. 'I think we'd better call it a day, Betty, before me customers start to believe yer. Yer'd cause trouble in an empty house, you would.' She jerked her head at Katy. 'Break the pieces as small as yer can, love, just to keep her quiet.'

Katy's mouth opened in horror. 'I haven't served any toffee yet, Mrs Edwards. I wouldn't know how to break it.'

'Holy suffering ducks!' Molly appealed to the woman who'd been patiently waiting to be served. 'Will yer hang on another minute, Mrs Wilson?'

The elderly white-haired woman smiled. 'Yeah, go 'ed, I'm enjoying meself. And it's warmer in here than it is in our 'ouse.'

Molly was huffing as she reached for the toffee tray. 'All this for a quarter of ruddy toffee.'

Betty winked at Katy. 'I don't need a quarter, Molly, I only want two ounces! I'm not made of ruddy money, yer know.'

When Katy burst out laughing Molly knew she was having her leg pulled. 'Yer'll have a quarter, Betty Mason, whether yer want it or not. I've a good mind to ram the flamin' stuff down yer ruddy throat.'

Doreen's mother wagged a podgy finger. 'Tut-tut, temper, temper.'

The next incident which Katy would relate to her mother that night in bed, was when Dolly Armstrong came into the shop, followed closely by Rita Williams.

Katy beamed at them. 'Ah, the terrible twins.'

Rita's eyes narrowed. 'Yer what?' She turned to Dolly. 'Did yer hear what she had the cheek to call us?'

'I did, and I've a good mind to clock her one.'

Undaunted, Katy carried on. She'd make friends with these women if it killed her. 'Have yer never heard the story about the terrible twins? They were little rascals, or better still, lovable rogues. They were holy terrors, always up to mischief and I used to love reading about them 'cos they made me laugh.'

The two women looked at each other, trying to decide if it was an insult or a compliment. They liked the sound of lovable rogues, though, so they came to the conclusion it was a compliment. As Jim was to say later, Rita grew at least a couple of inches in height, and Dolly's bosom took on a life of its own and stood to attention. They smiled at Katy when they were leaving and even stood at the door and waved to her. She'd learned how to be diplomatic over the last few days and that would stand her in good stead for the future. If customers liked you, they came to your shop. If they didn't, they shopped elsewhere.

It was six o'clock when Molly told Katy it was time she went home. As the girl was putting her coat on, the shopkeeper handed her two half-crowns. 'This is for today and the few nights yer've worked.'

Katy stared at the silver coins and backed away as though they were going to bite her. 'That's far too much, I couldn't take all that!'

'Oh, yer can afford to work for nothing, can yer? As a sort of hobby, like?'

'Well, no. But that's too much to take off yer.'

'Listen, love, I'm not daft in the head, I don't go around giving money away for nothing. You have earned that money, so take it.'

When Katy hesitated, Molly slipped it into her pocket. 'Off yer go now, and we'll see yer on Monday.'

'Would it be all right if I spent some of it in the shop now?

52

Not much, just to buy some tinsel and a couple of streamers to brighten our house up for Christmas.'

'Of course yer can. It's your money so yer can do what yer like with it.'

Happiness made Katy act on impulse, and she threw her arms around Molly's neck. 'Oh, thank you, Mrs Edwards, thank you, thank you, thank you.'

Molly blinked away a tear. 'Do I get a hug every week when yer get yer wages? I'd better not tell Jim, or he'll be paying yer daily.'

Katy remembered then that the woman she was hugging was her employer. She dropped her arms and looked embarrassed. 'I'm sorry, it's just that with you being so kind, and me not expecting so much, well I got carried away. I'll not make a habit of it, I promise.'

Molly smiled into the pretty face. 'Listen, sweetheart, if you want to hug me then you go right ahead. Unless, of course, we've got a shop full of people.'

Katy lowered her eyes and asked shyly, 'Shall I go the other side of the counter to be served?'

'Will you heckerslike!' Molly gave her a gentle push. 'Yer work here now so don't expect to be waited on.'

Katy hummed as she picked out the decorations that caught her eye. Three paper streamers that were cut into shapes – they could be hung across the ceiling. And the lengths of tinsel, in silver, green and red, could be draped across the mirror and pictures. That should well brighten up the room. She was turning away when she saw the packets of coloured balloons. There were twelve in a packet for tuppence, and they were all different shapes. Ooh, they would look a treat, but should she spend two whole pennies on them? In her mind's eye she could see the balloons hanging from the picture rail, and in the end she couldn't resist.

She placed her purchases on the counter and took one of the half-crowns from her pocket. 'Will you serve me, Mr Edwards, please? I'd rather not do it meself.'

After a nod from his wife, and a cursory glance at the decorations, Jim said, 'That'll be a shilling, Katy.'

'They come to more than that, I've added—'

Her words were cut short. 'I said a shilling, Katy, so hand it over and get home before yer mam thinks we're working yer to death.'

Katy felt as though she was walking on air as she made her way home. Wait until her mam knew she'd bought all the decorations and still had four bob left. She wouldn't half get a surprise. And it meant she could get Colin's shoes soled and buy him a cheap shirt for Christmas. That would be him seen to, and perhaps when Katy got her wages next week there'd be enough for something new for her and her mam. Not that they were going anywhere, but if the room was all dressed up it would be nice if they were, too.

Katy was expecting the shop to be quiet on the Monday before Christmas because people were usually skint after the weekend. But her mam had never been able to afford to go in a tontine, so she didn't know that the week before Christmas was pay-out time, when the housewives got back the money they'd paid in every week of the year, even on weeks they could ill-afford it. And today they were intent on getting the children's presents in before their husbands came home from work and cadged a few bob off them for the pub.

The women were all in a happy frame of mind and it rubbed off on Katy. She was bubbling with happiness as she brought selection boxes off the shelves, Christmas stockings filled with assorted bars, chocolate money in gold net bags, and a variety of chocolate animals covered in silver paper with a little red loop at the top for hanging on the tree. Some of the orders came to over a pound, and Katy wasn't taking any chances by trying to add it all up in her head. She didn't want anyone coming back and saying they'd been overcharged, so she asked Jim for some paper and a pencil and wrote every item down so the customer could see what she was paying for.

While Molly and Katy worked flat out, serving, Jim filled the shelves as quickly as they emptied them. They laughed and joked with the customers as they filled baskets and shopping bags, but there was no time to stand and hold a conversation. It was pleasant work, though, serving women who had wide smiles on their faces instead of scrounging around on a Monday, robbing Peter to pay Paul, they had some money in their well-worn purses. Many of them had big families and wouldn't be spending a penny on themselves, but as long as the kids came down on Christmas morning to find pillow-cases or stockings filled with goodies, that was good enough for them.

Molly went to open the door for one lady who was laden down, and as she came back behind the counter, she whispered to Katy, 'Am I glad you had an understanding headmistress! I'll say I am!'

Katy grinned. 'That makes two of us.'

It was late afternoon when Katy found herself facing Doreen across the counter. She was so taken aback, she didn't know how to react. They'd been friends all their lives and it was stupid to fall out. But she wasn't the one who'd caused the rift, so it wasn't up to her to make the first move. 'Can I get something for yer?'

'Hello, Katy.' The girl's face was flushed with embarrassment. 'I only came down to see how yer were getting on in yer new job.'

'I'm doing fine, thank you, I love it.' Katy regarded her friend thoughtfully. 'Did yer mam tell yer to come?'

Doreen shook her head. 'No, I came off me own bat. I don't want to be out of friends with yer, so shall we make up?'

'I never fell out of friends, Doreen, it was you.' Katy was conscious of the customers waiting to be served. 'I haven't got time to talk now, but yeah, of course we can be mates again. I'll slip up to yours tonight, that's best.'

Doreen passed an envelope across the counter. 'I brought yer a Christmas card.'

'Oh, that's nice, thank you.' As Katy picked up the card she was groaning inside. Oh dear, she hadn't got a card to give in return. In fact, she hadn't got a card for anyone. She hadn't even thought about it because there'd never been money for cards before. 'I'll bring yours up tonight. Thanks, Doreen.'

With a smile on her face, Doreen turned away. 'See yer later.' She was glad her mam had nagged her into coming because although she wouldn't admit it, she had missed her friend. And now they were getting old enough to go to the pictures at night, she had to have someone to go with or she wouldn't be allowed out.

As Katy served, her mind was on Christmas cards. They sold them in the shop, six in a pack for threepence. She had threepence in her purse because her mam had insisted she kept a few coppers out of her wages. And six cards would just about go around. There were the Edwards – they'd definitely get one for being so kind to her. Then there was Doreen and Billy, Mrs Campbell next door, her Grandma Baker and her mam and Colin. There was a smile on Katy's face as she handed a customer her change, but her mind was telling her only a magician could make six cards go around seven people. Then she solved the problem by deciding one card would do between her mother and brother. And she'd do the same as Doreen had – deliver them by hand. It cost too much to post them, and anyway, it was daft when you saw the people every day.

Katy worked until seven o'clock every night that week, and when Saturday came she was given ten shillings wages. She'd never had a ten-shilling note before, and oh, the joy of hearing the rustle as she fingered it in her pocket. She couldn't wait to see her mam's face when she handed it to her.

Dot had the dinner ready to put on the table when her daughter walked in. 'Oh, yer must be dog-tired, sunshine. It's a long time to be on yer feet.'

'I don't mind, Mam, I enjoy it.' When Katy took the note from her pocket she felt so important she thought her heart would burst. She waved it under her mother's nose, teasing, 'How about that then? Not bad, eh?'

Dot gasped and stared at the note for a second, then her face lit up. 'Not bad? It's bloody marvellous, love!'

Colin was by his sister's side in a flash. 'Ten bob! Ye're rich, our Katy.'

'Not yet I'm not, not by a long chalk.' Katy put her face close to his. 'But stick around, brother, 'cos one day I might be.'

'There's other riches in the world beside money,' Dot said.

56

'If yer've got love, a good family and friends around yer, and yer enjoy good health, then yer can call yerself rich.'

'It won't worry me if I never have a lot of money, Mam,' Katy said. 'I'd just like enough to live on without scrimping from one week to the next.'

'You're easy pleased, you are.' Colin was staring wide-eyed at the note. 'I'd like to have loads of dosh in me hand.'

'Well, ye're not getting yer hands on this, it's all for me mam.' Katy held the note out. 'Here yer are, Mam.'

Dot shook her head. 'No, yer've been working all the hours God sends, yer deserve some pocket money. We'll go half each, eh?'

Katy considered a moment. There was a haberdashery shop next to the sweetshop and the woman who owned it sold scarves, gloves and blouses, as well as cottons, ribbons and buttons. There was a pair of gloves in the window – black woollen ones that would keep her mother's hands warm when she went to work in the winter mornings. She'd like to buy them for her as a surprise, and a present for Colin. 'I'll tell yer what, Mam, just give me a shilling. I've promised to go in tomorrow to help with the last of the Christmas orders, and Mrs Edwards said she'd give me two bob for it.'

'Oh, not on a Sunday, sunshine, yer need some rest.'

'It'll be quiet after Christmas, Mam, so I might as well make the most of it while I can. It won't be a full day because there's not that much to do, the big orders have all been delivered. These are only for the women who didn't want the things until the last minute because they said their kids would strip the house if they knew Father Christmas had come early.' Katy pressed the note into her mother's hand and closed her fingers over it. 'Just give me a shilling and I'll have plenty with the two bob I get tomorrow.'

'I feel lousy takin' it off yer, sunshine, it just doesn't seem fair. Not after you puttin' all the hours in that yer have.'

'I'll be getting it back, won't I? If ye're buying me a present, something new to wear on Christmas Day, I'll be more than satisfied.'

Colin was all ears. 'Am I gettin' something new to wear, as well?'

'We'll see.' Dot gave Katy a knowing look. Colin's new shirt was already wrapped up and hidden on top of the wardrobe. But it wouldn't be there long if he knew about it. 'It depends how far the money will stretch.'

'I'll look well, won't I, if you two are dressed to the nines an' I'm sitting in me old shirt that's nearly fallin' off me back?'

Katy patted his cheek. 'Now, now! If Father Christmas hears yer moaning, he'll think ye're a naughty boy and he won't bring you anything.'

'Sit down, the pair of yer, or this dinner won't be fit to eat.' Dot bustled into the kitchen. 'I was hoping to go and see me ma tonight, 'cos I won't feel like it on Monday after working all day. And although we finish work at dinner-time on Christmas Eve, I'll be too busy getting the shopping in.' She carried a plate through and put it down quickly in front of Katy. 'Don't yer put her hands on that, sunshine, it's red hot.'

'If ye're going to Grandma's, yer won't forget to take me card, will yer?' Katy speared a sprout and blew on it. 'I wish I could buy her a present. I mean, yer should buy yer grandma a present at Christmas, shouldn't yer?'

'Me ma understands what the money situation's been, Katy. She knows if we could afford it we'd be up there every week.' Dot's widowed mother lived off Walton Road, which wasn't that far but it still cost eightpence in fares for the three of them to visit her. And until last week Dot had had to make every penny count just to keep her head above water. 'She's going to our Mary's for Christmas dinner, but next year, please God, we can invite her here.'

'Yeah, things will be different next year.' Katy's eyes went around the room. The decorations looked nice but they didn't hide the fact that the wallpaper was dirty. It was brown with age and the smoke from the fire, and on the ceiling, right over the gas light, there was a big black ring. 'This room will be nice by then, won't it, Mam?'

'I certainly hope so, sunshine, I'm fed-up looking at it. I'm frightened to invite anyone in, I'm that ashamed.'

'And the year after next will be better still.' Colin was swinging his legs back, kicking the bottom of his chair seat.

'I'll be fourteen then, and we'll be dead rich with three wages comin' into the house.'

'Don't speak too soon, son, it doesn't do to plan so far ahead.' Dot felt a sadness come down on her. They'd made so many plans, her and Ted, and look what had happened. But it wouldn't be fair to burden the children with her heartache; they had their whole lives ahead of them. And, please God, they'd have good lives. She gave a little shiver to rid herself of her memories then forced a smile to her face. 'But I do think that things are looking up for the Baker family.'

When the shop closed on Christmas Eve, Katy began filling a bag with the presents she'd wrapped for her mam and Colin, and the gift the Edwards' had given her. It had been a wonderful day, with the customers full of excitement and merriment, bringing a party spirit into the shop. They'd been mad busy from early morning right up to Jim Edwards finally putting the bar across the door and turning the sign to read *Closed*. Katy was very tired, but it was a nice tiredness, and she thought there could be no girl in the world more happy than she was right then.

Jim was clearing the counter while Molly swept the floor, and Katy was reluctant to leave while there was still work to be done. 'I'll mop it when yer've finished sweeping, Mrs Edwards. It won't take me long and you'll both be finished that much quicker.'

Molly shook her head. 'No, you get on home, love, yer've done enough.' She leaned her chin on the top of the broom handle. 'Yer've kept up with us all day, and that takes some doing for a fourteen-year-old. Me and Jim got a bargain when we got you.'

Katy picked up the bag and smiled. 'I got the best of the bargain, and I know when I'm lucky. I thank you for me present and I'm only sorry I couldn't give yer one back. But I'll find out when yer birthdays are and treat yer then.'

Molly pulled a face. She was a bonny woman, cuddly without being fat. Her mousy-coloured hair was peppered with grey, but she had rosy cheeks and a good complexion, making it difficult to tell her age. 'Listen to me, girl, if yer want to stay popular then yer won't mention birthdays. When yer've had as many as us yer don't want to be reminded.'

Jim gave out a loud guffaw. 'My dear wife has been forty for the last twenty years! She said I can grow old if I want to, but she's not coming with me.'

'My grandma says that ye're only as old as yer feel, Mr Edwards.'

'Then your grandma hasn't worked in a shop, Katy.' Jim walked across to his wife and put his arm across her shoulders. 'I think I can speak for Molly when I say we both feel as old as the hills right now. Eh, love?'

Molly grinned and ran a hand over his balding head, making the wisps of fine white hair stand on end. 'I feel tired enough to admit to fifty, but no more.'

Jim's eyes moved to the window where he could see a figure lurking. 'I think yer'd better go, Katy, 'cos young Billy Harlow has been hanging around for the last half hour.'

Katy tucked the bag under her arm. 'He's probably waiting to tell me how he got on today. He was going to see his dad's boss about a job.'

'Ah, I hope he got it,' Molly said. 'He's a nice boy.'

'Yeah, it would be a nice Christmas present for him.' Katy stood by the door. 'I'll see yer on Saturday, then. I hope yer have a lovely Christmas, and thanks for me pressie.'

'No opening it until tomorrow, d'yer hear?'

'I won't.' Katy lifted the bar from the door. 'Will you put this back after me, Mr Edwards? If not, yer might get more customers coming in.'

'If Clark Gable himself walked up to that door, I wouldn't let him in. And considerin' he's the most handsome man on two legs, that's saying something.' Molly's brows drew together and she tapped a finger on her chin. 'On second thoughts, I might just make an exception for Clark Gable. I mean, he wouldn't come back if I refused him once, would he?'

Jim feigned a sad expression as he took the bar from Katy. 'See what I'm up against, love? That's the worst of marrying a younger woman.'

Katy smiled, knowing the couple thought the world of each other. 'Good night, and thanks again for everything.' She stepped into the road and gave a cry of surprise when she found herself almost nose-to-nose with Billy. 'Oh, yer daft nit, fancy comin' up on me like that. I nearly jumped out of me skin!' She searched his face. 'Yer got the job, didn't yer?'

Billy's teeth were chattering and he was frozen to the bone. But his heart was glowing with pride. 'Yeah, I start the Monday after Christmas.'

'Ooh, I'm made up for yer, Billy. That's both of us got jobs right away – aren't we lucky? I bet yer mam's pleased, too.'

'Yeah, she's like a cat with two tails.' Billy lived in Province Road, just yards away from the block of shops, but he fell into step beside Katy, saying, 'I'll walk yer home.'

'Billy, yer look like death warmed up. Go home and get beside the fire. The last thing yer need now is a cold.'

'Nah, I'm all right. I'll walk with yer and I can tell yer about me job. Not that I'm goin' to stick at it for ever. I'm definitely going away to sea as soon as I can talk me mam round.'

'Some hope yer've got there, Billy, 'cos, knowing yer mam, she won't want her lovely son to leave home.'

Billy hunched his shoulders and dug his hands deep in his pockets. 'She's got me two brothers at home, and me dad, it's not as though she'd be on her own. And it wouldn't be for ever, just for a year or two. I've always had a hankering to go to sea, ever since I can remember. I want to see something of the world, and I'll not be content until I've got it out of me system.'

'If I were you, Billy, I'd keep that to meself for a while. Yer don't want to spoil yer mam's Christmas for her, do yer? Start yer job, and stick it for a while. Yer never know, yer might like it and forget all about going to sea.'

'No chance.' Billy had set his heart on a life on the ocean wave, and nothing would change his mind. 'One of me uncles goes to sea, and he told me yer can learn yer trade on the boats. Carry on with yer apprenticeship, like.'

They stopped outside Katy's house. 'I won't ask yer in, Billy, 'cos me mam will be up to her neck in work. But I hope yer have a nice Christmas, and I hope that sometime in the future yer get what ye're hankering after.'

'I hope you have a nice time, too, Katy, and I'll call in the shop to see yer after the holiday. Remember me to yer mam and wish her all the best for me.'

When Colin opened the door, he eyed the bag his sister was carrying. 'What have yer got in there – something nice?'

'Yer'll find out tomorrow, nose fever. Just you keep yer thieving hands off.' Katy found her mother in the kitchen peeling potatoes. There was a pan on the stove with carrots and turnips in, and another with sprouts. 'You've been busy, Mam.'

'You ain't kidding, sunshine. I haven't stopped since I got out of bed this morning. I went into town after work and got all me shopping in, and I've given the house a bit of a do since. And when I've finished these spuds everything will be prepared for the dinner tomorrow. All I'll have to do is put a light under the pans.' Dot threw the potato-peeler down and lifted the heavy pan on to the stove. 'I've got all the eats ready for tomorrow, but I've nowt in for tonight. Will yer have chips from the chippy?'

'Anything will do, Mam, as long as it takes the hunger off. How about toast?'

'You would say that wouldn't yer?' Colin was leaning against the doorjamb, a look of disgust on his face. 'A round of toast won't fill me, I'm a growing lad! Let me go to the chippy, Mam, and we'll have chips and scallops.'

Dot rinsed her hands under the tap and reached for the towel hanging on a nail behind the door. She shrugged her shoulders at Katy. 'Anything for a quiet life, sunshine, I haven't got the energy to argue.' She jerked her head at Colin. 'Pass me purse off the sideboard, there's a good lad. Threepence worth of mixed, and run all the way there and back.'

Chapter Five

John Kershaw had been out for a Christmas drink with the men he worked with. And as he cycled home, he was telling himself that the few pints he'd had were the only enjoyment he'd have over Christmas. In fact, tomorrow could be any old day as far as he was concerned. He turned into Willard Street, so lost in thought he didn't see the figure leave the pavement and run across the road directly in his path. He felt the impact of the collision and struggled to right the bike. Then to his dismay he heard a cry of pain and saw a boy lying in the road at the side of him. He quickly cocked his leg over the crossbar and laid the bike down. 'Are you hurt, son?' When John knelt down he could see the boy was crying. 'Tell me where it hurts.'

'It hurts all over, but me ankle's the worst – it's agony.' Colin tried to keep the tears back; after all, big boys shouldn't cry like a baby. 'And I've dropped me parcel of chips.'

John looked around. 'Here's your parcel, but that's the least of your worries. If I help you up, could you stand?'

'I'll try,' Colin sniffed, 'but I don't think so. Me ankle's not half paining me.'

'Which ankle is it?'

'Me left one.'

John ran his hand down from the knee, but when he came to the ankle the boy yelped in pain. 'I don't think you'll be able to stand on it, so we'll have to think of a way to get you home so we can see what the damage is. What's your name and where d'you live?'

'Colin Baker. I live at Edith Road, number twenty-one. I'll have to get home 'cos me mam's waiting for the chips for the dinner.'

John slipped one arm under the boy's knees and the other

under his arms. 'I'll sit you on the pavement while I see to my bike. If the wheel's not buckled, you can sit on the seat and I'll wheel you home.'

Although Colin was in great pain, he told himself this man must be awful strong 'cos he'd picked him up as though he was a baby. He also told himself it was his own fault for not looking before he ran across the road. He wouldn't half get a lecture off his mam.

John towered over him. 'The front wheel of the bike is so buckled I couldn't possibly push you home on it, we'd be all over the road. The only alternative is for me to carry you.'

Colin gaped. 'Yer couldn't carry me all that way, I'm nearly twelve!'

John chuckled. It was a long time since he was twelve, but he knew he'd have been mortified if anyone had suggested carrying him like a baby. 'Let me stand you up and see if you could manage to hop on your good foot if I support you.' He put a hand under each of Colin's armpits and lifted him effortlessly from the ground. 'Put your weight on your right foot first, now slowly lower your left foot.'

Colin let out a scream and would have collapsed if John hadn't been holding him. 'I can't, it hurts too much.'

Without a word, John scooped him up in his arms. 'Like it or not, son, this is the only way you're going to get home. It may be just a bad sprain, then again you could have broken your ankle and you'll need to have it seen to.'

'He's a long time,' Dot said, pacing the floor. 'I wonder what's keeping him?'

'There's probably a big queue, Mam,' Katy said. 'Lots of people will be having chips tonight for quickness.'

'If he's met one of his mates and is standing yapping, I'll have his ruddy guts for garters. The flaming chips will be cold when we get them.'

Just then the knocker sounded and Dot hurried out. 'Where the heck . . .' The words faded as she gazed in astonishment at the man standing before her. He looked about ten feet tall and was built like a battleship.

'Mrs Baker, my name's John Kershaw and—'

Dot suddenly realised he was cradling Colin in his arms and she let out a cry. 'Oh, my God, what's happened to me son? Has he been in an accident? Is he hurt bad?'

'He ran in front of my bike,' John explained, 'and he seems to have hurt his ankle. With any luck, he's just sprained it.' When Dot seemed struck dumb with fright, he asked, 'Is your husband in, to take him from me?'

'I'm a widow.' Dot's brain cleared when she realised she'd have to invite the man in. She couldn't manage to carry Colin, neither could Katy. The living room was clean, but that's all you could say for it; it was certainly no palace. But what the hell, she didn't know the man from Adam and would probably never see him again. 'Would you carry him in for me, please, and we can put him on the couch.' She opened the door wide and stepped on to the bottom stair to give him more room to manoeuvre in the tiny hall. 'Katy,' she called, 'will yer clear the couch for us, there's a good girl. Our Colin's been hurt.'

Katy had been listening from the living-room door, and when John carried Colin through, she asked, 'Is me brother hurt bad?'

'I don't think so, dear, but someone should take a look at his ankle.' John gently lowered the boy on to the couch before gazing into his anxious face. 'I think it's just a bad sprain and with cold compresses on, it should be all right in a few days.'

Dot pushed him none too gently because he was stopping her from getting to her son. 'Excuse me, please.' She dropped to her knees at the side of the couch and, cupping Colin's face, she kissed him. 'Where does it hurt, sunshine?'

'It's me ankle, Mam, it's murder.'

Dot's eyes travelled down to his feet and she gasped with horror. 'Oh, my God! Will yer look at his foot, it's swollen to twice the size and his shoe's digging into him.' She made to undo the shoelace but her son screamed at her to leave it.

'Don't touch it, Mam, it hurts too much.'

John bent to take a look. 'Your mother will have to take your shoe off, son, so we can see what the damage is.' He pressed on Dot's shoulder. 'Would you like me to do it for you, Mrs Baker?'

'Yes, let him, Mam.' Colin trusted the man who had carried

him all the way home and hadn't hurt him once. 'Go on, Mam.'

Dot shuffled on her knees to the end of the couch. 'Would you mind, Mr Kershaw? I know we shouldn't be keeping yer 'cos yer wife's probably got yer dinner ready.'

'I'm a bachelor, Mrs Baker, there's no one at home waiting for me.' John knelt down and smiled at Colin. 'This will probably hurt, but only for a couple of seconds, until I get your shoe off. I know you're going to be brave, so close your eyes and grip hold of your mother's hand.'

Colin did as he was told, and to prove he was brave he ground his teeth together to stop himself from screaming when the shoe was removed.

Dot felt a stab of shame when she saw her son's big toe sticking out of a huge hole in the toe of his sock. She had new ones for him to wear tomorrow but that was no excuse for the way he looked now. This man must think she was a bad mother who couldn't look after her children properly. She felt her hand being gripped tight as Mr Kershaw tried to ease the sock off, and she stroked the boy's head. 'There, nearly over now, sunshine. Yer've been a very good boy.'

John examined the swelling before asking, 'Would you be brave for another minute, Colin, while I touch it?' Without waiting for a reply, the big man gently touched the flesh, probing lightly for signs of a fracture. 'I don't think he's broken anything, but it might be just as well to let a doctor see him.'

Dot was silent for a moment. He'd seen the state of the room, and the state of Colin's sock, so there was no point in pretending things were different than they were. 'I can't afford to bring the doctor out, Mr Kershaw, I don't have the money. I've never borrowed from anyone because I don't believe in it. But if Colin's still in pain in a day or two, I'll get the money from somewhere.'

John could see what it cost her to say what she had, so the words he had ready to offer to pay for the doctor remained unsaid. 'If you keep putting cold compresses on it, they should take the swelling down. I'm sure it's only a sprain.'

'How did it happen?' Dot asked. 'I suppose he was running without looking where he was going, as usual.'

John raised his brows at Colin. 'I think I'll let the lad tell you that himself.' When he grinned he revealed a set of strong white teeth. 'As you can see, he wouldn't part with the chips. He's hung on to those as though his life depended on it.'

Dot had seen the parcel under her son's arm but she'd been too upset to give it a thought. Now she took it from him and handed it to Katy. 'They'll be stiff by now, but put them on a plate in the oven and I'll warm them up later.'

As Katy walked to the kitchen she asked over her shoulder, 'Shall I make the gentleman a cup of tea, Mam?'

Dot felt herself cringe inside. John Kershaw was well dressed and spoke without a trace of a Liverpool accent. He wouldn't appreciate a cracked cup with a saucer that didn't match. This would be another black mark against her. She was trying to think of an excuse when Colin piped up.

'Yeah, ask him to have a cup of tea, Mam.'

'I think Mr Kershaw would like to be on his way,' Dot said. 'He's wasted enough of his time on you.' She struggled to her feet and found she had to crane her neck to meet John's eyes. 'You mentioned you were on a bike – where is it?'

'I've left it parked against a wall in an alley. It won't get stolen because the front wheel is buckled and it would be useless to anyone.' His teeth flashed. 'I would very much like a cup of tea.'

Dot reached a decision. 'Look, Mr Kershaw, I'm very grateful for the way yer've helped Colin, it was very kind of yer. Most people would have left him to get on with it. And ye're more than welcome to a cup of tea. But I can't go on making excuses for our living conditions, so yer'll have to take us as you find us. My husband died ten years ago and I had to go to work to keep the family together. It's been hard going and there's never been enough to renew things as they wore out. So if yer still want a drink of tea I must warn you in advance that if the cup ye're given has a handle, yer'll be very lucky.'

John's rich laughter filled the room. 'Mrs Baker, I take my tea to work in an enamel billy-can and I drink from the top of it. It used to have a blue rim, but now there's no blue to be seen it's so cracked. I thank you for your honesty and I admire you for it, but I am not a snob.'

Colin was gazing up at him with wide eyes. He wasn't half a big man, he could probably take six men on in a fight and beat them all. 'There yer are, Mam, he wants to stay for a cup of tea. And he can have some of my chips to make a buttie with.'

Dot relaxed and grinned. 'No matter how badly hurt my son was, he'd still be thinking of his ruddy tummy. Sit down, Mr Kershaw, and I'll see if I can find a cup with a handle.'

Katy had come to the kitchen door when she heard John laughing. She couldn't ever remember hearing a man's laughter in the house before and it sounded nice. 'I started work last week, Mr Kershaw, so in a couple of weeks we'll have a new tea-set 'cos it's near the top of the list we've made out of things we want. Isn't that right, Mam?'

'Yes, sunshine, that's right. But I'm sure Mr Kershaw doesn't want to wait a couple of weeks for a cup of tea, so stick the kettle on, please.'

'Look, I've got an idea.' John put his hand on the arm of the chair to lever himself up. 'Why don't I go down to the chippy and get some fresh chips for you?'

'Certainly not! I wouldn't hear of it!' Dot wasn't having any of that. He seemed a nice bloke but that's as far as it went. She wasn't taking charity from him. 'While we're waiting for the kettle, I'll nip upstairs and root out an old sheet I can tear up to make a cold compress for Colin's ankle.'

An hour later, John was still sitting in the chair at the side of the fireplace. At first Dot had been willing him to drink his tea and go, so she could finish what she had to do. Then she told herself she was being miserable – it was Christmas Eve, after all. And it was nice for the children to have a man to talk to. He had a good sense of humour and had them roaring with laughter as he related some of the antics he'd got up to when he was at school.

'Does bachelor mean yer haven't got a wife?' Colin asked.

Dot was horrified. 'Colin, don't be so cheeky! You shouldn't ask questions like that.'

'I don't mind, Mrs Baker.' John smiled at her before turning his eyes to Colin. 'No, I haven't got a wife. You see, my mother

68

was an invalid and I looked after her until she died last year. I had a number of girlfriends, but none of them were prepared to take my mother on.'

Colin was still curious. 'Yer don't half speak posh. Are yer rich?'

'*Colin!*' Dot didn't know where to put her face for the best. 'Ye're going too far. Stop asking so many questions.' She appealed to John. 'Yer'll have to excuse him, he's not used to having a man in the house.'

'I can assure you I don't mind, Mrs Baker.'

'Well, I do. And for heaven's sake stop calling me Mrs Baker, me name's Dorothy.'

'Nobody calls yer Dorothy though, do they, Mam?' Katy said. 'Yer only ever get Dot.'

Dot threw her hands in the air and laughed. 'I can't win, can I? OK, it's Dot, and I know you're John. That's sorted that out.'

'Well, with your permission, Dot, I'll answer Colin's question. My mother used to be a school-teacher before I was born, and she was a stickler for good grammar. When I was young it was woe betide me if I didn't pronounce my words properly, and I'm afraid—' John's head swivelled around when there was the sound of something crashing against the wall at the side of him. When this was followed by a high-pitched scream and the sound of sobbing, he looked across the room to see Dot's hands covering her face. 'What on earth is going on?'

Dot sprang to her feet. 'We have a neighbour who likes to knock his wife around. I'll have to go in there and see if I can help her. He's a real villain and once he starts on her there's no stopping him. He's always been the same, but he's got to be stopped because she's . . . er, she's not well.'

John noticed the hesitation and the quick, concerned glance she'd given Colin. There was more to what was going on than she'd admitted. So when she was on her way out, he jumped up. 'I'll come with you.'

'He's a bad man, Mr Kershaw,' Katy shouted after him. 'Don't let him hurt me mam.'

Dot found Maggie O'Connor outside Mary's front door

and her husband hovering a short distance away. 'Sure, isn't there something wrong with a man when he'll hit a woman who's carrying his child? As sure as God's in His heaven, the divil will kill that girl one of these days. But we've got to do something, Dot, 'cos I'd not be resting in me bed if I thought I'd stood by and not raised a hand to help.' Maggie looked surprised when John loomed up behind Dot. 'I'm sorry, me darlin', I didn't know yer had a visitor.'

Dot was brief with the introductions. 'John Kershaw, this is Maggie O'Connor and her husband, Paddy.' Standing by the front window they could clearly hear Tom Campbell's raised voice and Mary's sobs. 'To hell with this, someone's got to put a stop to it.' Dot curled her fist and banged as hard as she could on one of the door panels. 'Open this door!' she commanded.

The shouting stopped and for a few seconds there was silence. Then they heard a string of obscenities before the door was flung open. Tom Campbell, the worse for drink, stood swaying on the top step and looked down at Dot. 'Oh, it's the bleedin' nosy cow from next door.' He belched loudly and the smell of beer was strong and sickening. 'Bugger off, back to yer own house an' yer two bastards, and mind yer own bleedin' business.'

Dot stood her ground. 'I'm making Mary my business. You keep yer hands off her or else yer'll be sorry.'

Hanging on to the doorframe for support, Tom Campbell bent his head and belched again in Dot's face. His speech slurred, he said, 'She's my wife an' I'll do what I like with 'er. Now just you bugger off. Why don't yer go down Lime Street with the whores an' get yerself a feller?' He began to laugh like someone deranged. 'Do you the world of good, that would. Yer'll have forgotten by now what it's like to have a man inside yer.'

Dot curled her fists and bent her elbows, ready to fly at him, but she felt herself being pulled back and her place was taken by John. Without a word, he reached up and grabbed Tom by the front of his shirt, pulled him off the step and slammed him back against the wall.

'Now, what you've just said to Mrs Baker, I want you to

repeat to me so I can be sure I heard correctly.'

Tom Campbell blinked rapidly to try and focus. Through the drunken mist, he could just make out that the man holding him was tall and hefty. And there were a few other people there but they were only shapes, he couldn't see their features properly. 'Who the bleedin' hell are you? Take yer hands off me or I'll get the police to yer,' he bluffed.

'I will personally escort you to the police station myself, after we've had a little chat. Now what was this about Lime Street and whores?'

'It's that bleedin' cow next door I was talkin' about. She wants to get herself a man, do her good, the miserable bitch.'

John turned to Dot. 'Would you and your friend see how his wife is?'

Dot nodded and beckoned to Maggie. Her foot was on the top step when she heard the sound of flesh hitting flesh, and she quickly stepped backwards, almost knocking Maggie over. She wasn't going to miss this. It was about time Tom Campbell had a man to stand up to.

He had yelped with pain when John struck, and he was now holding a hand to the side of his face when he growled, 'Who the bloody hell are you? I've never seen yer before, so just you piss off and take that cow from next door with yer.'

'Oh dear,' John said, 'you really are asking for it.' He drew his left arm back and aimed straight at Tom's cheek. It wasn't a heavy blow, not meant to break bones, but it brought a sharp cry of pain from the man who was sobering up quickly. 'Now I want you to apologise to Mrs Baker first, then I want your assurance that you will never raise your hand again to your wife. Do you understand?'

Tom Campbell had called into the pub on his way home from work. Well, it was Christmas Eve, he was entitled to a drink. It never entered his head that his wife might need money to get some shopping in for over the holiday. He had drunk seven pints of beer and it had filled him with Dutch courage. But the two blows had blunted that courage somewhat. Still, he wasn't having a total stranger telling him what to do, so he blustered, 'Yer what? Some hopes you've got, Mister-whatever-your-name is. I'm not apologising to no one, certainly not

71

some frustrated old cow. And as for me wife, if I want to hit her I'll bleedin' well hit her.' A sly look came over his face and his lips curled. 'I get it now. That one next door is yer fancy woman and ye're filling yer boots in there on the quiet. Not that I blame yer, she's not a bad bit of stuff. I'd have got me own leg over there if I wasn't gettin' all I want at home.' Little realising that every word was digging him in deeper, he went on: 'She's good in bed, is my wife, like havin' me own little slave. She does everythin' I tell her to – d'yer know what I mean?'

John couldn't remember ever feeling so angry and disgusted. That a man would speak so of his wife, and in front of two other women, repulsed him. He turned to Dot. 'Please take your friend inside, Mrs Baker.'

The women didn't need telling twice. Shocked and embarrassed, they stepped into the Campbells' tiny hall. Maggie blessed herself before saying, 'May the good Lord forgive him for his evil thoughts. If I hadn't heard it with me own ears, sure I wouldn't have believed a man could speak so dirty, and that's the truth of it, so it is.'

'God may forgive him, Maggie, but I certainly won't.' There was bitterness in Dot's voice. 'Not after the things he said about me. I hope John gives him a bloody good hiding.'

She pushed open the living-room door and when she saw Mary, her own feelings took second place. Her neighbour was crouched on the floor behind a chair in a corner of the room. A lock of lank hair was hanging down her tear-stained face and her clothes were in disarray around her thighs. Dot closed her eyes for a second, then, with Maggie's help, pulled the chair out of the way. 'Come on, sunshine, let me help yer up.'

Mary whimpered and shook her head. Her arms were wrapped around her thin body and there was a look of fear on her face, reminding the women of a trapped animal. 'Where is he?'

'He's outside, having a talk to a friend of mine.' Dot bent down, 'Maggie, will you take the other arm and help me get her to a chair?'

The gas light was turned so low the room was dark and

miserable. Dot could understand that Mary had to be economical, but this wasn't the time for trying to save a copper. 'I'm turning the light up, so we can see what we're saying.' She ignored Mary's protest and stood on one of the wooden chairs to pull on the chain hanging at the side of the glass shade. 'That's better.' It was as she was jumping down from the chair that she saw the reason for her neighbour not wanting the room lit. The bruising on both of Mary's cheeks was beginning to colour, there was blood coming from her nose and her bottom lip had been split. And around both wrists were angry red marks.

Dot could feel a headache coming on with all the upset, and she rubbed the heel of her hand across her brow as she walked to where Mary sat. Putting a finger under her neighbour's chin, she raised her face. 'Is this what he gave yer for yer Christmas present?'

Mary lowered her eyes in shame and humiliation. 'He's had a lot to drink.'

'Oh, so that excuses him, does it? He's allowed a belt for every pint, is that how he works it out? And you in the family way! Well, he wants hung, drawn and bloody quartered. You might not like what I'm going to do, Mary, but believe me, I'm only doing what I think is best for yer. I'm not getting at yer, sunshine, but me and Maggie worry about yer. We can't just stand back and let him belt that baby out of yer. So I'm asking someone in to see yer.' When she saw the look of terror in eyes that were already beginning to close over, Dot was filled with hatred for the man who could hurt someone as gentle as Mary. 'Maggie will stay with yer while I go outside for a minute.'

There was an argument raging in Dot's head. Part of her mind was saying she shouldn't get John mixed up in this, he was a total stranger and it wasn't fair. He did a good turn in bringing Colin home, then finds himself in a fight! But he'd followed her out on his own accord, she hadn't asked him to. Nor had she asked him to take Tom Campbell on. If he could just put the fear of God into the drunken bully, he'd be doing them all a favour. Paddy would do it, of that she was sure, but he had to live next door to the man and heaven only knew what retribution would be forthcoming. When Tom Campbell had drink in him he was capable of anything. But John would never see him again, never see any of them again.

John was still holding Tom prisoner, backed up against the wall. 'How is she?' he asked.

'Can I speak to yer for a minute?'

'Of course.' John released his grip, saying, 'If you know what's good for you, you'll stay right where you are.'

Dot turned her back on Tom. She could see Paddy standing near and knew he'd be ready if trouble broke out. 'Listen, Mr Kershaw – John – this is not your problem, so if yer want to walk away, I'll understand.'

'But it's not your problem, either, is it, Dot? And I don't see you walking away.'

'That's different, Mary's me neighbour and me mate – I owe it to her. But we're all strangers to you – you don't owe us anything.'

'No man who is worth his salt would ignore a woman in distress. So if you need my help, all you have to do is ask.'

'I'd like yer to see what Tom Campbell has done to his wife, then tell him what yer think of him. I know I've got a cheek, making use of yer like this, but yer see, she's having a baby and he's told her he doesn't want a brat in the house. And if he has his way, she won't have it. That's why me and the O'Connors are so worried.'

John glanced to where Tom was standing. 'He won't move, so lead the way.'

'Mary, this is a friend, John Kershaw. He's been having a talk with yer husband.'

John wasn't prepared for such a sight. If he'd known the brutality the man was capable of, he wouldn't have pulled his punches. 'I'm sorry we meet under these circumstances, Mrs Campbell. I'm also sorry to have to say your husband is a bully and a coward; he makes me ashamed of my own sex. But I've had a good talk to him and I think he'll see reason from now on.'

Mary kept her head down. 'Ye're right about him being a bully and a coward, but wrong about him seeing reason. Yer see, my husband doesn't know what reason is.'

'Oh, I think he's beginning to understand. He certainly knows that the reason I hit him the first time was because he said some dreadful things about Mrs Baker.'

Mary's head came up. 'Yer hit him?'

John nodded. 'Several times, Mrs Campbell. I asked him to apologise for the things he'd said, but he not only refused, he insulted her further. So I had no alternative but to defend a woman's honour and I hit him again.'

Mary's hand went to her mouth. 'Oh dear, I'm the one that'll bear the brunt of his anger. He won't fight with you, but I'm an easy target. I can't fight back.'

'Well, I'll have another word with him before I bring him in. If he refuses to behave and is a threat to you, I'll walk him to the police station.'

'Mary doesn't have to stay here tonight,' Maggie said. 'She can stay with us – we've got a spare bedroom.'

'That might solve the problem for tonight, Mrs O'Connor, but unless she wishes to leave her husband for good, she's got to come home sometime. Better get it sorted out once and for all.' John lifted his brows at Dot. 'Perhaps it would be better if you ladies left? He's not going to enjoy having his ego deflated in front of two women, that would be like rubbing salt in an open wound. And it might be best if you went out the back way.'

'Yeah, OK.' Dot squeezed Mary's shoulder. 'If yer want me or Maggie, just knock on the wall and we'll come running.'

'Thanks, Dot, and thank you, Maggie. I might be unlucky in me choice of husband, but I'm very lucky to have good neighbours like you.'

'John, yer will call in and let me know what happens, won't yer?' Dot asked. 'I'll lie awake all night if yer don't.'

'Of course I will. I wouldn't leave without seeing the invalid, anyway.'

'Yer mean yer hit him again before yer brought him in?' Dot's voice was high with surprise and more than a trace of pleasure. She couldn't get Mary's face out of her mind and she now hoped the devil was feeling the same pain he'd inflicted on his wife. 'What made yer do that?'

'Because I went easy on him with the first two punches, after he'd insulted you. But when I saw what he'd done to his wife – well, I'm afraid I let my anger and disgust get the better of me and I gave him a real belter.'

Colin was stretched out on the couch, his sore foot resting on a cushion. His face was alive with excitement and his head was moving from side to side as if he was shadow-boxing. Oh, he'd have given anything to see the big man knock the stuffing out of that horrible bloke next door. 'How many times did yer hit him, Mr Kershaw?'

'Colin!' Dot tapped a finger against the side of her nose. 'Just keep this out of it, it's not for your ears. Anyway, it's way past yer bedtime, although how we're going to manage that, heaven only knows. Any other night I'd let yer sleep on the couch, but not Christmas Eve, I've got too much to do.'

'I'll help him upstairs,' John said. 'That's no problem.'

'I want to go to the lavvy, Mam, I've been wanting to go for ages.'

'He has, Mam,' Katy said, 'but when I offered to fetch him the bucket he went mad.'

Colin glared at her. If looks could kill, Katy would have been a dead duck. 'Yer know what you can do, don't yer? I'm not using no bucket, so there.'

The look of utter mortification on the boy's face made John smile. After the carry-on of the last half hour, he was glad of a little light relief. 'I'm at your service, Master Baker. Would you like me to escort you down the yard?'

Colin grinned. 'I'll glad your mam made yer speak proper, Mr Kershaw, 'cos it doesn't half sound funny.'

'It does not!' Dot was horrified. After all the poor man had done for them, and now he was getting insulted all ends up. 'We'd all be better off if we spoke like Mr Kershaw.'

'Me mam's right.' There were daggers in the look Katy threw at her brother. 'My teacher used to speak like him, and the headmistress.'

John chuckled. 'You're out-numbered, my lad, so I'd give up if I were you.' He stretched his long arms over his head before getting to his feet. 'Come on, let's take you to the toilet, then up to bed.' With hands that were gentle, he sat the boy up, then helped him to stand on his good leg. 'If I put my arm around your waist to support you, I think you'll manage very well to hop the short distance.'

Mother and daughter smiled across at each other when they heard John giving some advice as he helped Colin down the back step. 'Take a tip from me, son, never try and get the better of a woman 'cos nine times out of ten you'll end up the loser. They'll have the last word if it kills them so far better to keep calm and give in gracefully.'

'Yeah, dead bossy, they are.'

Dot grinned. 'Cheeky blighter! I've a good mind not to give him his new shirt.' She tilted her head sideways. 'What have you got him?'

'I'm not telling yer.' Katy sounded very determined. 'And I'm not telling yer what I've got for you, either, so yer needn't bother asking. All me presents are wrapped up and they're going on the sideboard as soon as our Colin goes to bed.'

'Ye're a good girl, Katy.' Dot crossed her arms and hugged herself. 'Thanks to you we're going to have a good Christmas.'

'Don't keep saying that, Mam. You bring much more into the house than I do.'

'There's a big difference, sunshine! I'm yer mother and it's up to me to look after yer. But you didn't have to be as generous as yer've been. Most other girls would have kept more for themselves.'

'How long is it, Mam, since you had a half-a-crown in yer hand and nothing to do with it only spend it on yerself?'

'We've survived, Katy, and when yer dad first died I never thought we'd do that. I had visions of us being turned out on the street and ending up sleeping on yer grandma's floor.'

They didn't hear John carrying Colin back, nor did they know he'd been a listener to the last part of their conversation. 'Here's the wounded soldier. Shall I take him straight up to bed or lay him on the couch?'

'Straight up to bed, please. I've got stacks to do and I'll never get it done while he's here, asking this, that and the other.'

'Ah, ay, Mam! Can't I stay down until Mr Kershaw goes? Please?'

'Colin, I'm sure Mr Kershaw can't wait to get out of the house. God knows we've kept him long enough. And don't forget it's Christmas Eve. With a bit of luck Santa might call with a present for yer.'

Colin twisted in John's arms and looked up into his face. 'Yer see, I told yer they were bossy, didn't I?'

'And I told you what to do, didn't I?' John gave a conspiratorial, man-to-man wink. 'Best if you follow my advice.'

'Yeah, OK. Will you take me up?'

'I'll show you how to get up the stairs on your own, then you can come down the same way in the morning as long as your mother helps you to the top of the stairs.'

With Dot and Katy crowded behind him in the tiny hall, John set the boy down on the bottom stair. 'Now, keep your left leg straight out so you don't knock your sore ankle, and use your other foot to lever yourself on to the next stair.'

Colin soon got the hang of it and in no time was sitting on the top stair. 'Did yer see that, Mam? I did it!'

'That was very good, son, I'm proud of yer.'

'If I put him on the bed, will he be able to undress himself or shall I give him a hand?'

'Just put him on the bed, John, I'll see to him.' As Dot ran up the stairs she was thinking this man would expect her son to have pyjamas, a luxury they'd never been able to afford. 'I won't be five minutes.'

When she came downstairs she was shaking her head and grinning. 'He's not half going to give us the runaround. His lordship wants a cup of tea in bed, no less.'

'I'll make it, Mam.' Katy looked at John. 'Would yer like a drink, Mr Kershaw?'

Dot opened her mouth then quickly closed it. What a miserable article she was. She'd made use of this man, now she had no further use for him, she wanted him gone. If that wasn't being ungrateful she didn't know what was. She spread out her hands. 'If yer want to make a run for it, John, I wouldn't blame yer 'cos yer must have had a bellyful of the Baker family by now. What with one thing and another, we've spoilt yer whole night for yer.'

John smiled at Katy, who was still standing by the kitchen

door. 'I'd love another cup of tea, thank you.' He turned to Dot and said, 'I had nothing else to do tonight.'

'Well, sit yerself down, ye're that big yer make the place look untidy.' Dot's smile told him she was joking. When he was seated, she said, 'Before we go any further, I want to know about this bike of yours. If the wheel's buckled, and it was our Colin's fault, I want to help pay for it. Not this week, mind, but the week after.'

'Don't give it a thought – it won't cost me a penny,' John lied. 'I've got a friend who repairs bikes, he'll do it for me as a favour. Anyway, it wasn't all your son's fault, I was as much to blame. My mind was miles away instead of being on the road.'

'Are you telling me the truth?'

'It's hardly worth lying over a couple of shillings, is it?'

In the kitchen, Katy heaved a sigh of relief. They'd agreed that her next full week's wages would go on buying wallpaper and paint for the living room. She'd be very disappointed if they had to wait until the following week. It would be nice to see the house looking bright and cheerful, but she wanted it more for her mother's sake than her own. Her mam deserved to have a house she could be proud of, and she deserved to have some decent clothes, too.

Standing by the stove waiting for the kettle to boil, Katy listened to the conversation going on in the front room with a smile on her face. It was strange to hear a man's voice, but she liked it. And wasn't it funny that it all happened because their Colin never looked where he was going?

John stretched his legs out and ran two fingers down the crease in his trousers. 'There's been no sound from next door, has there?'

Dot shook her head. 'Not a dickie bird! Whether that's a good sign or not remains to be seen. If I can pluck up the courage tomorrow, I'll give a knock and wish Mary the compliments of the season.' Then she pulled a face. 'No, best not to. How can yer wish anyone a Happy Christmas when their face has been battered, when they've probably got no coal for the fire, no food in the cupboard and no one to pass them a civil word.'

Katy came in carrying two steaming cups of tea. 'I'll give a knock next door tomorrow, if yer like, Mam. If Mary answers the door I could ask her to come in here for an hour or two. She'd have someone to talk to and be nice and warm.'

'I wouldn't do that, Katy, because her husband is not a nice man,' John said quickly and decisively. 'If he came to the door the chances are he could be verbally or physically abusive.'

Katy grinned. 'I'm not frightened of him, Mr Kershaw, 'cos I'm a good runner. If he came near me I'd give him a good kick on his shins and scarper.'

Dot saw the concern on John's face and hastened to assure him. 'There's no way I'd let me daughter go near there. He's not fit to breathe the same air as her.'

'I could walk around tomorrow and give a knock, if you like,' John offered. 'It would set my own mind at rest if I knew he was keeping to his promise and she was all right.'

'Promise! I shouldn't think Tom Campbell has kept a promise in his whole life!' There was bitterness in Dot's voice as the image of Mary flashed before her eyes. 'He doesn't even know the meaning of the word.' She shook her head at John. 'I'd rather yer didn't come round; it might only make things worse for her. I'll have a word with Maggie and Paddy. We'll think of something – there's no need for you to get involved.'

Thinking a nod was as good as a wink when you were being told you weren't wanted, John drained his cup and handed it gratefully to Katy. 'Thank you, you make a very good cup of tea.' He pushed himself out of the chair. 'It's a very busy night for mothers and I know I'm holding you back, so I'll be on my way.' He held out his hand to Dot. 'Have a very happy Christmas, Dot, and I wish you and your children only good fortune in the future.'

'Thank you, and the same to you.' As she shook his hand, Dot was racked with guilt. She was throwing the poor man out, and he knew it. But she did have a lot to do, what with ironing and making the room look nice for in the morning. She wanted all the gaily wrapped presents arranged on the sideboard so they would be the first thing Colin saw when he limped into the room. He wasn't getting much, but it was a damn sight more than he'd ever had before. 'Yer won't mind if Katy shows yer out, will yer? I've still got a lot to do down here, then see to Colin and settle him down for the night. If I don't make an effort and get cracking soon, it'll be time to get up before I go to bed.'

Katy closed the front door and walked slowly back into the room. 'Yer were a bit mean with Mr Kershaw, Mam, I was surprised at yer. Yer never even asked if he'd like to call in any time he was passing.'

'I know, sunshine, and I'm not proud of meself. But I couldn't sit here gassing when there's so much to do and so little time to do it in. He seems a really nice bloke, but, after all, he is a complete stranger and we'll probably never see him again.'

'Oh, I think yer will because he said he'd call and see how Colin was getting on.' Katy stretched her arm behind the couch and pulled out the bag she'd hidden. There was a smile of satisfaction and anticipation on her face as she began to arrange the colourful parcels along the sideboard. After changing the position of them for greater effect, she stepped back to admire her handiwork. 'Don't they look nice, Mam?'

'They look lovely, sunshine.' Dot put her arm round her daughter's shoulders and hugged her tight. 'Wait until I add mine, they'll look even better.'

'Look what else I've got.' Katy's tummy was churning with pleasure as she delved into her bag once more and brought out a box of Christmas crackers. They were bright red and had little sprigs of green and gold paper stuck on them. 'They didn't get sold, so Mrs Edwards said I could have them for nothing.'

Dot held her tight as tears threatened. How different tomorrow was going to be from the last ten Christmases, when all the children got was an apple, an orange, some nuts and a paper comic. She couldn't wait to see her son's face when he came down in the morning. If Ted was looking down on them from heaven, she knew he'd be smiling with contentment that his family were finding their feet.

'Mam, I'll put a cracker each on the presents, then we can have another one on the table with our dinner tomorrow.'

'You do that, sunshine, while I sort out what I've got to iron.' Dot's hand went to her mouth and her eyes flew open. 'Oh, my God, I've just remembered our Colin asked for a cup of tea.'

'I'll see to it, Mam. It won't take long 'cos the water's still hot.'

When Katy came downstairs again, she said, 'Our Colin asked if Mr Kershaw was coming back and I told him he might. He said he likes him 'cos he didn't treat him like a baby. And I thought he was really nice, too, Mam, so if he does ever come, yer will make him welcome, won't yer?'

'I usually do make people welcome, sunshine, but a lot of upsetting things happened today and it put me off me stride. First our Colin's accident, then the trouble with next door – me nerves were gone.' Dot was remembering what the drunkard from next door had said about John filling his boots in this house. When he'd had time to think about it, John would probably decide it was in his best interests to stay clear. She hoped so, because she didn't want to get herself a bad name by having strange men coming to the house. 'I promise I'll make him welcome, sunshine, but I doubt we'll ever see him again. He might live the other side of Liverpool for all we know.'

'No, he doesn't.' Katy looked surprised. 'Didn't yer know, he lives in Springwell Road.'

'Springwell Road!' Dot's voice reached a high note. 'Yer mean at the top here?'

Katy nodded. 'He said if next door ever started any trouble, to let him know. He told me which house he lived in.'

'Well, would yer believe it! Fancy him living right by us and we've never set eyes on him! It's not as though yer could miss him, not the size he is.'

'It's a long road, Mam, there's probably hundreds of people we don't see. And Mr Kershaw lives right the other end.' Katy wasn't going to divulge anything else she'd been told, so she changed the subject. 'I'll finish the ironing while you do the pressies.'

Chapter Six

Dot raised her head from the pillow and blinked the sleep from her eyes. Something had woken her from a deep slumber but it wasn't the alarm clock because she hadn't set it last night. Looking at it now, the illuminated fingers told her it was six o'clock. It was pitch dark in the room and there wasn't a sound except for the gentle breathing of her daughter lying next to her. She must have been imagining things, she told herself as she laid her head down and pulled the blanket up to her nose. Either that or it was the pipe-cleaners she'd put in her hair to titivate herself up for Christmas Day. 'It serves me right for being so flamin' vain,' she muttered softly as she pulled the pillow down to fit comfortably into her neck. 'And I don't know why I bothered because we won't see a living soul all day.'

She closed her eyes and within seconds could feel herself drifting into sleep, thinking what a lovely sensation it was as your body floated on air and the troubles of the world were left behind. Then her eyes shot open. That was definitely a voice; she wasn't imagining it. She sat up and cocked an ear. Oh Lord, Colin was awake.

'Mam, what time is it?'

'It's only six o'clock, go back to sleep for an hour.'

'But me foot's sore, Mam.'

Dot sighed as she slid her legs from under the clothes. She'd have to go into him or he'd wake Katy, and it wouldn't be fair. It had been well after one o'clock when they'd come to bed, both weary after a long, hard day. The lino was freezing on her bare feet and she could feel the cold strike right through her body. 'Listen, son, it's far too early to get up. Go back to sleep for an hour and stop shouting.'

'But me foot's sore, Mam.'

Dot didn't believe him for a moment, but she wasn't so old she'd forgotten how she was at his age. She used to use every trick in the book to get her parents out of bed at an unearthly hour. 'If yer foot's sore, sunshine, then the best thing for it is to rest in bed. So behave yerself, just for another half hour.'

'Ah, ay, Mam!'

'Colin, for once in yer life, do as ye're told.' With her arms stretched out in front of her to avoid obstacles, Dot made her way back to the front bedroom. She felt like a block of ice and was careful to keep to her side of the bed, away from Katy. She was so cold she didn't even feel sleepy any more. So when Colin called out again ten minutes later, she was lying wide awake staring at the ceiling.

'Mam, I want to go to the lavvy.'

Dot smiled in the darkness. You had to hand it to the lad, he didn't give up easily. He'd keep at it until she finally gave in, so she might just as well surrender now because she'd get no peace. She slipped out of bed and felt on the floor for her old bedroom slippers. Then she pulled a cardigan on and tiptoed from the room.

'I don't want to hear one peep out of you, Colin, d'yer hear? I'm going down to light the fire so the room's warm for yer, so hold yer horses for another ten minutes. If you wake our Katy up I'll be real annoyed with yer 'cos she was on her feet for about eighteen hours yesterday. So don't be selfish, think of somebody else for a change.'

Now the wheels were in motion and turning, Colin was quite happy to promise a noise-free ten minutes. 'I'll be good, Mam.'

Dot was sitting back on her heels watching the flames from the firewood dance around the cobs of coal, when the door opened and Katy came in. 'Mam, why didn't yer wake me? I'd have come down to light the fire.'

'There's no rest for the wicked where our Colin is concerned, sunshine, so I'm just as well making meself useful as lying in bed wide awake.'

'He called out when he heard me.' Katy rubbed her eyes

with the heel of her hands. 'He said he wants to go down the yard.'

'I could say he was a bloody nuisance but I won't because it's Christmas Day, a big day in the life of a child. And he is only a child.'

'I know, Mam.' Katy crossed the room to drop a kiss on her mother's forehead. 'A Happy Christmas, Mam.'

'And the same to you, sunshine.' Dot gave a quick glance at the fire to make sure it had caught before pressing on the floor and scrambling to her feet. 'I can't give yer a hug, 'cos me hands are black. I'll give yer a double one later to make up for it.'

'You wash yer hands, Mam, and I'll make a pot of tea.' Katy made a move towards the kitchen but stopped halfway. 'I've got something on me mind, Mam, and I won't rest if I don't tell yer.'

Dot was full of concern. 'What is it, sunshine?'

'I wasn't going to tell yer, but when I heard yer saying to Mr Kershaw that yer didn't believe in borrowing – well, I've been worrying about it. Yer see, I didn't have enough money to buy decent presents for you and our Colin, and I wanted this Christmas to be special. So the woman in the little shop next to ours, she let me have two bob on tick. She said I could pay it back at sixpence a week.' When her mother just stared at her without saying a word, Katy felt her heart sink. 'I'm sorry, Mam.'

Dot looked down at her dirty hands, then at her daughter. 'Oh, to hell with it, what's a bit of dirt between mother and daughter.' She wrapped her arms around Katy and hugged her tight. 'There's no need to be sorry, sunshine. Yer did it to make someone happy and there's no harm in that.'

A voice came from above. 'Me foot's sore, I want to go to the lavvy and me throat's dry for want of a drink.'

Mother and daughter clung to each other, laughing. 'My God, he doesn't do things by half, does he?' Dot chuckled. 'I've had the foot and I've had the lavvy, but now he's added thirst for good measure.'

'Well, it is lousy for him when he can't get about. You put the kettle on and wash yer hands, Mam, and I'll help him out of bed and on to the stairs.'

85

Dot stood in the hall and watched her son negotiate the stairs on his bottom. 'Yer did well, son, as quick as yer would have done on yer two feet.' She helped him stand on his right leg then put an arm around his waist and the other under his armpit. 'Lean all yer weight on me – there, that's right. Now start hopping.'

Colin's eyes went straight to the sideboard. 'We've got crackers, Mam!' His eyes were as round as saucers. 'Oh boy, I've never pulled a cracker before.' He'd stopped by the couch expecting to be set down, but his mother wasn't having any.

'Oh no, you don't, young feller-me-lad, it's down the yard with you. And after that I want to take a look at yer foot and put another cold compress on it. Then we can all sit down to open our presents with a nice cup of tea and a mince pie.'

Colin howled with frustration. 'Oh, no!'

'Oh, but yes!' Dot pulled him towards the kitchen. 'Open the back door for us, Katy, there's a good girl.'

Ten minutes later Colin was sitting comfortably on the couch. His mother had examined his foot before putting the compress on, and was pleased that it didn't seem quite as swollen as yesterday. She'd given his face and hands a cat's lick and a promise with the flannel, and now he was ready for the big moment.

Katy passed the crackers around first. 'There's paper hats in them, so we can look all Christmassy when we open our pressies. Here yer are, Colin, you can pull mine with me.'

There was much laugher as crackers were pulled, mottoes read and paper hats perched on heads. 'You look like a queen, Mam,' Colin giggled, 'with a crown on.'

Dot laughed. 'Oh, aye, I can see Queen Mary with pipe-cleaners in her hair.' She patted her hair and adopted a posh accent. 'Don't you know, they're the latest fashion? Oh yes, anybody who is anybody is wearing them.'

Katy handed her brother four of the parcels off the sideboard. 'You first, seeing as you're the youngest. Those two are off our mam, and the other two off me.'

The pale blue shirt was greeted with a knowing nod. 'I knew yer wouldn't leave me out.' The selection box had his mouth watering. 'Can I start on them now?'

'No, wait until all the presents are open, then yer can give us all a square of chocolate.'

The first parcel he opened of Katy's brought forth a howl of delight. 'Ooh, ay, Mam, just look at these. A scarf and gloves to match. There'll be no holding me back when I've got these on, I'll be the cock of the north.'

Katy was pleased with his reaction. He wasn't to know that she'd got them for half price because, as the woman in the shop told her, they were classed as seconds on account of there being a flaw in them. Nobody would know there was anything wrong with them because you'd need a magnifying glass to see the small knot in the wool.

The last present had Colin bouncing up and down on the couch. It was a *Beano Annual* and he went into raptures over it. 'I can't believe it! Mam, I can't believe it's really mine! Oh, thank you, Katy, I'll love yer forever for this.' He stroked the hard-backed cover as though it was something precious. Indeed, it was precious to him. No more would he have to envy his friends who taunted him with their *Beano* and *Dandy* books. He was so overcome his eyes were brimming with tears when he looked at his sister. 'This is the bestest present yer could have got me, our Katy, and I'll take good care of it. I won't lend it out, I promise.'

'Doesn't yer sister deserve a kiss?' Dot asked quietly.

'Yeah, I'll say she does.' Colin laid the treasured book on his lap and held his arms wide. 'And a big hug.'

Katy could feel his cheek wet with tears and she filled up herself when he whispered, 'I love you, our Katy.'

'And I love you, too.' She ruffled his hair. 'Now you be quiet while me mam sees what Santa's brought for her.'

Dot shook her head. 'No, you first, sunshine.'

Her hands trembling, Katy picked up her three parcels. Colin had his head buried in his book and Dot was unrolling the pipe-cleaners from her hair as she watched, praying her daughter wouldn't be disappointed. Then the silence of the room was broken with Katy's shrieks of delight as each parcel was unwrapped. She'd never had grown-up clothes before, and now she was the proud possessor of two blouses and a skirt her happiness knew no bounds. The blouse off the Edwards' was in a pale blue with long sleeves, buttoned to the neck with pearl buttons and had a neat, pointed collar. The one off her mother was in a dusty pink, also with long sleeves and buttoned to the neck, but with a mandarin collar. And the navy blue skirt, fitted over the hips and then slightly flared, was, to Katy's inexperienced eye, the height of fashion.

Katy stared down at the clothes on her knee, savouring the moment and telling herself she wasn't dreaming. Then she placed them down and went to hug her mother. 'Thank you, Mam, they're lovely. I didn't expect so much and I'm a very lucky girl. But yer shouldn't have spent so much on me, really yer shouldn't. I bet yer haven't got anything new for yerself, have yer?'

'Yes I have, sunshine. I bought meself a skirt when I was getting yours. They're only cheap but I did the best I could with the money I had. I cut down a bit on food, like only getting a chicken instead of a turkey, but we won't starve.'

'Yer did right, Mam. I'd rather have something new to wear than stuffing meself with food, any day.' Katy tilted her head and asked, 'What's your skirt like?'

'Just plain, like yours, only in dark brown.'

'Then my present will go lovely with it.' Katy took the last parcel from the sideboard and handed it over. 'I was going to buy yer two small presents but changed me mind and got one good one. I hope yer'll like it.'

The jumper was in the palest of green, knitted in a delicate open-work pattern. It was so pretty, Dot was lost for words. How long was it since she'd had anything as lovely as this? For the last ten years everything she'd bought had to be cheap and hard-wearing. She couldn't remember the last time she'd gone into a shop and bought something just because she liked the look of it.

'D'yer like it, Mam? I thought the colour would suit yer 'cos of yer hazel eyes.'

'It's beautiful, sunshine.' Dot fingered the soft wool. 'It looks hand-knitted.'

'It was, Mam!' Katy leaned forward, her face eager. 'Some woman does knitting and sells it to Mrs Green in the shop to make a few bob. I was told she makes a couple every week, so she mustn't half be a fast knitter. Anyway, I'd gone in the shop to get a pair of woollen gloves for yer when the woman turned up with two jumpers. I fell for that one right away because the colour's so pretty.'

'And yer ended up getting tick.' Dot smiled. 'I'm glad yer did, sunshine, 'cos I'll feel like a million dollars in this.'

Colin had been staring at the same picture in his book while he listened to his mother and sister. Now he said, 'Yer'll look pretty in it, Mam, with yer new skirt and yer hair all done nice. And our Katy will look nice, too. We've all done well, haven't we? I never knew that Christmas Day could be like this.'

'Yes, but don't forget that Christmas is not just about giving presents, son, it's a celebration.'

'Yeah, I know that, Mam. And I won't half be in trouble for not going to Mass today. I'll likely get the cane for it.'

'No you won't, son, 'cos I'll give yer a note to take to school with yer. Me and Katy are going to eleven o'clock Mass, and if Father Kelly's on the altar I'll make it me business to see him afterwards and explain.'

'Mam,' Katy said, 'can I get washed in the sink before you start out there? I can't wait to get meself all dolled up. I'm spoilt for choice on what to wear. I think I'll put the blue blouse on this morning, then change into the other for this afternoon.'

Dot smiled, happy for her daughter. She was a pretty girl and she deserved to have pretty clothes. 'You get washed and see to yerself, sunshine. I'll need the kitchen to meself when I start 'cos I've got the chicken to clean, so it's ready to stick in the oven before we go to church. We'll just have a round of toast for breakfast because we'll be having a big dinner about one o'clock.'

Colin was propped up on the couch reading his book. His mam had placed a chair at the side of him and on it sat a cup of tea and a plate with a mince pie on. He was wearing his new shirt and feeling very pleased with himself and very contented. It was almost worth having a sore foot when you got waited on like this. He had just taken a bite out of the mince pie when a knock came on the door and his eyes rolled from side to side. Oh dear, what should he do now? He'd better call out and tell whoever it was to come back when his mam was in.

'Who is it?'

Through the letter box came the reply, 'John Kershaw.'

'Hang on a minute, Mr Kershaw.' Colin wasn't going to tell him to come back, even if he had to crawl on his hands and knees. He liked the big man and wanted to show him all the presents he'd got. Putting the book down at the side of him, the boy then pushed the chair back and swung his good leg over the side of the couch. Scratching his head, he looked down at the foot that was encased in a piece of sheeting. If he could hop to the end of the couch he could reach the door and hold on to that for support. 'I'm coming, Mr Kershaw. Don't go away, will yer?'

'Oh dear, oh dear.' John looked down from his great height at the boy who was grinning from ear to ear. 'Isn't your mother in? You really shouldn't be moving about because if you get another knock on that ankle you'll know about it.'

'I haven't been moving about, Mr Kershaw, I've been lying on the couch. But me mam's gone to Mass with our Katy, and there was no one else to open the door.'

'I could have come back later, Colin.'

'I didn't want yer to do that, Mr Kershaw. I wanted to show yer me presents now.' Hanging on to the door, the boy hopped back a step. 'Come on in, Mr Kershaw.'

'I'm not sure I should, Colin, not with your mother being out. She might not take kindly to the idea and send me packing with a flea in my ear.'

'Nah, me mam's not like that, she'll be made-up 'cos I've got someone to sit with me. Honest, she won't mind at all.'

'On your own head be it, Colin.' John was carrying a large canvas bag with handles of thin rope slotted through brass eyelets, and this he held in front of him as he mounted the top step. 'You go through and I'll close the door after me.'

Colin was sitting on the edge of the couch holding his book when John came in. 'Look what I got off our Katy.

Aren't I lucky? It's me bestest present.'

The big man smiled as he set the bag down carefully on the floor at the side of the couch. 'You are indeed very lucky. When I was your age, the *Beano* was always my favourite present, too. Look after it and you'll get years of enjoyment from it. I've still got all my copies and they're all in excellent condition even though they're well over twenty years old.'

'Go 'way! How many have yer got?'

'Six copies. When I was fourteen my mother decided I was too old for children's books. My dear mother wasn't often wrong, but she was on that score because I still get them out occasionally and I find them as funny now as I did then.'

'Wow!' Colin looked at his *Beano* and it suddenly became more precious to him. And it also increased his liking for John now they had something in common. 'I will look after it and I'll put it away and keep it, like you did.'

John was still standing and now he said, 'Get back to the couch properly, Colin, and rest that leg, otherwise it'll never get better.'

'Yes, Mr Kershaw.' Colin made himself comfortable then let his eyes travel the full length of the man standing before him. 'Ye're not half a big man, Mr Kershaw. How tall are yer?'

John chuckled. 'Six feet four and a half inches.'

Colin whistled through his teeth. 'D'yer think I might grow to be that tall?'

'How old are you now – eleven?'

'I'll be twelve in three weeks.'

'Well, you're certainly not small for your age, so I'd say there's a fair chance of you growing into a tall man.' John could see a question forming in the boy's mind, and before it reached his lips, he quickly added, 'You'll have to wait a few years to know for sure, though.' He pulled a chair near the couch. 'Now, I haven't seen this year's *Beano Annual*, so how about you and me reading it together?'

Dot linked Katy's arm as they came out of the church. 'I'm glad we hung back to let the crowd go first, it's given Father Kelly time to get round.' The priest was shaking hands with his parishioners and mother and daughter joined the small queue that had formed.

'A merry Christmas to yer, Mrs Baker, and to you, Katy.' Father Kelly shook their hands, his face beaming with good cheer. He was a fine figure of a man, tall and slim with a mop of pure white hair and rosy cheeks. With his soft lilting accent and that quick humour of the Irish, he was very popular in the parish. Not that he was always sweetness and light, far from it. Once he was in that confessional box, or taking the children for their catechism, he became the man who had taken holy orders to lead his flock on the road to righteousness, and take them he would, come what may. 'Is yer son with yer, Mrs Baker?'

'No, Father, he's laid up on the couch.' Dot explained what had happened and said she hoped Colin wouldn't be punished for missing Mass. 'There's no way he could have made it, his foot's out like this.' She held her hands about fifteen inches apart and when she heard the laugh that rumbled in the priest's tummy, she burst out laughing herself. 'Perhaps I exaggerated a bit, Father, but it is the truth, he is laid up.'

'Sure, I know yerself wouldn't be telling me a lie, Mrs Baker. It's sorry I am to hear about the boy's misfortune and you can tell him I'll remember him in my prayers tonight.' He smiled at Dot and patted Katy on the head. 'God bless you both.'

'Thank you, Father.'

They were walking through the church gates when Dot heard her name being called. She turned her head. 'It's Mrs Mason and Doreen.'

After greetings were exchanged, Betty told her daughter to walk on with Katy. 'I couldn't keep up with you two, so get going. Me and Dot can have a natter on the way.'

'But no one's had any breakfast yet.' Doreen's voice always seemed to have a wail in it. 'Me dad will go mad if we don't get back soon.'

'No, he won't, 'cos you'll be there to make him a pot of tea and some toast. Yer've got two hands, the same as me, so start learning how to use 'em.'

Doreen tossed her head. 'Tut, come on, Katy, it's no good arguing.'

Dot knew it would take her twice as long to get home because, carrying so much weight, Betty walked at a snail's pace. 'Katy, look at the chicken when yer get in and see if it's done,' she asked hastily.

'How will I know if it's done, Mam?'

Betty spluttered, 'Ask the bleedin' thing. Open the over door and say, "Are you ready yet, Mr Chicken?".'

Doreen pulled on her friend's arm. 'Come on, Katy, yer'll not get any sense where me mam is. Everything's a joke to her.'

'Well, it has been since you were born, girl, I've got to admit. I never used to laugh much before that, but the minute you were born and the nurse put yer in me arms, I started laughing and haven't stopped since.'

'Go on, girls, take no notice of her. Tell each other what yer got off Father Christmas.' Dot waited until they were out of earshot then said, 'Yer were a bit hard on your Doreen, weren't yer?'

'Not as hard as I'd like to be.' The smile left Betty's face as she waddled from side to side. 'She won't do a thing in the house, won't lift a finger to help. All she's fit for is standing in front of the mirror titivating herself up. I'm hoping she gets a job soon and finds out what it's like to get her flamin' hands dirty. That's if she can stick a job – she's a lazy bleedin' cow.'

'Betty, it's Christmas Day! Will yer stop swearing?'

'I haven't said no swearwords, girl, what are yer on about?'

'You, with yer bleedin' this, and yer bleedin' that.'

Betty stopped waddling and rested her face on a chubby hand. She was thoughtful for just a few seconds. 'That's not a swearword.'

'Oh, yes it is!'

'In that case, your Colin's not half starting young. Last time I was in your house he came running in after he'd fallen over, and I distinctly remember him saying, "Mam, me leg's bleeding".'

Dot bit on her bottom lip. She could tell the other woman was bursting with laugher inside, and didn't want to give her the satisfaction of knowing she saw the funny side of it. 'Yeah, but he *was* bleeding, wasn't he?' she said obstinately. 'That was real blood running down his leg.'

'Oh, I see what ye're gettin' at, now, girl! It's the real thing yer want! Oh, what a pity I don't carry me bread-knife around with me. I could have slashed me wrists and said, "Oh dear, Dorothy, look at me bleedin' arm".'

Dot shook her head and linked her arm through her friend's. 'OK, you win, I give up.' She tried to speed up Betty's walking pace but she'd have had more luck pulling a number 22 tram. 'I'm surprised yer didn't hear the commotion last night. Tom Campbell was giving Mary a hiding and we heard it through the wall. The bloke that knocked our Colin over was in our house and heard it.'

'Hang on a minute, stop right there. What's this about your Colin gettin' knocked over? No one told me nothin' about that.'

'Well, it was late last night, too late to be picked up by the grapevine. I'd sent him to the chippy because I was too tired to cook and . . .' Dot carried on with the story and didn't let Betty's 'Ooohs, aaaahs and bloody hells' distract her. She was up to the part where John had dragged Tom Campbell off the step, when they reached the corner of Edith Road. 'I'll tell yer in more detail another time, but the upshot was, this John feller gave Tom Campbell a bloody good hiding.'

'If yer think yer can leave me swinging at the most exciting part, Dot Baker, then yer can just sod off. Whether yer like it or not, I'm coming up to yours to hear the rest of it. I'll just give my feller a knock and let him know where I am.' Betty's way of letting her husband know, and everyone else in the street, was to bang on the window and yell, 'I'm goin' to Dot's, I won't be long.'

'Ye're right there, Betty, yer won't be long. I want to see to the dinner 'cos I'm starving. We only had a round of toast for breakfast.'

'Ah, yer poor bugger, me heart bleeds for yer.' Betty cocked an ear as she watched her neighbour turn the key in the lock. 'Can't be much wrong with your Colin, he's laughing his blinkin' head off.'

Dot pushed the door open but didn't mount the step immediately. A man's laughter had joined that of her son and daughter. 'Oh Lord, I've got a visitor.' She turned to her friend. 'If it's who I think it is, Betty, will her behave yerself and watch yer language, please?'

Betty's chins did a dance when she shook her head. 'Would yer like me to go home and put me best party dress on? The one with the frill around the bottom, what shows off me shapely legs? And when I bend down it shows off me shapely backside which my feller says reminds him of the rising sun?'

Dot grinned. 'No, I love yer just as yer are.' She had recognised the man's voice, but what the hell? If John Kershaw didn't like her friends that was just too bad; it was his worry, not hers. And anyway, what was he doing here?

Chapter Seven

John jumped to his feet when the two women entered the room. 'I'm sorry to intrude on Christmas Day. I really only knocked to see how Colin was, but he insisted I come in and see his presents. Particularly his *Beano Annual*.'

'That's all right.' Dot sensed his embarrassment and found herself feeling sorry for him. God knows why, because he was big enough to look after himself. And she could also tell by her son's face that he'd been a welcome visitor. She waved her hand. 'Betty Mason, this is John Kershaw.'

Betty pumped his hand up and down, her chubby face creased in a wide smile. 'So you're the one who gave the queer feller next door a good hidin', are yer? My God, when he saw the size of you he must have done it in his kecks.'

'Yer'll have to excuse my friend, John, she's inclined to say exactly what comes into her mind without thinking it through first. She'll get me hung one of these days.'

John had trouble keeping his face straight. 'At least you know where you are with someone who says what they think to your face, and doesn't go behind your back.'

Betty pulled a face at Dot. 'There yer are, a man after me own heart in more ways than one. Tell him to sit down so I can hear the rest of the story from the horse's mouth, so to speak.'

John shook his head. 'No, I won't intrude any longer. I'm sure Dot has a thousand and one things to do.'

'She's not going to get them done while I'm here,' Betty told him, 'and I ain't moving until I've heard all the gory details.'

Dot could see the eagerness in her son's eyes and knew she was outnumbered. 'Put the kettle on, Katy, please, and make a pot of tea. Oh, and take the chicken out of the oven for us, there's a good girl, or it'll be burned to a frazzle.'

'That's more like it.' Betty chose one of the dining chairs so her backside could hang over the sides. 'Sit down, John, and make yerself at home. Pretend ye're at yer grandma's.'

But John remained standing. 'There was another reason for me coming this way today, apart from calling to see how Colin was. I intended to knock next door to see Mrs Campbell.'

Dot's eyes travelled the length of him. He was wearing a beautifully tailored suit in light grey that most definitely hadn't come off the thirty-bob rail at Burton's. His white shirt was immaculate and his dark blue tie perfectly knotted. 'I wouldn't recommend yer to do that,' she said. 'If her husband saw yer there'd be blue murder, and we don't want the street up on Christmas Day.'

'I've bought something for her.' John moved from one foot to the other, obviously ill at ease. 'With you saying she'd have no food in, it's been playing on my mind. No one should go hungry today.'

'So you've bought food for her?'

John nodded. 'I get a turkey given to me every year by my boss and I never eat it all, it goes to waste. So I got up very early this morning and cooked it.' He made a gesture towards the canvas bag. 'It's in there, with a few other things.'

Betty had been listening intently, her chin cupped in her hand. 'Ye're a kind man, John, but where the hell can she say she got a ruddy turkey from?'

Dot laced her fingers and stared down at her clasped hands. He was a kind man, no doubt about that. Kind and generous. 'Colin, have yer heard any sounds from next door while we've been out?'

'I heard the grate being raked out, but I haven't heard no voices.'

'The queer feller's probably still in bed.' Dot pinched her bottom lip. 'I wonder if I could get Mary to come in here and see what she has to say. I don't see why she should go hungry because her dear husband spends all his wages on booze.'

Katy popped her head around the kitchen door. 'Mary's in the yard now, getting coal.'

Dot flew off her chair. 'I'll nab her before she goes back in the house.'

Mary was halfway up the yard with a shovelful of coal when she heard Dot call her name. Her nerves were shattered and every bone in her body ached, but Dot was one of the few friends she had and she couldn't ignore her. 'Yes, Dot?'

'Is your feller still in bed?'

'Yeah. He'll probably stay there all day with the pubs being shut.'

'Well, I've got something to show yer. Come over for a minute.'

'I don't want to see no one, Dot. I look a mess.'

'Mary, if yer slip out of the entry door, no one will see yer. Yer've got a choice – either yer come under yer own steam or I drag yer round.'

'I'll come, but just for five minutes.'

When Mary saw John and Betty, she turned to flee, but Dot held her around the waist. 'These are friends, Mary, and there's no need to fear yer friends.'

Betty gasped when she saw the state of her face. 'The bloody swine!' She left her chair to gather the trembling woman in her arms. 'There, there, don't cry.' When she held the frail body all she could feel were bones. If anyone wanted feeding up, it was Mary Campbell. And if anyone deserved to rot in hell it was her husband. 'Come and warm yerself by the fire, ye're shakin' like a leaf.'

Dot felt a lump form in her throat. Apart from the bruised and swollen face, and the far too thin body, her neighbour was dressed in rags. No one would believe her husband had a full-time job and earned a decent wage. With only the two of them, they should be living in style with a nice home, plenty of clothes and a full larder. Instead, the Campbells' house was bare of all creature comforts, the larder was empty and Mary was dressed like a tramp.

Her pity turning to anger at the injustice of it all, Dot caught John's eyes. She nodded first to where the bag stood, then to the kitchen door. And when she left the room he picked up the bag and followed her. 'I've got an idea,' she told him. 'It might not work but it's worth a try. Will yer empty what yer've got on to the draining board, please, John?'

Dot gaped when she saw the size of the turkey. 'My God, that would feed a family of ten! If I know Tom Campbell, he'd take one look at that and put it on the fire out of spite.'

'She needs plenty of nourishment, Dot, she's far too thin,' John said. 'If she's expecting a baby, as you say, she'll have to start getting some food down her, and she'd get several dinners out of that.'

'If she was allowed to.' Dot gazed at the other items he'd taken from the bag. A small Christmas cake, a tin of shortbread biscuits and a box of mince pies. Then her eyes turned to the pans on the stove. It wouldn't hurt them to have a roast potato and a few sprouts less. 'I'll see if I can get her to stay here for dinner. If her husband lies in bed all day he won't even miss her.'

'Then you must use the turkey.'

'I'd have to use some of it because we've only got a chicken and it's got to do us tomorrow, as well. But I'll make sure she gets a good dinner today, tomorrow and the next day. I can't promise anything after that because I'll be skint until me next payday.'

'It's not right that anyone should have to live the way she does, is it, Dot?'

'No, it isn't, John, but neighbours can only do so much. She's very proud, she won't ask for help. But we'll keep our eye on her, don't worry. Her husband's determined she won't have this baby, but me and the O'Connors are just as determined that she will. And when I've had a good talk to me mate in there,' Dot nodded towards the living room, 'we'll have her on our side, too. There'll always be someone watching out for Mary.'

'Good! Then I'll go on my way and leave you in peace.'

Dot followed him out of the kitchen. 'Going visiting, are yer?'

'No, I'm going home,' John said, before smiling down at Betty who was sitting next to Mary and holding the thin hands in her chubby ones. 'It was nice meeting you, Mrs Mason, and I wish you all the best. And you, too, Mrs Campbell. I hope the New Year will bring you better fortune.'

Mary raised her head and tried to smile, but the action brought a grimace to her face. 'Things couldn't get any worse, Mr Kershaw.'

Dot was standing behind him and all she could think of was that huge turkey in her kitchen while he was going home to an empty house.

'Ye're welcome to stay here for yer dinner, John.'

Katy and Colin had been as quiet as mice, now they both shrieked with pleasure. 'Oh yes, Mr Kershaw, say yer'll stay!'

'Thank you, but I think not. There's work to be done and I'd be in the way.'

Dot poked him on the shoulder. 'I'm not asking yer, John, I'm telling yer. Now sit yerself down in that chair 'cos, as I've told yer before, yer make the place look untidy.' With her hands on her hips, she turned to Betty. 'Mrs Mason, will yer do me a favour and send your Doreen up with two dinner plates and two knives and forks?'

'I'd have to go home to do that, girl.'

Dot leaned forward and pinched her cheek. 'Yes, I know that, Betty, and it's about time yer went home to see yer family.'

'Blimey! Talk about "here's yer hat, what's yer hurry?" isn't in it!' Betty patted Mary's hands before releasing them. 'I'm cut to the quick, I really am.' She winked at John who was now sitting in the fireside chair. 'I've got a very delicate constitution and I get upset real easy.'

John winked back. 'Yes, I knew as soon as I saw you that you were a very shy, vulnerable woman.'

Betty had half-pushed herself up from the chair; now she let her backside fall back on to the wooden seat. 'What did yer say I was?'

'Shy and vulnerable.'

Betty screwed her face up and her eyes disappeared in the folds of flesh. 'Shy I can understand, but what's that other thing yer said I was?'

John chuckled. 'Vulnerable.'

'And what's that when it's out?'

'It means you are easily hurt.'

'Oh yeah, I am! Ooh, aren't yer a good judge of character, eh?'

101

Dot grabbed her friend's arm and pulled. 'Missus, will yer get going so I can start on the dinner, please? Me tummy's rumbling like no one's business. I'll finish the story next time I see yer.'

'No need, girl, John told me while yer were in the back yard.' Betty leaned towards Mary and cupped her face. 'You stay here, love, and have a bit of company for a change. Do yer the world of good.'

A look of fear crossed Mary's face. 'Oh no, I'll have to get back in case he decides to come down. There'd be murder if I wasn't there.'

'If yer weren't there, girl, the only person he could murder would be himself and think what a blessing that would be. One less bad 'un in the world.'

'Mary's staying here for her dinner.' Dot lifted her hand when Mary moved to protest. 'No argument, yer'll have a good dinner here, then I'll take yer home and see how the land lies. If his nibs starts anything I'll clock him with the poker.' She took Betty's arm. 'Come on, sunshine, I'll see yer to the door. And don't forget the plates and things, otherwise they'll be eating from the pans with their fingers.'

While Dot was in the kitchen seeing to the dinner, she could hear laughter coming from the living room. John had started a guessing game and even Mary seemed to have relaxed and was joining in. It was her turn now. 'I spy, with my little eye, something beginning with M.'

Colin's hand shot up. 'Mirror.' Wrong.

'Mantelpiece,' Katy said. Wrong.

'Mat,' was John's guess. Wrong.

Dot poked her head around the door. 'Will yer take yer seats at the table, please? All except you, Colin, you'd better stay put.' As she was putting Mary's dinner in front of her, she asked, 'Was it the matchbox?'

Mary's nod brought a cry of complaint from Colin. 'Ah, ay, Mam, that's not fair, yer weren't even playing! I bet I'd have got it.'

'What you'll get, sunshine, if yer spill any gravy on me couch, is a thick lip.'

'Oh dear, oh dear.' John laughed. 'What a sorry sight that

would be. A thick lip to go with your thick ankle. No can walk, no can talk.'

Even Colin joined in the laughter and this set the seal for a very happy and jolly Christmas dinner. What they lacked in such niceties as serviettes, decent cutlery and crockery, they made up for in laughter. And it was John who brought forth much of the hilarity. He was a born story-teller with a marvellous sense of humour. Katy and Colin were delighted with him, he was the perfect finishing touch to the happiest and most exciting day of their young lives. And Dot was thanking her lucky stars that she'd asked him to stay because he brought Mary out of her shell. She looked so relaxed, laughing easily at John's jokes and contributing some of her own. And when the meal was over her plate was clean.

'That was a lovely meal, Dot.' Mary pushed her plate away and patted her tummy. 'I'm full to the brim.'

'Yer must have a little space left for a piece of Christmas cake?'

'I couldn't, I really am stored.'

'I'll wrap yer a piece up to take home with yer, then.' Dot began to stack the dirty plates. 'And a mince pie and some shortbread biscuits.' She was laying the knives and forks on the top plate when the door knocker sounded. 'I'll go, I'm on me feet.'

When she came back into the room, she jerked her head at Katy. 'Someone for you.'

'For me? Who is it, Mam?'

Dot kept her face straight. 'I couldn't tell yer, sunshine, I didn't recognise him.'

Katy's frown grew deeper. 'Yer must know him – yer know all me friends.'

'I didn't recognise him, Katy, and if yer don't get a move on he'll be turned to a block of ice 'cos it's freezing out there.'

When Katy turned her back, Dot put a finger to her lips for silence. 'Just listen.'

They didn't have to wait long for the squeal, followed by, 'Billy, yer've got long trousers on! Ooh, yer don't half look grown-up.'

Billy eyed her new skirt and blouse with admiration. 'So do you, yer look a cracker.'

'Come on in and let's have a proper look at yer.' Katy closed the door and pushed him ahead of her into the room. 'How about this, then, Mam? Quite the little gentleman, isn't he?'

Dot nodded, her face serious but her eyes laughing. 'I told yer, I didn't recognise him.'

His face the colour of beetroot, Billy shuffled his feet. 'Me mam bought me them for Christmas. She bought me these and another pair to go to work in.'

'Very smart, young man,' John said. 'But I don't know why Katy said you looked like a little gentleman because you're not so little. You must be about five feet seven or eight from where I'm sitting.'

Billy's chest expanded with pride. 'I'm five foot seven and a half.'

'I thought so.' John pursed his lips for a second. 'By the time you're eighteen, you'll be over six foot.'

This caused Billy to stretch to his full height. 'Yeah, that's what me dad said.'

Dot picked up the plates and made for the kitchen. 'Sit yerself down, Billy, we're just going to have a cup of tea.' She plonked the dishes on the draining board before popping her head back in the room. 'We don't mind yer standing if yer don't want to get yer new trousers creased.'

'Nah.' Billy moved his shoulders in a cocky manner. 'That don't worry me, I've had them on since I got up.'

'Sit down then, while I give me mam a hand.' As Katy walked towards the kitchen she was thinking she'd never even imagined there was such a thing as complete happiness. But she knew now what it was and to let her feelings out, she put her arms around her mother and hugged her tight. 'Mam, hasn't this been the most marvellous day?'

'It has, sunshine, it really has. God has been looking down on us this year.' Dot put her arms around her daughter's waist and the pair clung to each other. 'Let's hope it's the start of a better life for us.' A shadow crossed her eyes and she looked over Katy's shoulder to see John standing in the doorway. She smiled at him before releasing her hold on her daughter.

'We've always been a soppy family.'

'I think loving is the word. And that's how a family should be.' John nodded towards the pile of dirty dishes. 'I came out to give a hand with the washing up.'

'What – in that suit? Yer must be joking!'

'That's easily remedied.' John slipped his jacket off and hung it on the knob of the kitchen door before removing his cuff links and rolling his shirt-sleeves up. 'I'm house-trained and can wash dishes with the best of them.'

'I'll help me mam, Mr Kershaw,' Katy said. 'There's no need for you to get yer clothes dirty.'

'Oh, and what about your clothes? I didn't say it before because I didn't want to embarrass Mary, but you both look very pretty in your new clothes.'

Katy beamed with pleasure while Dot bowed from the waist. 'Thank you, kind sir.'

'You can thank me by allowing me to help with the dishes.'

'OK, if you insist.' Dot took the kettle of boiling water from the stove and poured it into the sink. 'I'll wash, you dry, and Katy can make a pot of tea. Mary will be on pins to get home so let's get cracking.'

'I'd rather go on me own, Dot,' Mary said, clasping her hands together to stop them from shaking. 'I'll be all right, honest.'

'I'm coming with yer to make sure. If he's come down, and the fire's gone out, he'll be like a raving lunatic.' Dot slipped her arms into her coat. 'If he's still in bed, then all well and good, I'll leave yer to it.' She linked her arm through Mary's. 'Hide those cakes from him and eat them tonight for supper.'

John didn't look very happy. 'I think it would be far better if I took her.'

'No, that would be like waving a red flag at a bull. I'll give a shout if we need help, don't worry, I'm not a ruddy hero.' Dot squeezed Mary's arm. 'Come on, sunshine, let's get it over and done with. Say goodbye to yer Auntie Mary, kids, and with a bit of luck yer might see her again for dinner tomorrow.'

When Dot opened the door from the entry into her

neighbour's yard, she felt a pull on her arm. 'What is it, sunshine?'

Mary's whole body was shaking. 'He's up.'

'How d' yer know?'

'I put a shovelful of coal down in the yard when yer called me. I thought I'd only be gone a few minutes. It's not there now.'

Dot felt her tummy tighten with fear. She didn't fancy facing the violence of Tom Campbell and it flashed through her head to shout for John. Then she remembered the horrible things Mary's husband had said about her and her fear turned to anger. 'Come on, love, there's two of us, he can't eat us.' She propelled Mary up the yard, opened the kitchen door and pushed her neighbour in ahead of her. She deliberately left the door open in case of emergency.

Tom Campbell was sprawled in a chair, his battered face almost as bad as his wife's, but he still managed to curl his lips in a sneer. 'Oh, yer've decided to come home, have yer? Where the bleedin' hell d' yer think yer've been?'

Mary didn't answer. She was shaking so much she couldn't have spoken if she'd tried. Fear was written all over her and it was enough to incense Dot. 'Mary knows where she's been, she doesn't have to think about it. I invited her to ours for an hour, and seeing as you were in bed snoring yer ruddy head off, what difference does it make to you where she's been?'

Tom put his hands on the arms of the chair and pulled his body forward. 'She's my wife, she should be here when I want her. Not that it's any of your business, yer nosy cow.'

'Oh, so when yer want something, yer remember she's yer wife, eh? That's convenient for yer, isn't it? What a pity yer don't remember when ye're propping the bar up at the pub every night, spending the money on ale that yer should give her to buy food and clothing for herself. Just look at the state of her,' Dot waved a hand towards the cowering woman. 'She's expecting a baby and she needs to eat good food, both for her sake and the baby's. If she was married to a real man he'd make sure she was getting looked after properly. But then, she's not married to a real man, more's the pity.'

'Oh, expectin' a baby, is she? Up the bleedin' spout, eh?'

'That's a funny thing to say, seeing as you gave it to her.'

'I gave it to her an' I can take it away from her.'

The evil written on his face sent shudders down Dot's spine. Afterwards she was to wonder how she had the guts to do it, but she crossed the floor and stood directly in front of him. Wagging a stiffened finger in his face, she ground the words out through clenched teeth. 'You ever again lay a hand on Mary and it'll be the sorriest thing yer ever did. I know two men at least, who would like nothing better than to teach you a lesson. And they're both within shouting distance of where I'm standing now. D'yer want me to call them?'

'This is my house an' they'll not get through the bleedin' door.'

'Oh no? If yer'd like to get off yer lazy, fat backside, yer'll see I've left the kitchen door open just in case. If I raise my voice, they'll come running and you won't be able to stop them. Yer see, yer'd have to get past me first and I wouldn't advise yer to try.'

A sly look crossed Tom's face. He knew she wasn't lying because she sounded too sure of herself. She was a nosy bleeding cow and he'd get her one of these days. And he knew exactly how he'd get back at her, through his wife. Mary would be made to suffer for this, by God she would, but it would be in his own sweet time. 'I don't know what all this commotion's about, just because I asked me wife where she'd been. Bloody hell, any husband would 'ave asked the same if his missus had gone missing.'

Dot knew what his tactics were and was filled with disgust. He'd wheedle and worm his way out of anything if he thought his precious hide was at stake. If she weren't so fond of Mary she wouldn't even want to be in the same room as this man. 'You're pathetic, d'yer know that? I'm not going to waste any more of me breath on yer.' She turned to Mary. 'One of us will give yer a knock later, just to make sure ye're all right. But if yer need us, all yer have to do is bang on the wall either side.' As she was going through the door Dot turned around unexpectedly and caught an expression of such fierce hatred on Tom Campbell's face it made her flesh crawl. It threw her for a second, then strengthened her resolve. 'I've asked Mary to come for dinner tomorrow. If yer've any objections, speak up now.' When there was no reply, she looked at the timid woman who was too afraid to speak up for herself. 'One of us will call for yer about one o'clock, Mary.' Then, glaring at Tom, she added, 'If yer don't come, we'll know why.'

With her head held high and her shoulders squared, Dot marched down the Campbells' backyard. But once out in the entry she leaned back against the wall and gulped in the cold, clean fresh air. She hoped she never had to go through that again. Standing in the same room as that man, you could almost touch the wickedness of him. He was evil through and through and capable of doing great harm to Mary without batting an eyelid.

'Well, how did it go?'

Dot was so lost in thought she jumped when she heard the voice. 'Ooh, yer gave me a fright! And that's the last thing I need after battling it out with the queer feller.'

'I'm sorry, I didn't mean to frighten you,' John said. 'But when you were so long the children began to get worried about you.'

Dot pushed herself away from the wall. 'I have never in my life met anyone who is as rotten to the core as Tom Campbell is.' She quickly related all that had been said, ending with a deep sigh as she told him, 'He said he could take the baby away from her, and yer don't need much intelligence to know what he means by that. And d'yer know what, John? I've got a terrible feeling in me heart that he'll carry out his threat.'

'We mustn't let him. Somehow we've got to put a stop to his shenanigans.'

'I intend to, believe me. I have no intention of sitting back and letting him harm Mary or her baby. But the biggest stumbling block is Mary herself. She's so terrified of him she gives in to him all the time. If he told her to stick her head in the gas oven, she'd do it. There's times when I could shake her, she's so docile. She wants this baby badly, so why the hell doesn't she start putting her foot down with him?'

'From what I've seen of Mary,' John said quietly, 'I would say she's given up on life.'

'Oh, aye? Well, we'll see about that. We've all felt like that at some time in our lives, and nobody knows that better than me. But we pick ourselves up and do something about it, and it's time she did the same. I'm blowed if I'm going to stand by and see an innocent, unborn baby suffer, because of its mother's weakness and its father's wickedness.'

'What do you propose to do?'

There was the ghost of a smile on Dot's face. 'I'm going to rally the troops. As soon as our Colin's in bed, I'm going to send for the O'Connors and Betty Mason. Between the lot of us we should be able to keep an eye on Mary. Betty and Maggie can see she gets a good dinner every day during the week while *he's* at work, and I'll take over at the weekend. Perhaps we can talk some sense into her at the same time.'

'Would you permit me to sit in on this council of war?'

'If you agree to certain conditions.'

'What might they be?'

'That yer don't talk posh and use big words that none of us understand.'

John lowered his head and ran a hand through his sandy hair. When he looked up, there was a twinkle in his blue eyes. 'OK, girl, I promise to keep me bleedin' gob shut.'

His thick Liverpool accent brought forth a peal of laughter from Dot. It was just what she needed after coming out of a house full of doom and gloom. 'There's no need to get carried away,' she chortled. 'Just don't use any words that have got more than five letters in them.'

Betty rested her elbows on the table and her eyes went from one to another. 'Bleedin' marvellous, isn't it? All this because of a jumped-up little no-good swine like him. If he was mine I'd have brained him long ago.'

Her husband, Alec, grinned. 'Ah, but you would never have married someone like him, would yer? Ye're too clever for that. You knew what yer were doing when yer married a soft touch like me. A gift from heaven, I was.'

'Huh!' Betty rolled her eyes as she pinched at the fat on her arm. 'Seeing as I make two of you, you got double yer money's worth.'

'Can we get back to the matter in hand?' Dot asked patiently.

'Are we all agreed to help Mary, or is there anyone present who would prefer to keep out of it?'

'Sure, it's glad I'll be to help,' Maggie said. 'I'm heartily sorry for the poor creature and Paddy feels the same, so he does. You can count us in, Dot.'

'Yer've no need to ask me 'cos I'd already made up me mind when I saw the state of Mary's face. Yer can put my name down with pleasure.' Betty clenched her fist and held it up. 'I just wish his face was at the receiving end of this – that would give me the greatest pleasure. But as my husband, my gift from heaven, thinks that any woman what fights is as common as muck, I'll leave the fisticuffs to the men.'

'Sure, my hands have been itching to have a go at Mr Campbell, so they have.' Paddy, the quiet man, surprised them all with the emotion in his voice. 'There's been nights when I had to cover my ears so I couldn't hear the violence coming from next door, it was so bad. I've been afraid to interfere, and that's the truth of it. But now there's a baby's life in danger I couldn't live with meself if I stood by and did nothing to help.'

'You can count me in, Dot,' Alec Mason said. 'I'm no good at making dinners or offering words of sympathy, but if yer need a pair of hands, then mine are available.'

'That's it, then.' Dot sat back and gave a sigh of relief. 'We women can sort out some sort of rota to make sure Mary gets fed properly, and we'll have the men to back us up if it ever becomes necessary.'

'What about John, here?' Betty asked. 'He hasn't opened his flipping mouth. Doesn't he get a look-in?'

'John's done more in one day than any of us have done,' Dot said, before gazing at the big man through narrowed eyes. 'Betty's right, yer haven't opened yer mouth. Don't yer agree with what we're doing?'

'Oh yes, wholeheartedly. And I'll give you any help you need, I'm sure you know that.'

'Then why have yer been so flamin' quiet?'

John's eyes were laughing at her. 'Because I couldn't string a sentence together using only words containing five letters or under.'

110

Dot's body shook with laughter. 'Oh, yer daft nit, yer knew I was only joking.'

When Betty leaned forward her folded arms completely disappeared under her ample bosom. 'Ay, girl, let us all in on the joke, will yer?'

'I was only acting daft! I told him he was too posh for us.'

'Oh, yer did, did yer? Well, he might be too posh for you, but not for me. I'll have you know I was brought up proper, I was, not like some I could mention.'

'I knew that the first time I set eyes on you, Betty,' John said, tongue in cheek. 'Good breeding always shows.'

The big woman's reply was not very ladylike but it had them all laughing. And with the help of John she kept them amused until it was time to call it a day.

Tom Campbell waited until the hands on the clock told him it was midnight. She'd be fast asleep by now, away to the world. He struck a match and held it to the wick of the candle standing in a saucer on the table. When the flame took hold, he blew out the match and threw it in the grate before reaching up and pulling the chain to extinguish the gas light. Excitement was building up inside of him as he climbed the stairs, and on his face was a look of pure malice. It was time for retribution and the very thought had his heartbeat racing.

After setting the saucer down on a chest of drawers, Tom walked to the bed and for a few seconds he gazed down on the sleeping form of his wife. Then he gripped the bedclothes and jerked them back. 'Get up.'

Mary blinked rapidly. She'd been in a deep sleep and for a while she couldn't make out what day it was. Had she overslept? Was Tom late for work? 'What time is it?'

'Time for yer to attend to yer husband needs.'

Mary reached for the clothes he'd pulled from her. 'Not tonight, Tom, I'm too tired.'

'I said get out of that bed now! You had yer pleasure this afternoon with yer pal from next door, now it's my turn. Get out of that bleedin' bed before I drag yer out by yer hair.'

An icy hand gripped Mary's heart at the threat in his voice. She knew he'd drag her out without a qualm, so she slipped

111

her legs over the side of the bed and stood up. All she was wearing was a vest and knickers, both bought from a second-hand stall and now so worn out they offered no protection from the cold. She clasped her hands together and dropped her head in shame.

'Lift yer bleedin' head and look at me, or else.'

The tone of his voice brought Mary's head up. There was no one to help her now. She couldn't knock on the wall at this time of night, and besides she'd be too ashamed. And her husband knew that. He had her where he wanted her, at his mercy.

His eyes on her all the time to make sure she was watching, Tom slipped the braces from his shoulders and began to undo the buttons on his trousers. He let them fall to the floor then kicked them to one side. He was in no hurry as he discarded his underpants; he wanted to make her sweat with fear. Then he slowly lifted his shirt. 'Take a good look at that, it's all for you.'

When Mary continued to look straight ahead, he became enraged. He grabbed her by the hair and pulled her head down. 'I said take a good look. Yer don't know how lucky yer are. That cow from next door would think it was her birthday if she had that to go inside her.'

In the flickering light given out by the candle, Mary could see the gloating on his face. He was really enjoying the power he had over her. She made one last try. 'Not tonight, Tom, please? In the morning, when I'm not so tired.'

'Get hold of it. Go on, do as I bleedin' tell yer or yer'll be sorry.'

Sick with revulsion, Mary stretched out her hand and touched him, in the hope that if she humoured him he wouldn't be so hard on her. But she didn't know the depth of his wish for revenge.

'Turn around and put yer hands flat on the bed.'

'Oh no, Tom, please! Not like that, yer'll hurt the baby.'

'Baby! What baby? I don't want no bleedin' kid! Now if yer don't want a bloody good hidin', do as ye're told and turn around.'

Sighing, and hating him with every fibre of her being, Mary

112

turned and put her hands on the bed. But her position didn't satisfy Tom and he took hold of the back of her neck and pushed her down until her face was buried in the clothes. Then he slipped an arm under her tummy and lifted her bottom from the bed. And as he did so a series of pictures flashed before his eyes. He was about eight years of age and he was standing outside the partly-open door of his parents' bedroom. His curiosity had got the better of him that night; he had to find out why almost every night he could hear sounds coming from the room next door. Low moans from his mother, as though she was in pain, and grunts from his father. So he had slipped out of bed and silently crept to stand outside the door next to his. There was a candle burning and he was able to make out the form of his mother, bent over the bed. His father was standing behind her, and he seemed to be holding her legs up off the bed as his body jerked and his grunts became louder. The boy was too young to understand what was happening, and afraid of being caught he'd crept back to bed. But he was excited by what he'd seen, and there were many nights he forced himself to stay awake just to spy and enjoy the sight of his father proving his dominance over his mother.

Mary was biting on the bedclothes waiting for the pain she knew was to come. This was one night she wished she had a weapon handy – a poker, iron, or rolling pin – anything that she could hit him with to stop him hurting and humiliating her and harming the baby she was carrying. But why was he waiting? Why prolong the agony for her? She turned her head slightly to the side and peered through lowered lids. He was just standing there with a silly smirk on his face, his eyes staring into space. For a brief moment she thought perhaps he wasn't going to go through with the act, then fear took over as she imagined him thinking of other ways he could hurt and degrade her. This would be the last time, she vowed. In future she would make sure she had a weapon within reach.

Tom's mind was miles away, reliving certain events in his life. His mother had died when he was fourteen, but he didn't know why. She just took to her bed one day and no amount of shouting and bullying would get her out. She refused to eat and eventually wasted away, lacking the heart to carry on with

113

the life she was being forced to lead. Neither he nor his father mourned her; in fact Tom was glad she was gone. It meant he had his father, his hero, all to himself.

There were many women brought to the house from the pub his father frequented, and each one seemed more than willing to mount the stairs to the bedroom. The boy would sit downstairs, excited at what he knew would be another conquest for his father, another woman satisfying his appetite for sex. It was when Tom was sixteen that two women were brought back from the pub, both women of the streets, and that night all four climbed the stairs. From that night on he had his father's appetite for sex and his need to control and dominate. He was nineteen when his father was killed in an accident at work but he'd never forgotten his words. 'Never marry a dominant woman, get one who's good in bed and who'll do as she's told. Always keep a firm hand on her and show her who's boss.'

Tom shook his head as his mind came back to the present and he looked down on Mary's body. 'I remembered, Dad, I did as yer said.' His voice was high as he thrust himself inside Mary with such force she had to stuff the blanket in her mouth to muffle a scream.

With each thrust and groan, Tom's excitement mounted to fever pitch. He was master, he had the power in his hands. He had his eyes closed and there was a maniacal smile on his face. He'd lost all sense of reason, for in his warped mind the woman he was hurting, humiliating and degrading wasn't his wife, it was the Baker woman, the bitch from next door.

For years she'd been asking for this, and at last he was getting his revenge and gasping from the pleasure of it.

Chapter Eight

Katy couldn't hold back the grin when Billy came into the shop on the Saturday afternoon. She'd seen him a few times since Christmas Day but still couldn't get used to the sight of him in long trousers. She had to admit that they suited him though, and made him look older than his fourteen years. He wasn't bad-looking, either, now she came to think about it. 'Work until one on a Saturday, do yer, Billy?'

'No, it's eight until half-twelve. I've been home and had me dinner.'

Molly walked along the counter to smile at him. 'How did yer first week's work go? D'yer think yer'll like it?'

'Yeah, it's all right. Mind you, it'll take me a while to get to know the difference between a valve, a washer and a ballcock. It's a good job they've put me with me dad, otherwise I'd have had me block knocked off by now, the questions I ask.'

'Yer'll soon get the hang of it, son, and it's only to be expected that yer'll ask questions. How else would yer learn?' Molly turned her head at the sound of the doorbell tinkling. 'I'll serve Mrs Roberts, Katy – you see to Billy.'

'Me dad wants twenty Woodbines and a box of matches.' Billy put half-a-crown on the counter. 'He wanted an *Echo*, too, but yer haven't got them in yet, have yer?'

'Not for another hour.' Katy put the cigarettes and matches on the counter and picked up the half-crown. 'I could put one through yer letter box on me way home, if yer like, save yer coming out again.'

'Nah, I'll come for it.' Billy changed feet while a blush started to creep up from his neck. 'Any chance of a game of cards in yours tonight, Katy?'

'None whatsoever.' Katy's tone was very definite. 'We're

115

starting to strip the walls in the living room tonight.' Her pretty face was lit up by a beaming smile. 'Me mam's buying the paper and paint this afternoon and I can't wait to see what the wallpaper's like.'

'Who's decoratin' it for yer?'

'We're doing it ourselves, of course! We can't afford to have a man in to do it for us, we haven't got that sort of money.'

Billy stuck out his bottom lip, a look of doubt on his face. 'Has yer mam ever done any decoratin' before?'

'No, but as she says, there's a first time for everything.'

'Well, it's to be hoped she doesn't buy paper with a pattern on that yer've got to match, 'cos that's a bugger to put up.'

'Billy! You swore!'

'Sorry, it just slipped out. All the men in work swear like troopers, yer see.' He looked suitably reprimanded. 'It's no good me saying I'll give yer a hand 'cos I'd only make a mess of it, but I could help yer scrape the old paper off and wash the woodwork down. An extra pair of hands and yer'd probably have it done in one night.'

'Ooh, yeah!' Katy's mind was working overtime. 'You could get on the ladder and reach the high-up bits, couldn't yer?'

'Yeah, I could do that, easy-peasy. I know I sound as thick as two short planks sometimes, but I'm not as soft as I make out. And scraping paper off a wall is child's play.'

'Good, ye're hired then. Yer wages will be a cup of tea and a biscuit. Does that sound fair enough to yer?'

Billy was over the moon. 'I'll be outside when the shop shuts an' walk home with yer.'

Katy nodded. 'OK, Billy, but will yer go now 'cos there's a few customers want serving and ye're holding me up.'

Molly had a smile on her face as she watched the boy walk to the door. He was definitely smitten with Katy, but it was hard to tell if the girl realised it, or even felt the same way. She certainly didn't treat him any different to anyone else. To her he was just a schoolfriend, one of the gang.

Molly screwed the top back on the sweet jar and reached up to put it back on the shelf. It would be interesting to see how that friendship developed, she thought. Still, only time would tell and that was something of which they had plenty.

Dot sighed as she put her shopping bags down on the kitchen floor. Her arms were tired from the weight of them and both hands had red weals across the palms where the handles of the bags had dug into them. Anyway, that was the food seen to. Now she had to go out again to buy the wallpaper and paint. 'Colin, will yer put all this stuff away while I'm out, please? And it'll be the chippy again tonight, I've no time to make a dinner.'

Colin rubbed his hands together in glee. 'That's the gear, Mam, me mouth's watering at the thought.'

'It'll have to water for another couple of hours, son 'cos we've got to wait for Katy to get in from work. I'm not putting cold chips down in front of her after she's been on her feet all day.'

'Can I make meself a buttie, then? Me tummy's not half rumbling.'

'Oh, all right, seven bellies, but don't eat the whole loaf and don't plaster the margarine on.' Dot stretched her shoulders. 'I'd better get cracking in case the shop in Hawthorne Road hasn't got any paper in that I like and I've got to traipse down to Stanley Road.'

'If yer've got a penny to spare, Mam, will yer get us a comic?'

Dot turned on her way to the door, intending to tell him she didn't have a penny to spare. But one look at the pleading in his eyes and she relented. All week he'd carried out the chores he was supposed to get sixpence for, and he hadn't kicked up a stink when she'd told him that this week he'd have to do without his pocket money because she needed every penny. Katy had understood the need to economise, but Colin wasn't twelve until next week; he was only a kid and would have preferred his pocket money to having the room decorated. 'I think I can spare a penny, son, I'll bring a comic in with me. But you behave yerself, d'yer hear?'

Her hand was reaching up to open the front door when the knocker sounded and she jumped with fright. 'Blast,' she said, under her breath. 'Who the hell can this be?'

'Oh, I've caught you on the way out.' John looked embarrassed as he held a bag towards her. 'I'll just hand this over and let you get about your business.'

It was the first time he'd called since Christmas Day and Dot thought they'd seen the last of him. 'What's in the bag?'

'A couple of things for Mary, nothing special.'

Dot held the door wide and stepped back. 'Yer'd better come in.' She didn't mean to sound so abrupt, and it wasn't that she wasn't glad to see him, it was just that he couldn't have chosen a worse time to call.

But if his mother's reception had been lukewarm, Colin's was just the opposite. He was overjoyed to see the big man again and it showed on his face. 'Hello, Mr Kershaw! I'm glad yer've come 'cos I was beginning to think we wouldn't see yer no more.'

'Hello, Colin.' John ruffled the boy's hair. 'A Happy New Year to you.' He turned to Dot and held out his hand. 'And to you, Dot.'

Feeling like a heel because of her rudeness, Dot took his hand. 'I'm sorry, John, I'm forgetting me manners. It's just that I've done nothing but rush around all day, like a cat chasing its ruddy tail. I've been to work, done me shopping for the house, and now I'm off to buy the paper and paint for this room. If I haven't got it when Katy comes home, she'll never forgive me.'

'You know how much of everything you need, do you? Tins of paint, rolls of paper and border?'

Dot's face fell. 'I'd forgotten about the border. I know I need six rolls of paper 'cos Betty Mason told me, and I'll get a big tin of paint.'

'At the risk of being told to mind my own business, Dot, you need a lot more than the paper and paint. The ceiling will have to be white-washed before you even think of putting paper on the walls, and the woodwork must have an undercoat.'

'I'm not doing the ceiling,' Dot said. 'I'd never be able to manage that. I get dizzy standing on the front step, never mind climbing to the top of a ruddy ladder.'

John's brows nearly touched his hairline. 'You are not intending to decorate this room yourself, are you?'

'I don't see anybody else around, do you?' Dot was getting

118

irritated. 'Of course I'm doing it meself, what's wrong with that?'

'I know I'm going to rub you up the wrong way, but I don't want you throwing good money away.' John pointed to the ceiling with its ten years of dust and soot-marks. 'That would have to be done before you put nice new paper on the walls, otherwise it'll stand out like a sore thumb.'

Dot's anger came because she knew he was right. 'I'm not doing the ceiling because I can't ruddy-well do the ceiling, so that's all there is to it.'

'I'll do it for you.'

Colin moved to stand beside John as though taking sides. 'Yeah, Mam, let Mr Kershaw do it. He's big enough to reach up there without the ladder.'

'The ceiling stays as it is,' Dot said, even though she knew she was cutting off her nose to spite her face. 'And if I don't get out now the shops will be shutting.'

'You're a stubborn woman, Mrs Baker,' John said quietly. 'Why won't you accept help from someone who is not only willing, but wants to help?'

'I am not a stubborn woman, I'm a practical one.' Then Dot met his eyes and pulled a face. 'Yes, I *am* a stubborn woman, ye're right. It's just that I've been both man and woman in this house for the last ten years and I can't get out of the habit.'

'Will you let me help, then?'

Dot nodded. 'Yes, and I'll be very grateful.'

'Then I'll come to the shops with you now because there's things you'll need that you won't even think about. Besides, you'll never manage to carry so much on your own.'

Dot was thoughtful for a while. She had been worried about how she was going to cope, she'd even thought of taking Colin with her but decided he'd be more hindrance than help. 'All right, but on one condition.'

'You've very fond of making conditions, aren't you?' John grinned. 'What have I got to agree to this time?'

'That I go out the front and you go out the back.'

'*What!* Don't you think that's carrying things a bit too far? Are you ashamed of being seen with me?'

'Of course not!' Dot eyed his good-quality suit and overcoat, and the trilby hat he was holding in his hand. With the old coat she was wearing, the boot should be on the other foot. 'But I'm not walking down the street with yer and setting all the tongues wagging. The gossips would have a field day, I'd never hear the end of it.'

John would have liked to have reminded her that she was a free woman and could please herself what she did, but wisely he kept his thoughts to himself. 'I'll meet you in Hawthorne Road, at the bottom of Willard Street. Does that suit you?'

Dot nodded. 'I know yer think I'm barmy, but I can't help the way I'm made.' She glanced at the bag on the table. 'Is there anything in that bag that yer can put in yer mouth and chew? If there is yer'd better warn my son to keep his hands off it or he'll scoff the lot.'

Colin was cut to the quick. 'I will not! I won't touch it, Mr Kershaw.'

'It's just a bit of fruit and a jar of malt and cod liver oil. I thought they might help to build Mary's strength up.'

'You're too good to be true, you are.' Dot smiled at him before pointing to the kitchen. 'Out yer go and I'll meet yer in five minutes.'

'I like that one the best.' Dot went back to the first roll of paper the man behind the counter had opened up for her. It had a light beige background with small sprays of flowers on. 'Do you like it, John?'

'Yes, it's nice and light and will brighten the room up. Also, the pattern's so small there'll be no need to match and so no waste of paper.'

'I'll take six rolls,' Dot told the assistant. Then, mindful of how much she had in her purse, she said to John, 'I'll buy the stuff for the ceiling and get the paint another time.'

'There's no need for you to buy whitewash, I've got plenty of it at home. I'll never use it all if I live to be a hundred, so it would be silly to waste your money when I've got bags of the stuff lying in my wash-house.' When Dot looked dubious, John bent down so their eyes were on a level. 'It costs coppers, Dot, for heaven's sake. You don't buy it in a tin, like paint, it's a powder that you have to mix with water.'

'Are you telling me the truth?'

'You'll see for yourself when I mix it in your bucket, with water from your tap.' John suddenly let out a loud chuckle. 'I've just thought of a good name for you – Doubting Dorothy.'

Dot scratched her forehead. 'That's not fair, I can't think of a word that goes with John. But when me mind's clear I'll come up with something. I'm not having you get the better of me even if yer are going to whitewash me ceiling with yer own whitewash.'

When the assistant came back with the six rolls of paper, John watched as Dot counted the money out to him. He could almost hear her counting up how much she had left and knew she was wondering whether she'd have enough for the other things she needed. 'Just get the undercoat for now, Dot,' he advised. 'Leave the gloss paint for another day. It's going to be near the end of next week before we need it because there's a lot to do before the gloss goes on.'

'OK, I'll do that. What size tin of undercoat do I need?'

'What colour do you want the paintwork?'

'I'd like a cream colour – the brown we've got on now gives me the willies.'

It was John who told the assistant. 'The lady would like a large tin of white undercoat.'

When Dot saw the size of the tin she nearly fainted. She'd never have enough on her for that! 'I don't need such a big tin, it's only a small room.'

'Yes, it's a small room, but if you want the paintwork cream, it'll need two coats to cover the brown. If you want the room to look nice, don't try and skimp.' John turned his back to the counter so the man couldn't hear him whisper, 'Stop doubting me, Dorothy.'

'I'll get me own back on you, just you wait and see,' Dot whispered back before smiling at the assistant. 'How much is it? I might not have enough money on me.'

'Three and sixpence.'

Dot's smile widened. Thank God for that, she could just make it.

John insisted on carrying both paper and paint. 'And I'm

121

walking down the street with you, no more cloak and dagger stuff for me. Besides, aren't you being a bit miserable, depriving your neighbours of some juicy gossip?'

'I'll tell them that ye're me long-lost brother what's been living in Australia for the last fifteen years. That should put a stop to any jangling.'

John laughed down at her as she tried to keep up with his long strides. 'You should have no trouble getting away with that story, because the resemblance between us is remarkable. We could easily pass for brother and sister, particularly in the dark.'

Dot pursed her lips. 'Yeah, ye're right. If yer hair and eyes were a different colour, if yer nose was turned up instead of straight and yer had a dark complexion and thick lips, we'd be the spitting image of one another.'

Much to Dot's embarrassment, two of her neighbours were standing talking in the street and when they saw John they made no attempt to hide their curiosity as they eyed him up and down. 'Hello, Dot, goin' to be busy, are yer?'

'I'm going to give it a try, Judy. Hello there, May.'

John inclined his head. 'You'll have to forgive me, ladies, I'm afraid I can't doff my hat to you because, as you can see, my hands are full. But I bid you a very good evening.' He gave each of the ladies a bright smile before walking on, leaving them to look at each other with wide eyes and open mouths.

Dot was bursting with laughter but she managed to control it until they were in her living room where she doubled up. 'Oh dear, oh dear! Did yer see their faces?'

Colin looked at the tears running down his mother's face and asked, 'What happened, Mam? What are yer laughing at?'

Dot fished in her pocket for a hankie and blew her nose. 'Two of the neighbours were in the street, son, and I'll bet any money that right now they're trying to figure out whether John's a nut-case or I've got meself a posy fancy man.'

'Why, what did he say to them?'

Dot reached up and took John's trilby from his head. When she put it on it was far too big for her and dropped down to cover her eyes and ears. Undeterred, she held out her arms as though she was laden down. 'It won't be word for word, but near enough. "You'll have to forgive me, ladies, I'm afraid I can't doff my hat to you because, as you can see, my hands are full. But I bid you a very good evening".'

While Colin put a hand over his mouth and shook with laughter, John chuckled. 'Not a bad impersonation. D.D.'

Dot narrowed her eyes when the penny dropped. Pushing the trilby to the back of her head, she said to her son, 'Your friend, John Kershaw, has given me a very unflattering nickname. Doubting Dorothy, he calls me. Now I'd like to return the compliment but can't think of a word beginning with "J".'

'I can, Mam! What about Jumping John?'

'No, that's no good. If he jumped in this room he'd put a ruddy hole in the ceiling. Anyway, it's not insulting enough. I'll just bide me time until I can come up with a belter.'

'While you're deciding on a name for me, I'll nip home and get changed,' John said. 'And I'll organise the whitewash and brushes.'

'Right.' Dot followed him to the front door. 'Alec is lending us his ladder and a paint brush . . . he's bringing them down later – and Betty said she'd come and give us a hand to get the old paper off.'

'Have you got a couple of scrapers? One is no good between four of you.'

'We'll have to use knives, won't we? Where there's a will, there's a way.'

'I'll see what I've got at home.' John stepped into the street. 'I'll see you later.'

'Don't come too early, 'cos Katy doesn't get in until just after six and we'll be having our meal then.' Dot gave a short snort. 'Some meal . . . chips from the chippy.'

'I'll be having the same myself, I'm afraid, so don't be feeling sorry for yourself.' John walked two steps away, hesitated, then came back. 'Would you mind if I brought my chips here to eat? For that matter I could get yours at the same time, save making two journeys.'

Dot folded her arms and leaned against the side of the door. 'Let's get something straight, John, and clear the air once and for all. Yer've been very good to us and I really appreciate it, but I've got to say what's on me mind. Yer might think I'm feeling sorry for meself again when yer hear what I've got to say, but I don't. Oh, there's been times when I've thought fate had dealt me a lousy hand, but I've never suffered from self-pity. I've got two lovely children and that's enough to want to live for. I've always been straight with them, explaining why we were hard-up and they couldn't have the things their friends were getting. We talk everything through, as a family, and each of us is entitled to an opinion. When Katy started work I told them that life wouldn't be any different for quite a while because I want to use her wages to make this house a halfway decent home for them – a nice place where they'd be proud to invite their friends in. And they agreed. So tonight, we'll be having threepenny-worth of chips and scallops between us. No fish, chips and mushy peas, we can't afford such a luxury, not for a while, anyway.' She took a deep breath and smiled at him. 'So now you have the picture and we know where we stand.'

'I've had the picture since the first time I set foot in your house, Dot. You're a very good mother and have done an excellent job in bringing up the children – they're a credit to you. And seeing as we're having a heart-to-heart, I'll tell you why, on the night I knocked Colin down, I didn't just dump him and leave. Most boys would have been crying, trying to save their own skins by laying the blame firmly at my door. He didn't, and I don't think the thought even entered his head. I took a liking to the lad for his honesty, and after meeting the rest of his family I took a liking to them, too.'

John pulled up the collar of his coat to protect his ears from the cold and turned, ready to walk away. 'Now you've said what you wanted to say, and I respect your wishes, I'll still call in the chippy on my way here and get fourpennyworth of chips and scallops which we'll share. And if it makes you feel better, I'll take your threepence then. Does that meet with your approval, D.D.?'

'It certainly does.' Dot half-closed the door before adding, 'I'll see you later, J.J.'

* * *

124

John tried not to let his surprise show when Katy handed him his share of chips in a piece of newspaper. He put them on his lap waiting to be handed a fork, but when the others sat down and proceeded to eat with their fingers, he followed suit. And he had to admit that chips had never tasted so good. He thought of his mother and how strict she'd been over good table manners. If she could see him now she'd be horrified. Then suddenly in his mind's eye there flashed a picture of her as she was a few years before she died, and she was smiling as though happy for him.

'Have yer finished, Mr Kershaw?' Katy was standing before him. 'I'll take the paper off yer and put it on the fire.'

He screwed the paper up before handing it to her. 'I enjoyed that, very tasty.'

'Yeah, yer can't beat chips, can yer? Here's Billy with a cup of tea.'

'I haven't brought yer tea,' Billy said, blushing. 'Mrs Baker wants to know if yer'd rather have a cup with a handle and no saucer, or a saucer and a cup with no handle?'

John chuckled. 'Bit of a tongue-twister that, eh, Billy?' He held his chin in his hand and looked serious. 'That's a big decision to have to make. I'll need to give it some thought.'

Dot poked her head around the door. 'Come on, slowcoach, make up yer mind before it's time to go to bed.'

'I'll settle for the cup with a handle. Oh, and Dot, I'll need to wash this ceiling and frieze down, the soot is caked on it. Would you put the kettle on for extra hot water, please?'

'Will do.' There came a hammering on the door and Dot grinned. 'That'll be Betty, she's got a real moneylender's knock. I keep expecting her to put the blinkin' door in.'

'Well, well, well!' The big woman breezed in, a wide smile on her chubby face. 'What have we here, then – a flippin' party?'

'Are we heck,' Dot said. 'We're just having a quick cuppa then we'll all roll our sleeves up and get stuck in.'

'I may as well take the weight off me feet while I'm waiting, then.' Betty lowered herself on to one of the wooden chairs. 'How's it going, John? I never expected to see you here.'

'I offered to do the ceiling for Dot, seeing as she can't stand heights.'

Dot prodded her friend's shoulder. 'Don't tell me the gossip hasn't spread to you yet? I'm surprised at yer, Betty Mason, you're usually the first to know what's going on in the street. Yer must be slipping.'

When Betty frowned, her eyes became mere slits. 'I can read tea-leaves, girl, and I'm not bad at reading cards or palms. But when it comes to reading people's minds, I've got to admit I've never been able to master the art.'

Colin was perched on the arm of the couch next to John. 'Ooh, it's dead funny, Mrs Mason, just wait till me mam tells yer.'

'I'm waiting, son, I'm waiting.' Betty jerked her head and sent her chins flying. 'Come on, Dot, I could do with a good laugh.'

Dot glanced at John who had come prepared to work in a pair of dark blue dungarees. 'Yer should have come dressed up and I could have borrowed yer trilby again. It won't be as funny without.'

'Do yer best, girl,' Betty said, 'and I'll use me imagination.'

'I know, I've got an idea.' Dot dashed out to the kitchen and came back with a large pan covering her head. She tapped the pan. 'Trilby.' Then she held out her arms and bent them at the elbows. 'Carrying wallpaper and paint. Everybody got the picture?'

'I'm with yer so far, girl, so carry on.'

A few minutes later the room was ringing with laughter. And when Dot put her hands on her tummy and doubled up, the pan fell from her head and the sound of mirth increased.

'Oh Mam, that was funny.' Katy wiped her eyes. 'I wish I'd been there.'

Billy didn't know who Judy and May were, but they'd be no different to any of the women in the neighbourhood who would be flabbergasted to have a man speak to them so politely. He himself had never heard of a bloke doffing his hat, or bidding anyone a very good evening. He could imagine the scene and thought it was hilarious.

The kitchen chair Betty was sitting on was taking a real

126

hammering; it creaked in protest as her body shook with laughter. With her fingers rubbing at the dimples in her elbows, her laughter was the loudest. 'Ooh, can yer imagine it, Dot? I bet Judy went home and belted her feller around the room 'cos he doesn't doff his working cap to her.' She grinned at John. 'It would serve her right if he did, 'cos he's a coalman and she'd get covered in coal dust.'

Dot bent to pick up the pan. 'Right, that's enough fun and jollification, let's get some work done. All the furniture's to be pushed into the middle of the room and I'll cover it with an old sheet.'

John jumped to his feet. 'Don't you ladies be lifting anything heavy. Billy and I will sort it out if you'll stand aside.'

My God, he can work, Dot was thinking five minutes later. The dining chairs were stacked in the hall, the fireside chair was in the kitchen, the couch and sideboard pulled to the middle of the room and the table upturned on top of them. She glanced at Betty and mouthed, 'He can move, can't he? I wonder what his job is?'

Betty, never backward in coming forward, had no intention of wondering while she had a tongue in her head. 'Where did yer say yer worked, John?'

'I didn't say, Betty, but if it satisfies your curiosity I work in the cable works.'

As though they'd rehearsed it, Betty and Dot spoke in unison. 'The cable works! Yer mean in Linacre Lane?'

John chuckled at the surprised expressions. 'Doubting me again, Dorothy?'

Dot tossed her head. 'I'd never have given it a thought if Betty hadn't asked.'

'That's right, blame me, I don't care.' Betty hitched up her bosom. 'What d'yer do there, John, if yer don't mind me asking?'

'I sweep the floors.' John bit on the inside of his cheek to stop himself from laughing. 'And make the tea. A general dogsbody in other words.'

'Take no notice of him, Betty, he's having us on. And I've just thought of a good name for him . . . Joker John.'

'I'll get it out of him before the night's over, don't worry.'

127

Betty was wearing a short-sleeved dress but she pretended to roll up her sleeves. 'He'll not get out of this house until I know everything there is to know about him. Even to how many blankets he's got on his ruddy bed.'

'Ay, missus, yer came down here to work, not gossip. If yer want to know John's history, ask him when he's walking yer home, later.' Dot went through to the kitchen and returned with the two scrapers John had brought with him. She handed one to Betty, saying, 'If yer do yer job properly yer'll be too tired by then to ask questions.'

'Bloody slave-driver,' her friend muttered. 'Which wall would yer like me to start on?'

'On the big one with me. Katy and Billy can do around the window while John washes the frieze on the other two walls and the part of the ceiling he can reach without drowning us in water. Then if we're all ready at the same time, we can swap around.'

Katy looked at the scraper her mother handed to her. 'How do I do it?'

'I'll show yer, I've helped me dad in our house,' Billy said, feeling very manly. 'Just don't dig too hard or yer'll take the plaster off the walls.'

'Ah, ay, Mam, what can I do?' Colin wailed. 'I'm not standing here twiddling me thumbs while ye're all working.'

'I thought you were going to be my mate,' John said. 'I was hoping you'd hold the ladder for me and help me change the water when it gets dirty.'

Colin was in his applecart. 'Oh yeah, I'll do that, Mr Kershaw. I'll hold the ladder real steady for yer.'

So with everyone assigned to their jobs, work started in earnest. The only sounds in the first half-hour were the scraping of walls, water being wrung out of a cloth, and a cry of delight when a strip of wallpaper came off in one piece. Then Betty thought enough was enough. There was no reason why you couldn't talk and work at the same time. She gave Dot a nudge. 'D'yer know what I feel like?'

All hands stopped work, grateful for the interruption and not wanting to miss what the big woman had to say. She came out with some belters when she was in the mood.

'This is not the time for a guessing game, sunshine,' Dot said, pushing a lock of hair out of her eyes, 'so I'll give in. What *do* yer feel like?'

'I feel like a ruddy monk in a monastery what's made a vow of silence.'

The laughter brought a smile to her face. 'That's better, cheer the place up a bit.'

Dot tried to put on a serious expression. 'May God forgive yer, Betty Mason, for what yer've just said.'

'Oh, He will, girl, He will. Take it from me, what's a very good friend of His, that God's got a smashing sense of humour. Well, I mean, it stands to reason, doesn't it? When He looks down and sees some of the antics we get up to, He must laugh His ruddy socks off!'

'I'll tell yer one thing, Betty Mason, and after that it's back to work. If you end up going to heaven, and I finish up in the fires below, I won't half kick up a stink.'

Betty looked aghast. 'What sort of a friend d'yer think I am? I wouldn't leave you behind, girl. Where I go, you go too – otherwise we're both staying put.'

After the brief humorous interlude, work started again in earnest. For exactly half an hour.

'I didn't half pull a fast one on my feller today, girl.'

'Did yer, sunshine?' Dot heard the silence and turned to find all eyes on her friend. 'Yer do know that ye're holding the job up, don't yer? When you open yer mouth everyone downs blinkin' tools.'

'I can't help it if they're nosy, can I?' Betty glared ferociously. 'Get those oars goin', the lot of yer, or I'll start cracking the whip.'

'Even a galley-slave is entitled to a breather, Betty.' John was standing on the bottom rung of the ladder. 'Come on, tell us all what trick you played on your long-suffering husband?'

'Well, I did a bit of washing this morning and I put the pillow-cases in the sink with the intention of steeping them in bleach water for a while to bring them up nice and white. But when I got the bleach bottle out it was empty, so after saying a few choice words I stood it on the draining board. Then I

129

got the idea of playing a trick on Alec.'

A picture of her husband's face flashed before her eyes. His jaw had dropped open and his eyes were wide with astonishment. She began to laugh silently and her huge tummy shook.

'When he got in from work I had a towel wrapped around me head and he asked if I'd washed me hair. I told him I hadn't washed it, I'd bleached it. Oh, yer should have seen his face. "What did yer want to go and do a thing like that for? Yer know I hate peroxide blondes," he said. I said, "I know yer do, love, that's why I didn't use peroxide." Then I walked to the kitchen and came back with the empty bleach bottle and handed it to him. "I used bleach instead."'

Dot could see the funny side of it, then she thought about the shock Alec would have had if he'd thought his wife was serious. 'That was a lousy trick, to play,' she commented. 'Yer could have given poor Alec a flamin' heart attack.'

'Ay, ye're right there, girl, I really thought he was going to have one. He sat in the chair and his face was green. He said, "Yer've done it good and proper this time. When yer take that towel off, there won't be a hair left on yer head. Yer'll be as bald as a billiard ball. In fact, yer'll be lucky if yer've got any scalp left because raw bleach will eat through anything." He sat shaking his head, then he said, "Yer haven't got the sense yer were born with, missus, d'yer know that?"'

'He's right – yer carry things too far, sometimes,' Dot said severely. 'And how long did yer leave him to worry himself to death?'

'Oh, I didn't leave him, girl, 'cos his face was as white as a sheet by this time and I got more of a fright than he did. So I whipped the towel off to prove I still had me head of beautiful, thick glossy hair, then I did a little twirl and bowed to him.'

'And what did Alec have to say?' John asked. 'Did he see the joke?'

'Well, it's like this, yer see, John. My husband is a very mild-tempered man most of the time, but when he does get in a paddy then he really lets fly. I can't tell yer what he called me, not in front of the children anyway. All I'll say is, it wasn't very flattering to me, or me mother, God rest her soul.'

130

'No more than yer deserve,' Dot told her. 'Now, we've only got a tiny bit to do on this wall then we can change around and let John come over here. So will yer keep that hole in yer face closed, please? Let silence be yer punishment for what yer did to Alec.'

By ten o'clock all the walls had been stripped except for a few bits of paper by the picture rail where the women couldn't reach. And Colin had been busy; he'd brushed the floor and put all the old paper in a sack. 'I'll do those fiddly bits,' John said. 'It'll only take me a few minutes.'

'It's a wonder your arms aren't dropping off,' Dot said, 'stretching up all that time.'

'No, I'm all right. Just a bit of a kink in my neck, that's all.'

Dot looked over to where Katy and Billy stood talking. The pair had worked like a couple of Trojans; the room would never have been finished without them. 'Billy, sunshine, yer've been a little brick, so has Katy. But it's nearly a quarter past ten and I'm worried about yer mam. She'll wonder where yer've got to.'

'Nah, she'll be all right, she knows I'm here.'

'Even so, I think yer should be making tracks. We'll just put the furniture back, then I won't be long out of bed meself 'cos I'm nearly asleep on me feet.'

'Can I come tomorrow, then, Mrs Baker?' Billy asked. 'I can give a hand rubbing the paintwork down.'

'Of course yer can, sunshine, but leave it until after dinner.'

'I'll see yer out, Billy, but first yer'll have to bring the chairs in or we won't be able to open the front door.'

When Billy had gone, Dot went into the kitchen where her son was watching John emptying the bucket. She heard him say, 'It's me birthday next Saturday, Mr Kershaw.'

'Is it, now?' John saw Dot standing in the doorway and winked. 'Well, we'll have to do something to celebrate, won't we?' He reached down to put the bucket on the floor. 'Will you do me a favour and check that all the bits of paper have been picked up, please?'

'It's way past his bedtime,' Dot said. 'He should be in dreamland by now.'

John smiled at the boy. 'You've got two minutes, Colin.'

When Dot made to follow her son, John motioned for her to stay. 'I wanted a word with you on your own. Would you mind very much if I took Colin to a football match next Saturday, as a birthday treat?'

'Oh, he'd be over the moon! He's never been to a football match.' Dot tilted her head and screwed up one eye. 'As long as I can pay for him.'

John sucked in his breath with frustration. 'I heard you telling Betty tonight that she sometimes goes too far. Well, she's not the only one, because you really do take things to the extreme. Why won't you let me take Colin to the match as a birthday present from me? Would it hurt you so much to allow me that little pleasure?'

Dot held his eyes for a few seconds, then said, 'I am a miserable bitch, aren't I? Me mam's always telling me that there's such a thing as having too much pride.' Without turning her head, she called, 'Colin, come here a minute, sunshine.'

'Yes, Mam?'

'Mr Kershaw's got something to tell yer. I'll finish off in there and then make a pot of tea before Betty starts giving me a mouthful.'

When the cry of pleasure reached her ears, Dot smiled. The fates had certainly been on Colin's side the night they decided that if he had to run in front of a bike, then he couldn't pick a better one than John Kershaw's.

The furniture was back in place, the children were in bed, and Dot, Betty and John were enjoying a well-earned cup of tea. 'This time next week you won't know this room.' John cast his eyes over the walls and ceiling. 'Nice white ceiling and paintwork, and light wallpaper, it will look a treat.'

Dot was too tired to say she wouldn't have the money to buy the gloss paint or the border until Saturday when she and Katy got paid. She'd tell him tomorrow when she felt more like it. 'Thanks for offering to take Colin to the match, he's absolutely delighted,' she said instead. 'I've never seen him so excited – he probably won't sleep all week.'

'I'll enjoy taking him, he'll be company for me. Liverpool are playing at home so it should be a good match.'

'When it's my birthday, will yer take me?' Betty grinned. 'My feller wouldn't object – he'd be glad to get rid of me for a few hours.'

'You've certainly got the voice of the Kop, Betty,' John said, 'but I don't think I could handle you, you're too much for me.'

Betty leaned forward and touched Dot's knee. 'Insult or compliment?'

'Oh, definitely a compliment, sunshine, a big compliment for a big woman.' Dot suddenly put a hand to her mouth. 'Oh strewth, John, I'd forgotten the things you brought for Mary. I'll pass them over first thing in the morning, before her beloved gets up, I promise.'

'How is she?'

'She gets a good dinner every day from Monday to Friday, Betty and Maggie see to that. But Saturday and Sunday are difficult with him being home, so all I can do is take her a dish of porridge and a couple of rounds of toast for her breakfast. She says she's fine, and there's no sign of bruises or anything.' Dot curled her hands around the cup. 'But I'm not satisfied in me mind that all is as she says it is. I wouldn't trust him as far as I could throw him.'

'Me neither,' Betty said grimly. 'He's a rotten bugger and I wouldn't put anything past him. But if Mary's says everything's all right, there's nowt we can do to interfere.'

John sighed and shook his head. 'What an existence for a young woman.' He put his cup on the floor and stretched his long arms over his head. 'I think I'll hit the trail, I feel quite tired.'

'Yer've worked hard, John, and I'm beholden to yer. Get home to yer bed, and drop me mate off at her door, will yer?'

'I'll leave her at her door, I haven't got the energy to drop her there.'

'Ay, excuse me! Don't you two be talkin' about me as though I wasn't here.' Betty forced a hurt expression to her face. 'Ye're only picking on me 'cos I'm little.'

'Get off yer backside, Betty Mason, and toddle off home.' Dot gave a wide yawn. 'Even me flamin' eyelashes are tired.'

'Come on, Betty.' John cupped the big woman's elbow.

'Let's make a move.' He smiled at Dot. 'I'll come early in the morning and see if I can get the ceiling done before it's time for you to put the dinner out.'

'Not before ten, please, give me time to wake up. And I'll peel an extra spud so yer can have a bit of dinner with us.'

'Am I included in the invitation, girl?'

'You can go to blazes, Betty Mason. I don't want to see *you* before three o'clock.'

Betty's smile was sweet. 'Sod you, too, girl.'

Chapter Nine

Katy chewed on a piece of toast as she watched her mother sweep things off the top of the sideboard into an open drawer. 'You go, Mam, or yer'll be late for work. I'll see to the fire and our Colin will tidy around while we're out.'

'He doesn't do it properly, he leaves all sorts lying about. Oh, I'm not blaming him, he's only a kid, after all. And as it's his birthday he'll think that's a good enough excuse not to do anything. I'm coming home from work at dinner-time instead of going straight to the shops so I can make sure he's neat and tidy to go to the match with Mr Kershaw.' Dot chuckled. 'If it was left to him he'd go out without polishing his shoes and with a dirty big tidemark around his neck.'

'Is Mr Kershaw still coming for tea?'

Dot nodded. 'I asked Colin if he'd like to invite a friend for tea, seeing as it's his birthday, but he said he'd rather have John than any of his schoolfriends. So I didn't have much option.' She stood in the middle of the room and looked around. 'I still can't get used to this room looking so light, I keep thinking I'm in the wrong house.'

'Yeah, it looks lovely. And it'll look even better when the border's up and the paintwork finished. We couldn't have managed without Mr Kershaw, Mam, he's practically done the whole place on his own.'

'Yes, I know, sunshine, we're in his debt, that's for sure.' Dot reached for her coat off the hook behind the door. 'I'll get the rest of the stuff while I'm out shopping, and with a bit of luck the place should be finished tomorrow.' She tied a scarf round her head and picked up her purse. 'I'll have to scoot or I'll be late clocking in. When yer wake our Colin, tell him to give himself a good wash and brush his shoes. I should be home about one, plenty of time to see he looks respectable before John comes at half-past.' She bent to kiss her daughter. 'I'll see you about six, sunshine, and I'll have a little spread ready. Not much, just some boiled ham and sausage rolls. And I've left a jelly in the larder to set.'

'Our Colin won't know himself, having a party for his birthday.'

'He's more excited about going to the match.' Dot turned to the door. 'Especially as he's going with John. He thinks the sun shines out of his backside.'

Katy grinned. 'I wouldn't go that far, Mam, but he is a nice man.'

'Yeah, I suppose so. Anyway, I'll see yer later. Ta-ra for now.'

As soon as she heard the door closing, Katy picked up her plate and pushed her chair back. With twenty minutes to spare before she had to leave for work, she could use the time to clean out the grate and set the fire. It was her brother's job really, that's what he got sixpence a week pocket money for, but as her mam had said, he was a bit slap-dash. It didn't matter on most days, but today was special and Katy knew her mother wanted the place to look nice for Mr Kershaw coming. No one knew what his home was like, but he spoke posh and dressed posh, so it would follow that his home was posh, too.

Still, Katy mused as she raked the ashes out, we've made a start with this room. In another couple of months, please God, the whole house will be redecorated and we'll be able to stick our noses in the air. We might even have some new crockery, that would be smashing.

'I couldn't sleep.'

Katy, on her hands and knees in front of the grate, turned to see her brother framed in the doorway blinking fifteen to the dozen. His hair was standing on end, reminding Katy of Stan Laurel, and she grinned. 'Happy birthday, brother.'

'Yeah, I'm twelve now. It won't be long before I'm working.'

Katy ran a wet cloth over the hearth before getting to her feet. 'Me hands are dirty so I can't give yer a hug, but I can kiss yer.' She planted a noisy kiss on his cheek then told him,

'You are the best brother in the world and I love yer to bits.'

Colin blushed with embarrassment. 'Yer needn't have done the grate, Katy, I'd have seen to it. But thanks all the same.'

'I'll put a light to the fire as ye're up early, but don't be putting coal on every half-hour, we can't afford it. Bank it up with some slack when I've gone and it should last until me mam gets in at one.' She struck a match and held it to the rolled-up newspaper under the firewood. 'Keep yer eye on that and give a shout if it goes out. I'll just rinse me hands and then get cracking. I'll bring yer birthday card in with me tonight, I haven't forgot.'

'Mr Kershaw's coming at half-one to take me to the match, yer know.'

'Yes, I know, Colin, yer've told me at least six times every day. And I know he's coming to tea, as well.'

'I can't wait. I'm that excited I couldn't sleep and I feel sick.'

'The morning will soon pass; it'll be half-one before yer know it. In fact, if I don't move meself it'll be that time before I get to work.' Katy went on talking as she slipped her arms into the sleeves of her coat. 'The tea in the pot is still hot so get a cup before it goes cold, and make yerself a couple of rounds of toast.' She was opening the front door when she shouted, 'For heaven's sake keep yer fingers off the new wallpaper and stay away from the fire.'

Colin scratched his head as he walked to the kitchen. 'Blimey, she's worse than me teacher and he's bad enough.'

'By Jove!' John smiled down at the eager face. 'You do look very smart.'

Colin's heart was bursting with excitement and pride. 'Me mam said if I didn't wash behind me ears proper, she'd use a scrubbing brush on me.'

Dot was standing behind her son, a hand on each shoulder. 'I've told him that a boy of twelve should be able to keep himself clean and tidy without his mother having to look behind his ears or search for tidemarks.'

'You are coming back for tea, aren't you, Mr Kershaw?'

137

'I'd be delighted, as long as your mother isn't sick of the sight of me by now.'

'I'd have been a damn sight more sick without yer, John, that's for sure. I was full of big ideas and intentions but I know now I'd never have managed to decorate this room on me own – I'd have been at it until Pancake Tuesday. So you're more than welcome to come for tea as long as yer know yer'll be the only invited guest. There'll only be the four of us and that hardly makes up a party.'

'I thought Billy was coming!' Colin looked disappointed. 'You said our Katy could ask him if she liked.'

Dot grinned. 'I'd forgotten about Billy. I'll have to bring a chair down from the bedroom.'

John made a sweeping gesture towards the door. 'Come along, young man, otherwise we'll be caught up in the crowd.'

'How will you get there?' Dot asked, following them to the door.

'By bus. I came a bit early so we could avoid the crush.' John stepped into the street and Colin stood beside him. 'Don't worry, Dot, I'll take good care of him.'

As they walked down the street, Colin looking up into John's face and chattering away, a stray tear ran down Dot's face. She was remembering the day Colin was born and how happy her Ted had been. 'We've got one of each now, a girl for you and a boy for me,' he'd said, looking down with love on the small scrap of humanity in his arms. 'When they're older, you can take Katy around the shops while I take me son to the football match.' How proud he'd have been, walking down the street with his arm across his son's shoulder. Instead, Colin was going to see his first match with a man they'd only known a couple of weeks. How unfair life was, and how cruel.

Dot watched until they reached the corner and returned their wave before going back into the house. She felt so sad, even the brightness of the room failed to lift her spirits. For a while she stood in front of the fireplace and let memories invade her mind. Then she shook herself and said aloud, 'Buck yerself up, girl, because there's no way you can change things. Yer've got to carry on for the sake of the children. And it's your son's birthday, yer don't want to be miserable when he comes home.' She reached for the coat she'd flung on the couch when she came home from work and was putting it on as she walked to the kitchen for her shopping basket. 'I'll be all right when I get out in the fresh air and start shopping; it'll take me mind off things.'

With her basket cradled in the crook of her arm, Dot was passing next door when Mary appeared on the step. It was so well-timed, Dot thought her neighbour must have been looking out for her. 'Everything all right, love?'

'Yes, fine! I just wanted to return yer plate.' Mary held out the deep plate which Dot had given her that morning filled with porridge. 'I thought you might need it.'

'I'll need it in the morning for yer breakfast, but can yer hang on to it until I come back from the shops? I've got a lot to get and I don't want to have to cart that around with me.'

'Yes, OK. But in case my feller's in later on, I'll slip it into your backyard now. The entry door is open, isn't it?'

Dot nodded. 'Where is the queer feller?'

Mary shrugged her shoulders. 'He never tells me where he's going, but I think he's probably looking for a bookie to have a bet on.' She lowered her eyes. 'Dot, d'yer know where I can get a cheap poker from?'

'A poker? Haven't yer got one?'

'Yes, I've got one, but I need another. It's got to be cheap, though, 'cos I've only got a couple of bob to see me through.'

'Yer'd get a second-hand one at a market for about tuppence. If I didn't have so much to do this afternoon I'd try and get yer one, but I just don't have the time. Anyway, yer can't be that desperate when yer've already got one. I don't know what yer want two ruddy pokers for, anyway.' Then a smile crossed Dot's face and she leaned forward. 'Every woman gets a craving for something when they're expecting, yer know. With me it was chocolate when I was carrying Katy, and with Colin it was coconut. I remember poor Ted had a terrible time trying to get hold of coconut. But I've got to say I've never heard of anyone having a craving for a poker.'

Mary glanced nervously up and down the street. 'Will yer step inside, Dot, just for a minute? I won't keep yer.'

'One minute, Mary, that's all the time I can spare. I've got an awful lot to do.'

When they were standing in the tiny hall, Mary closed the door to. 'I want one to keep in the bedroom in case Tom ever takes off,' she confided in a scared whisper. 'I'm terrified of him giving me an unlucky belt and me losing the baby.'

'He's not up to his old tricks, is he?'

'No,' Mary lied, 'but I don't trust him.'

'I don't blame yer, I wouldn't trust him either.' Dot tilted her head; she couldn't imagine Mary having the guts to protect herself. 'Would yer really hit him with a poker?'

'If it was to protect meself, yes I would. I've taken a lot off him since we've been married, but I'll not let him harm the baby.'

'Good for you, sunshine! I'm glad to see ye're coming to yer senses. It's not before time but better late than never. I'll see if I can scrounge around for anything that looks like a poker. And if yer nerve fails yer at the last minute, Mary, yer can always use it to knock on our wall. I'd have no compunction about wrapping it around his neck.'

Mary gave a faint smile. 'If I haven't got the nerve to hit him, at least I could pluck up enough courage to hold him while *you* belt him.'

'That's the style, sunshine. You start getting tough and that should tame him.' Dot put her hand on the door. 'I'll have to go, I've got an awful lot to do and only three hours to do it in. If I don't see yer before, I'll see yer over the wall in the morning. Ta-ra, Mary.'

'Ta-ra, Dot, and thanks.'

Dot was running a comb through her hair when the knock came. She'd only been in the house fifteen minutes, just enough time to change into her one decent jumper and skirt. She could hear her son's excited voice before she opened the door. 'I don't need to ask if you enjoyed yerself, sunshine. I think the whole street can hear yer.'

'Ooh, ay, Mam, yer should have seen how many men were there! Must have been easy a couple of thousand. And they were all singing and shouting, ooh, it was the gear.'

140

John smiled as he stepped past Dot. 'I'm afraid his calculations are way out. There were at least twenty-five thousand there.'

'Did he behave himself?'

John put his trilby down on the sideboard. 'It was a pleasure to have him with me. I can't remember enjoying myself so much at a match. He was so keen and excited it rubbed off on me and my throat is sore from shouting.'

'Ay, Mam, yer should hear the crowd roar when a goal's scored! They must be able to hear it in London. It was magic, Mam, just magic.'

'Who won?'

'Liverpool, of course.' Colin, who had never been to a match before, sounded as though he was an authority on the game. 'They ran circles round the other team.'

'And have you thanked Mr Kershaw for taking yer?'

'Yeah, course I did. And he said he'll take me again.'

Dot was about to protest when John beat her to it. 'Now, Colin, that's not quite what I said, is it? What I said was, if your mother had no objections I would take you.'

'Me mam won't have no objections, will yer, Mam?'

Dot's mind was torn in two. She had to admit to herself that she was resentful of the way her son was getting close to John. Resentful and jealous. This was unfair to the man, she knew, because he'd shown them nothing but kindness. And to deny her son the chance of going to a football match now and again, like his friends did, would be making him suffer because of her personal feelings. 'I'll let you go if yer pay for yerself out of yer pocket money.'

'Yeah, I'll do that, Mam, I will!' The boy smiled up at the big man. 'Yer see, Mr Kershaw, I told yer it would be all right.'

John returned his smile. 'That's settled then. The next time Liverpool play at home you and I will be in there shouting as loud as the rest of them.'

'Take yer coat off, John, and hang it up. There's no charge.'

While he was doing so, John asked, 'Did you get the border and paint while you were out?'

'Yes, they're in the kitchen. What with that lot, and me

own shopping, me arms were nearly dropping off. That paint isn't half heavy.'

'Well, I did offer to get it for you, Doubting Dorothy, but you are too independent to take me up on the offer. I could have got it on my way home from work.'

'Ay, Mam,' Colin tugged at his mother's arm, 'Mr Kershaw's a boss where he works. He is, 'cos he told me so.'

John closed his eyes briefly before saying, 'I can see I'm going to have to be more selective on which of your questions I answer.' He looked at Dot. 'Colin makes it sound as though I've been bragging and I can assure you I haven't. He just has a way of going around things until he gets what he wants without you realising it.'

'Well, I knew yer must be a boss 'cos yer speak so posh.' Colin wasn't the least bit put out by John's statement. 'And I was right, yer see.'

Dot sighed. 'Colin, it might be your birthday but that doesn't mean I can't give yer a clip around the ear. How many times do I have to tell yer not to ask people personal questions? Yer curiosity will land yer in trouble one of these days.'

'There's no harm been done, Dot, all children are curious.' John raised his brows, his eyes asking her not to make an issue out of it. 'What I didn't tell Colin is that I'm only a very minor boss, not a big one of any importance.'

Dot grinned, sympathising with his embarrassment. 'Big boss or little boss, yer'll still be getting a cup with no handle.'

'Am I entitled to a request?'

'Well now, that depends upon what the request is.'

'I would like to forego the saucer and have a cup with a handle.'

Dot wagged her head from side to side and tutted. 'I don't know, some folk are not half fussy, there's no pleasing them.' Talking about the state of her crockery reminded her of Mary. 'Colin, slip down the yard and see if Mary's left a plate on the ground. Then lock the entry door, there's a good boy.'

'Funny place to put a plate, isn't it?' John said, when Colin had left the room. 'Why couldn't she hand it to you?'

'I was on me way out when Mary wanted to give it to me and I didn't have time to come back in the house. Anyway, the plate was just an excuse – she'd been watching out for me.' Dot searched his face for a few seconds before making up her mind. 'I think she's having trouble with Tom, although she said she's not. It's a long story and I can't tell yer now because our Colin's got big ears and as yer've already found out, he can't keep anything to himself. But d'yer know if in that wash-house of yours, the one that seems to contain everything under the sun, yer don't happen to have a spare poker in there, do yer?'

John looked surprised. 'A poker?'

'It's for Mary. She asked me if I knew where she could get one cheap.' Dot heard the kitchen door close and put a finger to her lips to remind him not to say anything in front of her son. 'The one she's got is no good. It doesn't matter if yer haven't, it was just a thought.'

'I have got one, as a matter of fact, and she's more than welcome to it. Shall I go home now and pick it up?'

'No, it's not that urgent. Bring it with yer in the morning if yer will.'

'What d'yer want Mr Kershaw to bring with him, Mam?'

'Oh, ye're there, are yer, nose fever? Well, it's nothing that concerns you, so go and find yerself something to do. Entertain Mr Kershaw while I get things ready for tea.'

'I'll give you a hand,' John said quickly. 'You've worked hard today, so let me help. I'm pretty good at making sandwiches.'

'I'll take yer up on that,' Dot said, to his surprise. 'Me feet are practically talking to me 'cos I've been on them since half-six this morning. So if you'll cut the bread and butter it, that would be a big help. I'll clear the table and yer can do it in here because once you get in the kitchen there's no room for anyone else.'

'So my size is against me, too, is it?'

Dot looked him in the eyes for a couple of seconds before deciding he was pulling her leg. 'Go on, yer big daft ha'porth, take yer jacket off and get stuck in.'

'Mam, can I go up to Spud's to tell him about the match?' Colin couldn't wait to boast about his afternoon of excitement. 'Just for ten minutes.'

143

'Make sure it is only ten minutes, d'yer hear? And don't be showing off to Spud, 'cos his mam has to count every penny, same as meself.'

Colin was out of the door before she'd finished speaking, and Dot smiled at John. 'You've started something now, Mr John Kershaw. He'll pester the life out of yer and yer've only yerself to blame.'

'I can take care of him, never fret.' John removed his cufflinks and began to roll up his shirt-sleeves. 'As a matter of fact, he was very well-behaved while we were out.'

'Yeah, he's not a bad kid, even though I say it as shouldn't. Anyway, I'll get a clean cloth for the table and yer can start cutting the bread.'

'Before you go, Dot, what is all this about Mary and a poker?'

Dot told him what Mary had said, then added, 'I think he's been having another go at her, but she won't admit it. Something drastic must have happened for her to want to protect herself; she's not the type to go for someone with a poker unless it was serious. But for the life of me I can't see her using it – she's far too meek and gentle.'

'Everyone has a breaking point, my dear, and perhaps Mary has reached hers.'

'Aye, that may be so, but I'd rather she knocked on the wall for me or Maggie than have a go at him herself. He's such a violent man she could end up getting herself killed.'

'She could do both, actually. Knock on the wall *and* fend him off until help arrives.'

'Blimey, it sounds like a film, the way you say it. One of those old-fashioned ones where two men meet in the park at daybreak to defend their honour. They're asked if they want pistols or swords and when they've decided, they turn around and walk away from each other. Ten slow paces, then they turn and fight it out until one of them is dead.'

John chuckled. 'It's easy to see where Katy and Colin get their sense of humour from.'

Dot turned away, uneasy now they were alone in the house. 'I don't know whether ye're a big boss at work, or a little one. But while ye're in this house, I'm the big boss. Big Chief

Sitting Bull, that's me. So get cracking on that bread and cut the slices as thin as yer can.'

John stood to attention, clicked his heels and saluted. 'Yes, sir! Right away, sir!'

'I'd have to stand on a chair to do it, but any more lip out of you, Joking John, and I'll box yer ears for yer.'

'Is that a threat or a promise, Doubting Dorothy Baker?'

But Dot was already in the kitchen pretending she didn't hear, so he never found out.

'I'll stay behind if yer like, Mrs Edwards, and give yer a hand to clean up,' Katy said. 'It would give yer more time to get ready for the pictures.'

'No, love, thanks all the same. It won't take me five minutes to make meself presentable. After all, Clark Gable won't be able to see me, will he?'

'Yer've really got a crush on him, haven't yer?'

'I think he's very handsome, Katy, but I'm a bit long in the tooth to have a crush on a film star. I only keep on about him to wind my Jim up.'

'One of the customers was telling me she'd seen the picture and she enjoyed it. I won't tell yer what she told me 'cos it would spoil the story for yer. It's called, *It Happened One Night* so it could be a mystery. Yer'll have to hold yer husband's hand if it is.'

Out of the corner of her eye, Molly saw her husband come in from the storeroom and decided to pull his leg. 'Fancy holding my feller's hand and watching Clark Gable's face on the screen. I've got a good imagination, but not that flamin' good.'

Jim winked at Katy before saying, 'I've changed me mind about going to the Broadway, love. I'd rather go to the Carlton to see Dick Powell and Ruby Keeler.'

Molly was taken in by his straight face. 'Well, yer can just change yer mind back again, unless yer want to sit in the pictures on yer own.'

'Oh, I don't think I'd be on me own for long. There's plenty of women go to the pictures by themselves, so I might just get lucky. After all, not every woman is crazy about Clark Gable.'

'Wishful thinking, my love.' Molly gave him a look that said where he was concerned, the film star wasn't in the running. 'Act yer age and take the bar off the door for Katy. Young Billy has been kept waiting long enough.'

Katy picked up the birthday cards and comics she'd bought for her brother. 'Have a nice time and enjoy the picture. I'll see yer on Monday.'

Outside, Billy was none too happy. 'I thought yer were never coming. Yer've been standing there gabbing for nearly half an hour.'

'Don't you bite my head off, Billy Harlow, I didn't ask yer to wait. I can quite easy walk home on me own, yer know, I'm not helpless.'

'I know that, but I met yer mam early on and she said she'd have the tea ready for a quarter past six. It's gone half-past now.'

'Shall we agree to agree, Billy, or shall we agree to disagree?'

Billy chuckled. 'I'm goin' to follow me dad's advice and agree. He's always telling me never to argue with a woman, 'cos yer can't win. They'll have the last word if it kills them, that's what he says, so I'll agree with him and I'll agree with you.'

'Ye're a coward, Billy Harlow.'

'I know, Katy Baker, a hundred per cent one at that.'

They were laughing when John opened the door to them. 'You two seem very happy.'

'It's down to agreements, Mr Kershaw.' Katy gave him a bright smile as she slipped past him. 'We now agree that I talk too much and Billy is a coward.'

Colin was standing by the table when they entered the room and he turned wide eyes on his sister. 'I've got a birthday cake, Katy.'

'Ooh er, aren't you lucky?' She squeezed his shoulder with one hand while handing him the comics and cards with the other. 'There's one each off me and me mam.'

'Here's a card from me,' Billy said gruffly, 'and a bar of chocolate.'

'Thanks, Billy, and you, our Katy.' Colin closed his eyes for a second. What a day this had been, his heart was beating

146

like a tom-tom. 'Look what me mam's done.' He moved away from the table so they could have a better look. There were plates of sandwiches, sausage rolls, a glass dish filled with red jelly topped with pink blancmange, a plate of iced fancy cakes and a jam swiss roll. And in the centre on a glass stand, was a Victoria sponge sandwich cake with twelve candles on it. 'Doesn't that look the gear? Me mouth's watering just looking at it.'

'Yer've done well, Colin,' Katy said, feeling quite emotional. They'd never had a birthday cake in the house before; in fact, a birthday was just like any other day except for hugs and kisses. 'I hope yer've thanked me mam for it.'

'He's thanked her at least a dozen times to my knowledge,' John said, standing by the kitchen door. Being in this house was a joy he'd never known before. He was filled with admiration for this small family who had come through ten years of hardship without a trace of bitterness or complaint. They'd been deprived of all the material things that other families took for granted, but they had something that was worth far more than a few shillings in their pockets. They had a loving mother who was prepared to work her fingers to the bone for them, who had taught them right from wrong, respect for others, how they should never be afraid to show their love, and who had always found time to listen to their problems. And she had passed on to them her pride and her sense of humour – both qualities that had made her the fine woman she was.

'Will yer move out of the way, please?' Dot gave John a gentle dig. 'Ye're holding up the traffic. I'm trying to get through with a pot of tea and you're standing there looking all gooey-eyed. Come on, shift yerself.'

John grinned as he stepped aside. 'Ever since I gave you a nickname you've been picking on me. I'll have to re-think my tactics. Instead of Doubtful or Doubting Dorothy, I'll re-christen you and call you Delightful Dorothy, see if that puts me in your good books.'

Dot set the teapot on the table. 'The only time I'm delightful, John, is in me dreams. I was going to say when I'm fast asleep, but then I've got me dinky curlers in and I look like Granny Grunt. Not to mention when I take me false teeth out and put them in a cup at the side of the bed.'

'Oh, Mam!' Katy looked horrified. 'Don't say that! Mr Kershaw will think yer've got false teeth, and yer haven't, yer've got nice teeth.'

'It's not her false teeth I'm worried about, Katy,' John said, his smile wide. 'It's where she keeps her wooden leg. Does she prop it against the wall or leave it at the bottom of the bed?'

'Any more lip from you, Mr John Kershaw,' Dot wagged a finger at him, 'and I'll take it off and wrap it round your ruddy neck.'

And so Colin's first ever birthday party started with laughter. He'd been allowed to sit at the head of the table, while John and Billy faced Dot and Katy. 'Be careful with the dishes,' Dot warned. 'They've got to go back to Mrs Mason's when we've finished with them.'

'We'll have our own for the next party, though, won't we, Mam?' Katy's deep blue eyes were bright with happiness. 'Yer won't need to borrow them.'

Dot's head went back and she roared with laughter. 'Don't let Betty hear yer say that, she won't be able to keep tabs on us. She knows what we're having to eat by the dishes we borrow off her. She wouldn't lend me the glass dish until I told her what colour the jelly was.'

John looked from mother to daughter. Apart from the colour of their eyes, they were the image of each other. The same thick auburn hair, well arched black eyebrows, strong white teeth, and even the same laughter lines at the side of their eyes. 'We're lucky, aren't we, Billy?' he said. 'Having two pretty girls to look at.'

'Yeah.' Billy flicked a crumb from his sleeve. 'Dead pretty, they are.'

Dot raised her brows. 'Thank you for the compliment, but I don't think by any stretch of the imagination I can be classed as a girl.'

'Excuse me, D.D., but Billy and I were having a private conversation. If we want to say you are a girl, and a pretty one at that, it really doesn't have anything to do with you. Am I right, Billy?'

Billy spluttered and had to put a hand over his mouth to stop crumbs from flying everywhere. He swallowed hard before looking at Katy. 'Mr Kershaw hasn't met me dad, has he?'

Katy was laughing too much to speak, so John asked, 'What's your father got to do with this, Billy?'

'It's all to do with agreements, Mr Kershaw,' the boy said, 'and me being a coward.'

Katy had calmed down by now and took over. 'He's been advised by his father that it's no good arguing with a woman 'cos yer can't win. Women will have the last word if it kills them. So Billy's decided to become a coward and agree to everything.'

John pursed his lips and nodded. 'Your father is a wise man, Billy.'

Dot groaned when a knock came on the door. 'Oh no, who can this be?'

'Shall I go, Mam?' Katy asked. 'It'll only be one of the neighbours looking for change for the gas.'

'No, you stay where yer are, I'll go.'

Silence reigned over the table as all ears were cocked. Then they heard a shriek of delight and Dot's voice. 'Mam, oh it's lovely to see yer.'

Colin's chair nearly toppled over as he jumped up. 'It's me grandma.'

Katy left her chair too, and brother and sister tried to elbow each other out of the way to be first to greet the slightly built, white-haired lady who was beaming at them. She gathered them close and hugged them. 'Hello, me darlings, how are yer?'

'It's me birthday, Grandma.'

'Yes, I know, son, that's why I'm here.' She handed Colin a card and bag. 'Happy birthday, sunshine.'

'Mam, this is John Kershaw – he's the bloke I told yer about over our Colin. This is me mam, John, Mrs Baker.' Dot laughed when she saw the puzzled expression. 'I know, how can she have the same name as me? Well, yer see, she's me mother-in-law, really. I was an only child and me parents were both dead, so when I married Ted I took on his whole family.

149

His mam and dad became my mam and dad, and his sisters became my sisters. And I couldn't have wished for a better family.'

John took the frail hand in his. 'I'm very pleased to meet you, Mrs Baker.'

'Likewise, son, likewise.' The old lady's smile was warm as she craned her neck to look up at him. 'Ye're a big lad, I'll say that for yer.'

'Come on, take yer coat off, Mam.' As Dot began to undo the buttons on the faded grey coat she said over her shoulder, 'Don't be taken in by the size of her, John, she's a proper little live-wire. Still goes out to work every day, even at her age.'

'It's a case of having to, to pay me rent.' Mrs Baker pushed Dot's hands away and slipped her coat off. 'It's either that or the workhouse.'

'Only because ye're too independent.' Dot hung her coat up. 'Your Mary wants yer to go and live with them but, oh no, yer'd rather work yerself to death, wouldn't yer?'

'Hard work never killed no one, girl – in fact, it keeps me going. Another thing, I can please meself when I come and go, and that suits me fine. And I just hope that when me time comes I'll be carried out of me own little house.'

'It'll be a long time before you're pushing the daisies up, Mam, yer'll probably outlive the lot of us.' Dot gave her a hug. 'Anyway, it's a nice cheerful subject for a party, isn't it? You sit yerself down in Colin's chair and I'll make a fresh cuppa. There's still some eats left, so help yerself.'

The old lady's eyes swept the room. 'I see yer've been busy, girl. It looks nice – yer've made a good job of it.'

'Not me, Mam, it was John who did it. He's got the border to put up yet and the gloss paint to put on, but when it's finished we won't know ourselves. We'll be proper posh.' Dot was at the door of the kitchen when there was a loud knock. 'That'll be Betty. I think when she gets in a bad temper she comes down here and takes her spite out on my door.'

'I'll go, Mam,' Katy said, hurrying from the room.

Dot stayed by the door until her friend came in. 'What do you want, Betty Mason? Have yer come to check we haven't broken any of yer dishes?'

150

Betty nodded and smiled at Mrs Baker before saying, 'No, girl, I came because yer forgot. I don't blame yer like, 'cos I know yer've been busy and it must have slipped yer mind.'

Dot looked puzzled. 'What did I forget?'

'To invite me to the party, of course! But don't get upset over it, 'cos as I said, I know yer've been rushed off yer feet.'

'You are one cheeky so-and-so, Betty Mason. I didn't invite yer 'cos it's a child's birthday party, not adults'.'

Betty snapped her fingers. 'Blast, I've left me dummy at home.' She stuck her thumb in her mouth and sucked loudly on it. 'I'm only nine, Auntie Dot.'

'Aye, and the thirty years yer've forgotten about.' Dot flared her nostrils and glared. 'It's no good me telling yer to go home because I know yer won't, and it would take a flaming crane to shift yer. So, Billy, will yer take yer plate and sit on the couch, there a good lad.'

When Billy stood up, Betty eyed his plate. 'If that's one of mine, just watch where ye're putting it. If it gets cracked, so does your head.'

Billy grinned. 'Me head's already cracked, Mrs Mason, me mam dropped me when I was a baby. That's why I'm always agreeable and a coward.'

Katy laughed and joined Billy on the couch. He was delighted to be so close to her but his happiness was short-lived when Colin wriggled his bottom to sit between them. 'Look what me grandma gave me, Billy – a dozen ollies. Will yer have a game with us tomorrow?'

'In me long kecks? Some hope you've got, Colin. Me mam would kill me if I knelt in the gutter in these.'

Billy didn't realise everyone was listening until there was a roar of laughter.

Mary heard the laughter coming from next door as she lay in bed, her knees pulled up to her chest to try and keep warm. How marvellous it must be to belong to a family who laughed as much as the Bakers. A family where there was love and warmth and respect. She had had all that when she was at home with her parents and brothers, but she'd thrown it away to marry a scoundrel like Tom Campbell. He made her life a nightmare, never knowing when the next punch was coming. He didn't hit her in the face any more, or on her neck or arms, he was too crafty for that. Now he aimed for the small of her back or her chest – places that were hidden from the eyes of neighbours. He was a rotter, a down-and-out rotter and she hated him. She also feared him, that was why she'd come to bed so early. Some Saturdays he came home rotten drunk, hardly able to stand and incapable of harming her. She welcomed those nights and was able to sleep without fear. But other times, like last Saturday, when he was only half-drunk . . . those were the nights she dreaded.

Mary tucked the bedclothes around her and lay awake listening for the key in the door. She'd vowed to herself that never again would she allow herself to suffer the pain and degradation he'd put her through that night. She had thought about bringing the poker up with her, but he sometimes used it to liven the fire up when he came home so he could get a warm while smoking his last cigarette of the day. He'd have the house up if he couldn't find it. But she'd get one from somewhere on Monday and hide it under her side of the bed. And if he started his tricks tonight she'd scream the house down and to hell with the consequences. He'd soon stop if he heard the neighbours banging on the door.

She lifted her head from the pillow at the sound of a key turning and listened with her heart in her mouth. Then she heard him fall into the hall, sending the door crashing against the wall and she sighed with relief. She'd seen it so often she knew he wouldn't be able to stand up straight, never mind climb the stairs. So tonight she had the bed to herself and tomorrow she'd find him either on the floor or flat out on the couch. And when she woke him to suggest he came to bed to sleep it off, the smell of stale beer would sicken her and his bad language would put her to shame.

But for now, please God, she could sleep in peace and forget the drunken, wicked bully to whom she was tied.

Chapter Ten

Dot opened the door to John on the Sunday morning with her finger on her lips and her eyes rolling upwards. 'Don't make a noise, the children are still asleep. If they don't wake up yer might get an hour's work in before our Colin's down and getting under yer feet.'

Maggie O'Connor passed at that moment on her way to Mass and she smiled from one to the other. 'Top of the mornin' to yer, me darling. And to you, John.'

'Good morning, Maggie.' Dot could feel herself blushing to the roots of her hair. How must it look, John calling at a quarter to nine in the morning? And Maggie must have heard her saying that the children were still in bed, which meant she'd be on her own with him. It was a good job it was Maggie and not one of the other neighbours, otherwise she'd be the talk of the wash-house.

But John looked quite unconcerned as he doffed his hat. 'Good morning, Maggie. Off to church without Paddy, I see.'

'Sure, doesn't he enjoy a lie-in on a Sunday? And the man deserves it, so he does, for he works hard all week. But Paddy will not be missing Mass, he'll go to the eleven o'clock one. It suits me, all right, because I go home to a cooked breakfast and while he's at church I see to the dinner. We share things, me and Paddy, which is just as it should be in a marriage.'

Dot felt an explanation was necessary. 'John's been decorating me room, as yer know, Maggie, and he's come early to try and finish it off today. It'll be a load off his mind because he must be sick of the sight of us.'

'Not for a minute would I believe that, me darlin'. Sure he'd have to be a hard man to please if he didn't get on with you and the children.'

153

'I get on very well with them, Maggie.' There was a smile on John's face as he gave a quick glance at Dot. 'Unfortunately, Dot worries too much about nosy neighbours thinking she's a loose woman.'

'Well, if they're talking about you, me darlin', they're leaving someone else alone. And wouldn't it be a pity if they had nothing else to do? Anyway, I'd better be off or I'll have to stand all the way through Mass and me corn is giving me gyp.' With a smile and a wave, Maggie went on her way, her feet covering the ground quickly to make up for lost time.

Dot went into the living room, leaving John to close the door behind him. He entered the room to find her standing with her hands on her hips. 'Why did yer have to go and say that about nosy neighbours thinking I'm a loose woman?'

'Why? Isn't that what you were thinking?'

Dot became flustered and lowered her eyes. 'It doesn't matter what I was thinking, yer had no right to say it.'

'Actually there was no need for me to say it, it was written all over your face. And for the life of me I can't think why. If you had something to hide I could understand it, but what is the harm in my coming to decorate your room? Only a very narrow-minded person would make something out of that.'

'There's quite a few narrow-minded people in this street, I can tell yer.' Dot was beginning to feel a bit silly. She was making a mountain out of a molehill but was too stubborn to admit it. 'All they've got to do all day is stand on the doorstep and gossip, and I don't want to be the one they're gossiping about.'

John tilted his head and raised his brows. 'I'm going to take the advice of Billy's father and agree with everything you say. You and I are up to no good and, while the children are asleep upstairs, I am going to have my wicked way with you. Is that dramatic enough for you?'

Dot was lost for words. He was right, why should she worry about a few nosy people who had nothing better to do than pull someone to pieces? And he mustn't half think she was big-headed for even thinking he fancied her. 'We'll call it quits, shall we? Yer could have had the border up by now, if yer didn't talk so much.'

John chuckled. 'There's never a dull moment with you, is there, Dot? Anyway, seeing as your temper seems to have calmed down, I think it's safe to give you this.' He handed her a long thin parcel wrapped in newspaper which he'd been holding down by his side. 'It's the poker you asked for and it's for Mary, not for hitting me over the head with.'

As she ripped the wrapping away, Dot said, 'Your head's so hard I'd probably end up bending the blinkin' thing.' She crumpled the paper up and eyed the poker, which looked as though it had never been used. It was a strong one with an ornate brass handle. 'Trust you,' she said, smiling, 'even yer ruddy poker's posh.'

'Can we be serious for a moment, Dot?'

Her face showed surprise. 'Yeah, of course. What is it?'

'I brought the poker because you asked me to, but I really don't want you to give it to Mary. Defending yourself is one thing, but to hit someone over the head with such a lethal weapon is a different matter entirely. What if she struck him an unlucky blow and it killed him? That would be murder, Dot, and they hang people for murder.'

'No, she wouldn't hit him that hard, she'd just jab him with it.'

'When you're in a state of fear, your mind isn't thinking straight. And I know that there must be times when Mary is so terrified she'd do anything to stop him from hurting her. Any woman would feel the same – it's just a natural instinct to protect yourself. But it would only take one unlucky blow and she'd be in serious trouble.'

'So she just sits there and lets him belt hell out of her? Is that what ye're saying?'

'That's not what I'm saying at all and, if you viewed it with an open mind, you'd realise I'm not just talking through my hat.' John ran his fingers through his fine sandy hair. 'Let's see if I can prove something to you. Pretend you and I are alone in this house and I'm the same type of man as Tom Campbell. If I made a grab for you to hurt you, or to make an attempt to force you into a sexual act, what would you do?'

Dot's eyes were wide. 'I'd belt the living daylights out of yer if yer even looked sideways at me.'

155

'What would you belt me with?'

'If a man was using force, I'd belt him with the nearest thing to hand.'

'A poker, for instance?'

'Yes, if it was the only thing to hand! I'd not let any man lay a hand on me if I didn't want him to.'

John spread his hands in a gesture of resignation. 'I've said what I think, I can't do any more. But when you've calmed down I'd like you to think about what I said. If you want to take the responsibility then that's your business, but I want nothing to do with it.'

Dot took a deep breath. This was ridiculous. He'd come to do some work for her and here they were, shouting at each other. 'I've got her porridge on the stove now, I'd better see to it before it sticks to the bottom of the pan.' She was very thoughtful as she spooned the porridge on to a plate. The more she went over what John had said, the more sense it made. If she hadn't been so quick off the mark and so sure she knew best, she'd have listened to his reasoning instead of arguing the toss with him.

John laid his coat and trilby neatly on the couch before going into the kitchen to mix some paste for the border. 'I'll get started. It should only take me an hour to put the paper up and then I can start on the paintwork.' When Dot didn't answer he bent his head until their eyes were on a level. 'Have you got a cob on with me? Aren't we speaking?'

'I'm surprised ye're still here. I don't know why yer bother putting up with me. I mean, it's not as though yer've got to. I'm a rude, ungrateful, big-headed Mrs Know-it-all.'

'I won't argue with that.'

Dot grinned. 'I don't blame yer, 'cos I am a rude, big-headed know-it-all. But I've been thinking over what yer said and yer have a point. I wouldn't want to see Mary being carted off to jail for that no-good so-and-so.'

'I'm not suggesting she shouldn't protect herself, far from it. But that poker is made from hard steel; one heavy blow on the head and it could kill. There must be other things she can use that might knock him out but not do any serious damage.' John grinned now. 'Like me giving him a good hiding. That should teach him a lesson and keep him quiet for a while.'

Dot sprinkled sugar over the plate of porridge. 'I'll give a knock on the wall then pass this over. The queer feller's probably still in bed.'

John laid a hand on her arm. 'Just a minute, there's something I've been wanting to say to Mary ever since that first night when I saw the state of her. I couldn't bring myself to say it, being a complete stranger to her, and I haven't had the nerve since. And I'm taking a chance now of you flying off the handle at me. Nevertheless, I think for Mary's sake it's worth the risk.' He stared hard into Dot's eyes. 'Will you promise not to thump me one, or banish me from your house forever?'

'Oh, for heaven's sake, John, of course I won't thump yer, or banish yer. But will yer hurry up or else this porridge will be stiff.'

'There's an easy way for Mary to stop her husband in his tracks when he starts his shenanigans. It won't be possible in every situation, like when she's in bed, but it will come in handy in most cases. All she has to do if he comes near her, and his intentions are unwelcome, is to bring her leg up hard and knee him between the legs, in his groin. That will double him up with pain and give Mary a chance to make for a place of safety.'

Dot was silent for so long John was beginning to doubt the wisdom of speaking his mind. Then a smile spread slowly across her face. 'The bloody gear. He's put her through enough pain over the years, it would do him good to have a taste of his own medicine.'

'Will you tell her then? Not in front of me, of course, it would embarrass her.'

'Oh, I'll tell her all right – too true I will. First chance I get.' Dot was grinning as she reached out to open the door. 'Oh boy, wouldn't I like to hold him while she did it.'

When she heard the neighbour's kitchen door open, she called softly, 'Mary, can yer talk?'

'Yeah, he's in bed, dead to the world. He only went up an hour ago, he's been on the floor all night, too drunk to see the stairs, never mind climb them. He'd been sick all over the floor, I've just been clearing it up.'

Dot closed her eyes and shivered. Fancy having to live with an animal like that. 'Come over here and have yer breakfast; it must stink in your place.'

'It smells like a muck-midden, Dot, I've been retching for the last hour.'

'Get over here and have a decent breakfast. Come on, no arguing.'

Mary gasped when she saw John. She looked a sight in her old dress and she hadn't even run a comb through her hair. She'd had a struggle getting Tom up the stairs, he was still drunk and a dead weight, then she'd been ages cleaning up after him. She could smell the vomit under her nose and it was making her feel sick. 'Dot, why didn't yer tell me John was here? I haven't even been washed yet, I'm not a fit sight for anyone to see.'

John ran a hand down the dungarees he was buttoning. 'I'm in my working gear, Mary, I'm not exactly dressed up.'

'And do I look as though I'm going to a ball?' Dot cupped Mary's elbow and led her into the living room. 'Sit down and I'll have me porridge with yer. We'll just ignore John and let him get on with his work.'

While they were eating, with John in the kitchen mixing a paste, Dot brought up the matter of the poker. Keeping her voice low, she told her neighbour why she didn't think it was a good idea. 'It would only take one wrong blow, sunshine, and they'd be carting you away in a Black Maria.'

'I hate him, Dot, and there's been hundreds of times I've wished him dead, but I certainly wouldn't kill him. Even if I had the guts, I wouldn't.'

'I know yer wouldn't mean to, love, I'm not saying that. But if we could think of something a bit less dangerous than a poker, that would be better. And in the meantime there is a good way to put a halt to the queer feller's gallop.'

The paste was ready but John stayed in the kitchen, leaning against the sink. He could hear the low murmur of voices and could pick up enough to tell him what the conversation was about. He didn't want to walk in now and spoil everything. Dot was doing a good job and he took his hat off to her. She wasn't making heavy weather of it, just saying what she would do if she were in Mary's shoes. Then he heard her chair being scraped back over the lino as she said, 'I'll make us some toast now, eh, and a fresh pot of tea.'

When she went into the kitchen, John winked at her and gave her the thumbs up. 'Nice work, D.D. Will it have any effect, d'you think?'

'Only time will tell.' Dot put the dirty plates in the sink before giving him a push. 'Get a move on, before the kids get up.'

While the women sat at the table drinking tea and talking about things in general, John finished putting the border on the second wall. Using a clean dry cloth, he patted the paper, saying over his shoulder, 'How does that look, D.D.?'

Dot turned her head and her face lit up. 'Ooh, doesn't it make a difference? It sets the wallpaper off lovely. Ah, yer've worked hard, John, come and sit down and have a cuppa.'

'The room looks very nice,' Mary said wistfully. 'Mine looks like a dungeon.'

'And have yer noticed that John doesn't even have to stand on a ladder? It comes in handy to have long arms and legs, doesn't it?'

'You'd never have managed it on yer own, Dot, not the ceiling anyway. My mam does all her own papering but she wouldn't attempt the ceiling, she leaves that for me dad.'

'The next job is the back-kitchen. It looks worse than ever since this place was done. I should be able to do that on me own, it's so small yer couldn't even swing a cat around in it.'

Mary was more relaxed now, feeling more at home here than she ever did in her own house. She smiled at Dot. 'Ask John to do it for yer. He could stand in the middle and do it all without moving a foot.'

'No!' Dot answered quickly. 'I've got to learn how to decorate because the whole ruddy house wants doing. The bedrooms are an eyesore, dark and dismal, enough to give yer the willies or a flaming nightmare.'

John winked at Mary. 'Will you manage the hall and stairs on your own, Dot? You need a ladder and a plank of wood to stand on to reach the top, and all the strips of paper are different lengths. It's definitely a job for a man and I'm quite prepared to do it for you.'

'I'll have a bash meself, I've got to learn sometime.' Dot tossed her head, sending her thick auburn hair swinging about her face. 'D'yer want me to make yer some toast, John?'

'I'll have another cup of tea, please, but no toast. I had a good breakfast before I came out.'

Dot rolled her eyes. 'He's that bloody organised, this feller, he puts me to shame.'

'It would take a better man than me to put you to shame, Mrs D.D.D.D.D. Baker.'

'Oh Lord, what have I done now? What does all that stand for, or have yer suddenly developed a stutter?'

'It stands for Doubting, Difficult, Determined and Delightful Dorothy.'

'Get away with yer, yer daft nit.' Dot cursed the blush she could feel creeping up from her neck. 'I'm none of those things.'

'You are *all* of those things – at different times, of course.' John drained his cup and set it down on the saucer. Then he stared straight into her eyes and she could see a message there. She couldn't fathom out what it was, but he was trying to tell her something. 'I couldn't help hearing you and Mary talking about a poker. If I may be so bold as to make a suggestion, would you or Mary object?'

He waited until both women shook their heads, then went on: 'I could have something made for you in work, Mary – something small and neat that you could keep under your pillow. It would serve the purpose if your husband started any shenanigans. It might cause a few bruises, even knock him out, but it wouldn't kill him.'

'Don't put yerself to any trouble, John – I'll get by. I feel as though I'm being a nuisance to everyone. At my age I should be able to take care of meself instead of expecting others to do it for me.'

'Ye're not a nuisance!' Dot was quick to defend her neighbour. 'It's not your fault that yer've picked a bad husband.'

'A bad husband, Dot? If he was only bad I could put up

with that. No, my husband is evil and wicked. He loves to torture me, as though he derives great pleasure from it. Sometimes he looks and acts like a madman, and that's what terrifies me. He's not normal – no normal man would do the things he does.'

'Then start fighting back,' Dot said. 'Take John up on his offer and also remember what I've told yer to do. Give the bugger a taste of his own medicine.'

'Give who a taste of their own medicine, Mam?' Katy stood in the doorway, yawning and rubbing sleep from her eyes. 'Who are yer talking about?'

'Icky the fire-bobby, sunshine.' Dot sprang to her feet. 'Come and sit down and I'll see to yer breakfast. Is Colin awake, d'yer know?'

'I didn't hear him, Mam, shall I go up to him?'

'No, I'll give him a shout when his breakfast's ready. He should be going to Mass, we all should, but this decorating lark has upset our routine.'

'I'll get back, Dot,' Mary said, giving Katy a hug as she sat down beside her. 'I'd better peel some spuds in case my dearly beloved feels hungry when he finally sobers up.' With the palms of her hands on the table she pushed herself from the chair. 'I won't forget what yer said, John, and I would appreciate one of those things yer mentioned, just in case.'

'You'll have it in a couple of days. I'll drop it off here one night on my way home from work. Take care of yourself, Mary, and if things get out of hand don't be afraid to shout out. You have plenty of friends who you can call on.'

'Would yer like me to come with you?' Dot asked, following Mary through to the kitchen. 'In case he's up?'

Mary shook her head. 'He won't be up, he couldn't see straight when I took him to bed. With a bit of luck I won't set eyes on him all day. If he doesn't put in an appearance I'll be sleeping on the couch tonight.'

Dot went back into the house and closed the kitchen door. John was pasting a piece of border on the draining board and he gave a sigh as he raised his brow. 'There goes one very sad lady. I can't understand why she doesn't leave him and go back to her parents.'

161

'John, she hasn't even told them she's expecting. She went up to see them last week and I was sure she'd told them, but no, she never said a dickie-word. She can get away with it now because, although she's four months, she's not showing. But she won't be able to hide it much longer and her mother's not blind. But yer can talk to Mary until ye're blue in the face and it won't do no good. I've even thought of going to see her mam meself, but I don't want to go against Mary and lose her as a friend. She's determined to keep her troubles to herself and not burden her family with them.'

John lifted the end of the strip of border and began to hang it into eighteen-inch folds ready to carry through. 'It's a sorry business, but you have to respect Mary's wishes. All we can do is help when she asks for it.'

Dot watched him walk back into the living room. He was a nice bloke and a very good worker; he seemed to be able to turn his hand to anything. He'd made decorating that room look like child's play. Quick and efficient, he was, and everything done with a smile on his face and a joke on his lips. It was someone like him Mary should have married; he'd make a really good husband.

'Colin, for heaven's sake watch that door, the paint's wet.' Dot's heart was in her mouth as her son dashed out to the kitchen with his dirty plate. 'If you smudge it I'll break yer ruddy neck for yer.'

'I never touched it, Mam, I was careful.' The boy grinned at her before getting down on his knees next to John, who was painting the skirting board. Since he'd got out of bed at eleven that morning, he'd followed the big man around like his shadow. 'Me mam thinks I'm daft, yer know, Mr Kershaw. She forgets I'm twelve now.'

'Yes, but your mam is right to tell you to watch the doors, lad. It'll be at least twenty-four hours before the paint's dry enough to touch, and if you brush against it you won't only be spoiling my work, you'll get paint all over your clothes.'

'I just wish yer'd leave the poor man alone and let him breathe.' Dot was getting more flustered as the day wore on. If he'd had the room to himself, John could have pulled all the furniture away from the skirting board and given himself a clear run. But Billy had turned up at six o'clock to see if he could give a hand, at least that was the excuse he used which didn't fool anyone, and he was sitting on the couch with Katy. And to top it all, Doreen had called round to see if her friend would go for a walk with her and she was now sitting at the table and looked as though she was set for the night. The room was crowded and it was ridiculous to expect anyone to work in these conditions. 'Katy, why don't you and yer friends go for a walk? Mr Kershaw would be finished in half the time if he had the place to himself.'

'Yeah, OK, Mam. Come on, Billy, get yer coat on and we'll walk down as far as the North Park.'

'The park will be locked up by now,' Doreen said, her lips pouting. She hadn't really called to go for a walk, she'd come to see if Billy was there. 'They lock the gates early in the winter, as soon as it gets dark.'

'We'll go for a walk along Stanley Road, then, and look in the shop windows.' Katy pulled her coat on. 'We'll be back about half-nine, Mam, is that time enough?'

'That's fine, sunshine.' Dot followed the three young ones to the door. She stood on the step and watched with interest and amusement as Doreen linked arms with Katy, putting herself between her friend and Billy. Oh, he's not going to like that, Dot thought to herself. And she was proved right before they'd taken a dozen steps.

'Move over and let me in the middle, Doreen.' Billy's voice was gruff. 'You can walk on the outside.'

'I want to walk next to Katy, she's my friend.'

'What yer want and what yer get are two different things, Doreen Mason.' Without further ado, Billy stretched an arm between the two girls, pushed Doreen aside and took her place. 'There, that's more like it.'

Dot was chuckling as she went back into the living room. 'There's high-ding-dong out there because Doreen wanted to walk between Billy and Katy. But she didn't get away with it; Billy soon put her in her place.'

John sat back on his heels after resting the paint-brush on the top of the tin. 'Billy's sweet on Katy, it sticks out a

163

mile. I see a budding romance there.'

'Go on, he's daft, Billy is,' Colin said, a look of disgust on his face. 'He sits there looking at her with cow eyes. Sloppy thing.'

'You'll change your tune when you're older, Colin. When you meet the girl that's the one for you, you'll be looking just the same as Billy.'

'Nah,' said Colin. 'I'm going to be like you, I'm not going to get married.'

Dot tutted. 'Colin, ye're getting personal again and that's very naughty. How many times do I have to tell yer?'

'Leave him, Dot, this is man-to-man talk,' John said, keeping his face straight. 'The only reason I didn't get married, son, was because I had a mother who needed looking after. Because she'd been a very good mother, and I loved her dearly, I decided that caring for her was more important than me taking a wife.'

'I've got a very good mother,' the boy nodded his head knowingly, 'and I love her dearly as well.'

'You have indeed, Colin. You have a very good mother and a very pretty one. You should be really proud of her.'

'Oh, I am! And I'm going to look after her when she gets old.'

Dot's tummy was shaking with laughter. 'I'm hoping it'll be another thirty or forty years before I need looking after, sunshine, and by that time you'll be well married with a grown-up family of yer own.'

'Nah, I don't want no children, they're nothing but a blinkin' nuisance.'

'If your mother and father had thought like that, you wouldn't be here, would you?' John was smiling as he picked up the paint-brush again. 'You'll change your mind.'

'He can change it in bed,' Dot said. 'It's a quarter to nine and time to climb the stairs to dreamland.'

'Ah, ay, Mam, I didn't get up until eleven! I don't feel a bit tired.'

'You will at half-seven in the morning when I'm trying to get yer out of bed. So don't give me any lip, just say good night to Mr Kershaw and poppy off.'

164

Out of the corner of his eye the boy could see John watching and waiting, with a look on his face that said he wouldn't get any help from that quarter. Best thing he could do was give in gracefully. 'I will see yer again, won't I, Mr Kershaw? Even though the room's finished.'

'Yes, I'll be slipping in one night to drop something off to Mrs Campbell – I'll see you then, Colin. And I think Liverpool are playing at home the Saturday after next, so with your mother's permission we'll go to the match.'

'Ooh, the gear!' After kissing his mother good night, Colin took the stairs two at a time, whistling a happy tune. He had something to look forward to now and everything in his little world was rosy.

'Have yer got much more to do, John?'

Dot was standing with her hands on her hips and John smiled. 'Don't stand like that, Dot. I always feel as though I'm in for a telling-off.'

She was quick to drop her arms. 'To hear you talk, anyone would think I was a complaining, bad-tempered so-and-so. And I'm not, really.'

'No, you're just very outspoken.'

'If yer mean I say what I think, then yes, I am outspoken. I think it's the best way to be 'cos then folk know where they stand with yer. Anyway, yer didn't answer my question. Have yer got much to do?'

'Only this stretch. Fifteen minutes should see me finished.'

'Right. I'll wash the few dishes, then peel the spuds for tomorrow. Yer should be finished by then and I'll make yer a cup of tea before yer go home.'

It was half an hour later when John sat down. He stretched out his long legs and gave a sigh of contentment. 'That's a good job done.'

'It certainly is – yer've done wonders.' Dot sat with her feet tucked under her, a cup of steaming tea in her hand. 'I don't know how to thank you, yer've been so kind. I know I've got a big mouth that says I could manage on me own, and I'd definitely give it a bash, but I could never have done such a good job as you. Yer've turned a grotty little room into a palace.' She grinned and her hazel eyes twinkled. 'The kids will have

165

all their friends traipsing through over the next few days, they'll be showing off like mad. Mind you, it won't bother me, the poor blighters have never had anything to show off before.'

'There is one way you can thank me.' John watched a tea-leaf floating around on the top of his tea. Was that a sign of good luck, or was it supposed to mean you were coming into money?

'What way is that, John?'

'Let me decorate your hall and stairs.'

'Oh, come on, John, I can't let yer do that! Yer've spent enough time and energy on us as it is! Over the past couple of weeks yer've hardly seen yer own home.'

'Time and energy I've got plenty of, Dot, and it's very lonely at home now that my mother isn't there. I get very tired of talking to the flowers on the wallpaper because they can't answer back. So in offering to do a bit of work for you, I'm being selfish really. I enjoy being with you and the children and I'd hoped we could be friends.'

'Of course we're friends, and the kids think the world of yer. But we can be friends without you working yourself to death for us.'

'I want to do it, Dot, please?'

'Right, here's me being outspoken again.' Dot reached down and put her cup on the floor. 'I haven't got the money to buy all the material in one go, it'll take a few weeks. So the job would have to be done in stages. Besides, I promised our Katy I'd buy a teaset next week, she's set her heart on it. And I'm sure yer'll agree that we could do with a few cups and saucers that matched.'

John thought of the dinner and teasets that filled the cupboards at home. More than he'd ever use in his lifetime. But he knew better than to offer them. So he grinned at Dot, and said, 'Oh, I don't know, I rather enjoy being asked if I want a handle on my cup or would I prefer a saucer. It's more homely and friendly. But I agree you can't let Katy down. And in any case it will take quite a while to strip the landing, hall and stairs, so you'd have plenty of time to buy the necessary.'

He's got an answer to everything, Dot thought. But you

166

couldn't fall out with him, he was kindness itself. 'I think ye're a sucker for punishment, John, but if you want to do it, then be my guest.'

'I'll be calling one night with the thing for Mary, so I can measure up for the paper and paint while I'm here, then start scraping next Saturday.'

'What is it yer've got in mind for Mary? I'm curious.'

'Something the same shape as a policeman's truncheon, only much smaller. You'll see it when I bring it.'

They heard Katy letting herself in and Dot whispered, 'Not a word.'

'Ooh, I see yer've finished, Mr Kershaw. It looks lovely, doesn't it, Mam?'

'It does that, sunshine, he's made a damn good job of it.' Dot narrowed her eyes. 'You look down in the dumps, sunshine, what's wrong?'

'Those two have done nothing but argue since we left the house. They got on me flippin' nerves. It was Doreen's fault really, she never stopped moaning. We'd only been out five minutes when she said she was freezing, then her feet were aching, then the cold wind was giving her a headache. Honest, she can be a real misery-guts at times. I didn't blame Billy for telling her to shut up. If he hadn't I'd have done it meself.'

Dot was dying to laugh but didn't think it would be appreciated. 'So a good time was had by all, from the sound of things, eh?'

'Yer should have heard Billy when we got outside her house.' A smile came to Katy's pretty face. 'He told her to go in and get warm by the fire, put her feet to soak in a bucket of warm water and take a headache tablet. I don't think Doreen saw the joke but I thought it was funny.'

'Sadly for her, Doreen hasn't been blessed with her mother's sense of humour, sunshine. She's a moody girl, yer can see it in her face.'

'Anyway,' Katy said, throwing her coat on the couch, 'Billy said, "Don't ever ask me to go out with her again, Katy Baker, or I won't be responsible for me actions".'

Dot grinned across at John. 'Yer know where yer are with

167

Billy. He's outspoken, says what he thinks. Does he remind yer of anyone?'

'Yes, he does, actually, but he's not as pretty.'

Dot aimed a cushion at his head and was bang on target.

Chapter Eleven

'My God, girl, there's no flies on you, now, is there?' Betty Mason gripped the bannister as she lowered herself down the stairs. 'Only ruddy bluebottles, eh?'

'I'm over the moon, Betty. I have to keep pinching meself to make sure I'm not dreaming.' Walking slowly behind her neighbour, Dot let her eyes linger on the newly decorated walls and the white paintwork. Everywhere looked lovely and bright and she'd been so proud to show her best friend around. 'I can't believe the difference it's made.'

Betty carefully negotiated the last stair then made a beeline for the living room and one of the straight wooden chairs. 'He's made a bloody good job of it, my girl, I'll say that for him. And he's been quick – the whole house decorated in just two months! He must have gone like the bleedin' clappers 'cos it takes my feller that long just to think about papering one room.'

'He's quick, all right,' Dot said, pulling out a chair and sitting to face her friend. 'And he's a clean worker, too, always tidies up after himself.'

Betty folded her arms and hitched up her bosom. 'Yer dropped in dead lucky, there, girl.' She nodded her head knowingly. 'Your Colin did yer a great big favour the day he let John knock him down.'

Dot grinned. 'I wouldn't go as far as to say he let John knock him down. It was his own fault, but he didn't do it on purpose. And he did *himself* a favour 'cos he thinks the world of the man. John can do no wrong in my son's eyes.'

'And what about you, girl?' Betty asked gently. 'How are you getting on with him?'

'I suppose yer mean John, not Colin? Oh, I get on well with him, he's a good friend.'

'Friend be buggered!' Betty snorted. 'Yer can't tell me he comes around here so often just 'cos he wants to be a friend to yer. He's never away from the place.'

Dot could feel herself colour. 'He's a friend, Betty, nothing more. So don't you be trying to read anything into it.'

'Come off it, girl, I wasn't born yesterday! The man's got a soft spot for yer – anyone with half an eye can see that. And as for you, you couldn't do better. That John is a good bloke.'

'Betty, we like each other and respect each other, nothing more. I am certainly not in the market for a husband, so let's leave it at that, eh?'

'Then ye're a bloody fool, girl, that's all I can say. If I was in your shoes I'd be giving him the glad eye, I can tell yer.'

'But ye're not in my shoes, are yer? So can we drop the subject, please?' Dot placed her palms flat on the table and pushed herself up. 'I'll put the kettle on and yer can have a drink out of me new cups. And I think I'll give Mary a knock, get her to join us. I saw her feller going out half an hour ago so the coast should be clear.'

'I'll go for her, girl, while you put the water on.' Betty paused on her way to the door and called through to the kitchen: 'Oh, and I hope yer've got a couple of biscuits to put on the new plate ye're going to set before me.'

'Sod off, Betty Mason. If yer want biscuits yer'll have to go home for them.'

'Oh, charming, that is,' Betty grumbled as she opened the front door. 'A posh house and her as common as muck.'

Dot grinned as she reached up to take three of her new cups, saucers and plates from the kitchen shelf. She was lying about the biscuits, she did have some. But she also had a cake, a rare treat. It was only a small sponge sandwich, but it was the first time in years she'd been able to offer visitors a slice of cake.

'Ooh, I'm dead envious every time I come in here.' Mary smiled a welcome. 'It always seems like night-time in our place, it's so dark and dismal.'

'Sit yerself down, sunshine, I'll bring the tea in.'

'I was telling Mary she gets bonnier every time I see her,' Betty bawled. 'Six months she is, and the size of a ruddy house already.'

'It's the dinners you lot are feeding me.' Mary smiled valiantly with her face but not her heart. Her friends made sure she had a hot meal every day and John brought her fresh fruit. They did this because they wanted her to have a healthy baby. But the man she was married to told her repeatedly he wasn't having a brat in the house. So whenever he was there she feared for her unborn child.

'Ooh er, I'll have to lay off the dinners.' Betty's cheeks moved upwards when she grinned. 'It must be them making me look like a pregnant pup, 'cos it certainly isn't me feller. The poor bugger can't rise to the occasion these days, he says he's past it. Would yer believe it? He's only forty-one and past it already. I've told him if he doesn't buck his ideas up I'm going to look for a bit on the side.'

'What did he have to say to that?' Dot asked, coming through with a wooden tray bearing her new crockery and which she placed on the table with pride. She was hoping that Betty was about to begin one of her far-fetched tales which were always hilarious. 'That's if he wasn't speechless.'

'He said one of his mates in work has got a wife what's gone past it, so he'd introduce me to him.' When Betty started to laugh her tummy raised the table a couple of inches off the floor, causing tea to spill from the cups into the saucers. Dot huffed and glared, but nothing would stop her friend once she started. 'His name's Joe, and my feller said he likes his women big.'

Dot stared at the tray. The whole effect was spoilt now, with more tea in the saucers than in the cups. But what the hell, wasn't a laugh better than a cup of tea any day? So she joined in the mirth. 'Does he also like his women to wear pink fleecy-lined bloomers?'

'D'yer think I'm soft, girl? If we fancy the look of each other, yer know what I mean, like, then I'll buy meself some of those French knickers I've seen in the window at Etam's.' A chubby hand cupped several layers of chin as Betty's eyes sought help from the newly painted ceiling. 'Mmm, white I think, trimmed with fine white lace.'

'Oh, definitely,' Dot said. 'Always white for a virgin.'

'Yeah, and a lovely lacy brassière to match.' Betty's face took on a dreamy expression as she fluttered her eyelashes. 'I can see it now, me and Joe staring into each other's eyes longingly. I'd be all shy and coy, of course – I mean, I wouldn't be all over him. Not at first anyway. I wouldn't want him to think I was a trollop.'

Dot and Mary were sitting forward, their elbows resting on the table, their eyes wide as they waited for what was to come. They waited in vain, though, because the big woman had closed her eyes as though she was in a world of her own. 'Well?' prompted Dot, when she could wait no longer. 'Go on, what happens next?'

Betty opened her eyes and looked the picture of innocence. 'Alas, it was not to be. It wasn't the time for us, or the place.'

'Oh, ye're not getting away with that, Betty Mason!' Dot said. 'Going so far and then not telling us what happened.'

'What d'yer mean, what happened? What *could* happen when we were standing in Irwin's shop doorway and the world and his friend were walking past? And anyway, I didn't fancy this Joe feller. He had a big red conk and terrible bad breath.' She flicked an imaginary crumb off her sleeve before grinning. 'So I'm taking the French knickers and the brassière back to Etam's on Monday and I'm asking for a refund. I know it's not their fault that Joe had a big conk and bad breath, but I can't be wasting me money on things that don't work. Then I'm going straight to church to pray that my Alec soon gets his health and strength back.'

Dot and Mary looked at each other as they wiped the tears from their eyes. 'She's a nut-case, isn't she, Dot?'

'Yer can say that again, sunshine. But we're bigger fools that she is 'cos we've sat here for half an hour listening to her. There's an excuse for you, you don't know her that well. But there's no excuse for me, she's me best mate.'

Mary glanced nervously at the clock. 'Can I drink me tea now? I don't want to be out too long in case Tom comes home.'

'I'll have to make a fresh pot and rinse the cups out. Just

172

look at the state of them, and me mate not even batting an eyelid.'

'No,' Mary said quickly. 'I'll pour the tea out of the saucer back into the cup. It'll be all right, don't worry.'

'And I'll do the same.' Betty reached for a saucer. 'No use letting good tea go to waste when it's wet and warm.'

'Yer just won't let me be posh, will yer? It's jealousy, that's what it is,' Dot sighed. 'But time is getting on, I should be seeing to the tea. Colin's gone to the match with John, and they'll be home in an hour or so.'

Mary gulped her tea down and put the cup back on the tray. 'I'll get going if yer don't mind, Dot. There'll be ructions if I'm not there when he comes home.'

'I'll see Mary to the door, girl, while you clear the mess away.' Betty counted to three, then heaved herself up. 'You start to wash, then I'll dry when I come back. Otherwise yer'll be calling me fit to burn for leavin' yer with a mess.'

Mary had just stepped on to the pavement when her husband came along. The colour drained from her face and her eyes darted from left to right, as though seeking a way of escape.

'I'll break yer bleedin' neck for yer.' Tom's nostrils flared with anger and his eyes were blazing as he walked towards her. 'I told yer to keep away from that cow's house. Now get back home, quick, before I belt yer one.'

Betty was down the step in a trice and placed herself firmly in front of him. 'Who the bleedin' hell d'yer think you're talking to?'

'Not to you, yer bleedin' fat cow.' Tom smirked. 'Yer've got an arse the size of an elephant's, d'yer know that? Now, out of me way before I belt you one as well.'

'What! A bleedin' fat cow and an arse like an elephant's!' Betty pushed him in the chest, forcing him to step back to keep his balance. 'No one talks to me like that an' gets away with it.' Again she pushed, this time hard, sending him reeling back against the wall. 'Ye're a slimy little sod, Tom Campbell, lower than a snake's belly. Go on, belt me one, I dare yer.' Every time the man moved away from the wall, she pushed him back. And she wasn't gentle. The hand that pushed him

173

had her whole seventeen stone behind it. 'Go on, belt me one. Give me an excuse to land one on yer that'll knock yer into the middle of next week.'

Dot came flying into the street and her mouth fell open when she took in the scene. 'What's going on here?'

'The bold lad here called you a bleedin' cow, and me a fat one with an arse like an elephant's. He's not getting away with that, Dot, by God he's not. I'll brush the bleedin' street with him before I'm finished.'

'I wouldn't waste yer breath on him, Betty, he's not worth it.' Dot put a protective arm around Mary, and when she felt the trembling her anger rose. 'And I certainly wouldn't dirty me hands on him.'

'Oh, I can wash me hands, that's no problem. I might have trouble getting rid of the smell from under me nose, though.'

'I've got no argument with you.' Tom tried to wriggle out of it. He nodded to where Mary stood cowering, her arms folded across her swollen tummy. 'It's that stupid bitch's fault. If she'd done what I told her, none of this would have happened. But she'll not disobey me again. I'll sort her out when I get her in the house.'

'Over my dead body yer'll sort her out.' Betty grabbed the front of his coat, pulled him away from the wall, then slammed him back. Over and over she did this, venting her anger on a man who talked of his pregnant wife as if she were a piece of dirt, a chattel he could do what he liked with. 'Sort me out, instead. Go on, I dare yer.'

Tom had no intention of tangling with this woman; she had muscles on her bigger than any man he knew. 'Just move out of the way and let me get to me own bleedin' house.'

The O'Connors had come out and Paddy made a move to interfere but his wife put her arm out and stopped him. 'Leave it for now, Paddy,' Maggie said. 'I think Betty is more than a match for him.'

Several of the neighbours on the opposite side of the street had come to their doors, having seen the confrontation through their windows. One of them, who lived directly opposite the Campbells, was Miss Amelia Green. Many times, from behind her net curtains, she'd seen Mary being ill-treated, so she had no love for Tom Campbell. She was an elderly lady in her eighties, small and thin, but very wiry and fiercely independent. With one hand in the deep pocket of her floral wrap-around pinny, and the other smoothing her snow-white hair, she shouted encouragement. 'Go on, Betty, give him a go-along. If I was younger I'd do it meself 'cos he's a bad bugger if ever there was one.'

There were murmurs of agreement from the other neighbours. Tom Campbell wasn't a popular man with the women in the street because of his arrogant nature. No one ever got a friendly greeting or a kind word from him. Nor was he popular with the men who frequented the corner pub. Even hardened dockers, far from being shrinking violets themselves, found his crude jokes too near the knuckle and his language offensive.

Betty's eyes slid sideways. 'Take Mary back in yer house, girl. This is no place for someone in her condition.'

'Come on, sunshine, Betty's right.' When Mary was reluctant to move, Dot used gentle force to get her up the steps and into the house. 'It'll be all right, so don't be getting yerself all upset. It'll blow over, mark my words.'

As soon as the women disappeared into the house, Betty turned her attention back to Tom Campbell. With the picture of his terrified wife in her mind, she gripped the neck of his coat and shook him as though he was a rag doll. 'Now, where's that belt yer were going to give me? Come on, have your go first, then I'll have mine.'

A sly look came over the man's face. There was no way he was going to give the fat cow a chance to belt him one because he knew she was capable of knocking him out cold. But a kick in the shins should release her hold on him long enough for him to make good his escape. Betty, however, was too quick for him. Before he'd had time to lift his foot, she'd clenched her fist and let fly. It caught Tom on the jaw and he yelped with pain. 'Yer stupid bleedin' cow.' He was bent double, holding his face and moaning. 'Yer've broken me jaw! I'll have the police on yer for this.'

With a smile of satisfaction on her face, Betty dusted her hands together as though ridding herself of something unpleasant. 'Be my guest, yer snivelling little worm. I'll tell them yer threatened me and I was acting in self-defence.'

'I'll back yer up on that, Betty,' Miss Green said. 'I heard him threaten yer.'

'I'll be a witness for yer, Betty,' shouted the old lady's neighbour, Mrs Armstrong. 'With me own ears I heard him.'

And Mr Armstrong went as far as to say, 'I was standing next to the missus when he said it, so yer can count me in.'

Betty waved and smiled her thanks. 'He won't do nothing, though, he hasn't got the guts. He'll crawl home like the animal he is, and lick his wounds.' She jerked her head at Maggie and Paddy. 'Are yer coming in Dot's for a minute? I think this little episode calls for a meeting of the committee.'

When John walked in with Colin, it was to find the room full. He knew immediately by the set of their faces that it wasn't a social gathering. 'Something happened?'

'Yer could say that,' Dot said, sighing. 'Betty here had a fight with Tom Campbell and she gave him a fourpenny one.'

'Hey, hang on a minute!' Betty looked really put out. 'The way you say it, anyone would think I'd just gone up to him and landed him one for no reason at all. If ye're going to tell the story, get yer bleedin' facts right.'

'That wasn't a criticism of yer, sunshine, 'cos I'm proud of yer. I'll have you fighting in my corner any day of the week.'

Betty hitched up her bosom and smiled. 'I'll forgive yer, girl. But someone else can tell John what happened, then I can see the whole thing through another pair of eyes. Sort of neutral, like, if yer know what I mean.'

'I was the cause of it, John.' Mary's voice was low and unsteady. She was sitting on the couch next to Maggie, who had an arm across her shoulders. 'My husband surpassed himself today. He managed to make a show of me, which is nothing new, and he insulted Betty and Dot. And why? Because he doesn't like me coming in this house and has warned me against it. I think he was made up to see me leaving here, it gave him something to have a go at me for. But he'd reckoned without Betty.' Her voice gaining strength as she spoke, Mary repeated every word and action. 'Then Dot brought me in here and I didn't see or hear any more, except when Tom cried out. That must have been when Betty hit him. But if ever anyone was asking for a thump, then it was Tom Campbell for the things he said.'

It was Paddy, the quiet Irishman, who finished the tale. 'Sure, Mary's right, so she is. The man is an out-and-out rotter, and if the truth were known he got off lightly for insulting the women the way he did. I'll not be repeating the words he used, that I'll not, but his use of them showed how little respect he has for them. What Betty gave him, he had more than asked for.'

Betty's face was doing contortions as she leaned forward. 'Paddy, ye're a gentleman and I admire yer for it. But as I'm no lady, I'll tell John what he said.' She sat back in the chair and gazed at John. 'Mary is a stupid bitch who had the nerve to disobey him and who he was going to sort out when he got her home. Dot, of course, is a bleedin' cow, which we've all heard him say before. But he saved the best for me.' For the life of her, Betty couldn't keep the smile from her face. She wasn't a proud woman and could see the funny side of it. 'I'm a bleeding fat cow who's got an arse as big as an elephant's.'

John, perched on the arm of the couch with Colin sitting at his feet, smiled back at her. 'And a heart the same size. I take my hat off to you, Betty. My only regret is that I didn't witness it. He must feel a right fool, being beaten by a woman.'

'Ay, we'll have less of that, John Kershaw.' Betty feigned indignation. 'I'll have yer know that Elizabeth Margaret Mason is not just any woman. I can hold me own with any man.'

Dot closed her eyes and tried to chase a thought away. Now wasn't the time for jokes. But in the end she couldn't resist. 'Any man except one called Joe, who has a big red conk and bad breath.'

Betty's chair threatened to collapse as she rocked back and forth with laughter. Even Mary raised a smile. 'Ah, ay, girl, that's a bit below the belt, isn't it?' The big woman's hands were pressing on her tummy to stop it from shaking. 'The poor man can't help how God made him, now can he?'

Dot chuckled. 'God doesn't usually make them with bad breath, sunshine.'

John could see that Maggie and Paddy were as puzzled as himself. 'Would someone mind telling us who this Joe bloke is?'

'He's a friend of Betty's,' Dot giggled. 'And now as I come to think about it, he's to blame for all this. If it hadn't been for him, Mary would have been out of here earlier and the queer feller wouldn't have known the difference.'

'But who is this Joe?' John asked, puzzled. 'And what was he doing here?'

Dot groaned. Why couldn't she keep her big mouth shut? 'He wasn't here, John – in fact he doesn't even exist. He's a figment of Betty's vivid imagination and I'll tell yer about it some other time. Right now we've got to think of what to do about Mary.'

'Can I go and put the family's tea out, first?' Betty asked. 'I mean, Mary won't be going home yet, will she? Not while her feller's in such a temper. And I'll have to tell my Alec what happened before some nosy bugger gets their oar in before me.'

'Yeah, you toddle off, sunshine, Mary can have some tea with us. I'll have to get cracking because our Katy will be in before I know it.'

Paddy reached for his wife's hand to help her up. 'Will it be all right with yerself, Mrs Baker, if we come back later as well? Me and Maggie want to help, so we do.'

'Of course yer can come back – say about seven o'clock? But for heaven's sake, Paddy, will yer call me by me first name? Yer make me feel as old as the hills, calling me Mrs Baker.'

'Sure, I'd not be wanting to make a fine-looking woman such as yerself feel as old as the hills.' Paddy's smile was as gentle as his voice. 'It's meself that'll be honoured.'

Dot saw her neighbours out then made straight for the kitchen. 'It's only egg and chips, like it or lump it.'

'Don't do any for me, I'll go home for a bite,' John said. 'You have enough on your hands without worrying about me.'

'Stay where yer are, one more egg and a few chips won't kill me. Besides, what would yer have if yer went home? Nowt, I bet. And it's odds on yer haven't even got a ruddy fire in the grate.'

'I'm a bachelor, Dot, I'm not used to creature comforts.'

'I'll give yer a hand to peel the potatoes,' Mary said, disappointed that John was staying because she'd been hoping to have a quiet word with Dot. 'I may as well make meself useful instead of sitting on me backside.'

'There's no need, sunshine, I can manage on me own.' Dot looked to where Mary was framed in the kitchen door. 'Go and rest yer legs.'

Mary moved towards her, speaking softly. 'I wanted to talk to yer, private, like.'

'Oh.' Dot pinched her bottom lip and was thoughtful for a while. Then she nodded her head and walked past Mary into the living room. 'Will you do us a favour, John? Walk down to the shops for an *Echo*, and take our Colin with yer.'

'I've got an *Echo* in my coat pocket – I bought it on the way home from the match.'

Dot stared him out. 'Yer'll want to take that home with yer and I'd like one for meself. When the house is quiet I can put me feet up in front of the fire and have a good read, see what's going on in the world.'

'But you don't read the paper, Mam,' Colin said. 'I've never seen yer.'

'There's a first time for everything, sunshine, so put yer coat back on, like a good boy, and go with Mr Kershaw.'

'Yes, come on, Colin, we know when we're not wanted.' John had read Dot's signal correctly. 'I'll treat you to a comic.'

'Ay, don't you go spoiling him, John Kershaw, 'cos he'll come to expect it from me, and I can't afford to be forking out all the time.'

'I'm being selfish, Dot, not generous. I'd look daft going into a shop for a comic, wouldn't I? So I've got a good excuse in Colin. You see, I can borrow it when he's finished with it.'

Dot's pursed lips and shaking head told him she didn't believe him for one moment. 'Go on, yer big daft ha'porth, out with yer while I get the tea ready. And if ye're going to Katy's shop for the paper, tell her to come straight home, her tea will be on the table.'

When she went back into the kitchen, Dot told Mary, 'They

won't be out long, so yer'd better make it snappy. I'll do the spuds while you're talking.'

Mary picked at the wool on the sleeves of her shabby cardigan. She was so embarrassed she didn't know where to start. 'D'yer remember telling me what to do if Tom ever looked as though he was going to hurt me? You know, with me knee? Well, twice I've done it to him, and that's the reason for him taking off today. He's only looking for an excuse to have a go at me.'

Dot rested the potato-peeler on the draining board, her eyes wide with disbelief. 'Go 'way! Yer mean yer kneed him?'

Mary nodded. 'Yeah, twice. *And* I've used the cosh that John gave me. Each time he's doubled up with pain and it's given me a chance to run down the yard and into the entry. But he's determined to get his own back, and he thought he had the chance this afternoon. Once he'd got me in the house I wouldn't have been in a position to defend meself. Yer see, he didn't notice Betty, as she was standing in the hall.'

'Well, I be blowed! I never thought yer had it in yer, sunshine, I really didn't. So the bold lad hasn't been getting things all his own way, then?'

Mary lowered her eyes. If Dot could see the bruises on her body she'd know her husband had ways of getting his own back. She only had to look sideways at him and he'd punch her with a curled fist. She never knew when or where the blows were going to land; it could be in the small of her back, chest, thighs, and once or twice on the side of her tummy. 'He gives me a belt now and then, but nothing like he used to.'

'I should hope not, sunshine, for the baby's sake.'

'I know that, Dot, and I am careful.'

'Yer need to be, with that bastard.' Dot finished peeling the potato and threw it into a pan of water. 'Yer'll have to excuse me language, Mary, but that husband of yours would make a saint swear. Me blood boils just thinking of him. I don't know how yer can stand to be in the same house as him.'

'I've got to stay in the same house as him, but I've made up me mind I'll never sleep in the same bed as him again.

What happened today is the final straw. He'll have to kill me before I ever sleep with him again.'

'Ay, watch out, sunshine, he won't stand for that.'

'If you only knew some of the things I've had to stand for, Dot, yer'd be horrified.' Mary's voice was choked. 'There's never a word of endearment, and no such thing as a kiss or a cuddle. He just uses me, that's all. He takes what he wants, snarling like a wild beast from the jungle, then tosses me aside. Well, the worm has turned and he'll use me no more.'

Dot swished the potatoes around in the pan to clean them, then emptied the water into the sink. She wiped her wet hands down the front of her pinny before putting them gently on Mary's arms. 'I know I'm the one who's always telling her to stick up for yerself, sunshine, but it's easy for me to talk, I don't have to put up with it. It's the easiest thing in the world to give advice 'cos words are cheap. But it behoves the person giving advice to know exactly what she's talking about. And while I know Tom Campbell is a violent, no-good man I wouldn't give the time of day to, I really don't know the extent of his wickedness. So I'm afraid for yer, sunshine, I really am. Especially in your condition, when the last thing yer need is worry. All I'll say to yer is, you do what yer think is best. And do it in the knowledge that if things get bad then ycr've got friends either side of yer who will help yer, day or night.'

'I know that, Dot, and I thank God for you and Maggie, and Betty and John. I really don't know what I'd do without you, I'd be lost. And it's only because I know I've got you to call on that I've made up me mind to stand up to the bully I'm married to. From tonight on, I sleep on the couch and nothing he says or does will make me change me mind.'

Dot dropped her arms and sighed. 'So ye're going home tonight?'

Mary nodded. 'I'll go before he leaves for the pub, and tell him. Now I don't like asking this, Dot, and I know yer'll all think I've got a flaming cheek, but just this once, just to get tonight over, d'yer think John or Paddy will come in with me? Tom won't pull any stunts if he sees there's a man with me.'

'They'll both come with yer, sunshine, for good measure. And I'll keep me ears open all night just in case.'

181

Mary leaned forward and kissed Dot's cheeks. 'Thank God for me wonderful friends. I'll pay yer back one day, I promise.'

Dot turned away, picked up the small sharp knife and began to chip the potatoes. It grieved her to see Mary in the state she was in, having to ask neighbours for help. She was a young woman, kind, gentle, and if she was dressed as she should be dressed, would be a real knock-out for looks. Any man would be proud to call her his wife, except the one she was married to.

'Yer can pay us back by having a beautiful, bouncing, healthy baby,' she said in a cheery voice, but with her eyes full of tears. 'Whether it's a boy or girl, it'll have loads of aunties and uncles to love it.'

'I'm going to sort me life out when the baby's born,' Mary promised. 'I might go back to live with me mam and dad and try for a divorce. Me mam would be dead against it, being a good Catholic, but I'm not spending the rest of me days being married to Tom Campbell. There's got to be a better life than the one I've got now.'

'One thing's certain, sunshine, there couldn't be a worse one.'

Chapter Twelve

Katy leaned across the counter and put a halfpenny in the palm of the little girl's hand then closed her fingers over it. 'Keep tight hold, now, Ella, and don't lose it.'

'I won't.' The happy face smiled back. Ella was more interested in the bag in the other hand which contained two ounces of Dolly Mixtures. 'I'll run all the way home.'

Katy watched as the little tot opened the shop door and dashed out, leaving the door wide open. She was about to round the counter to close it when John and Colin came in and her face lit up in welcome. 'Hello, Mr Kershaw, and you, our kid.'

'Hello, Katy.' Every time John looked at her, he could see her mother as a young girl. He glanced along the counter to where Molly was serving and waved a greeting. 'Busy as usual, Mrs Edwards?'

Molly grinned. 'It puts the bread on the table, John. And on a very good day we can even afford butter, as well.'

John smiled before turning back to Katy. 'I'll take an *Echo*, please, and my young friend here would like to see the comics you have.'

Katy folded the paper and pushed it towards him. 'Did yer enjoy the match?'

'Yeah, the match was great,' Colin butted in. 'But when we got home—'

John gripped his arm, cutting off his words. 'I'm sure Katy doesn't want to hear all that, Colin, and if she does she can hear it from your mother when she gets home.'

'OK, Mr Kershaw. Can I have a look at the comics, then?'

'Yes, choose two and then I can take one home with me. We can do a swop when we've read them.'

Colin's face was a picture of happiness as he moved to where the comics were spread out on a shelf near the front window. 'Thanks, Mr Kershaw.'

Katy clicked her tongue on the roof of her mouth and shook her head. 'Ye're not half spoiling him, yer know.'

John chuckled loudly. 'Katy, you are your mother all over. You're the image of her in looks and you have the same mannerisms. You also have the same expression on your face when you're telling someone off. I got a ticking-off from her before we left the house about spoiling Colin, but a treat now and then won't spoil him. He's a very well-behaved boy, never asks for anything and is always appreciative.' He leaned across the counter and said softly, 'When I said you took after your mother, it was meant as a compliment. I think you are both delightful and adorable.'

Katy gave a little curtsy. 'Thank you, kind sir.'

'Don't tell her I said that, though, or I'll get another ticking-off. Not that I mind – in fact, I quite like the way she puts her hands on her hips and tilts her head before putting me in my place.' John laughed. 'Especially when she has to crane her neck to do it.'

'Me mam always says what she thinks, Mr Kershaw, and I believe it's best that way, don't you? At least yer know where yer stand with her.'

Colin came back and laid two comics on the counter. 'These two look good, Mr Kershaw, so shall we have them?'

'Yes, but remember I'm taking one home with me to read in bed and we're doing a swop when we've read them.' He raised his brows at Katy. 'That's fair, don't you think?'

'I'd think it was fair if I didn't think yer were telling a fib, Mr Kershaw. You don't really read comics, do yer?'

'Cross my heart and hope to die, Katy, I really do read them. Part of me hasn't grown up, you see, I'm still a little boy at heart.'

Katy's eyes travelled the length of him. 'There's nothing little about you, Mr Kershaw, but I know what yer mean. Yer see, if I had a doll I'd play with it, even at my age. I'd make clothes for it and have it sitting on the chair in me bedroom. And I'd call her Victoria. So yer see, I must still be a little girl at heart, mustn't I?'

'Stay that way, Katy, never grow up, at least not in your heart.'

Colin pulled on his coat. 'Are we going home, Mr Kershaw? Me mam will be wondering where we've got to.'

John looked at his watch. Dot and Mary should have had long enough by now to say what they had to say. 'How much do I owe you, Katy?'

'Fivepence halfpenny. But our Colin can pay for one of the comics – he gets pocket money, yer know.'

'He paid for himself to go to the match, dear, so I don't think he'll have much left.'

Katy took the silver sixpence and notched one up for her brother. Good for him, paying for himself. At least he wasn't scrounging off Mr Kershaw *all* the time.

'We'll see you later, Katy, and your mother said not to be late because she'll have the tea on the table.' Raising his trilby to Molly, John put his hand on Colin's shoulder and walked towards the door, but he held the boy back when he saw the door being opened from the outside. 'Let the gentleman in first, Colin.'

The man looked surprised to see John. He wasn't wearing a cap but he put his hand to his forehead in greeting. 'Hello, Mr Kershaw.'

'Good evening, Jim, how's the wife?'

'Oh, she's coming on a treat now, thank goodness. Yer can tell she's gettin' better 'cos she's started to throw her weight around again.'

'That's always a good sign.' John propelled Colin forward. 'I'll see you on Monday, Jim.'

Katy had the evening paper ready for the man who was as regular as clockwork. As she handed it to him, she asked, 'D'yer know Mr Kershaw, then, Mr Grimes?'

'Yeah, he's me boss.'

'Go 'way!' Katy's eyes shone with interest. 'Is he yer supervisor?'

Jim Grimes smiled as he passed a threepenny joey over. 'No, he's the manager of the factory, Katy, which means he's boss over everyone.'

Ooh, fancy that, Katy thought. Then with a touch of pride she said, 'He's a friend of ours, Mr Grimes. That was me young brother with him.'

'Then it's well blessed yer are with yer friends, Katy, 'cos he's a real gent, is Mr Kershaw. He's the best boss I've ever had, I can tell yer. Always fair and treats everyone alike.'

'Yeah, he is nice. I like him a lot and me brother thinks the world of him.'

Jim was about to say it was a pity Mr Kershaw wasn't married with a family of his own because he would make a very good husband and father, then he thought better of it. This was the time for prudence, in case anything he said was repeated. So he smiled at Katy and said, 'I'll have some liquorice allsorts with the penny change, lass, to give my dear old wife a treat. Put her in a good mood for when she sees me puttin' me coat on to go to the pub.'

Katy wagged a finger at him before reaching up to take a sweet jar from the top shelf. 'Just wait until I see Mrs Grimes, I'll snitch on yer.'

'Yer won't see hide or hair of her before Monday, lass,' Jim grinned as he watched her weighing the sweets, 'and the cob she'll have on tonight will have gone by then.'

'I'm getting to know all the tricks you men get up to.' Katy passed the cone-shaped bag over to him with a smile. 'It's surprising what yer learn standing behind this counter, it's a real education. When I'm old enough to get married, my poor husband won't get away with anything because I'll be wise to all the tricks and excuses.'

'Yer'll have to be married a long time for that, lass. The excuses only come when the novelty of being married wears off.'

Molly walked down the counter after serving the last customer. 'Oh, aye, Jimmy Grimes, and when did the novelty wear off for you? After two weeks of wedded bliss, was it?'

'More like twenty-two years, Molly. I've got no complaints in that department. Me and the missus have a good life, just like Darby and Joan.'

'Ay, Jim Edwards, come and listen to this,' Molly called

186

through to the stockroom. 'Get in here and take a few lessons from yer namesake.'

'What's that, light of my life?' Jim's head appeared around the door. 'Am I missing something?'

'Only how a wife should be treated, that's all. Here's Mrs Grimes being complimented to high heaven and I never even get a goodnight kiss! It's no wonder I go to sleep and dream of Clark Gable.'

Her husband grinned. 'Is he a good kisser?'

'Is who a good kisser?'

'Clark Gable of course, your dream man.'

'How the hell do I know?' Molly's tummy was rumbling with laughter. 'He's a good kisser in me sleep, but when I wake up I can't remember what it felt like.'

Jim Grimes was chuckling as he put the newspaper under his arm. 'He can't be that good if yer can't remember. I mean, if it was earth-shattering yer'd fall out of bed.'

'Ooh, er, fancy you saying that! Three times I fell out of bed last week and I blamed my feller for kicking me out! While all the time it was Clark Gable . . . well, I never.'

'Well, next time he can come and pick yer up off the floor.' Her husband grimaced as he put his hands on his hips and squared his shoulders. 'Last time I picked yer up I nearly did me back in.'

'I'll rub it for yer tonight, sweetheart, with Sloan's Liniment.' Molly grinned up into his face and nipped his cheek between two fingers. 'Let Jim out and then put the bar on the door so no one else can sneak in. We're closed for the day, thank God, and me feet can't wait to put themselves up. Oh, and yer'd better let young Billy come in to wait for Katy. He's been walking up and down that long he's probably worn a groove in the pavement.'

'Are we all right for timing?' John queried when Dot opened the door. 'We couldn't stay any longer, Molly was waiting to close the shop.'

'Yeah, everything's under control.' Dot sighed as she closed the door behind them. 'At least Mary thinks it is; I'm not so sure.'

John hung his coat on the hook behind the door before taking his trilby off and running his fingers through his fine sandy hair. 'Where is Mary?'

'In the kitchen keeping her eyes on the chips for me. Come through and have a word with her.' Dot winked at Colin when she saw the two comics. 'They should keep yer quiet for the rest of the night, sunshine.'

'Only one is his, the other's mine.' John intended to keep up the pretence; he didn't fancy another ticking-off for spoiling the boy. 'We made a deal and Colin must stick to it.'

'Oh, I will, Mr Kershaw, I won't touch yours. Look, I'll put one behind the cushion so yer'll know I'm not cheating.'

John grinned and ruffled the mop of thick black hair before following Dot into the kitchen. 'So, you two have hatched a plan, have you?'

'Mary has,' Dot answered. 'She'll tell you about it herself.'

Mary took a deep breath to try and steady her nerves. Talking about what she was going to do was one thing, carrying it out was another. 'I'll go home after tea, John, before my husband leaves to go to the pub. There's something I've got to have out with him, and if I don't do it tonight I'll never do it. He's not going to like what I intend telling him, and I'm afraid of being on me own with him, so can I play on your good nature and ask if yer'll come with me, please?'

'Of course I will. I've told you I'll do all I can to help.'

There was a look of concern on Dot's face as she used a fish slice to turn the chips in the spluttering fat. 'In all fairness, Mary, I think yer should tell John everything. If he's going in there with yer, he has a right to know he could be walking into real trouble. Because if I know your husband, he'll try to tear yer limb from limb.'

Mary dropped her head, wishing the floor would swallow her up. 'It's too embarrassing.'

'Holy sufferin' ducks! Mary, John is a grown man, not a little boy.' Dot rubbed her arm where a spurt of hot fat had landed. 'For heaven's sake, go and sit in the living room and I'll tell him meself.'

But when push came to shove, Dot found it wasn't that easy. With his eyes staring at her intently, she couldn't find the right words. So she played for time by licking the burn on her arm while willing herself to get it over with.

It was John who broke the silence. 'Dot, as you've just told Mary, I *am* a grown man.'

'I know ye're a flamin' grown man, soft lad, haven't I got a crick in me neck from looking up at yer? It's just finding somewhere to start.'

'Then perhaps I can make it easy for you. Just tell me, in as few words as possible, what Mary is going to tell her husband.'

'That she'll never sleep in the same bed as him again, she's going to sleep on the couch.' Dot got it all out in one breath. Then she looked at John and saw a smile playing around his mouth. 'I don't know what ye're laughing at, it's not funny.'

'I'm not laughing at Mary's plight, I can assure you. It was the expression on your face I found funny. You're not as tough as you make out, D.D. You were every bit as embarrassed as Mary would have been.'

'Well, it's not an easy thing to talk about to a strange man.'

'A strange man? Is that what I am, Dot? I thought we were friends.'

'Don't yer be trying to twist me words, John Kershaw, like yer always do. I regard Alec Mason as a friend, but I wouldn't dream of discussing sleeping arrangements with him, would I?'

John put a hand across his mouth to hide the smile. If she saw it, sure as eggs she'd clock him one. 'Well, I wouldn't advise it if Betty was in earshot. She's got a fantastic sense of humour but I doubt if it would run to you discussing what you call sleeping arrangements with her husband.'

Dot glared, but only for a moment, then her face relaxed into a smile. 'I do take things to heart too much, I keep telling meself that. Sometimes I wish I was like Betty, she wouldn't care if her backside was on fire. If she was me, living here, she'd have sorted Tom Campbell out years ago. A couple of good hidings off her and he'd be reduced to a quivering jelly.' She shrugged her shoulders in a gesture of resignation. 'But me, I'm all mouth and no action.'

John leaned forward and touched her arm. 'Dorothy Baker, you are just right the way you are. You are a good mother, a good manager and a good friend. I wouldn't ever like to say you were good with your fists. You are too much of a lady for that.'

Dot flushed as she turned away. 'Yer won't be saying I'm a good housewife, though, when I put yer chips down to yer and they're burned to a flamin' cinder. Now get out of me kitchen and let me get on with it.'

John saluted. 'Aye, aye, sir!'

'Oh, hang on a minute,' Dot said. 'Will yer nip up to the O'Connors' and explain there's no need for them to come down? I don't feel like having a house full of people tonight, me head's splitting as it is. But ask them to keep their ears open, just in case.'

'What about Betty? She's supposed to be coming down as well.'

'Oh Lord,' Dot groaned. 'There's no rest for the wicked, is there?'

'I'll call and tell her the same as the O'Connors. I like Betty, she's a good woman, but she wouldn't do your headache much good.'

'Tell her I'll see her tomorrow to give her all the news. And don't stay out long because these chips are ruined as it is.' When he reached the door, she called him back. 'Thanks for everything, John, ye're a good pal.'

'Would your headache put up with me staying for a few hours? We could have a quiet game of cards with Katy and Billy.'

'Oh, all right, but at ten o'clock I'm off to bed. All this excitement has worn me out.'

'I'll leave at the stroke of ten and take young Billy with me. Does that suit you, D.D.?'

'Down to the ground, J.J.'

John's eyes gleamed. 'Am I still Joker John? Or have you finally managed to come up with another name for me?'

'No, not really, I've given it up as a bad job. So it's got to be Just John.'

His chuckle was deep and infectious. 'That'll do to be going on with.'

* * *

'I wonder what's going on next door?' Dot couldn't settle and was pacing the floor. It was fifteen minutes since John had taken Mary home and there hadn't been a sound. She'd been expecting Tom Campbell to take off, roaring and swearing, but they hadn't even heard a voice being raised. 'It's too quiet for my liking.'

'Mr Campbell won't start any trouble while Mr Kershaw's there, Mam,' Katy said from her seat on the couch, Billy by her side. 'He's not that daft.'

Colin looked up from the comic he had spread out on the table. 'If he tried anything, Mr Kershaw would make mincemeat of him.'

In spite of her worry, Dot smiled. 'I bet you think he could make mincemeat of King Kong, too, don't yer?'

Colin pursed his lips as he gave that some thought, then he said, 'He couldn't fight him, but he could out-manoeuvre him.'

Dot stared. 'Out-manoeuvre him! That's a big word for you, sunshine.'

Billy chuckled. 'Have yer swallowed a dictionary?'

Katy giggled. 'I bet yer couldn't spell it.'

'I could, yer know, 'cos it's in this comic.' Colin pulled tongues at his sister. 'So there, that's one in the eye for you, clever clogs.'

'D'yer know what it means, sunshine?'

'Of course I do, Mam! Mr Kershaw told me.' The boy raised his eyes to the ceiling before going back to the excitement of his comic. Grown-ups could be really stupid at times. Except for Mr Kershaw – he knew everything, he did.

The knock on the door sent Dot flying out to answer it. 'I've been worried sick, wondering what was going on.'

'There was absolutely nothing for you to worry about, Dot, I told you that as Mary and I were leaving. As a matter of fact, Mr Campbell was ready to go out when we arrived and after Mary had said what she had to, he walked out. On his way to the pub, no doubt.'

There was a look of amazement on Dot's face. 'I don't believe it! Yer mean he just walked out and left the two of you there?'

'You'll have to believe it because that is precisely what happened.' Then John added, 'Oh, you can tell Betty she didn't break his jaw, but he has got a whopping big bruise on the side of his chin.'

'I don't know what to make of it – it doesn't sound a bit like him,' Dot said. 'What did Mary actually say to him?'

'Just what she told you,' John said, but the message in his eyes was reminding her it wasn't the sort of thing to discuss in front of children. 'Not much, really.'

'Oh well, yer live and learn.' Dot shrugged her shoulders as though dismissing the matter from her mind. 'Move yerself from the table, Colin, and Katy will get the cards out.'

'Can I have a game, Mam? Just the one and then I'll go to bed.'

'OK, but no acting the goat, d'yer hear? Any messing and it's right up the stairs, on the double, and I mean it.' Dot turned her back on the children and rolled her eyes at John. 'I'll make us a cuppa before we start and you can give us a hand setting the cups out. That's if yer don't mind, of course.'

'It will be my pleasure.'

With the sound of the running water drowning her words, Dot asked, 'Now, what really did happen in there? Did Mary say what she wanted, and did the queer feller just stand there and take it?'

'I didn't go right into the room, I thought that would make matters worse, so I stood in the doorway. I was surprised at Mary, she seemed quite calm and totally in control of her emotions. She told him in no uncertain terms that she would no longer play the part of his wife, in any shape or form. And that from now until the baby is born, she intended to sleep on the couch.'

'And he didn't say a dickie-bird?'

'What he said was, "Good riddance to bad rubbish", but his face spoke volumes as he said it. I'm certain that if I hadn't been there, his reaction would have been very different. As it was, he pushed past me with a sneer on his face and went on his merry way. I've warned Mary to be on her guard when he comes home. Particularly if he's downed half a dozen pints.'

'She's got more guts than me, I can tell yer.' Dot put the

192

sugar basin on the tray and reached into a drawer for spoons. 'I wouldn't stay in that house for a big clock.'

'I waited until she brought some bedding down, and she said she'll stay awake until she knows he's in bed. And if he does try anything, she has the cosh with her. That should keep him at arm's length.'

'I dunno, what a life. If I had a husband like him I'd put me ruddy head in the gas oven.' Dot sighed. 'Anyway, you take the tray in, John, and I'll bring the teapot.'

To the amazement of everyone, Colin won the first hand of rummy, and he did it without cheating or help from anyone. He jumped up and down, as happy as a cat with two tails. 'I wish we'd been playing for money, I'd be loaded.'

'When you play cards for money, Colin, it isn't a pleasure any more,' John said, shuffling the deck. 'It's gambling, and only mugs gamble.'

'Doreen came into the shop today, Mam,' Katy said, watching John deal the cards. 'She asked me if I'd go to the pictures with her next Saturday.'

Before Dot could answer, Billy made his feelings known. 'I hope yer told her to go and jump in a lake, a deep one?'

'No, I didn't! I told her I'd have to ask me mam. Anyway, if we did go, you could come with us, couldn't yer?'

'Ye're joking, aren't yer, Katy? I'm not going anywhere with *her*, she's a real misery-guts. I bet even Laurel and Hardy couldn't get a smile out of her.'

'If yer go to the first house, could I come with yer?' Colin pleaded. 'If it was a comedy they'd let me in if I was with an adult.'

Billy leaned his elbows on the table, his hazel eyes glinting with mischief. 'I've got a good idea! Colin can go with Doreen and I'll take Katy.'

The only one sitting around the table who didn't see the funny side of this was Colin. 'Ye're not palming me off with her, she's a pain in the neck!'

John finished dealing, placed the remaining cards in the middle of the table and turned the top one face up. 'It's ages since I went to the pictures, so why don't we all go together? Then nobody gets left out and we're all happy.'

'Oh, yeah!' Colin was so excited at the prospect he banged his two fists on the table, scattering the cards in all directions. 'Ay, Mam, wouldn't that be the gear?'

'I'm not going to no pictures on a Saturday night! I have to go to work in the morning, do a bit of tidying-up when I get home, go to the shops for all me messages and then make the dinner. I'm always worn out by the time I've finished.'

John deliberately kept his eyes averted. He knew he couldn't persuade her, but he'd be surprised if she held out long against the children.

'Ah, ay, Mam!' Colin's voice was high. 'That's mean, that is.'

'Go on, Mam,' Katy said. 'It would do yer good, yer never go anywhere.'

Billy grinned into Dot's eyes. 'Say yer'll come, Mrs Baker. That would be five of us to share Doreen. I wouldn't mind putting up with a fifth of her, that wouldn't kill me.'

Colin had another try. 'I think that's mean, Mam, 'cos I never get to go to the pictures. All me mates go, but not me.'

Dot knew she was on to a losing battle but wasn't ready to give in yet. She didn't like the idea of them all going to the pictures with John, just like one big happy family. People would start getting ideas and that was the last thing she wanted. 'It's out of the question because Katy doesn't finish work until six o'clock – that's too late to get to the first house.'

'I can get off early, Mam,' Katy told her. 'Mrs Edwards is always telling me if I want to go a bit early all I've got to do is sing out. She says I should be out enjoying meself at my age.'

Dot closed her eyes. Molly Edwards was right. Her daughter should be out enjoying herself – *and* Colin, come to that. They had ten years to make up for and it would be wrong of her to spoil their chance of pleasure because of her own misgivings. 'Oh, all right. Yer've talked me into it.'

John let his breath out and hid his smile. Dorothy Baker wasn't an easy woman to get close to, that was a fact. But wasn't that what had attracted him to her in the first place? She didn't flirt or act coy, didn't flutter her eyelashes or simper like some of the women in his office. With Dot, what you saw is what you got. And he liked what he saw.

* * *

Tom Campbell hung his head as he walked past the pub on the corner. He was giving that a miss tonight, he'd be a laughing stock if he tried to make an excuse for the bruise on his chin. He could still remember the jeering and cat calls he got last time, and he wasn't leaving himself open to that again. Especially if it had gone the rounds of the nearby streets that it was Betty Mason who'd clocked him one. He'd have a hard job to live that down. But revenge is sweet, and he'd get his revenge all right; no one was going to make a fool of him and get away with it. But it wouldn't be the big fat cow he got his own back on, he wouldn't tangle with her for all the tea in China.

As he turned the corner into Walton Road, his thoughts and anger were directed at his wife. It was all her fault, and by God she'd suffer for it. Standing there tonight telling him she wasn't going to live as his wife any more, who the hell did she think she was? A husband was entitled to his rights by law, and he had every intention of claiming those rights whenever, and however he chose. She'd been brave tonight because the big feller was with her, but it would be a different story later when he got home. She'd soon learn who was boss.

There was a pub just past the gates of Walton Hospital and Tom stood outside for a while. This should be far enough from home, nobody here would recognise him. He pushed open the door of the public bar and elbowed his way through the mass of people until he reached the bar. While he was waiting to be served he spotted a vacant seat on the bench that ran along the wall, and when he had his pint in his hand he made his way towards it. He didn't excuse himself as he pushed past people to get to the seat and he gave no heed to the murmurs of disapproval. Sod them all, he thought, as he sat down and put his pint on the small round table, I'll never see them again, so why worry?

He was on his third pint when he felt something brushing against his leg, and he turned to find the woman sitting next to him was smiling. 'I've been watching yer,' she said, rubbing her leg against his. 'Are yer all on yer own?'

Tom looked into her face for the first time and his pulse

195

quicken. She was giving him the 'come on', no doubt about that. She was no spring chicken, probably the same age as himself, and her face was cracked with make-up. But she wasn't bad-looking, and from what he could see of her figure, it was voluptuous. 'Yeah, I'm on me own.'

This time her hand touched his knee. 'What's a handsome lad like you doin' out on yer own on a Saturday night? Wife at home with the kids, is she?'

'We haven't got no kids.' Tom sipped on his beer as his mind ticked over. 'Me and the wife don't really get on, she's a real misery.'

Her hand was stroking his leg now, sending his heart pounding. 'That's hard on you, love, isn't it? A cold fish, is she?'

'Yer can say that again. Cold as a bleedin' iceberg, she is.'

'That's no good for a man with fire in his belly.' She leaned closer and the cheap perfume she was wearing wafted up his nostrils. 'What you need is a woman with passion. A woman who knows how to please a man.'

Tom put the glass down on the table and wiped the back of his hand across his lips. 'Where would I find such a woman?'

'It all depends how much yer need one.' Her hand was now creeping higher up the inside of his leg. 'And how much ye're prepared to pay for one.'

'How about a glass of gin? That is gin ye're drinking, isn't it?'

'I like the look of yer, so I won't charge yer me usual. I'll have a glass of gin and a tanner to go with it.'

Tom wasn't prepared to part with his money so easily. 'How do I know I'll get me tanner's worth, and where will I get it?'

'There's a jigger in the road opposite. Safe as houses it is, I've used it before.'

'Will I get me money's worth?'

'I think I can trust yer, so yer needn't pay me until after. If ye're not satisfied, yer can keep yer money. I can't be fairer than that, now can I?'

Tom stood up and lifted the two empty glasses. 'I'll get us a refill.'

When he came back with their drinks, he let his eyes run

over her. She had a good pair of legs and looked attractive from a distance. It was only when you got close you could see the word 'tart' written all over her: the hard expression on the heavily made-up face, bleached blonde hair, and cheap clothes worn to show off her figure. All the trademarks of a woman of the streets. But right now Tom Campbell couldn't care less what she was. His passion was roused and she would serve his purpose.

He set the glass down in front of her. 'We'll drink this and then go, shall we?'

Over the rim of her glass, Alice Butler weighed him up with cynical eyes. It was funny how many men used the excuse that their wives didn't understand them. She wasn't taken in for a minute when he said his wife was a misery. Her experience of men told her that any problems in his household were down to him. She could read him like a book – arrogant, bad-tempered and violent. 'What's yer name, love?'

'Er, Tom. Tom Smith.'

'And I'm Elsie Jones. Funny how we've both got common names, isn't it?' She watched his face turn red with embarrassment. 'Still, they wouldn't be common if a lot of people didn't have them, would they?'

Tom put his empty glass on the table. 'Drink up and let's go.'

'My, my, we are eager, aren't we?' Alice drained her glass. This wasn't her usual stamping ground – in fact, she'd never been in the pub before. And the only reason she'd pulled Tom was because she was bored. And because she was bored she intended using him for a bit of fun. He was used to having things his own way, she could tell that. Well, when she got him down that jigger he'd find he wasn't the one giving orders tonight. He'd get his tanner's worth, and more, while she got her kicks out of watching him grovel.

Chapter Thirteen

Tom Campbell came out of the entry fastening his fly buttons. He was having to walk quickly to keep up with the woman who had given him half an hour of the most exciting, sexual torture he'd ever known. 'Will yer be in the pub next Saturday, Elsie? I'll meet yer there if yer like.'

Alice, alias Elsie, stopped in her tracks and turned to face him. 'No, I was only in there by chance because I couldn't make it to me usual haunt. I twisted me bleedin' ankle runnin' for the tram and I thought I'd be laid up for the night. Blasted thing went all right when it was too late for me to go.'

'Where is it yer usually go? I want to see yer again.'

'Look, I go to a pub on the Dock Road, opposite the Seaforth docks. I have me regulars down there, plus when the ships come in the seamen make a dive for the place. It's easy money for the girls 'cos the seamen come ashore after weeks at sea and they're very generous.'

'I'll pay yer, like I did tonight.'

There was sarcasm in Alice's laugh. 'Listen, lover boy, you got the bargain of yer life tonight. The full works for a tanner! Yer'll never get that again, not off me, anyway.'

'How much d'yer charge, then? I'm willing to pay more.'

Speaking as though she was an assistant behind a shop counter, Alice rattled off the price list. 'Ten minutes down a jigger is a shilling, half an hour in bed is two bob, and all night in bed is four bob.'

'In bed!' Tom's voice was high with excitement. What he wouldn't do to spend a whole night with this woman. 'D'yer mean yer take the men home with yer?'

'There's no chance of that – my neighbours think I'm a respectable woman. I work the pub with ten other girls and we rent two rooms off an old lady who lives in one of the streets nearby. We pay her a tanner for every punter we take there and she's glad of the money.'

'I know the pub yer mean, I've passed it on the tram. I'll be down one night to see yer, maybe Tuesday.'

'If I'm not there, one of the other girls will fix yer up. And don't worry, yer'll get the same treatment off any one of them.' She turned to walk away. 'But not for a tanner.'

Tom watched until she was out of sight, then walked in the opposite direction. My God, it was a stroke of luck he'd picked that pub and that particular seat. OK, so she was a common prostitute, but she certainly knew her business. There was no messing around; she got straight down to it when they got in the entry, taking over as though it was a job of work. Which it was to her, of course. And she was good at it. There were times when he thought his heart, lungs and head were going to burst. He would definitely be after more of the same, even two bob's worth next time. The only way he could afford that was to cut down on his drinking, but it would be worth it.

His body was still tingling from the effects when he opened the front door. And when he saw the living-room door was firmly closed his lips curled into an unpleasant smirk. Who would want to be bothered with someone as pathetic as his wife? Someone who balked at doing the things that made him happy. She wouldn't even get undressed in front of him, he had to rip the clothes off her. No, he didn't need her any more, he'd landed on his feet tonight, all right. And he had Betty Mason to thank for it. If she hadn't thumped him one he would have gone to his local as usual and probably never found out what he was missing.

Mary lay in the darkness, waiting for her husband's return with apprehension. She'd forced herself to stay awake, knowing she needed to be alert in case he came in drunk and took off on her. And when she heard the key in the lock her heart began to pound. She lifted her head from the cushion and gripped the cosh tightly in readiness. Seconds passed and there was no sound, none of the usual fumbling or stumbling which would tell her how drunk he was.

Then she heard his footsteps on the stairs and her brow furrowed. She sat up and slid her legs over the side of the couch. What was he up to? Never in a million years would Tom Campbell let her get away with what had happened earlier. She'd made a fool of him and he'd be down to punish her, she was sure of that. Then she heard a thud from upstairs and recognised it as the sound of shoes being flung across the room. He did that on purpose, she thought in terror, to make me think he's getting into bed. But I know him too well to fall for that.

Mary covered her shoulders with a blanket and felt her way to the fireplace. She found the box of matches on the hob, and as she struck one she stood on tiptoe to see the time on the clock on the mantelpiece. It was only a quarter to eleven, he never went to bed so early. He was biding his time, making her sweat. Perhaps he was hoping she'd be asleep and he'd catch her unawares and knock hell out of her. Well, she'd be ready for him. So wrapping the blanket closely around her, cosh gripped tightly in her hand, Mary sat on the edge of the couch and waited.

Her nerves shattered by the long wait, and shivering with the cold, she struck another match. She couldn't understand it, he'd been upstairs half an hour and there hadn't been a sound in all that time. It didn't make sense. There was no way he'd sit up there in the cold all this time; he liked his comfort too much. And if he was fast asleep there was no point in her sitting up all night waiting and worrying. The only way to find out what was going on was to go up and see for herself.

Mary opened the living-room door slowly and popped her head out. No sight nor sound. So she put her hand on the bannister and trod each stair carefully, keeping to the sides to avoid any creaks. Halfway up, she stopped and wrinkled her nose. What was that sweet smell? She sniffed up again and again. It was definitely a woman's scent! But how on earth did the smell of scent get in here? She couldn't afford soap, never mind scent. Urged on by the mystery, Mary climbed the remaining stairs to the landing. The smell was much stronger up here. She put her ear to the bedroom door and her husband's snoring told her he was in a deep sleep. So she plucked up enough courage to open the door quietly, ready to flee if he was only feigning sleep. The smell of the cheap perfume was overpowering now, and she put her hand across the bottom of her face as she backed out. He's been with a woman, she thought, as she trod down each stair carefully. He must have been in very close contact with her too, because his clothes reek of it.

Back on the couch and with the scant bedding wrapped around her, Mary thought it all through. She knew now why he'd left her alone tonight – he'd been satisfied elsewhere. She rubbed her swollen tummy and whispered, 'Thank God for that. If he's found favour with someone else, I'd like to shake her hand, whoever she is.' She shuddered at the thought of the things he'd made her do, sadistic and degrading. Would another woman put up with that? Or did she let him get away with it simply because she didn't have the guts to fight him? Mary turned on her side to try and find comfort for herself and the child she was carrying. As her eyes closed and she began to drift away, her last thought was that she hoped the woman, whoever she was, would put up with Tom Campbell's antics at least until after the baby was born.

'Don't blame me for the time, Dot,' John said, slipping his arms into his coat. 'I did offer to go at ten o'clock as promised.'

'It's all right.' Dot put a hand across her mouth when she felt a yawn coming on. 'The game lasted longer than I thought.'

'You won, anyway, Mam,' Katy laughed. 'Ye're richer by ten matches.'

'Better than a kick in the teeth, sunshine.' Dot looked anxiously at Billy. 'I hope you won't get into trouble with yer mam. She'll think I'm a fine one keeping yer here till this time.'

'Don't be worrying, Mrs Baker, me mam won't mind. She knows I'm here an' she said it's better than me walking the streets and getting in with the wrong crowd.'

'It's only ten to eleven,' John said. 'It's not too late.'

'It is for my eyes. I could do with using those matchsticks to keep them open. And as for me feet – well, they were ready for bed hours ago. So off yer go, the pair of yer. Katy will let

202

yer out, to save banging the door and waking Colin.'

'We'd better go quietly, young man, before D.D. gets serious and kicks us out.' As John pushed Billy ahead of him, he asked, 'Will it be all right with you if I call tomorrow to see how Mary fared?'

'I suppose so,' Dot stifled another yawn, 'but don't you dare show yer face until the afternoon because I won't be fit company before then.'

Katy came back from seeing them out to find her mother clearing the table. 'Shall I rake the fire out, save a job in the morning?'

'If yer would, sunshine, while I tidy up.' Dot shook the green chenille cloth before throwing it over the table. 'There's nothing I hate more than coming down to an untidy room.'

Katy was on her knees in front of the grate, rattling the poker between the bars to send the ashes through to the ashcan. 'Mr Kershaw's so nice, yer wouldn't think he was a boss, would yer, Mam?'

'Well, he's only a little boss,' Dot said, plumping a cushion. 'Probably a floorwalker or something like that.'

Katy turned her head to look over her shoulder. 'He's not, yer know, he's the manager of the whole factory. He's over all the men.'

'No, he's not, sunshine. Whatever made yer think that?'

'It's true, Mam, honest! One of our customers works there, and he came in the shop as Mr Kershaw was leaving with our Colin. He told me, and he said he's never had such a good boss in his life.'

Dot stood with the cushion pressed to her chest. She was silent for a minute, then asked, 'Are you sure yer've got it right, Katy?'

'Of course I'm sure, Mam. I'm not thick.'

'Well, I think he's got a bloody cheek! Fancy him coming here all this time and not telling us. Ooh, I'm that mad I could spit feathers.'

Katy scrambled to her feet. 'What d'yer mean, Mam, he's got a cheek? He hasn't done nothing wrong.'

'He should have told us, that's what he should have done.'

'But why?' Katy couldn't understand her mother's attitude.

'If he'd told yer, it would seem as though he was bragging, and Mr Kershaw's not like that. He's not big-headed or anything, he's just nice.'

'If what you say is true, Katy, he'll earn more in a week than we do in a year. And yet he's sat here and drunk tea from chipped cups, ate chips from a newspaper and sat in a chair with the springs coming through.' Shame made Dot feel anger against the man. 'He probably has everything of the best in his own house, so why does he spend so much time here? Does he like slumming? Or perhaps he just wants to see how the other half live.'

Katy was stunned. She'd never disagreed with her mother before, but she did now. 'I can't believe ye're saying those things about Mr Kershaw. Because he's a boss and earns good money doesn't mean he can't be a good man. And if he does live in a posh house, that doesn't make him a snob.'

'I'm not saying he's not a good man, or that he's a snob, but he's not the same as us and he should stick to his own kind.'

Katy was shaking her head in disbelief. 'Mam, I think ye're being horrid about Mr Kershaw. He doesn't come here because he likes slumming, he comes because he likes it here and he likes us. It's not an act he's putting on, yer can see how comfortable he is. Perhaps he prefers us to what you call "his own kind".' Katy waved her hand around the room. 'Look at the house now, to what it was before. Look how good he is to Colin, and to Mary, next door. He's a good man, a kind man, and I think it's mean of yer to say those things about him.'

Dot had her head bent over the cushion she was holding. When she looked up there were tears glistening in her eyes. 'Me pride's been dented, sunshine, and it's pride that's kept me going all these years. I've been remembering the night John first came here, carrying our Colin. I can still see the big hole in Colin's sock when we took his shoe off. I can hear meself saying we couldn't get a doctor out to him because we didn't have the money. And I can remember how me heart sank when you asked him to have a cup of tea because I knew we didn't have one decent cup in the house. I felt ashamed that night, but it didn't really worry me because I thought we'd never see the man again.'

Katy could hear tears in her mother's voice and hastened to put her arms around her. 'Don't be getting yerself all upset, Mam, otherwise yer'll have me crying as well. But yer've always told me it's best to say what yer think, and I think ye're being unfair to Mr Kershaw.'

Dot swallowed the lump in her throat. 'Me own common sense should have told me, by the clothes he wears and the way he speaks.'

'Yer can't hold that against him, Mam. Even if he wore a suit made of pure gold, and spoke as though he had a dozen plums in his mouth, he's still a nice man. And yer must know that he doesn't come here because he's nowhere else to go. He comes because he likes it here. I'd be very sad if yer stopped him from coming, and our Colin would be heartbroken.'

Dot disentangled herself from her daughter's arms and threw the cushion on the couch. 'I'll not stop him from coming, but things won't be the same. When I think of the way I've spoken to him – ordered him around as though he was a skivvy . . . I won't be able to look the man in the face again.'

'If he didn't like it, Mam, he wouldn't keep coming back for more. He really does think a lot of yer, anyone can see that, so don't let on I've told yer. Don't spoil things.'

Dot cupped her daughter's face and kissed her. 'We very nearly had our first row, sunshine, and it would have been my fault. You were right to put me in me place. Me and my blinkin' pride, it'll be the ruination of me one of these days.'

'So yer won't say anything?' Katy asked. 'To Mr Kershaw, I mean.'

Dot stretched up to pull the chain at the side of the gas light and plunged the room into darkness. 'Of course I'll say something to him – he'll get the length of me blinking tongue.' She reached out for her daughter's arm. 'But don't worry, sunshine, I won't fall out with him.'

Katy opened the door to John the next afternoon and, looking up into his face, she whispered, 'If me mam starts shouting at yer, it's all my fault. I let the cat out of the bag.'

John smiled and chucked her under the chin. 'I don't know what the cat you let out of the bag said, but don't look so downcast. I think I'm too big for your mother to put me over her knee and spank me.'

Katy closed the door behind him, crossed her fingers for luck and prayed that her mother had mellowed. If she said all the things to his face that she'd said last night, the chances were Mr Kershaw would walk out of the house and they'd never see him again.

John entered the room to find Dot standing with her hands on her hips and her head tilted. This was the stance she took when about to argue and the one John found so endearing. 'Oh dear, what have I done now, D.D.?'

'Shall I take your coat for you, Mr Kershaw?' Dot asked without a flicker. 'I'll hang it up for you.'

'Why this attention all of a sudden? I usually hang my own coat up.'

'Ah yes, but that's before we knew who yer were. I mean, fancy me giving the manager of a factory his chips to eat with his fingers out of a newspaper, and with a cracked cup on the arm of the couch. I really made yer pig it with the rest of us, didn't I?'

John heard what she said but was more interested in the way she looked. With her rich auburn hair framing her face, her hazel eyes practically giving out sparks, and her stand of defiance, she looked alive and glowing. 'You know, you should always be in a temper because it suits you. You look so pretty, I think today is a Definitely Delightful Dorothy day.'

Dot was momentarily knocked off-course, but only momentarily. 'Don't you be trying to wriggle off the hook, John Kershaw, 'cos I won't let yer. I don't appreciate being made a fool of.'

'Only fish wriggle off hooks, Dot, but I don't think you meant it in that sense, did you? So will you please tell me what I've done to bring on this tantrum?'

'Tantrum! Tantrum, did yer say? I am not a child, John Kershaw, that cries because they can't get their own way. This is no tantrum, this is me being bloody angry.'

'And very pretty you look with it, if I may say so.'

'No, you may *not* say so! What yer can say is why yer didn't tell us what yer job was. I think it was underhanded of yer and I don't mind telling yer.'

'I didn't think it necessary to tell you. There was no reason – unless you judge a person by the material things they have in life, not what they are like as a person. If that is the case, I'm very disappointed in you. I thought you were more fair-minded than that.'

Katy was watching with interest, a smile hovering around the corners of her mouth. She thought Mr Kershaw was doing very well, but then, she wasn't her mother.

Dot glared at him for a few seconds, then asked, 'How come I always end up getting the blame when I argue with you? I haven't done nothing wrong, you're the one who's been sly and underhanded.'

'I am neither sly nor underhanded.' John's face was serious now. 'But if that is your opinion of me, perhaps you would like me to leave?'

Dot tossed her head. 'Please yerself.'

'No, if I leave it will be to please you, not myself. I like being here, I always feel contented as if I am among friends. But if you do not wish to be friends, if I am no longer welcome, then I will leave.'

It's a good job our Colin's out playing, Katy thought. He'd be screaming his head off if he heard what was going on here. Her mam was being very stubborn and if she didn't unbend soon, they'd lose the best friend they'd ever had. She crossed her fingers again and sent up a silent prayer. Don't let my mother send him away, please.

Dot once again stared him out. Then she held out her arm. 'Give us yer coat and I'll hang the ruddy thing up.'

John slipped his coat off and handed it to her. 'Don't you ever do that again, Dot Baker, it's not good for my indigestion.'

'Sod yer indigestion, John Kershaw, what about my heart? When Katy told me that you were Mr Moneybags I nearly had a fit. It's a ruddy good job we've got some new crockery, otherwise yer wouldn't be getting asked if yer want a cup of tea.'

John waited for her to hang his coat on the hook, then when she turned around he said, 'At the risk of bringing forth your displeasure once again, can you tell me what difference it makes how much money I earn, or what my job is? If I were a roadsweeper I would still be the same man inside.'

Katy could see her mother had no intention of telling him the truth, so she piped up. 'Tell him what yer told me, Mam.'

'Katy, just leave it. I'm too quick off the mark, that's my trouble. I shout me mouth off first, before thinking, instead of the other way around.'

'If you won't tell him, I will.' Katy's lips set in a determined line. 'Me mam doesn't begrudge you yer job, or yer money, Mr Kershaw, that's not why she was so mad. She was thinking back to the time yer first came here and we were so poor we had nothing. The house was a mess, everything in the kitchen was cracked or broken, and me mam didn't even have the money to get the doctor out to see to our Colin. She was ashamed that yer saw us like that at the time, but when I told her what Mr Grimes had told me, it made it ten times worse. We're still poor, Mr Kershaw, but as I told me mam, that's nothing to be ashamed of. As long as we've got each other, that's the main thing. Being in a loving family beats all the money in the world.'

'It's a wise head you have on your shoulders, Katy.' John looked from daughter to mother. So alike in looks but different in sentiments. But while Katy might have had to go without things she would have liked during her short life, she hadn't had the worry of finding enough money to keep the family together. Dot had to be strong and tough, or none of them would have survived. And after eleven years it was difficult for her to cast off the hard outer shell and her stubborn pride.

'Are you going to remain standing, Mr Kershaw?' Dot raised a brow. 'Or would you care to take a seat?'

'Ring for the butler,' John said, waving a hand airily. 'I'd like the chair dusted before I sit down. I can't afford to get my fifty-pound suit dirty.'

'Would Mr Kershaw care to sod off?' Dot grinned. 'The chair doesn't want dusting, John, it wants throwing on the tip with everything else in the room. But seeing as it's all we've got, I'm afraid yer'll have to like it or lump it.'

'If it's a lump he wants, Mam, he'd better sit on the couch,' Katy joked, her heart lighter now the danger had receded, 'then he can have as many as he likes 'cos it's all lumps.'

'Oh, I've mastered the couch, Katy,' John chuckled. 'I know exactly how to—' His words were cut off by loud hammering on the front door.

'In the name of God,' Dot said, a hand on her fast beating heart, 'I nearly jumped out of me flippin' skin! Do they think we're deaf or something? Even Betty's got more sense than to make a racket like that.'

'It sounds urgent, Dot,' John said, 'Shall I go?'

'No, I'll go meself. If it's only someone after change for the gas meter they'll get a piece of me mind before I wring their neck.' Dot made her way to the front door, muttering, 'Damn cheek, they're nearly knocking me door down.' But when she opened it to see Mary standing there looking distraught, her eyes red-rimmed from crying, Dot's anger turned to fear. 'Oh, my God, Mary, what on earth's the matter?'

'Dot, will yer help me please?' Mary held out her open hands as she begged. 'I've no one else to turn to.'

Dot stepped on to the pavement and cupped her neighbour's elbow. 'Come inside, sunshine, and tell us what's happened. Yer know we'll help yer.'

John jumped to his feet, his face anxious. 'What is it? Has that husband of yours been up to his tricks again?'

Her whole body shaking, Mary struggled to get her words out. 'Me dad's been taken ill. He's been rushed to hospital.'

Dot put her arm across her neighbour's shoulders and held her tight. 'How did yer find out, sunshine?'

'Me mam sent a message down with one of the children in her street. She said me dad was bad and I should go to Walton Hospital right away.' The tears flowed unchecked. 'How can I go looking like this? I haven't told me family I'm expecting and I don't think this is the time to give me mam a shock. But I can't hide it because the only coat I've got won't fasten on me any more and me dress is too tight. And I haven't got the tram-fare to go to the hospital.'

'Isn't your feller in?' Dot asked. 'Surely he can give yer the tram-fare?'

'He said he's got no money but he's telling lies.' Mary rubbed a hand across her forehead. 'He's sitting there with a smile on his face and I feel like killing him. He's glad me dad's ill, Dot, because he hates my family. If I got down on me knees and begged him, he wouldn't give me the fare to go and see them, even though me dad might be dying.'

'That's because they know him for what he is, sunshine. Yer told me yerself they didn't want yer to marry him. But forget about him for now, he's useless. Yer've got to get to the hospital or yer'd never forgive yerself. I can give yer the money for the tram, and I can lend yer me loose swagger coat, that would help hide yer condition a bit. But I haven't got a dress that would be loose on yer, 'cos the only dress I possess is tight-fitting.'

John decided that under the circumstances he had to take a chance on Dot getting on her high horse again, and he leaned forward. 'I hope you won't take offence, Mary, but I have a wardrobe full of clothes that belonged to my late mother, and fashions haven't changed so much that they'd make you look like an old woman. She was about the same height as you, but had a fuller figure, so they may well serve the purpose. However, if you don't care for the idea, I will understand.'

To his surprise, it was Dot who answered. 'Of course she won't take offence, will yer, sunshine? If the clothes fit she'll be glad of them.' Dot fingered the old raggedy dress that was stretched tight across Mary's abdomen. 'This thing is falling to pieces. It's too tight on her now and she's still got three months to go.'

Mary turned her tear-stained face to John. 'I'll be very grateful for any help, thank you.'

'In that case, I'd better move quick.' John crossed the room in two strides to reach for his coat. 'I'll be back in twenty minutes – that should give you time to wash your face and borrow some powder off Dot to hide the trace of tears.' He was gone before they could answer.

'That man is full of surprises,' Dot said. 'And I'll say this much for him, he's very generous and thoughtful. Doesn't let the grass grow under his feet, either. Yer only have to mention something and it's done before yer can turn around. No wonder he's a manager, and a ruddy good one, I'll bet.'

'He's a man in a million, Dot,' Mary said, nodding her head. 'There's not many like him around; they're few and far between.'

'Well, let's get you ready before he comes back. Yer'll have to douse yer face in cold water, I'm afraid, because I don't use face powder. Neither does Katy, but she does have a lipstick yer can use. That should brighten yer face up.'

Mary sighed as she stood up. 'I keep asking meself what I've ever done to deserve all these troubles heaped on me. As far as I know, I've never harmed anyone in me life.'

'No one goes through life without trouble, sunshine,' Dot said, following her neighbour out to the kitchen. 'I've had my share, believe me. But the cause of all your troubles is sitting next door. He's selfish, mean and wicked. But he'll get paid back at the end of the day, when he has to face his Maker.'

Dot went back into the living room to fetch a clean towel and happened to glance at the window as a shadow passed. 'Oh Katy,' she groaned, 'it's young Billy. Will get yer coat on and take him for a walk for an hour? We can't have him in here now. Mary doesn't want the whole world to know her troubles.'

Katy was up like a shot. 'Yeah, OK, Mam.' She went to the sideboard and brought a lipstick out of one of the drawers. 'This is for Mary. Tell her I hope there's good news for her when she gets to the hospital.'

'Ye're a good girl, Katy, I got a real treasure when I got you. I don't know what I'd do without yer, I really don't.'

'Oh, you'd think of something, Mam.' Katy got to the door and turned. 'Are yer going to tell Mr Kershaw that yer think he's generous and thoughtful, or shall I tell him?' Without waiting for an answer she waved before answering the door to Billy's impatient knocking.

Dot was smiling as she took a towel out of the cupboard built into the recess at the side of the fireplace. She had two lovely children and she loved the bones of them. While she had them her Ted would always be alive in her heart. Without them, life would have no meaning.

When John came back carrying a large suitcase, Dot grinned. 'I was going to be my usual sarcastic self and say only you would have a suitcase the size of a single bed. But I won't say it, John, so yer can see I am trying. Mind you, the size of yer, yer'd look daft walking along with a tiny case in yer hand.'

John laid the case on the couch before facing her with a smile on his face. 'Will I ever get used to you, D.D.?'

'Oh, yer don't do so bad for yerself, John Kershaw. We've had a few little squabbles, I'll admit, but the last time I counted, you'd won every one.'

'I prefer to think they were amicable squabbles and they all ended in a draw.'

When Mary walked through from the kitchen John's eyes registered his surprise at the change in her. The untidy mousy hair had been brushed back off her face and tied at the nape of her neck with a piece of black ribbon. It was a severe style but it suited her, giving prominence to two of her best features, her deep brown eyes and her full lips which were now painted a deep pink. 'By Jove, you look a different person.' As he spoke, John was asking himself what was wrong with the man next door that he didn't realise how lucky he was to have a wife who was not only a nice person, but also a very attractive one. The man was not only a rotter, he was a fool as well.

'Ay, come on, let's see what yer've got in the case.' Dot gave him a sharp dig in the ribs. 'Mary hasn't got all day.'

John snapped the locks either side of the case and threw back the lid. 'I didn't have time to sort them out properly, but I chose the ones I thought might suit.'

'Ooh, ay, that looks nice.' Dot lifted out a coat in brown and black small check. She could tell by the feel that it was made from the purest of wool and must have cost a fortune, but she wisely kept her thoughts to herself. 'Try this on, Mary, it looks as though it might fit yer.'

Mary slipped her arms into the coat and then wrapped it around the front of her. The fit was perfect and, for the first time, her smile was a genuinely happy one. She closed her eyes and stroked the material. 'This feels so comfortable, like an old friend.'

'It looks a treat on yer, sunshine. Anyone would think it had been made to measure for yer. Honest, kid, yer look a million dollars in it. And it hides what yer want it to hide.'

Mary looked at John as she gloried in the luxury of the coat. 'Will it be all right if I borrow this, John, just for today?'

'Mary, the coat is yours if you want it. And everything else in the case.'

Dot had been rooting through the clothes and now brought out a dress in dark brown. 'This would go well with the coat, lovey. Why not run upstairs and try it on? And put a move on. Yer need to get to the hospital, don't forget.'

Mary took the dress from her. 'I haven't forgotten, Dot. Me inside's turning over at the thought of what I'll hear when I get there.'

When Dot heard Mary reach the landing, she said in a low voice, 'It must be serious or they wouldn't have sent for her. Poor soul, she's got nothing going for her at all. Her life is one long misery, thanks to her beloved husband.'

'She's got some good friends, Dot – you in particular. You really are a good and loyal friend to her.'

Dot nodded at the case, and the clothes spilling out of it. 'It was very generous of yer to bring those, John, very generous.' She put her hand over her mouth and the words that came out were muffled. 'And thoughtful.'

John bent his long frame to gaze into her face. 'What did you say, Dot?'

She rolled her eyes. 'Would it be very wrong of me to laugh at a time like this?'

'Of course not! Your laughing isn't going to have any effect on Mary's problems.'

'Well, I said yer were generous and thoughtful.' Her body began to shake. 'I'm telling yer that because our Katy said that if I didn't, she would. So if she snitches on me, she'll get her eye wiped.'

'You've lost me somewhere along the way, Dot, but am I right in thinking there's a compliment in there from you to me? That can't be true, surely?'

Dot was spared from answering by the sound of Mary's footsteps on the stairs. And when her neighbour entered the room both she and John were too stunned to speak. In place of the dowdy woman who had knocked on the door just over half an hour ago, stood an elegant young lady who would turn heads.

Mary stood inside the door waiting for comments. Her hands, clenching and unclenching, were the only sign of her nervousness. But inwardly she was shaking like a leaf. And the silence that greeted her appearance caused her to believe the clothes didn't suit her as well as she thought they did. She gave a deep sigh and asked, 'You don't like them on me?'

'Oh, sunshine, ye're a sight for sore eyes.' Dot felt quite emotional. To think someone with Mary's looks had to walk around like a middle-aged tramp when she could appear as glamorous as this. 'They look marvellous on yer.'

'You look lovely, Mary,' John said sincerely. 'Very lovely.'

'Thanks to you.' Mary crossed to where he was sitting and cupped his face between her hands. Before kissing his cheek, she said, 'I will always be indebted to you. Thank you from the bottom of my heart.'

'Are yer going in to see yer feller before yer go to the hospital?' Dot asked. 'He'll get the shock of his ruddy life.'

Mary shook her head. 'No, I don't want him to see me in these clothes, I know I'd get the height of abuse from him. I'll go out the back way, save passing the window.'

'But he'll see yer in them tonight, so why worry? If it was me I'd parade up and down in front of him, with me tongue sticking out a mile.'

'If my husband saw me in these clothes, Dot, he'd rip them off me back. I'm not allowed to look nice, you see. He likes me in the gutter, where he says I belong. He'd take a pair of scissors to them, I know he would. So, if yer don't mind, I'll call after the hospital and leave them here. Then in a couple of days I'll tell him I got them off me mam.'

Dot blew out her breath in anger. 'It's a pity his mother didn't drown him when he was a pup, she'd have done us all a good turn. Anyway, sunshine, you'd better be on yer way.'

'I'll put a bit more lipstick on, if yer don't mind. John's got most of it on his cheek.'

When she left the room, John handed Dot half-a-crown. 'Give her this for her tram-fare. It looks better coming from you.'

'I've got a shilling in me pocket for her, that should be enough. Put yer money away.'

'Please, Dot, let me help her.' John narrowed his eyes as he looked into her face. 'Do my eyes deceive me, or are your nostrils flared, ready to do battle?'

He was right, Dot *was* ready to do battle. But, looking at him now, she was having second thoughts. He always got round her in the end, so why cause a fuss, especially as Mary would hear them. She took his half-a-crown and closed her hand on it. 'Ye're so clever, John Kershaw, can yer tell me how to un-flare me nostrils?'

'That's easy, you just smile and they'll fall back into place.' John touched the curled fist holding his silver coin. 'You are often stubborn and infuriating, D.D., but there are times when you are simply delightful.'

Dot brushed his hand away when Mary came into the room. 'I'll walk down the yard with yer, sunshine, to make sure the queer feller isn't around.'

'I don't know how long I'll be, John, so in case ye're not here when I get back I'll say my thanks now. I really am grateful.'

'Unless you're very late, I'll still be here when you get back. I'd like to know how your father is. And as for the clothes, I was glad I could help.'

After seeing the other woman safely out, Dot came back to stand in front of the fire. 'That March wind is bitter. I'll be glad when the month's over.' She rubbed her arms briskly. 'Did yer ever see such a change in anyone? Yer wouldn't believe it was the same woman.'

'She should always look like that, she's a very attractive woman.'

'Ye're fond of her, aren't yer, John?'

'It would be difficult not to be fond of Mary, and sorry for her.'

'It's a pity she's married 'cos yer'd make a lovely couple.'

John lowered his head and clasped his hands between his knees. This woman had no idea how he felt about her. Why couldn't she see it? Where was he going wrong? 'I'm fond of Mary, yes, the same as I'm fond of Katy and Colin. But even if she was single, I'm not fond enough of her to want to marry her.' He looked up to see Dot grinning like a Cheshire Cat. 'What is so funny?'

'Yer've got a bright pink Cupid's bow on yer cheek, soft lad. I'd give yer something to wipe it off with, but I'll bet a pound to a penny that yer've got a pure white, folded-up hankie in yer pocket, so I won't bother.'

John fished the hankie out of his pocket and shook it out of its creases. 'Where is it?'

'On yer cheek.'

'Which one?'

Dot rubbed her nose. 'Er, yer left cheek.'

'Show me.'

'Oh, in the name of God, can't yer do anything for yerself?' Tutting loudly, Dot took the hankie and wet it on her tongue. Holding his chin in one hand, she rubbed at the lipstick mark. 'How the hell you ever came to be a manager is beyond me. Ten foot tall and yer can't even keep yerself clean.'

John closed his eyes, enjoying every second. It was the closest Dot had been to him and she was only here because she was helping him. Suddenly he knew where he'd been going wrong. He'd been so keen for her to like him, he'd been doing everything for her. It would have found favour with most women, but not with Dot. She liked to do things for people – look how she was with Mary. Well, in future he was going to act helpless, see if that would do the trick.

The rubbing stopped and John found himself wishing Mary had kissed him on both cheeks.

Chapter Fourteen

Dot pulled a face when she looked at the clock for the umpteenth time. 'Half past ten – I wonder where she could have got to? I thought she'd have been home long before this.'

'It's not a good sign, I'm afraid,' John said. 'They only allow visitors to stay until this time if the patient is on an urgent note.'

'That's all Mary needs, isn't it? Just one thing after another for her.' Dot looked across at Billy, settled comfortably on the couch next to Katy. 'I think you'd better go home, sunshine, it's work tomorrow. And if yer mam is waiting up for yer she'll be cursing me up hill and down dale for keeping her from her bed.'

'Yeah, I'll make tracks.' Billy yawned and stretched. 'I hate Monday, it's the worst day of the week.'

'If yer went to one of the wash-houses yer'd find all the women agree with yer. Monday's wash-day in most homes, which is no joke if yer've got half a dozen kids. And those that aren't in the wash-house will be down at the pawnshop getting a few bob on their husband's Sunday trousers or shoes.' Dot grinned at the boy who was like a second son to her. 'So yer see, sunshine, ye're not on yer own – *everybody* hates Monday.'

Billy returned her grin. 'I don't think me mam goes to the pawnshop now, not with all of us working.' He patted his trouser leg. 'But just to be on the safe side, I'll put these under me bed tonight.'

'I'll see Billy out, Mam,' Katy said, 'then I think I'll go straight up. I'd like to wait for Mrs Campbell but I can't keep me eyes open.'

'You go to bed, love, yer'll be on yer feet all day tomorrow. Ta-ra, Billy, sleep well.'

'Ta-ra, Mrs Baker. Ta-ra, Mr Kershaw.'

After Katy had seen Billy out, she came back into the room to give her mother a good-night kiss. 'Did yer tell Mr Kershaw what yer said about him, Mam?'

Dot feigned surprise. 'No, what was that, sunshine?'

'Oh you, Mam, you're awful!' Katy turned to John and although her nostrils weren't flared, he'd swear they weren't far from it. 'Me mam was supposed to tell yer something and she didn't, did she?'

'Do you mean did she tell me I was very generous, thoughtful, caring, kind, compassionate and lovable?'

Katy's jaw dropped. 'She didn't tell yer all that, did she?'

John looked to where Dot was sitting, eyes and mouth wide. He chuckled. 'No, she didn't say all that – just that I was generous and thoughtful. But I know she meant all the other things; she was just too shy to say so.'

On impulse, Katy bent and kissed his cheek. 'Well, I'm not shy and I think ye're all those things, so there.' She left the room feeling very satisfied with herself for saying what she thought. He *was* a nice man and there was no getting away from it.

'Ye're doing well for kisses, John Kershaw,' Dot laughed. 'Yer can't beat it, can yer? Two in one day – that's good going, that is.'

'That's two more than I usually get.' The words were just out when they heard a light tapping on the window and John jumped to his feet. 'This will be Mary, I'll go.'

Dot followed him to the hall and as soon as she saw her neighbour's face she held her arms wide, and Mary walked into them, her loud sobs telling of her heartache. 'Me dad's dead, Dot, he's gone and I'll never see him again.'

'There, there, sunshine.' Dot held the shaking body close for a few seconds before leading her into the living room. She pressed Mary's head on to her shoulder and, stroking her hair, she rocked her gently. 'You have a good cry, sunshine, and get it out of yer system. John will make yer a drink, and when ye're ready, yer can tell us all about it.'

'He died an hour after I got there.' Her voice was choked, her words muffled. 'One hour, that's all I had with him.'

Dot could feel the dampness of Mary's tears through her dress as she comforted her. Her heart was full of pity, knowing that once her neighbour left here tonight there'd be no arms to comfort her, no one to offer soothing words of sympathy. 'Did yer dad know yer were there, sunshine?'

'Me mam and me brothers were there, they said he was unconscious. But when I got hold of his hand and bent over him to tell him it was me and that I loved him, I felt him squeeze me hand and he seemed to smile. One of me brothers, our Gordon, said I was imagining it, but I know I wasn't. And me mam said she saw it, too.'

'Of course yer weren't imagining it. Your dad would know you were there, take my word for it.' Dot looked over Mary's shoulder to see John standing in the kitchen doorway. 'Dry yer eyes, sunshine, and have a cup of tea. I'll get yer something to wipe yer face.'

John came forward, his outstretched hand holding his hankie. 'Here you are, Mary. I've only used it to wipe your lipstick off my cheek.'

Mary sniffed up as she took the hankie. 'Thank you.'

'Sit down and I'll pour the tea.' Dot waited until Mary was settled and then bustled out to the kitchen. A faint smile hovered around her mouth when she saw John had set out three cups and saucers in readiness, and a knitted tea cosy was keeping the pot warm. 'Mmm,' she said softly, 'generous, thoughtful and ruddy domesticated.'

Mary sipped at her tea, her hands wrapped around the cup for warmth. 'I'm sorry I've kept yer up so late, but me mam was in a terrible state so we all went home with her. Our Gordon is sleeping there tonight, just to keep an eye on her. She's out of her mind; it all happened so quick she can't take it in.'

'What was wrong with yer dad, sunshine? Had he been ailing?'

Mary shook her head. 'He's never been sick, me dad, never had a day off work in his life. Me mam said he was fine, he'd eaten his dinner and told her he'd enjoyed it. Then he went into the kitchen with his plate and the next thing me mam hears a loud crash. She rushed into the kitchen to find me dad lying on the floor. He was just staring at her, couldn't talk or move. She was terrified out of her wits and ran for the man next door. He lifted me dad on to the couch and then went for the doctor. It was a severe stroke, the doctor said, and had the ambulance there within twenty minutes.'

'I'm sorry, sunshine, I really am. Sorry for you and yer family.'

'It must have been terrible for your mother,' John said. 'Such a shock.'

'That's what I'm frightened of – the shock could kill her. They were very close, me mam and dad. One never went anywhere without the other.'

'You and yer brothers will have to take care of her for a while, make sure she's not left on her own for any length of time.'

'I'm going up there tomorrow, as soon as Tom leaves for work. I'll stay with her during the day, then one of me brothers will take over at night.'

'Will your feller be waiting up for yer, to see what happened?'

'You are joking, aren't yer? No, there was no light on when I passed, so he must have gone to bed. I'm glad because I couldn't put up with his taunts. I know what'll happen when I tell him me dad's dead. He'll laugh his head off and jump for joy.'

Dot snorted. 'He's a devil's disciple, that man. And that's where he'll end up, in the fires of hell.'

Mary stared down into her cup, and when she spoke her voice was low, as though she was talking to herself. 'If I had one wish, I'd wish me dad back. If I had two wishes, I'd wish Tom Campbell dead. I never in me life thought it was possible to hate anyone as much as I hate him right now. When I think of all the time I could have spent with me dad over the years, but I wasn't allowed because my husband forbade me. And I, the weak stupid person that I am, I was too frightened of him to go against his orders. Now me dad's gone, I'll never be able to make up those lost years and never be able to tell him how sorry I am.'

Dot swallowed the lump in her throat before saying, 'Listen, sunshine, I'm not a religious person, as yer know, but I believe that when a person dies they can look down on us from heaven and know how we feel. They watch over us, like. So your dad will know exactly what ye're thinking and how yer feel.'

'I hope so.' Mary could feel the tears stinging the back of her eyes and she bent to put her cup on the floor. These people had been very good to her; she didn't want to inflict her sorrow and worry on them any more. 'I've kept you up long enough. I'll go home now and let yer get to bed.'

'Are yer sure yer feel up to it?' Dot looked anxious. 'I can fix yer up here, on the couch, if yer like.'

'No, I'll be all right. I'll settle meself down in the living room and cry the rest of these tears away. I've got to be strong for me mam, tomorrow. And I've made up me mind that if Tom does ask me, I'll look straight through him. I won't give him the satisfaction of knowing that me dad's dead. In fact, I'll let him rot in hell before I tell him anything about my family. He's not fit to lick their shoes.'

'Aren't yer going to change yer clothes?' Dot asked. 'I thought yer said yer wanted to change back into yer old things.'

'That was when I was still frightened of Tom Campbell. He means nothing to me now. He can go to hell and back for all I care.'

'I'll see you safely inside the house, Mary, then I'll make my own way home.' John sighed as he took his coat down off the hook. 'If Dot doesn't mind, I'll call in tomorrow night and she can tell me how things are.'

'What d'yer mean, if Dot doesn't mind?' Dot's hand went to her hips and her head tipped sideways. 'Yer'd still come whether I say yea or nay!'

'Yes, but it would be nice to be invited.' She looked so appealing, John wondered what he'd have to do to make her hold him as she'd held Mary. '*Am* I invited?'

'John, ye're here that often, ye're practically part of the ruddy furniture. Of course yer can come, yer big daft ha'porth.' She pushed him aside so she could give Mary a hug and a kiss. 'If yer need anything, let me know when I pass your porridge over in the morning. Otherwise, slip in when yer get back from yer mam's and let us know how things are. And for heaven's sake don't worry yer head over money. There's things yer'll need, but me and Betty and Maggie will see yer right, so don't fret.' She jerked her head to John. 'Go on, big boy, see the lady home.'

And as the tall man ushered the smartly-dressed but tragic young woman out of the home, Dot's smile quickly faded. If anyone had their bellyful of trouble it was Mary. Catching sight of her reflection in the mirror, Dot pulled a face – it's a great life if you don't weaken.

'That'll be Mr Kershaw, Colin, open the door to him.'

The boy's face lit up and he couldn't get to the door quick enough. 'Hello, Mr Kershaw, me mam said it would be you.'

John was smiling as he came in the room. 'Oh, she did, did she? Now, I know she can't see through walls, so I wonder how she knew?'

'Because I could set the clock by yer, that's how.' Dot had slipped her shoes off and was relaxing on the couch. It was hard going standing all day on a concrete floor watching the machines winding the thread on the cones, and she was now giving her feet a well-earned rest. 'Eight o'clock, on the dot, it couldn't be anyone else but you.'

'Don't move, stay where you are.' John hung his coat up and grinned at her. 'You look so comfortable it would be a shame to disturb you.'

'No, I've got to make a move.' Dot slid her legs over the side of the couch and slipped her feet into her shoes. 'Betty and Maggie are coming to see if Mary needs anything for the funeral. Maggie's got a black coat she can borrow, so that's one less thing she'll have to worry about.'

'Have you seen Mary, then?'

'Yeah, she called just after I got in. She wouldn't stay because the queer feller was due in for his tea, but she said the funeral's on Friday. Her brother took a couple of hours off work and did all the running around, getting the death certificate, seeing the insurance man and arranging things with the undertakers. She said if Tom goes out for a pint she'll pop in tonight, if not, tomorrow night.'

Colin was perched as usual on the arm of John's chair, his

elbow resting on the big man's shoulder. 'Are we still going to the pictures on Saturday, Mr Kershaw?'

'I think so, unless your mother's changed her mind.'

'My son is a bit like you in one respect,' Dot said. 'He has a way of getting round me. If I said we weren't going to the pictures, I'd never hear the end of it. Me life wouldn't be worth living.'

'There's your answer,' John told the smiling boy. 'Saturday night at the pictures is on.'

'I'll pay for meself, Mr Kershaw. It'll only be half-price for me.'

'If your mother will forget her pride for once, I'd like it to be my treat.'

'Uh, uh! We all pay for ourselves, John, otherwise we don't go.'

'Would you really let me go to the pictures on my own, on my birthday?'

Dot narrowed her eyes and tilted her head. 'If ye're having me on, John Kershaw, I'll knock yer ruddy block off.'

John chuckled. 'I have a healthy respect for your temper, D.D. – I wouldn't dream of having you on. My birthday is on Sunday, but I'd like to celebrate it on Saturday by taking you and your family and friends to the pictures.' He decided to go for her sympathy, see if he had as much success as others did. 'You wouldn't condemn me to spending my birthday in solitary confinement, would you?'

'Nah, me mam's not like that,' Colin said. 'That would be mean, and me mam's not mean, are yer, Mam?'

'Yer've done it again, John Kershaw! Yer have a happy knack of turning things around so I'm always in the wrong.' Dot tried to look severe but her eyes were smiling. 'One of these days I'll take a leaf out of your book and see how you like it.'

'If it doesn't suit you, D.D., I could always alter my birthday to a date that finds favour with you. It is my intention to please you at all times.'

'I've often wondered how a softie like you ever got the job of manager – well, now I know.' Dot smiled as she played with a lock of her hair. 'Yer ruddy-well talked them into it. They gave in to yer to shut you up.'

223

'Mam!' Colin was impatient with all this talk, he didn't know what they were on about, anyway. 'Are we goin' to the pictures on Saturday or not?'

'Yes – on one condition.'

'Oh dear, here we go.' John looked up into the boy's face and winked. 'Your mother and her conditions.'

'Ah, ay, Mam! What d'yer mean?'

'Well, yer wouldn't like poor Mr Kershaw to be on his own on his birthday, would yer? So we'll let him treat us on Saturday and we'll have him to tea on Sunday. How about that?'

'Yippee! We're having a party for yer, Mr Kershaw, isn't that the gear?'

'It most certainly is, Colin. Your mother is both generous and thoughtful. In fact, I'll go so far as to say she is also kind, caring, compassionate and, at times, lovable.'

While Colin was trying to figure out why his mother and Mr Kershaw were laughing so much, there was a loud knock on the door. 'Here comes Betty, with her money-lender's knock. Open the door to her, sunshine, before the knocker comes off in her hand.'

'Oh aye!' Betty breezed in, her wide hips swinging, with Maggie following in her wake. 'What's tickled your funny bone, or is it a secret?'

Dot jerked her head and cast her eyes to the ceiling before answering, 'Blimey, Betty, there's not a soul in this street allowed to have a secret from you. I'll bet a pound to a pinch of snuff that yer even know how many shirts Judy had on her washing line today.'

Not to be outdone, Betty came back quickly with, 'Five, smart arse. And I'll tell yer something else for nothing – one of them wasn't her husband's.'

Dot took in the sight of her friend looking every inch a local gossipmonger, with her arms folded and hidden beneath her mountainous bosom, lips pursed and head nodding knowingly.

'Go 'way!' Dot decided to play along. She stretched her eyes wide, pouted her lips and folded her arms across her tummy. They didn't disappear from view like her neighbour's, but when it came to breasts, hers weren't in the

224

meg specks compared to Betty. 'Ooh, er, fancy that now! When Judy goes to Confession on Wednesday night she won't half have some explaining to do about whose shirt it was.'

'I can tell the priest for her if she's shy. Yer see, girl, I know who the shirt belongs to.'

'Well, I never, yer don't say.' Dot and Betty were facing each other, both thoroughly enjoying the exchange. While John chuckled softly, Maggie was doubled up with laughter and Colin was wondering what difference it made whose blinking shirt it was. 'Go on, Betty, yer know anything yer tell us won't go any further than Bootle and Orrel Park. So start dishing the dirt out, sunshine.'

'It was Eddy's. And they needn't bother telling me any different because I've seen the bleedin' thing on him.' Betty's chins rippled in rhythm with her head. 'Now can yer give me one good reason why his shirt should be hanging on Judy's line?'

Dot held her chin in her hand, deep in thought. 'Ooh, that's a puzzler, all right.' Then her face cleared. 'I've got it! Because he lives there!'

'Yer got it in one, girl.' Betty turned a beaming face to John. 'She's not half clever, this landlady of yours.'

'Just hang on a minute,' John said, 'until I get my facts straight. Who is Eddy?'

'Which Eddy?'

'The bloke whose shirt was hanging on the line, of course.'

'Oh, that Eddy! He's Judy's eldest son.'

John screwed up his face. 'Ouch! I walked straight into that, didn't I?'

Betty turned to Dot, shaking her head. 'He's a bit slow, this lodger o' yours.'

John waited for it and sure enough it came. Hands went on the hips and the head fell sideways as Dot roared, 'He's not me flamin' lodger!'

'No, I am not her lodger,' John said, wishing with all his heart that he was so fortunate.

'Well, yer could have fooled me. I thought yer'd taken root here. Every time I come down ye're here, and sitting in my bleedin' chair.' Betty put on a pained expression. 'That chair was always reserved for me 'cos it's the only one I can get me backside off.'

'Oh dear God in heaven.' Dot threw her hands in the air. 'I give up, I really do. We've got four wooden chairs, all exactly the same, and she wants that particular one. How awkward can yer get?'

'Ah, now, girl, be fair.' Betty, her pale blue eyes as innocent as a new-born baby's, held out her chubby hands, palms up. 'Be truthful, they're not all exactly the same.'

'Oh yes they are! I can't tell one from another and I'm ruddy sure that you can't either.'

'It grieves me to tell yer, girl, but ye're wrong there. My chair, the one I always sat in before his nibs came on the scene, is facing south and the others aren't.'

While she joined in the laughter, Maggie was thinking she'd have to remember every word and every action to tell Paddy. He liked a good laugh, did her husband.

John stood up, bent from the waist and waved a hand at the now vacant chair. 'I will never again sit on your chair, Betty, you have my word on it.'

Wearing a smile of satisfaction, Betty sat down. The chair would only accommodate half of her backside and the rest hung over the sides. 'It's not that I want to be awkward, you understand, John, it's just that if I'm not facing south I get all dis . . . er . . . distated.'

'I quite understand, Betty, and I know how easy it is to become disorientated.'

'I knew that word all along, yer know. I was only testing yer.' Parting her legs wider for comfort, and showing an expanse of her blue fleecy-lined knickers, Betty winked across at Dot. 'He's well educated, this lodger of yours.'

'Betty Mason, will yer be told, he's not my lodger! If yer say it one more time, so help me, I'll throttle yer.'

Betty fluttered her eyelashes at John, and said coyly, 'Yer'll be looking for more digs, then, John, if she's thrown yer out. I have a spare bedroom yer can have, and it's nicely decorated and well furnished. I'd only charge yer ten bob a week, and that's all in. And yer'd get a good laugh for yer ten bob a week, I'm not as straitlaced as some I could mention. I'll not name no names, but just follow me eyes.'

Colin was horrified. His mam was always saying that once you got in Mrs Mason's, yer could never get out. If Mr Kershaw went there, he'd never see his friend and hero again. 'You haven't got no spare room, so there! We've got stacks more space than you, so Mr Kershaw can live here if he wants to be a lodger.'

'Which he doesn't,' Dot said, turning to glare at Betty. 'See what yer've started now, you and yer fancy tales. By dinner-time tomorrow every kid in our Colin's class will know, and by tea-time the whole ruddy neighbourhood. John won't be able to walk down the street without being accosted by women wanting to offer him digs.'

'As long as that's all they're offering, girl, he won't come to no harm. But I think it would be only right and proper to warn him that if Rita Williams offers him bed and board, she might just forget to mention that she goes with the bed.'

Oh dear, Dot groaned inwardly. Once Betty starts on bedroom jokes she'll never stop, and Maggie won't know where to put her face for the best. Besides, Colin was sitting listening intently and this sort of talk was not for young ears. 'That's it for now,' she said briskly. 'Comedy time is over. Up to bed with you, sunshine, while me and me mates get down to brass tacks.'

'Ah, ay, Mam, just another ten minutes, please?'

'No, it's nine o'clock, plenty late enough for yer. So go on, poppy off and be a good lad.'

Colin walked behind the couch, trailing his hand along the top. 'Will yer be here tomorrow night, Mr Kershaw?'

Before John could get a word out, Betty said, 'Of course he'll be here! He ruddy-well lives here, doesn't he?'

'Don't answer, Colin, just go to bed like a good lad.' Dot kissed him on the cheek and hugged him. 'Yer know what yer Auntie Betty's like, she'll harp on it all night if yer let her.'

'Well, Mr Kershaw's not going to lodge with her, is he?'

'He's not going to lodge with anyone, sunshine. He's got a perfectly good house of his own. Better than any of ours, I'll bet.'

His mind reassured, Colin waved good night and made his

way to bed to lie awake for a while contemplating the visit to the pictures on Saturday. He wished it was tomorrow, but five days would soon pass over. If he had a calendar he could mark them off, day by day; that would make them go quicker. But it was too late to buy a calendar; he wouldn't get his money's worth now that three months of the year had gone. As his eyes closed and sleep was seconds away, he was wishing he'd be as tall as Mr Kershaw when he grew up.

Downstairs, Dot flopped on to the couch, next to Maggie. 'Yer've caused enough mischief for one night, Betty Mason, so can we be serious for a change? It doesn't look as though Mary's coming, which means her feller hasn't gone out.'

'Did yer say the funeral was on Friday, girl?'

Dot nodded. 'Yes, but I don't know what time.'

'I've been thinking,' Betty said, fingering the dimples in her elbow. 'Wouldn't it be nice if one of us went with her? With her feller not going it means she's really got nobody on her side. Her brothers will have their wives and children with them and Mary will feel terrible being on her lonesome.'

'I'd go if I could,' Dot said, ''cos it does seem lousy her going on her own, as though she hasn't got a friend in the world. But I can't afford to lose a day's pay. It takes me all me time to manage as it is.'

'I'll go with her, girl,' Betty said. 'I'd have nightmares if I let her go through that without someone to lend her a hand, or a shoulder to cry on.'

'I'll come with yer, so I will,' Maggie said. 'Sure, in her condition the poor soul needs someone to keep an eye on her.'

Dot sighed. 'That's a load off me mind, I have been worried about her.' She banged her fist on the arm of the couch. 'I'm that angry with Tom Campbell I could strangle him with me bare hands. He should be the one standing by her side giving her the support she needs.'

'He should be, girl, but he won't, so me and Maggie will look after her.'

'If you find out which church the service is at, I'll take a couple of hours off work,' John said. 'I'd like to support Mary and also pay my respects to her family.'

'Tom Campbell won't go two nights without his ale, so she'll definitely be in tomorrow night and we'll get all the details then. But to save embarrassing her, can we talk about having a whip-around between us to help her pay for a wreath?'

'She needs more than a wreath, girl, she needs some decent black clothes. She'll feel bad enough as it is, without having to go to her father's funeral dressed like a tramp.'

'Maggie's lending her a black coat, Betty, so that's a big worry less. But she could do with black stockings and a good pair of shoes. There's not much I can do about it, I'm afraid. I can throw a couple of bob in the kitty, but that's about all.'

'I'll buy the stockings,' Maggie said, 'and I'll throw a couple of bob in the kitty as well. Sure, aren't I in a better position than yerself, Dot? With Paddy working all the hours God sends and us with no family to keep, we can afford to help Mary.'

'May I make a suggestion, ladies?' John asked. 'If you three can club together to sort her clothes out, I'll pay for the wreath. I'll get the address off Mary and have the wreath delivered to her mother's house on Friday morning.'

'There yer go!' Betty flung her arms wide. 'The man has solved all our problems in one single sentence. No wonder Dot keeps him on a tight lead, he's too good to lose. If he was my lodger I'd sit on him all day to make sure no one ran off with him.'

'If you sat on him, no one would be able to run off with him – he'd look as though he'd been run over by a steamroller. As flat as a ruddy pancake.' Dot grinned. 'Like one of those cardboard cut-outs yer see outside a picture house.'

'Ho, ho, very funny. Ye're livening up now, are yer, girl?'

'No, I'm not! I'm bone weary, if yer must know. So, if yer don't mind, I'm giving you yer marching orders. I've got a stack of washing to get in steep, then I'm off to bed.'

'What!' Betty's eyebrows nearly touched her hairline. 'Don't we get a cup of tea out of yer brand-new cups and saucers?'

'Not tonight, sunshine, I'm too tired. It's all right for you, ye're not standing on yer feet all ruddy day. Yer'll get a cup of tea tomorrow night, when Mary's here, and if ye're a good girl I'll throw in a biscuit. And don't forget to bring the money with yer to save her worrying, and give her time to buy what she needs.'

Maggie stood up and cupped Betty's elbow. 'Come alone, me darlin', it's time we were on our way, so it is.'

Allowing herself to be propelled towards the door, Betty grumbled, 'Fine bleedin' way to treat yer friends. Common as muck, she is, no bleedin' manners at all.' She looked over her shoulder when she reached the door and nodded towards John. 'Isn't he getting thrown out, as well?'

'In about two minutes,' Dot said. 'I want him to shift me mangle first, so I can pull the dolly tub out. I may as well make use of him while he's here.'

Betty pulled herself free of Maggie's hand and spun around. 'Blimey, girl, couldn't yer do better than that? I've never heard such a lame excuse in all me bleedin' life. Ye're up to no good, the pair of yer, and ye're too miserable to let yer best mate in on it.' Her chins waved from side to side with the shaking of her head. 'I dunno, I'll not get a wink of sleep tonight with wondering what ye're up to.'

'I wouldn't want you to lose any sleep because of me, Betty, so I'll tell you.' John managed to keep his face straight. 'I'm going to have my wicked way with her.'

Betty just had time for a mischievous smile before Dot made a dive for her, and with Maggie's help got her down the step into the street. 'Well, that's charming, I must say.' Shrugging herself free, she struck up a dramatic pose. 'It's coming to something when yer best friend throws yer out on yer backside. Just wait until I tell my Alec I've been manhandled.'

'In case yer haven't noticed, sunshine, me and Maggie are not men.' Dot cupped the chubby face and planted a noisy kiss on each of her cheeks. 'Yer do know I love the bones of yer, don't yer?'

'Yeah, I know that, girl. And I know ye're tired. The trouble with me is, I never know when to stop. But I'll see yer tomorrow. Good night and God bless.'

'Good night and God bless, and you too, Maggie. Thank you for coming down.'

'Sure I wouldn't have missed a second of it for the world.

230

It's a good laugh my Paddy will have when I tell him. And it's meself that'll be going to sleep with a smile on me face, and that's the truth of it.'

John was still standing in the same spot when Dot went back into the house. 'I didn't know whether you meant it, about me moving the mangle, so I thought I'd better wait.'

'Of course I meant it! And while ye're doing it I'm going to give yer the length of me tongue for encouraging Betty. The things she comes out with, I don't know where to put meself at times. So don't you be egging her on, especially in front of Colin.'

John didn't answer until he'd shifted the heavy mangle. Then he smiled at her. 'You are not really angry with me, I can tell. Which is a pity, because you look your best when angry.'

Her head fell sideways as her hands moved to her hips. 'John Kershaw, I know when I'm angry, and I'm angry now.'

Fighting back the desire to hold her in his arms, John nodded. 'Yes, D.D., all right, I can see you are angry – and very pretty you look, too. In fact, I'd go so far as to say you look adorable.'

'Don't be acting the goat, yer daft ha'porth. Pull me dolly tub out for us, then be on your merry way and let me get me clothes in steep.' Dot smiled. 'I keep forgetting ye're not used to being spoken to like that, so I'll ask nicely, shall I?'

'No need, you've already done it beautifully. And I don't ever want you to change, I like you the way you are.'

'Ye're easy pleased, then, Mr Kershaw. Now, if yer'll make yerself scarce I can get the tub filled and me clothes in steep.'

John hung back. 'Katy's late, isn't she?'

Dot attached the hose to the tap and turned the water on. 'She's only in Billy's, playing cards. I'm expecting her any minute.' She gazed at him for a few seconds, then said, 'You've got something on yer mind, haven't yer? And whatever it is, yer don't know how to say it. Well, spit it out, John. I can't eat yer.'

'Come into the living room and I'll tell you. The tub takes ages to fill so you don't have to stand and watch it.'

Dot followed him into the room. 'Well, why all the mystery?'

231

'Give me your hands to hold, then I know you can't let fly at me.'

'What! Are yer crazy or something? You can get lost, I'm certainly not going to hold hands with yer.'

John shrugged his shoulders, praying he was going to get it right. 'OK, forget I ever asked. It doesn't matter, it wasn't important.'

Dot was silent as she studied his face. She couldn't read anything from it and her curiosity got the better of her. 'OK, if you want to play silly buggers, don't let me stop yer.' She held out her two hands. 'I don't know who's the daftest, you or me.'

John held her hands and felt a shiver run down his spine. He was getting there, but it was a very slow process. 'I want you to give Mary a pound to help pay her fares and anything else she needs. I would hate to think she was walking around without a penny to her name. And I don't want the other ladies to know. So, if I let go of your hands now, will you promise not to smack me across the face?'

'If you were offering *me* a pound, John, I'd get on me high horse because I'd think yer were feeling sorry for me. And because I couldn't stand that, I'd probably smack yer across the face. But not when ye're offering to help Mary. God knows the woman needs all the help she can get. I think it's very generous of yer,' Dot grinned, 'and thoughtful.'

'And what about kind, caring, compassionate and lovable?'

'Ooh, I'll have to think about that. Can I have me hands back now, please?'

It was with reluctance that John released the hands that were making his pulse race. But he knew he'd gone as far as Dot would allow. Try to go any further and he'd be sent packing a damn sight quicker than Betty had been. And there wouldn't be a welcome for him ever again. So, patience was the name of the game, to win the only woman he'd ever really wanted as his wife.

On the Tuesday night, Mary watched her husband spruce himself up. He never bothered when he was going to the corner pub, all the men went in their working clothes. So there was definitely something in the wind tonight. She didn't care where he went, or who he went with, as long as he left her in peace. He never spoke to her, but then they'd never had a real conversation since the day they got married. He'd given her a punch last night as she was passing his chair, for no other reason but that he enjoyed it. Tonight however, she might not have been there for all the notice he'd taken of her. That suited her fine, and as soon as he'd gone she'd go next door, to be with the only friends she had.

Tom Campbell slipped the comb into his breast pocket and gave one last look in the mirror over the fireplace. Satisfied with his appearance, he walked past his wife without a word and left the house. He could feel the excitement building up inside him as he walked down the street. He hoped Elsie would be there, but if not he'd try one of the other whores. She said they all gave the same service so it didn't really matter. And with two bob in his pocket it meant he would get half an hour in bed with one of them.

His steps quickened as his eagerness mounted. He was walking to Seaforth to save the tram-fare and it was a fair walk. But he needed to count his pennies so he could go again on Saturday. He had it all planned in his head. Twice a week he could have sex any way he wanted it. Those whores would do anything you wanted for a few bob.

Whistling as he walked, Tom Campbell had no idea that some time in the not-too-distant future he would have cause to remember this night. And curse it.

Chapter Fifteen

'A quarter of walnut toffee, Katy, and a penny bar of Fry's chocolate cream.' Doreen studied her reflection in the glass of the counter and noticed her hair was not hanging right. She twisted the offending curl around her finger before putting it in the position that suited her. She was a vain girl, couldn't pass a mirror or a shop window without checking her appearance. Not even a hair on her head was allowed to be out of place. 'What time are we going tonight?'

Katy pushed the sweets across the counter and held out her hand for payment. 'We're all meeting outside here at a quarter to six. Mrs Edwards is letting me go off early.'

'That doesn't give us much time to get to the pictures,' Doreen pouted. 'We'll be lucky if we get in, it'll probably be full.'

Katy sighed as she handed over the change out of sixpence. Why was her friend always so blinking miserable? 'You can go on without us, if yer like, then yer'll be sure of getting a seat.'

'No, I'll wait for yer.' Doreen put on her hard-done-by face. 'I wouldn't care if we didn't get in, anyway, 'cos Joan Bennett is on and I don't like her at all.'

Katy bit on the inside of her mouth to keep back the hot words that sprang to her lips. Billy was right – Doreen *was* a pain in the neck. 'I'm surprised at yer coming, then. Why don't yer go somewhere else?'

'No, I'll come,' Doreen said, her expression and tone condescending. 'After all, it is Mr Kershaw's birthday and I wouldn't want to disappoint him.'

Katy was stung into saying, 'Doreen, he wouldn't even miss yer! He's got me mam and our Colin, as well as me and Billy. And me mam was trying to persuade Mrs Campbell to come with us, to try and cheer her up a bit.'

Doreen's eyes nearly popped out of her head. 'Oh, not her! She always looks a sight! I'm afraid I wouldn't want to be seen out with her.'

'Yer don't have to, Doreen, yer can please yerself. Now yer'll have to go because there's people waiting to be served. If ye're not here by a quarter to six I'll know ye're not coming.'

With that, Katy turned away and smiled at a little old lady. 'Hello, Mrs Fitzsimmons, what can I get for yer?'

'Mix me a pennyworth of Mint Imperials and treacle toffees, queen. I can't chew them but they're nice to suck on.'

Out of the corner of her eye, Katy saw her friend leave the shop. She'd be there tonight, she wouldn't miss it for the world. She might not like Joan Bennett or Mary Campbell, but she certainly had a liking for Billy Harlow.

'There yer are, Mrs Fitzsimmons.' Katy passed the bag over and took a penny from the old lady's frail hand. 'I gave yer an extra toffee 'cos ye're one of me favourite customers and I think ye're a little doll.'

The lined face creased into a smile, revealing toothless gums. 'And ye're one of me favourite people, queen, a proper little lady if ever there was one. And as pretty as a picture into the bargain.'

Molly Edwards had been watching and listening. 'Have you two formed a mutual admiration society, or what?'

'Ah.' The old lady tapped the side of her nose. 'That's a secret between me and Katy, and we ain't telling.' She shuffled across to the door, opened it and turned to wink at Katy. 'I'll see yer on Monday, queen.'

Molly grinned. The best thing she and Jim ever did was to take Katy Baker on. With her pretty face, winning smile and a cheery word for everyone, she was very popular with the customers, men, women and children. 'I'll tell yer what, sweetheart, that old lady has more gumption in her than that friend of yours. Doesn't anything ever please her?'

'There must be something, somewhere, that pleases her, but I've never found it.' Katy reached up to put the jar of sweets back on the shelf. 'She finds fault with everything.'

'I've never been able to understand how Betty Mason ever

gave birth to someone who turned out as miserable as Doreen. Yer'd think some of her mother's humour would have rubbed off on her, wouldn't yer? And Betty's one of the most open, generous people I know, straight as a die, but I wouldn't trust her daughter as far as I could throw her. She's selfish through and through, and to my mind she always will be.' Molly put her arm across Katy's shoulder. 'Keep yer eye on Billy, sweetheart, or sure as eggs she'll have him off yer, just for the hell of it.'

'Nah, Billy's me best mate.' Katy grinned at the thought. 'He can't stand the sight of her.'

They both turned when the shop doorbell tinkled and Katy's face lit up when she saw Rita Williams and Dolly Armstrong struggling through the door side by side, arms linked. 'Ah, here come the terrible twins. Good afternoon, ladies, I hope yer've come to cheer me up with a few jokes.'

Dolly, her face as miserable as sin, grunted, 'Yer won't be gettin' any bleedin' jokes off me, I've got nowt to joke about.'

Rita Williams grimaced as she rolled her eyes upwards. 'This one has done nothing but moan for the last hour. I was in a good mood before I met her, now she's got me feeling down in the bloody dumps.'

'Ah.' Katy looked sympathetic. 'Are yer not feeling well, Mrs Armstrong?'

The words were spat out. 'No, I'm not, I feel as sick as a pig.'

'Perhaps yer'd have been better staying in if yer feel sick.'

'Oh, it's not that kind of sick, Katy,' Rita said. 'She's had a flaming row with her husband and she's making everyone else suffer for it.'

Molly was at the other end of the shop serving a man with half an ounce of Golden Virginia, but while she was smiling at him, her ears weren't missing a thing that was being said further down the counter. She gave him his change and hurried to stand beside Katy. 'Yer haven't been belting your Arthur with the brush again, have yer?'

'I'd have belted him with the bleedin' rolling pin if I could have remembered where I'd put the ruddy thing.' The big bosom was thrust out, the head held stiff and lips pursed. 'I'd have killed the stupid bugger if I could have got me hands on him, but he can run faster than me and I got out of breath.'

'What on earth did he do to bring this on?' Molly asked. 'Lost his money on the gee-gees, did he?'

'No, he lost his ruddy false teeth, that's what.'

'Ah, be fair, now, Dolly,' Rita said. 'He didn't lose them.'

'Of course he bloody-well lost them! He hasn't got them, has he? And why hasn't he got them? Because he's lost the bloody things.'

Rita shook her head. 'No, ye're not right there, queen. When yer say yer've *lost* something, it means yer don't know where it is. Your old feller knows where his teeth are.'

Molly and Katy exchanged puzzled looks. Then Katy dared to ask, 'If he knows where they are, what did yer belt him for?'

Dolly huffed and turned her head away. 'You tell them.'

Rita's mouth was twitching at the corners with suppressed laughter. 'They fell down the blinkin' lavvy.'

Katy had the desire to shriek with laughter, but the look on Dolly's face said that if anyone found it remotely funny, she'd clock them one. So the girl wisely pinched hard on her bottom lip to take her mind off it.

'How the hell did his teeth fall down the lavvy?' Molly asked, genuinely curious. 'They mustn't have been a good fit.'

'Oh, there was nothing wrong with the *teeth*,' Dolly put in, bright red patches of anger on her cheeks, 'it was that stupid get of a husband of mine! He was always moving them around with his tongue, I was fed-up telling him about it. Used to put me off me grub, it did.'

'This is not the sweetest-smelling conversation I've ever had,' Molly said, 'but seeing as we're talking about the lavvy, couldn't he have fished the teeth out? It wouldn't have been very pleasant, but he could have boiled them.'

Dolly looked at her friend. 'You tell them,' she asked again.

Rita took a deep breath before meeting Dolly's eyes. 'Listen, girl, my tummy has been aching with laughter since yer told me the sorry tale an hour ago. So while I'm telling Molly what really happened, d'yer think yer could try and put it out

of yer mind that it's your husband we're talking about, and
see the funny side of it? Because I don't only think it's funny,
I think it's bloody hilarious.'

'Well, you would, wouldn't yer? It's not you what's got to
fork out for a new set of ruddy teeth, is it?'

'Dolly, will yer shut yer gob and stop moaning, for God's
sake?' Rita winked at Molly. 'If yer don't see the funny side of
life, yer might just as well die off, that's my motto. Anyway,
from what I can gather, Arthur looked down as he pulled the
chain and that's when his teeth went down the pan. They got
flushed away and are probably floating somewhere in the River
Mersey by now, frightening the life out of the fish.' A gurgling
sound left Rita's mouth before her raucous laugher filled the
shop. 'And this miserable cow can't see the joke. Yer should
go and see yer doctor, Dolly, there's something not right with
yer.'

Molly kept her face straight and squeezed Katy's hand before
saying, 'Ay, this could be serious, yer know. What if some
sailor looks over the side of his ship and sees a set of false teeth
floating in the water? He might think there's a body in the sea,
belonging to the teeth. It could start a full-scale search.'

'Ha, ha, ha!' Rita's whole body was shaking as her
imagination took over. 'Oh, bloody hell, what a laugh! I think
Arthur should go to the police station right away and report
his teeth missing.'

Dolly looked on, not knowing whether to laugh or cry.
'Molly, you've got more sense than this silly sod, d'yer really
think my feller should go to the police?'

'No, sweetheart, we're only pulling yer leg. I know at least
four people who have lost their teeth in the sea when they've
been making the trip from Ireland and the crossing's been
rough. Hanging over the rails, they were, vomiting their hearts
out – and their teeth.'

'Oh God, I've wet meself.' Rita was bent double and the
sounds coming from her ranged from the high squeal of a pig
to a horse's neigh. 'I can't wait to tell me feller, he'll laugh his
ruddy socks off.'

'So will my Arthur,' Dolly said, in a tit-for-tat, 'when I tell
him yer wet yer knickers.'

'Ha, ha, ha, blackmail now, eh, girl?' Rita put an arm across her friend's shoulder. 'I'll tell yer what, I won't tell about Arthur's teeth if you don't tell about me knickers. It'll be our little secret, just between you and me.'

'Yeah, OK, queen.' Dolly tried to put an arm around Rita's waist, but her arm was either too short or her friend's waist was too big. 'Just between you and me.'

Katy's laughter was bubbling beneath the surface when she asked, 'How can it be a secret between you two, when me and Mrs Edwards know?'

'Ooh, aye, Reet.' Dolly was almost cheerful now, 'what about these two?'

'Well, let's see now.' Rita tapped a finger on her lips. 'If Molly Edwards opens her spout, she'll lose two of her best customers. If young Katy lets the cat out of the bag she'll lose two of her front teeth.'

Katy's head fell back and her clear laugh filled the room. 'We're back where we started, with teeth! But seeing as yer asked so nicely, Mrs Williams, I promise I won't breathe a word to a living soul.'

Molly saw the *Echo* delivery van pull up outside. 'Here's the papers, Katy, we'll have a rush on in a few minutes. I'll see to the papers, you serve these two customers.' She got halfway down the counter and turned, a wide smile on her face. 'Thank you, ladies, for the best laugh I've had in a long time. And for the warning. Yer see, what happened to Arthur could easily happen to my feller.'

While Katy was weighing a quarter of banana splits for Rita and a quarter of Everton toffees for Dolly, she was giggling inside as she listened to the two women talking. They had no idea how funny they were.

'It's all very well laughing about it,' Dolly said, 'but where are we goin' to find the money from to buy him a new set? It doesn't grow on bleedin' trees, yer know.'

'Oh, don't start off again, Dolly, for God's sake! What's done is done and yer can't do nowt about it. He's said goodbye to his ruddy teeth, so let him say goodbye to a pint of ale every night and save up for a new set.' There was more than a hint of laughter in Rita's voice as she said, 'Anyway, it'll do his gums good to let the fresh air get at them.'

'Go in the back room and titivate yerself up, love,' Jim Edwards said. 'Me and Molly can manage now. I think yer look fine as yer are, but my wife said yer need to comb yer hair and put some lipstick on.'

Katy glanced at the clock. 'Yeah, they'll all be here in five minutes and I'd like to freshen up a bit. Give us a shout if yer see any of them, will yer? I don't want to keep them waiting.'

'Never be on time for a feller, Katy,' Molly called down the counter. 'It does them good to be kept waiting.'

Jim pulled a face. 'Half an hour she used to keep me waiting. Even to this day I'll never know why she made the dates for seven-thirty when she knew damn well she had no intention of turning up until eight o'clock.'

'She was worth waiting for, Mr Edwards.'

'I know, lass, but it wouldn't do to keep telling her that, she's big-headed enough as it is.'

Katy washed her hands and face then stood in the crowded stockroom and combed her thick auburn hair. It was naturally curly and apart from running the comb through it, it needed no attention at all. Then she stood on tiptoe to try and see in the mirror on the wall as she put her lipstick on, but there were too many boxes in front of it to get near enough to see properly so she had to hope for the best that she hadn't smudged it. Anyway, it was dark in the picture-house so no one would know the difference.

Molly popped her head in. 'There's a big crowd of people outside the shop, sweetheart, and they look as though they're waiting for someone.'

'I'm ready.' Katy slipped her arms into her coat. It was the only one she had and was a bit scruffy, but it would have to do. 'As ready as I'll ever be.'

Molly could read her thoughts. 'Clothes don't make the person, Katy, and anyway, if you were wearing sackcloth yer'd still knock spots off a certain girl who shall remain nameless. With your smile, no one will even notice what yer've got on.'

On the pavement outside, smiling faces greeted Katy. She was glad to see her mother had been able to persuade Mary

Campbell to come, and the two women were linking each other. John Kershaw had his arm across Colin's shoulder and Doreen, the only one without a smile on her face, was standing as near to Billy as she could get. The lad wasn't very happy with the situation and as soon as Katy closed the shop door behind her he was by her side. 'Don't you leave me with her all night,' he growled in a low voice, 'or I'm warning yer, I'll end up giving her a thick ear.'

Dot and John exchanged amused glances. Young Billy didn't believe in mincing his words; if he thought it, he said it.

'Come on,' John said, 'we've got ten minutes to get to the Carlton.' With his arm still on Colin's shoulder he set off and the others followed.

Dot squeezed Mary's arm as they brought up the rear and whispered, 'Just watch the antics of the three young ones, they're dead funny.'

Billy started as he meant to go on. 'I'm walking on the outside, which is the proper place for a man. Katy, you walk next to me and Doreen can walk on the other side of yer.'

'Why can't yer walk in the middle?' Doreen wailed. 'That's what yer should do.'

'Because I don't want to, that's why. And stop behaving like a spoilt brat and move yer legs a bit faster so we can keep up with Mr Kershaw.' They'd only gone a few steps when he said, 'Next time yer come out with us, don't forget to bring yer dummy. They're good for keeping babies quiet.'

'All right, Billy,' Katy said, 'give it a rest now. Remember what yer dad told yer about arguing with women.'

'Doreen's not a woman, Katy, she's still a baby. In fact, I don't know why she's not still in nappies.' He hunched his shoulders and stuck his hands in his pockets. 'Even then I bet she'd have something to moan about, saying the pin was sticking in her.'

Dot chuckled as she glanced sideways at Mary. She'd had a hard job persuading her neighbour to come with them, but she was glad she did now because there was a smile on the pale face. She looked nice, too, did Mary, in the dress and coat she'd got off John. 'Love's young dream, eh, sunshine? Remember when we were that age?'

'I wish I was that age now,' Mary said. 'I would certainly choose a different path in life than the one I've got.'

'I know ye're going through a bad patch, with losing yer dad, but yer've got the baby to look forward to and a baby always brings love with it.'

'You try telling that to Tom Campbell. He told me he hates the baby and doesn't want anything to do with it.'

'Then you'll have to love it twice as much, won't yer? Oh look, there's John waving for us to hurry. Come on, a hop, skip and a jump.'

When John was at the kiosk getting the tickets, he bought four small boxes of Cadbury's chocolates. 'One each for the ladies, and perhaps they'll share them with us men.'

'Oh, yer shouldn't have bothered,' Dot said, thinking how long it was since a man had bought her chocolates. 'It's your birthday, we should be buying for you.'

John chuckled as he led them towards the door. 'I'd look a right cissie, letting a lady buy me a box of chocolates.'

The lights were still on in the cinema when the usherette took their tickets and motioned for them to follow her. When she stopped at the end of a row where there were seven empty seats, Billy was ready to organise the seating to his liking. 'You go in first, Doreen, then Katy and then me.'

When Mary was following Billy, John whispered to Dot, 'I'm going to have to take a few lessons from that young man. He knows what he wants and goes for it.'

'And gets it,' Dot answered, making for her seat and pulling Colin behind her, leaving John to sit next to her son at the end of the row.

John pulled his seat down, thinking it was coming to something when a fourteen-year-old boy could teach him a thing or two about women. But as the lights went down, he told himself he'd get his marching orders if he tried to pull a stunt like the one Billy had just pulled. Dot needed careful handling, with kid gloves.

The first short film was a Charlie Chase comedy and the antics of the funny man, in his trademark spectacles, had the audience roaring with laughter. All except Doreen. 'He's stupid,' she said to Katy. 'I don't know what they're all laughing

243

at.' When there was no reply, she leaned across her friend with the open box of chocolates in her hand. 'Billy, d'yer want one of me chocolates?'

Billy's eyes never left the screen. 'No! And keep quiet, can't yer?'

'Go on, have one. There's a hazelnut whirl, yer'd like that.'

'Why don't yer put them all in yer mouth at once, Doreen? That should keep yer quiet.'

Doreen sat back in her seat, not the least bit put out. 'I'll save them for the interval, then yer can choose which one yer want.'

When the lights went up, the only one who wanted an ice-cream was Colin. So John gave him the money and pointed to where the usherettes were serving the ices. 'You go, then you can pick what you want.'

'Thanks, Mr Kershaw.' The boy was off like a shot, leaving John to take advantage of the situation and move next to Dot. 'How are you and Mary? Did you enjoy Charlie Chase?'

It was Mary who answered. 'There's more fun next to me than there is on the screen. That Doreen's got a hide like a rhinoceros; she will not be insulted.'

John grinned and looked past her to where Billy was sitting. His hands were clasped in front of him and his face was like thunder as Katy chatted to Doreen across him so her friend wouldn't feel left out. 'All right, Billy?'

Billy bent towards him. 'If I can make a suggestion, Mr Kershaw, perhaps next time yer could buy gob-stoppers instead of chocolates. That's if there *is* a next time, which I very much doubt.'

Dot grinned. 'Hard going, is it, son?'

'Hard going! Did yer ever see that film with James Cagney in? The one where he's in prison and all the prisoners are chained together and they have to work like slaves breaking hard rocks with pick-axes?'

Chuckling inside, Dot said, 'I know the one yer mean. Where his hands are all cut and bleeding, and all they get to eat is bread and water?'

Billy nodded. 'That's the one, Mrs Baker. Well, James Cagney thought he had it tough, but he'd have found it harder

244

to get a smile or a laugh out of a certain person than he did breaking those blinking rocks.'

It was unusual for Mary to laugh out loud, but she did now. 'Perhaps that person *can't* laugh, Billy, have yer thought of that? Perhaps she's like Boris Karloff, put together with nuts and bolts. He never laughed, either.'

Billy's good humour was slowly being restored. 'Yeah, I never thought of that. Yer mean like Frankenstein's monster?'

Katy pulled on his coat. 'Billy, will yer sit down so we can hear what ye're talking about? All we can see is yer back.'

'According to me mam, Katy, me back's as good as me front.' Billy pulled his seat down and held it until he was safely re-installed. 'In fact, she said she can't tell the difference, except when I'm eating, of course.'

'Oh, that's daft,' Doreen said, to everyone's amazement and amusement. 'I can easy tell the difference.'

'God love her,' Dot whispered to John. 'The girl's more to be pitied than laughed at.'

'I'm back, Mr Kershaw.'

John turned to see Colin standing beside him with a tub of ice-cream in one hand and a little wooden spoon in the other. Crossing his fingers and pretending to make a move, he asked, 'Oh, you want your seat back?'

'No, you stay where you are, I'll sit here.' For months now the boy had been harbouring hopes that Mr Kershaw and his mam would become friends. Well, not just friends, they were that already, but more boyfriend, girlfriend. He'd grown very fond of the big man, who never talked down to him and was always kind and gentle. He knew Mr Kershaw liked his mam, he could tell, but his mam didn't seem interested one way or the other.

'Is it all right with you, Dot, if he sits there?' John asked, holding his breath. 'I'll change back if you'd prefer.'

Dot hesitated, then said, 'No, he'll be all right for now. But if there's any frightening bits in the picture then he's to come back to sit beside me.'

'If there's any frightening bits in the picture you can sit between us and hold both our hands. I go very sick at the sight of blood.'

Dot smiled at him. 'Yer can close yer eyes if yer get frightened, and I'll tell yer when it's safe to open them. When the goodie kills the baddie and the girl rushes into his arms.'

'I wonder if the day will ever come when a girl rushes into my arms.'

'Oh, it'll happen, John, never fear. The right one will come along one day, you'll see. Ah, the big picture's starting.'

It was a romantic mystery, nothing exciting but pleasant enough to watch. Or it would have been but for the continuous drone of Doreen's voice. She shared her thoughts and her complaints with everyone. Joan Bennett's eyes were too small and too close together. Her hair was a mess and the style didn't suit her. She couldn't act for toffee. Ronald Colman would never fall for her in real life because she wasn't pretty enough. How did she ever get to be a film star?

Katy was embarrassed and tried to shut her up, but her efforts fell on deaf ears. In the end a woman sitting in the row behind had had enough. She thumped Doreen on the shoulder and hissed, 'I paid good money to see a picture, not listen to your ruddy voice all night. Now shut up or I'll get the usherette to throw yer out.'

A smile lit up on Billy's face as he folded his arms and turned his head. 'Thanks, missus, yer've done us all a favour.'

Dot leaned towards John, and without thinking, she put her hand on his arm. 'The woman's right, Doreen is one ruddy nuisance,' she murmured into his ear. 'I'll never come out with her again.' Then, realising she was touching him, her face flamed and she withdrew her hand sharpish.

'Ah, what did you do that for?'

'What did I do what for?'

'Take your hand away.'

'It's *my* hand.'

'I'll grant you that, but what about my poor arm?'

'What's wrong with your arm?'

'It was enjoying the feel of your hand on it.'

'Shut up, John Kershaw, or yer'll be getting us all thrown out.'

John lost all interest in the picture then. Was tonight one step forward? He thought and he hoped so, but Dorothy Baker was so unpredictable it was best not to count his chickens before they were hatched.

When the lights went up the aisles quickly filled with people pushing and shoving. 'Let's hang on a minute,' Dot said, 'until the crush dies down.' She beckoned to Katy to lean towards her. 'Will you go in Billy's for a couple of hours, sunshine?' she whispered. 'I haven't had time to ask Mary how things went yesterday and how her mother is. We can't talk properly, not about personal things, when there's a stranger there.'

'Yeah, OK, Mam, but what about you-know-who?'

'She ain't coming to ours, that's for sure,' Billy huffed. 'Let her go home and make her own family miserable.'

'I wouldn't worry too much about her, sunshine. John will walk her to her door to make sure she gets home all right.'

'She'll have a right cob on, Mam, getting dumped like that.'

'She never looks any different, Katy, so how will anyone know she's got a cob on?' Billy said. 'If she won a million pounds she'd still moan because it wasn't two million. There's just no pleasing that girl at all.'

Dot noticed the aisles were clearing and she pulled herself up by the back of the seat in front. 'We'll take her with us, whether she likes it or not, and that's that. Now come on before they start letting the second house in.'

Colin had gone to bed and Mary sat at the table with Dot and John. Her finger running around the rim of her cup, she said, 'Me mam was in a terrible state yesterday. Me brothers had to hold her back when they were lowering the coffin into the grave. She won't know what to do without me dad, they'd been married for nearly forty years.'

Dot nodded sympathetically. 'A long time, sunshine, almost a lifetime. I'd only been married for four years when Ted died, and I felt as though half of me had died with him. It took me years to get used to him not being here, and it'll be a damn sight worse for yer mam, after all that time.'

John listened in silence. It wasn't the first time Dot had mentioned her husband, she brought his name up quite often. But never before had she said how much she'd missed him.

Mary let out a long, deep sigh. 'I was going to tell me mam

247

about the baby and suggest that when it was born, we could go and live with her. I thought it would be company for her instead of her being on her own, and I could have got a job to help out with money.'

'Oh, that's a good idea, sunshine, yer'd be company for each other. And the baby would bring her a lot of happiness, help to fill the void and give her a reason for living.'

'Yeah, that's what I thought. I had it all planned out in me head, but now I know why people say yer shouldn't plan ahead, it's bad luck. With the rotten luck I've had over the last few years, I should have known better than to expect a miracle.'

'Yer mean yer mam doesn't want yer to go and live with her?'

'I never got the chance to ask her, Dot. I didn't know, but the day after me dad died our Gordon told her she wasn't staying in the house on her own, she could go and live with him and his family. It was all arranged before I knew anything about it.'

'But surely there's still time for her to change her mind, if yer explained?'

'I couldn't bring meself to do it. Our Gordon idolises me mam, he'll take good care of her and see she doesn't want for anything. I love her, too, but I can't match what he can give her. All I could offer her is a load of trouble and heartache. And she deserves better than that, does my mam.'

'Yer've been dealt a lousy hand of cards, sunshine, no doubt about that. But I'm not going to cluck and sympathise with yer 'cos that won't get yer anywhere. What yer've got to do is look to the future, hold yer head up high and keep telling yerself that ye're as good as anybody and ye're going to make something of yer life. Don't let your feller walk all over yer, stand up to him. There's a baby on its way, and yer need to make sure it comes into the world welcomed and loved.' When Mary opened her mouth to speak, Dot held her hand up. 'No, let me finish, sunshine. OK, so its father doesn't want it and won't love it. Well, sod him, sunshine, 'cos that's his loss. Forget about him and concentrate on the baby. Start knitting and getting things together for when it's born. We'll all help yer out, yer know that. Maggie's already started knitting a matinée coat and she's quick, is Maggie – she'll have half a dozen ready in a week or two. Betty is making yer baby blankets and pillow-cases, and I'll buy a couple of nightdresses for it. And our Katy said she's not going to be left out; she's paying so much a week off nappies for yer.'

Tears rolled down Mary's cheeks and for a while she was too overcome to speak. Then she said, 'I don't know what to say, how to tell yer how much I appreciate all that's being done for me. I've been lying awake at night wondering where I was going to get the money for all the things I'll need. I know I shouldn't have to rely on neighbours, but Tom Campbell doesn't turn enough up to pay what needs to be paid every week as it is. If I asked him for more he'd either laugh in me face or belt me one.'

John spoke for the first time. 'I know this is woman's talk, but can I put my two-pennyworth in? You see, I'm hoping to be an uncle to this baby, so would you allow me to buy a present for it? Everyone else is doing their bit, and I don't want to be left out.'

Dot was quick to answer. 'Of course yer can buy it a present. Mary would be only too happy, wouldn't yer sunshine?'

'Yes, John, I would. Perhaps some bootees or mittens?'

'Oh, I'll leave those sort of things to the ladies, they're more knowledgeable than me. Would you allow me to choose what I buy?'

Dot grinned at him. 'A teddy bear, I'll bet.'

'No, if it's all right with Mary, I'd like to buy the pram.'

Mary was too stunned to speak, so Dot did it for her. 'She'd be over the moon, John, thank you. You really are a very generous and thoughtful man. And on this occasion I'll go as far as to add that ye're lovable as well.'

Seeing the laughter in her eyes, John dared to ask, 'Do I get a kiss off Mary for being very generous and thoughtful, and one off you for being lovable?'

'Don't push yer luck, John Kershaw, yer've had the word, yer don't need the action.'

'I don't know,' John sighed. 'I never get a kiss off anyone.'

'Ah, yer poor thing, me heart bleeds for yer.' They were the words that came out of Dot's mouth, but the words in her head were saying he wouldn't ever get a kiss or a hug because he was all alone in the world. And God knows, he'd do anything for anybody, fall over himself to help. Look at the way he'd said he'd buy Mary a pram, that would cost him a few pounds. There's not many people would do that, even if they had the money. So she jerked her head at Mary. 'Come on, one either side and give him a kiss before he starts bawling his ruddy eyes out.'

Mary's kiss was on the middle of his cheek, Dot's was about to land somewhere in the region of his ear. But he got daring and twisted his face around, hoping her lips would end up on his mouth. But Dot was too quick for him and grabbed his chin. 'I told yer, John Kershaw, don't push yer luck.' But she was smiling as she kissed his nose. 'That's for being generous and thoughtful.'

'Where's the one for being lovable?'

'Hey, it's Mary ye're buying the pram for, not me.'

'I'll buy you one, if you like.'

'No, thank you very much. Them days are over for me.'

'There's no pleasing you, D.D., is there?'

'Yes, there is. Yer can stick the kettle on and make us another cuppa before it's time for Mary to leave.'

'I'm in no hurry, Dot, my feller won't be in before half-ten. He spent the whole afternoon getting himself spruced up so I imagine he's gallivanting further afield than the corner pub.'

'Has he said anything about the clothes, or hasn't he even noticed?'

'He passed some sarcastic remark, I can't remember what it was, and I said I'd got them off me mam. He's never mentioned them since.'

'I've still got the case upstairs, yer know, if yer want anything else out of it.'

'D'yer mind if I leave it here for a while, Dot, until I feel a bit better? At the moment I feel completely drained after the events of this week. But I will pull meself together and do as you say. I'll look to the future and me new baby.'

'That's the idea, sunshine.' Dot looked up as John came in carrying the teapot. 'My God, you've been ruddy quick!'

'I only had to boil the kettle, we can use the same cups.'

'Frightened of missing something, that's your trouble.'

'As a matter of fact, I was thinking of ways to please you ladies.' John put the teapot in the middle of the table and sat down. 'You can be mother, and pour.'

'We'll let it brew for a while.' Dot eyed him with suspicion. 'Go on, tell us how yer can please us.'

'Well, it's more like you pleasing me, really. I was wondering if you'd let me take both of you to the pictures next Saturday, without the children. We could go to the second house, then.'

'What about our Colin? I'm not going out and leaving him on his own.'

'I'm sure Katy and Billy would be pleased to stay in with him and play cards. Anyway, Liverpool are playing at home next week so he'll have plenty of excitement for one day.'

Not wanting to be a spoilsport, Dot pinned her hopes on her neighbour refusing. 'How about it, Mary?'

'I'd love to get out of the house for a while, but it's up to you.'

So the ball was back in Dot's court and she had no option but to agree. 'Yeah, OK, then.'

They chatted until ten o'clock, then Mary said she'd make a move. 'I want to be settled before Tom gets in. If the light's off, he'll go straight up to bed.'

'John will see yer in safely.' Dot saw the disappointed look on his face but pretended she hadn't. 'Come on, big boy, you're on yer way as well.'

'Can you hear the way she talks to me, Mary? She makes me feel like a schoolboy who never gets picked for milk monitor.'

Dot grinned as she handed him his coat. 'I'll give yer a note to take to yer teacher, asking her to give yer a go.' She saw them out and was about to close the door when she heard John say, 'Hang on a minute, Mary, I've forgotten something.'

He mounted the step and before Dot had any idea of what he was going to do, he cupped her face and kissed her on the lips. 'That's what you give to someone you think is lovable.'

With that he was gone, leaving Dot touching her lips. It was over so quickly, she found it hard to believe it had happened. His kiss had been gentle, like a feather brushing her lips. She willed herself to feel angry with him, but she couldn't stop her heartbeats from racing. It had been so long since any man had kissed her.

Dot closed the door and leaned back against it. He'd thrown her for a while, but she soon reverted to her normal self. 'Cheeky devil! Next time he pulls a stunt like that I'll clock him one.'

But as she cleared the cups away, she was smiling. She touched her lips, and chuckled again, 'Cheeky devil!'

Chapter Sixteen

Tom Campbell stared at his reflection in the mirror and, pleased with what he saw, he bared his teeth in a smile. Not bad, he thought, I look more like twenty-five than thirty-five. It was a Friday night and he'd made up his mind to go down to the pub in Seaforth, instead of waiting until Saturday. All day in work his body and mind had been crying out for the delights he enjoyed two nights of the week, and by the time he got home he knew he couldn't wait another twenty-four hours to savour those delights. The trouble was, he was threepence short of the two bob he needed, and those prostitutes were hard-hearted when it came to money. Especially the one he went with regularly now, who'd do anything you asked without turning a hair. She told him her name was Esmée but he took that with a pinch of salt. She had bright red hair and her face, like her voice, was coarse, but her looks didn't interest him. He'd been with several of the women before her, but none since. She was the only one where nothing was off-limits, and half an hour in bed with her was spectacular. She certainly knew her business, and was very businesslike with it. Until she had the money in her hand she wouldn't set foot outside the pub. And the half-hour you paid for was exactly what you got, not a minute over. One night she'd said to him, 'I don't turn a trick until I've got the money in me hand. I'm not in the business for the good of me bleedin' health.'

Tom slipped the comb into his breast-pocket and sauntered through to the kitchen where Mary was washing some clothes in the sink. She was eight and a half months pregnant now and very heavy with the child she was carrying. She turned towards him when she felt his presence behind her. 'Make sure yer've got the key with yer.'

He eyed her swollen tummy and his lips curled. 'God, look at the state of yer, it's enough to put anyone off.'

'Nobody's asking yer to look at me; go about yer business.'

'I need threepence, hand it over.'

Mary looked at him in amazement. How could he expect her to have money on a Friday night? 'I haven't got a penny to me name! How the hell do yer expect me to have any money left out of the pittance you give me? Yer get yer wages tomorrow, do without yer ale until then, it won't kill yer.'

Without warning, his two curled fists aimed blows at her belly, first one hand, then the other. And Mary, fearful for her baby, turned from him as quickly as she could and stood facing the sink. The blows kept coming, so hard she really believed if he kept it up he'd break her back. The man is mad, she thought, he'll kill me. 'There's a couple of coppers on the shelf there,' she gasped. 'I keep it for the gas meter. Take that and get out.'

She heard the scrape of coppers as he scooped them from the shelf and she could imagine the gloating she'd see on his face if she turned around. But she didn't turn, she wouldn't give him the satisfaction of seeing the tears rolling down her cheeks. She just wanted him to go so she could sit down and try to find some ease from the pains in her back. She heard the front door bang and made to move, but a wave of dizziness came over her and she gripped tight hold of the edge of the sink. *Please don't let me faint, please!* she cried inwardly as the window in the kitchen kept moving nearer to her and then fading away. She could feel herself swaying on her feet but sheer determination and the support of the sink kept her upright as she dipped a hand into the cold water and doused her face with it, over and over again until the feeling of weakness passed. Then her anger took over. How dare he treat her as though she was a piece of dirt! If he'd harmed her baby she'd kill him. Even if it meant going to the gallows, it would be worth it. Tom Campbell had no right to live on this earth; he was a devil and the place for him was hell.

Holding on to the wall and pieces of furniture, Mary slowly made her way to the couch. The pains in her back were excruciating and she cried out as she lowered herself on to the seat. What sort of a man had she married? He certainly wasn't normal. As the father of the baby, he should be proud and looking forward to it being born. He should be a shoulder for her to cry on, not to be the one to cause the tears.

Mary grimaced as she reached for a cushion to put behind her back. The pains might ease off soon, please God. Then she'd go upstairs for the bedding for the couch and settle herself down. She had the urge to release some of the pressure in her head by crying, but her tears of anger, frustration and sadness would have to wait. They said that unborn babies feel all the emotions of the mother and become distressed. So for the baby's sake she must try to keep calm. After the birth, when she felt stronger, she'd make up her mind what she intended doing with her life and the baby's. And her plans didn't include Tom Campbell. She had to get away from him to keep her sanity and for the sake of her child's happiness.

Mary rubbed a hand over her swollen abdomen. Speaking softly, she said, 'It might take some time for me to get yer away from this house of evil, sweetheart, because I haven't the money to do it. But I promise yer I'll never let him hurt yer, not while I have breath in my body.'

'It's a beautiful morning, sunshine. Summer has come with a vengeance. The sky's a lovely clear blue with little white clouds bobbing about like balls of cotton wool.' Dot placed a plate of toast in front of her daughter and grinned down into her face. 'Makes yer feel good to be alive on a morning like this. It would be even better if we had the summer clothes to go with it. You and me could do with one or two cotton dresses. I'll be sweltering working in this ruddy jumper and skirt.'

'One of the customers was saying there's a sale on in TJs, and they've got cotton dresses for four and eleven.' Katy bit into a piece of toast. 'You could buy yerself one this week and I'll wait until next week. It's not so bad for me, it doesn't get that hot in the shop.'

'Or we could dip into the money we've been saving towards a new three-piece. We can make it up over the next few weeks.'

Katy's face lit up. 'Yeah, let's go mad and do that, Mam.

255

You go down this afternoon and get us one each. I'd love a new dress, in blue or green, with short sleeves.'

'I'll see what I can do, sunshine. Now I'd better get Mary's porridge over to her then put me skates on or I'll be late for work.'

Dot was spooning the porridge into a dish when Katy called, 'There's someone at the door, Mam, and if I'm not mistaken, it's Mary. Shall I go?'

Dot bustled through. 'No, I'll go and she can take her porridge back with her. I haven't got time to talk so I hope it's nothing important.'

But one look at her neighbour told her it was important. There was pain etched on her face and her eyes were red-rimmed from crying. 'In the name of God, Mary, what is it?'

'Me back is killing me, I've hardly slept a wink. But I didn't come to moan, Dot, I only came to tell yer I wouldn't be going to the pictures with you and John tonight.'

Dot nodded knowingly. 'Yer know what the sign of a bad back is, don't yer? It means the baby's not far off.'

'No, it can't be, I've got another couple of weeks to go.'

'Any midwife will tell yer, Mary, that a first baby can come two weeks early or two weeks late. Now I haven't got time to help yer, I should be on me way to work. But I'll give yer the dish with yer porridge in and while ye're getting that down yer I'll give Maggie and Betty a knock. They'll keep their eye on yer until I get back. I won't go to the shops, I'll come straight home. It might be a false alarm, then again it might not.'

Dot handed the dish over and watched as her neighbour walked away. Every step was agony, she could tell, and it set her wondering. She remembered having backache just before her two were born, but she couldn't remember it being too painful to walk, or so bad it made her cry.

'Listen, sunshine, I'll have to fly,' she told Katy, 'but will yer tell our Colin not to leave this house no matter how many mates call for him? I think Mary's baby might be on its way and if it is I'll want to stay with her. That means Colin will have to get all me shopping in, and he'll have to go to John's to tell him it's not on for the pictures tonight. Have yer got that, sunshine?'

'Ooh, er, is Mary's baby going to be born today?'

'I really don't know, Katy, we'll just have to wait and see. Don't you breathe a word to anyone, not even our Colin.' Dot reached the door and grinned. 'Most definitely *not* our Colin.'

Betty and Maggie stood with worried looks on their faces as they gazed down at Mary. 'I think the best place for you is bed, me darlin',' Maggie said. 'Anyone with half an eye can see ye're in pain.'

'Shall we send for the doctor, girl?' Betty asked. 'Just to be on the safe side?'

Mary shook her head. 'Mrs Wainwright's coming to deliver the baby, but I don't know whether the pains I'm getting are labour pains. I don't want her to come and find it's a false alarm.' Just then a cramp gripped her and she doubled up. 'It was me back before, but now I'm getting pains in me tummy.'

'How often are yer getting them, girl?'

'That was the third bad one.'

'Yeah, but what I mean is, how long between the pains?'

'I don't know – about twenty minutes.' There was fear in Mary's eyes and it struck right through to the hearts of her two neighbours. 'I'm getting frightened.'

'There's nothing to be frightened of, girl, it'll be over before yer know it.' Betty thought about the racket she'd made when hers were being delivered, but she wisely kept that to herself. Mary wouldn't think it funny if she told her that if she had a choice between giving birth or a quarter of walnut toffee, the toffees would win hands down. 'I think yer'd better be getting into a nightie and going to bed. Maggie will help yer do that while I run round for Mrs Wainwright.' For all her size Betty was light on her feet and in no time at all she was bouncing down the street to fetch Mrs Wainwright, who had retired from nursing many years ago but was still favoured by most women in the neighbourhood to deliver their babies.

Mary hadn't worn a nightdress for years, didn't even own one. When you didn't have enough money for food and coal, a nightdress was an unaffordable luxury. But she'd found one in amongst the clothes John had brought round months ago, and she'd kept it in the cupboard at the side of the fireplace for this very day. She got it out now and said shyly, 'I'll go up and get undressed, Maggie, then I'll get into bed and give yer a shout.'

'Sure, yer shouldn't be going up those stairs on yer own, me darlin'. I'll give yer a hand up, so I will.'

'I'll be all right, honestly. Yer can stand at the bottom of the stairs if yer like.'

'Mary, don't you be worrying yer head about things that don't really matter, like the bed not being changed or the bedroom untidy. Sure, it's yerself we're concerned about, not the state of yer house.' Maggie patted her arm. 'Off yer go, me darlin'. I'll stand on the stairs and wait until ye're ready.'

Mary was in bed when Maggie entered the room, and her clean nightdress was a stark contrast to the rest of the dismal room. The Irishwoman kept a smile on her face but her heart was sad. This was a room that had never known love. The wallpaper was dark brown with age, the ceiling was badly in need of whitening, the blankets on the bed were frayed and the sheets and pillow-cases were discoloured and threadbare. The room wasn't dirty, it was obvious Mary did the best she could, but it was an unwelcoming room, one you would like to get out of as quickly as you could. By God, Tom Campbell would have a lot to answer for when he met his Maker.

'We'll wait until Mrs Wainwright has a look at yer, me darlin', and if she says the baby's on its way I'll nip home and get all the things yer'll need. But while we're waiting, would yer like me to make yer a nice cup of tea?'

'The gas has gone, Maggie, and I've no coppers.' Mary didn't like to lie to this good woman but she felt bound to make an excuse. 'I used the last one during the night.'

'Well, that's no problem. Haven't I a stack of them on me kitchen shelf? But I'll not be leaving yer until Betty gets back, so try and relax until then.' Maggie plumped the pillow and smiled at the woman who had a look of terror on her face. 'Sure, it'll be a mercy if the baby comes today and yer get it over with. I've never had a baby meself, but back in Ireland

258

all me friends had. And they all said that once the baby is laid in yer arms, yer forget all the pain and the worry.'

'I think I heard a knock on the door, Maggie.'

'It's sharp ears yer have, me darlin', I didn't hear a thing.' Maggie ran down the stairs talking to herself. 'Too busy jabbering, I was, to hear anything but the sound of me own voice.'

Betty gestured to Mrs Wainwright to lead the way, then followed her into the hall. 'I was just in time, Gertie was ready to go to the shops. Another couple of minutes and I'd have missed her.'

'How is Mary?' Gertrude Wainwright was sixty-eight years but as spritely as someone half her age. She was small and slim with white hair that was always neatly waved, and she still had all her own teeth. 'I examined her last week and it looked then as though she'd go her full term.'

'I hope we've haven't brought yer on a wild-goose chase, Mrs Wainwright,' Maggie said, 'but I'll be glad if yer'll have a look at her. The poor soul is frightened out of her wits.'

'Right, let's not waste any time.' The older woman was up the stairs before Betty reached the third step. 'Well, now, Mary, what's all this, then? The baby's decided to enter the world early, has it?'

'I don't know, Mrs Wainwright.' Mary lowered her eyes. She wasn't afraid of giving birth, she was used to pain. But she was afraid of the shame that would burst on her any moment now. 'I hope so, to get it over with.'

'Then let's have you lying down, dear, so I can see what's going on.' When Mary's eyes went to the two women standing at the foot of the bed, the old lady waved them out. 'Let the girl have some privacy, I'll call you when I'm finished.'

Betty and Maggie were standing on the landing when they heard a cry. 'Oh, my God! Mary, my dear, how did this happen?'

'To hell with privacy.' Betty opened the door and barged in, Maggie close on her heels. 'What is it, Gertie?'

'This.' Mrs Wainwright pulled the sheet back a little and heard the two women gasp with horror as they looked on the swollen tummy, covered in angry black and blue bruises. 'One of you will have to run for Dr Gray, I can't take the responsibility of delivering a baby with the mother in this condition.' She bent to stroke Mary's damp hair. 'What happened, my dear? You must tell me.'

'I'll tell yer for her,' Betty cried, anger and pity fighting for supremacy. 'It was that bleeding, no-good husband of hers, and I'll strangle him when I get me hands on him.'

'Oh, no, surely not?' In all her years of delivering babies, Gertrude had never encountered anything like this. 'Mary, is your husband responsible for these injuries?'

The young woman's eyes were closed and her voice was a mere whisper. 'Yes, my brave husband did that to me, last night. All for the sake of threepence, he was prepared to kill my baby.'

'The man is an animal.' The old lady's voice was low, but the three women heard it and agreed. 'Betty, run for Dr Gray and tell him it's urgent. The baby might be stillborn.'

Mary grasped her arm. 'No, the baby's alive, I can feel it kicking.'

Maggie, crying silently in the background, blessed herself and said a little prayer. 'Please, God, she's suffered enough, don't let her lose the baby.'

'I'll be as quick as I can, Gertie,' Betty said as she left the room. 'I'll bring the doctor back with me if I have to drag him every foot of the way.'

'He'll come if you tell him I said it's urgent,' Mrs Wainwright called after her as she covered Mary with the sheet. 'While we're waiting, my dear, perhaps your neighbour here could make sure there's plenty of hot water on the go, just in case. And you'll need some clean towels and plenty of old sheets.'

'Everything is ready, so it is.' Maggie was happy she could say that for Mary's sake. At least it would allow the poor soul to hold on to what little pride and dignity she had left. 'Sure, doesn't my back bedroom look like a nursery? She has everything ready, has Mary, all neatly folded on me spare bed.' She saw the query in the older woman's eyes and told her truthfully, 'Mary didn't want the things here because of her husband. He's a devil of a man, right enough, and that's the truth of it. He doesn't want the baby, and with the violent temper he has, it was thought best he didn't see the baby things in case he destroyed them. And nobody doubts for one moment that he's wicked enough to do that.'

Gertrude shook her head. If this baby was born alive, what sort of life did the future hold for it? Unloved by a brutal father, perhaps it would be merciful if it *was* stillborn.

'I'll slip home, me darlin', now ye're in safe hands, and make yer a nice cup of tea. And while I'm waiting for the kettle to boil, I can be sorting out what the nurse needs.'

'Thanks, Maggie.' Mary was smiling at her neighbour when suddenly her eyes and mouth opened wide and she let out a loud shriek as she clutched her tummy. She tried to sit up but the effort was too much and her head sank back into the pillow. 'Oh, dear God, this is the worst one I've had.'

'How long since the last one, my dear?'

Mary didn't hear her; the pain was so great she thought it would split her insides. Her breath coming in short bursts, she gripped the blanket with both hands and rocked from side to side. 'Oh, dear God, help me.'

'The last pain was over half an hour ago,' Maggie said. 'Me and Betty had just got here and Mary said it was the third spasm.'

'You go and make the tea, then, Maggie, there's still a long way to go. I won't touch her until the doctor gets here because I have to cover myself, you understand?' Gertrude rolled her eyes towards the door, a sign that she wanted to say something that wasn't for Mary's ears. Out on the landing, she said softly, 'The bruises you've seen on her tummy are nothing compared to the ones on her back. Heaven alone knows what injuries that maniac has caused and I'm not qualified to say. After the doctor's examined her, it wouldn't surprise me in the least if he sent her into hospital.'

'It's the demon she's married to that should be sent to hospital – one for the criminally insane.' Maggie had never felt more like cursing than she did at that moment. And it was with great difficulty that she restrained herself. 'There's a few men in the street who would like to whip him for what he's done to Mary, and my Paddy is one of them. Not only the men, either! Didn't Betty herself take her fists to him not so long ago?'

A faint smile crossed Gertrude's face. 'Ah, Betty, she's a great one for sticking up for the underdog. What a pity she didn't finish him off altogether.'

'Sure, yer might have the pleasure of seeing her do that before the day's over.' Maggie started to go downstairs. 'I'll make Mary a drink, the poor soul hasn't had one all morning.'

'Make it in a big pot, Maggie, I think we could all do with one.'

Dr Gray couldn't hide his disgust after examining Mary. 'What sort of an animal are you married to, Mrs Campbell?'

'What yer've seen of me should tell yer what sort of an animal he is, Doctor.'

'He must be barking mad, that's all I can say. Didn't he realise he could have killed you and the baby?'

'My baby's not dead, is it, Doctor?' There was pleading in Mary's voice. 'I couldn't stand that, not after all I've been through.'

'No, your baby is alive, Mrs Campbell, I can tell you that. And everything seems to be in order, the head is in the right position to be born. But it is my duty to warn you that your husband's vicious attack may have caused untold damage to the wee mite.' Dr Gray was a tall, thin man in his fifties. He was a kind man who cared deeply for his patients, many of whom were living in abject poverty. 'I'm quite concerned about the conditions in which you live, Mrs Campbell. If your husband is such a violent man, I'd be fearful for the safety of yourself and the baby. I would like you to go into hospital for the birth, and spend two weeks in there until you have regained your strength.'

'No, please, Doctor, don't send me into hospital, my friends will see I'm all right.'

He sighed as he pushed his horn-rimmed spectacles back into place. 'I'll ask them to come in and we'll hear what they have to say.'

Gertrude, Betty and Maggie listened as he explained the position. 'Mrs Campbell doesn't want to go into hospital but

I feel I would be neglecting my duty if I left her here, where she would be in danger.'

Betty, her arms folded and her lips set firm, said, 'Yer don't need to worry about her bleedin' husband, Doctor, 'cos I'm going to kill him when I get me hands on him.'

'That, Mrs Mason, would indeed be a just reward for what he's done. But as it's not likely to happen I'm still concerned for Mrs Campbell's safety, and the baby's. Good neighbours as you obviously are, you cannot be with her twenty-four hours a day.'

'I can,' Maggie said. 'I've got a spare room she can have and I'll make sure she's well looked after for a few weeks. Everything is there now, all the baby things, so there'd be no problem. She could be moved now, couldn't she? Sure, we'd have her settled in, all nice and comfy, before the baby comes.'

Mary lifted herself up on an elbow and reached for the doctor's hand. 'Please, let me stay with me friends, they're all I've got.'

Just then the door burst open and Tom Campbell rushed in, his face contorted with anger. 'What the bleedin' hell's going on? Get out, the lot of yer.' He pointed a finger at his wife. 'You, get downstairs and see to me dinner.'

Disgust was written all over the doctor's face. 'Your wife is in labour.'

'You can sod off. She's not going to drop the thing now, is she? So she can just get down those stairs and see to me bleedin' dinner.' Tom Campbell moved towards the bed, his arm outstretched to pull the bedclothes back, but his hand never touched them as Betty grabbed him by the scruff of his neck and swung him around.

'I've got a bone to pick with you, yer yellow-livered bastard.' Betty moved her hands quick to grab the top of his coat. Lifting him a foot off the floor, she looked up into his snarling face. 'You and me, outside.' She carried him aloft to the top of the stairs, threw him on to the floor then dragged him by the back of his coat down the stairs. He screamed with pain as his body came down heavily on each stair, but Betty didn't care, his cries were like music to her ears.

In the bedroom, Gertrude looked at the doctor. 'Would

you excuse me for a minute, Dr Gray? I wouldn't miss this for the world.' With that, she took Maggie's hand and they fled.

Dot was hurrying up the street when Betty dragged Tom Campbell down the two front steps and on to the pavement. 'Oh, my God, what's going on?' Dot muttered aloud as she ran the last few yards. 'Betty, for heaven's sake, what are yer doing?'

'Keep out of it, girl, this is just between me and this thing that calls itself a man.' Betty slammed Tom against the wall, and in one movement, curled her fist and aimed. Not for his face as he expected, but for his beer gut. In pain, and winded, he tried to double up, but she wasn't having any of that. Another blow was aimed at the same target, but Betty wasn't seeing Tom Campbell's pain, she was seeing Mary's swollen tummy and an unborn baby fighting for its life.

Dot grabbed her arm. 'Stop it, Betty, that's enough.'

'Leave her, Dot, me darlin', he deserves it, so he does.'

'But what's he done, Maggie?'

'Go upstairs and see what he's done to Mary, then yer'll understand why Betty wants to hurt him.'

Dot gazed at her neighbour for a few seconds then almost fell over the two steps in her haste to get to Mary. As she scrambled up the stairs, she was praying, 'Oh no, please God, don't let him have hurt her.'

A few minutes later Dot ran back down the stairs. She didn't look at anyone, just made for her own front door and dashed inside. 'Colin, I want yer to run round to John's and ask him to come as quick as he can,' she panted out. 'Tell him it's trouble and I need his help.'

'What's the matter, Mam?'

'I've no time to tell yer now, sunshine, but I will later, I promise. Just run as fast as yer can, there's a good boy.'

'What number is Mr Kershaw's house, Mam?'

'I don't know! Yer've passed it often enough, yer'll know it when yer see it. If I'm not in when yer get back, I'll be next door.' Dot put her bag down and slipped out of her coat. 'Oh, go out the back, son, it'll be quicker.'

When she got outside, Paddy was holding Betty away from

Tom Campbell. His overalls at his feet, where he'd thrown them, he was trying to calm the big woman. 'Come on, Betty, leave him be.' He knew a little of the reason for the onslaught, for Maggie had run to meet him when he'd turned the corner, but, angry as he was, he could see Campbell had suffered enough. 'Ye're even with him now.'

'No, by God, I'm not! Nothing I could do to him would be as bad as what he's done to that poor girl. You haven't seen her, Paddy.' Betty covered her face with her hands and her whole body began to shake as she sobbed her heart out.

Dot rushed to her friend's side and took her in her arms, while Paddy helped Campbell up from the ground, where he'd slumped. He was moaning as the Irishman walked him inside the house and pulled him roughly on to the couch. But while Paddy put a cushion under his head, he was not prepared to do more for a man who had so little respect for the woman he'd married and who was carrying his child. So he went out without a backward glance and closed the living-room door behind him.

The neighbours who had come to watch out of curiosity drifted away, and Mary's friends stood in a small group. 'Dry yer eyes, Betty, if yer intend going back in to see Mary,' Dot said. 'The last thing she needs is to be upset. Just play the whole thing down.'

Maggie was telling Paddy she was sorry there was no meal ready for him. 'Me and Betty have been with Mary all morning, me darlin', I haven't had time to cook yer anything.'

'Sure, it wouldn't be the first time I've eaten bread and jam, and been glad of it. Food is the least of me worries now, sweetheart. It's young Mary that's on me mind. How is she going to stay in that house as things are?'

'The doctor wants her to go into hospital, but the poor girl doesn't want to. So I did suggest she could come to us and we'd look after her and the baby for a few weeks. That's if you have no objection, me darlin'.'

'Have I ever objected to you doing anything, sweetheart?'

Maggie stood on tiptoe to kiss him. 'It's a man in a million, yer are, Paddy O'Connor.'

'That's a marvellous idea, Maggie. You and Paddy are a

couple of crackers,' Dot told them. 'We'll all muck in and give yer a hand, yer know that. So let's see if we can talk the doctor round and ease Mary's mind. She's got to go to hell and back very soon, she needs her friends around her. I wouldn't change places with her right now, not for a big clock.' Dot cupped Betty's elbow, saying, 'And you keep yer tears until yer get home, like me. Anyway, the sight of yer standing in the street bawling yer eyes out, I never thought I'd live to see the day.'

'It takes a lot to get me so worked up, girl, but when I saw the state of Mary I just blew me top, couldn't help it.'

The midwife was standing outside the bedroom door when the three women reached the landing. 'Doctor's examining Mary again, so you can't go in just yet.'

'How are things looking, Mrs Wainwright?' Dot asked. 'Is Mary going to be all right?'

'I hope so, my dear, but we'll know more after she's been examined.' Gertrude Wainwright had been delivering babies for more years than she cared to remember, but this was one day she would never forget. 'Whether she has the baby at home or in the hospital, she's going to have a hard time. She's in agony with the injuries to her back, never mind having to cope with labour pains as well.' She glanced at Betty and smiled. 'D'you know that first punch you gave her husband? Well, can I say you gave him that one from me, with my blessing?'

'Yeah, of course yer can,' Betty said sheepishly. 'It was a good punch, that one.'

'And the second one was from me,' Maggie said. 'With my blessing.'

'Hey, hang on a minute! If yer carry on like that, it'll end up that I didn't get a punch in for meself! It's me what's got the sore knuckles, and it's me what'll get a name like a mad dog when my feller hears about it. Fair play, now, ladies.'

The bedroom door opened and Dr Gray appeared, crowding the tiny landing and causing Betty and Maggie to step down on to the two top stairs. 'I've made her as comfortable as possible, but she is in a lot of pain. I really believe she would be better in hospital – they could give her something to relieve the pain – but she got very distressed when I suggested it.'

Gertrude's eyes swept over the three neighbours before she asked, 'Are you expecting it to be a normal delivery, Doctor?'

'Yes, I'm sure it will be. But I'm not so sure what condition the baby will be in.'

'We'll cross that hurdle when we come to it.' The old lady was once again the brisk nurse who was used to making decisions. 'I suggest we move Mrs Campbell to Maggie's house right away, while there's still time. Her good friends will be on hand to help me if needed, and if at any stage I'm concerned, I will send for you.'

The doctor's spectacles were resting on the end of his nose, pinching his nostrils, and he pushed them back into place with a forefinger. 'One woman I would argue with, Gertrude, two I might be tempted to argue with, but I would never be silly enough to consider taking four of you on in a fight. So Mary can have her baby at home and I will call first thing in the morning, unless you need me before. But there's one thing I must point out, and it is important. The baby's head is engaged, so under no circumstances must she walk. She'll have to be carried. And quickly, too, because the contractions are now coming every fifteen minutes.'

'We've got two strapping men to carry her, Doctor,' Dot said. 'There'll be no problem there, they'll treat her like a piece of Dresden china.'

'Right, well, I'll be on my way – I've got several other calls to make. Don't hesitate to contact me if you're concerned, Gertrude, no matter what the time.' Holding his black leather bag in front of him, he squeezed past the women and made his way down the stairs, followed closely by Maggie.

'Doctor, I'd be grateful if yer'd have a look at Tom Campbell. My husband carried him in and put him on the couch, but no one knows how badly hurt he is. I've no love for the man, but sure he might be lying there dead for all we know.'

'You wait here.' The doctor opened the living-room door and disappeared inside, leaving Maggie biting nervously at her fingernails. She didn't mind the man being in pain, in fact she hoped he was suffering the same agonies as Mary, but she'd not wish him dead.

'He's complaining about severe pains in his stomach,' the doctor said, closing the door behind him, 'but I've given him a quick examination and I don't think there's any serious damage been done. He is badly bruised, and I can assure you he'll still be in agony long after Mary's labour pains are over.'

He opened the front door and stepped into the street. 'Which is your house, Maggie? I'll need to know for my next visit.'

'Next door, on the left.' The doctor was walking away when she called, 'We'll take good care of Mary, Doctor.'

He turned. 'I'm sure you will, my dear, I'm sure you will.'

Mary sat on the side of the bed and lifted first one arm and then the other, for Dot to put her coat on over her nightdress. 'I hope there's not a crowd in the street to see me being carried next door. I'll feel so stupid.'

'Paddy's going to carry you, John will walk at the side of yer and I'll walk in front. No one will see yer, it's only a few yards. Anyway, that should be the least of yer worries, sunshine, fretting about the ruddy neighbours. Yer don't owe them nothing; they don't pay yer rent for yer.'

'It was just for something to say, Dot, to take me mind off things. I don't know what I'm going to have to go through and I'm terrified.'

'Yer wouldn't be normal if yer weren't, sunshine, every woman feels the same. Having a baby isn't as easy as falling off a bike, that's for sure. But after yer've fallen off a bike, yer don't end up with a beautiful baby in yer arms, do yer? So if yer just concentrate on what you're doing yer'll come through with flying colours.' Dot had borrowed a pair of bedroom slippers off Maggie and she slipped them on Mary's feet. 'I'll call the men up now and get yer next door before yer next pain starts. Maggie's in there now, with Betty, getting everything ready for yer.'

The street was deserted except for one man, and he was walking with his back to them. There were no women standing at their doors gossiping, because Saturday was payday and the weekend shopping had to be done. So the only one to witness the scene was Miss Amelia Green from her vantage point opposite. She had seen what Betty had done to Tom Campbell and, guessing the reason, she had applauded every blow. And now, observing Mary being carried into the O'Connors' house, she put two and two together and came up with the right answer.

'Put her on the bed, Paddy, and we'll see to her.' Maggie could see Mary was in pain and she quickly shooed the men away. 'Off with yer, this place is out of bounds for men.'

Paddy patted Mary's shoulder. 'Don't you keep us waiting too long, me darlin'. Sure I can't wait to see the wee baby.'

John kissed her cheek. 'You'll be fine, Mary, just you wait and see.'

Mary gritted her teeth until they were out of the room, then doubled up in pain. 'Oh, dear God, I'm in agony with me back and me tummy. I don't know which is the worst.'

'Let's get you lying down, my dear.' Gertrude beckoned to Betty to give her a hand. 'You're the strongest, Betty, lift her gently.'

When the worst of the contraction had died away, Mary gasped, 'How much longer, Mrs Wainwright?'

'It's hard to tell, my dear, only the baby knows that. It could be a couple of hours, it could be longer.'

'Dot, why don't you and Betty go home for a short break?' Maggie suggested. 'See to yer families and get yer shopping in. Me and the nurse can manage fine, so we can.'

'I'll have to get to the shops,' Betty said, 'otherwise the cupboards will be as bare as Old Mother Hubbard's. There'll be nowt in for the Sunday dinner.'

'I can send our Colin for me shopping, he's sensible enough. So I'll make a list out for him and come back and relieve yer in an hour or so, Maggie, give yer a break.' Dot took hold of Mary's hand. 'I'll see yer later, sunshine, OK?'

Mary gripped her hand. 'Yer won't be long, will yer, Dot?'

'No, of course I won't. Me and Betty will take turns sitting with yer, to give the nurse and Maggie time to have a cuppa. Yer'll be sick of the sight of us before this is over.'

Mary clung to her hand. 'I'm sorry I've burdened yer with

269

all me troubles over the last year. I've been nothing but a worry to yer and yer must be fed-up with me.'

'Never in a million years would I get fed-up with you, sunshine, never in a million years. Me and you are mates and we're here to help each other.' Dot bent to stroke the fevered brow. 'I'll have to go now, but before I do, I'd better tell yer about yer husband. Yer haven't asked, but I know yer must be wondering. Well, our other mate, Betty, gave him a good hiding which he richly deserved. But the doctor's seen him and he's all right. He's flat out on yer couch and I bet any money he'll be in the pub tonight, as usual.'

'That's where all his money will go this week, he won't give me any to pay Maggie for me keep. And he wouldn't dream of putting the rent-money away.'

'Listen, sunshine, sod Tom Campbell and sod the rent-man. Right now yer've got enough on yer plate.' Dot saw her wince as the pains started again. 'I'll be back before yer know it, so behave yerself and do as the nurse tells yer.'

John heard Dot and Betty coming down the stairs and he quickly drained his teacup. 'I'll go home with Dot, see if she wants me to do anything for her. But if you need me, Paddy, just shout out.'

The minute she got back inside her own house, Dot bent over the table, scribbling a shopping list for Colin. 'Ask the butcher for half a shoulder of lamb, and tell him I said if it's not lean I'll come and wrap the ruddy thing around his neck.' She tapped the pencil on her teeth as she tried to think of what groceries she needed. 'Yer'll have to make two trips, son, yer'll never do it all in one go. Leave the potatoes and veg for the second trip because they'll be heavy.'

'Would you like me to go with him?' John asked. 'I wouldn't mind.'

'No, you stay put in case of emergency.'

'Is Mrs Campbell having her baby today, Mam?'

'We hope so, son, we hope so. Now you scarper and I'll have poached egg on toast ready for when yer come back.'

With the shopping list in his hand, the basket nestling in the crook of his arm, Colin left the house whistling cheerfully.

'Oh, what it is to be young and innocent, eh?' Dot said, pulling a face. 'Just wait until he's married and his wife's having a baby, then he'll find out what life's all about.'

'Come on, I'll give you a hand in the kitchen.' When John stood up and stretched his arms above his head they nearly reached the ceiling. 'I'm pretty good at doing poached eggs on toast, believe it or not.'

'No, the kitchen's too small for two of us, particularly with the size of you. We'd only get in each other's way, so you sit down while yer've got the chance. I've a feeling it's going to be a long day. Mind you, you don't have to stay until the baby's born, yer could go home and come back tonight. It may all be over by then, please God.'

'No, I'm staying.' John settled himself back in the chair. 'I want to be one of the first to see the baby. I've never held a newborn baby in my arms and I'm really looking forward to it.'

Dot went into the kitchen and John could hear her filling the kettle and lighting the gas stove. He was thinking about Mary, wondering what was going to happen after the baby was born and she had to go back to her own house and her brutal husband. His thoughts were interrupted by a sound which he couldn't make out. Then he realised he could no longer hear Dot bustling around in the kitchen, and the sound he could hear was sobbing. He jumped to his feet and crossed the small room in three strides to find Dot leaning against the sink, her hands covering her face to muffle the sound of her weeping.

'What is it, Dot? Why are you crying?'

'I'm crying for the girl lying in Maggie's bed, scared out of her wits.' Her sobs became louder. 'She's not got one good thing in her life, nothing to look forward to. Even the baby is a worry to her because she knows what life's going to be like for both of them with Tom Campbell.'

John pulled her into his arms and rested her head on his chest. Stroking her hair, he said, 'Don't get yourself upset, Dot, or Mary will know you've been crying. You've done all you can for her, she couldn't ask for a better friend. And when this is over, we'll all pull together to help her.'

Dot raised a tear-stained face. 'You don't understand, John. She hasn't got a doting husband standing by her bed now, holding her hand and helping her through the agony of childbirth. All she's got is worry. D'yer know what the last thing she said to me was? That he, that swine of a husband of hers, would spend all his wages on ale. He wouldn't give her any money to pay Maggie for her keep, and he wouldn't think of putting the rent-money to one side. Fancy being in labour and having those worries on top! It just isn't fair.'

John pressed her head against his chest and rocked her like a baby. 'Hush, now, Dot, I don't like to see you upset. I'm sure Maggie wouldn't take money if it was offered to her. And as for the rent-money, I'll see that Tom Campbell pays up. I'll get if off him myself.'

Neither of them heard young Colin come into the living room and stop in his tracks to stare through the open kitchen door at the sight of his mother in the arms of Mr Kershaw. Without making a sound, he placed the full basket on the table and backed out of the room. He didn't hear his mother's sobs; all he could hear was his own heart singing with happiness.

Chapter Seventeen

Maggie handed a small hand-towel to Gertrude. 'I don't know whether that's any good, but it's all I can think of.'

'That should do fine.' The nurse twisted the towel lengthways until it was as tight as she could get it. 'Here you are, Mary, take an end of this in each hand. When the pains start, pull at it as hard as you can and bite on it at the same time. It will help to make the pain more bearable.'

Dot was standing beside the bed wiping her neighbour's brow with a cool, damp flannel. 'It won't be long now, sunshine. Another half-hour and it should all be over.'

'Can I have a drink of water?' Mary's voice was barely audible. 'Me mouth's dry.'

'Sure, yer can, me darlin'.' Maggie poured some water from a jug into a cup and handed it to Dot. 'I'll have to go down for a refill, the jug's empty.'

'Why don't you stay down there for a while, Maggie, and rest yer feet?' Dot said. 'Betty will bring the water up.'

'What about Gertrude? Sure, isn't she more in need of a rest than meself?'

The old lady shook her head vigorously. 'I won't leave this room until the baby's born. It should be any time now. The head is ready to come out, so with the next contraction Mary will have to start pushing like mad.' She closed her eyes briefly as she said a little prayer that the baby would be perfect. After all the girl had gone through, she deserved nothing less than a beautiful child. 'Away you go, Maggie, and put your feet up for ten minutes. I'll get plenty of rest tomorrow, there's nothing to stop me staying in bed all day.'

Three pairs of anxious eyes focused on Maggie when she

273

opened the living-room door. 'Any sign yet, Maggie?' John asked hopefully.

She shrugged her shoulders. 'According to Gertrude it should be any time now. It depends how much strength Mary has left. It's been hard for the girl, and that's the truth of it. And haven't I said more prayers in the last couple of hours than I've said in the whole of me life?'

'Here yer are, girl, you take my chair, I'll go up now.' Betty lumbered to her feet. 'Until today, I'd forgotten what it was like having a baby. So although he'll never know it, Mary has done my feller a big favour. He'll be able to rest easy in bed every night now, without me trying to rouse some passion in him. Not that I've ever had much success, like, but I'm off it altogether after today.'

Maggie handed her the jug. 'Will yer fill that and take it up with yer, me darlin'? Mary's mouth is as dry as sandpaper.'

They could hear the big woman muttering to herself as she filled the jug. And when she was passing through the living room she narrowed her eyes to glare at John and Paddy. 'The things you men put us women through, yer want horsewhipping. There's not one of yer worth a light, not one.'

The two men looked at each other and laughed. 'And here's us, begorrah, without a child between us,' Paddy said. 'Sure, the dear woman has got her wires crossed, so she has.'

'Anyone watching us for the last few hours, Paddy, would be forgiven for thinking one of us is the father of the baby being born upstairs,' John chuckled. 'We've paced the floor, bitten our nails to the quick and jumped every time Mary screamed. I can't think of anything we haven't done that an expectant father would do.'

Maggie had just settled herself on the couch, with her legs stretched out, when there came a loud scream from above. It was quickly muffled, and she had visions of Mary biting on the towel. 'I wonder if I should go up?'

'Rest yer legs, sweetheart. If yerself is needed they'll give yer a shout.'

Within minutes there came another scream, so tortured it turned their blood cold. 'I'm going up.' Maggie slid her legs over the side of the couch. 'I want to be there when the baby's born.'

After she'd left the room, the two men sat in complete silence, their ears cocked for any sound. Then it came, the cry of a newborn infant. Both men jumped to their feet, and Paddy, his eyes filled with tears, blessed himself. 'Thank God, thank God.'

John was too full of emotion to speak. He'd never experienced anything like this, never felt as close to anyone as he did towards these people. And that new baby upstairs, he hadn't even seen it, didn't know if it was a boy or a girl, but he knew he was going to love it.

The door burst open and Dot appeared, laughing and crying. 'It's a girl! A beautiful little girl!' She clapped her hands as the tears rolled down her face. 'Hot water, Paddy, quick! And will you carry it up? I'm shaking that much I'd spill the lot.'

While she hopped from one foot to the other, she said, 'Oh John, she's gorgeous. Absolutely bloody gorgeous. It's the first time I've seen a baby being born and it has to be the most wonderful experience in the whole world.'

'How is Mary?'

'Very weak, but very happy.' When Paddy came through from the kitchen carrying a large bowl of steaming water, Dot made for the stairs. 'I'll take it off yer outside the door. Mary would die of shame if yer went in the room. And we'll need plenty of hot water so keep the pans on the go. Oh, and could yer bring an empty bucket up and leave it outside the door, please?'

The next half-hour was bustling with excited activity. The women took it in turns to bring down the bowls of dirty water, which they poured into the lavatory in the backyard and pulled the chain to flush it away. Paddy was waiting for them as they came back up the yard to hand them a bowl of fresh water. Everything was so well organised, John was filled with admiration and respect. He had good neighbours where he lived, but their kindness and generosity had never been put to this sort of test. He doubted if they would compare with this lot, who had, in the last few hours, shown him what real neighbourliness was all about. And been cheerful about it, too!

Paddy held a bowl out to his wife. 'Is there any chance of me and John seeing the baby yet, sweetheart? Sure, it's on pins, we are.'

'Not for a while, me darlin'. Betty is washing the wee mite and the nurse is still working on Mary.' Maggie took the bowl from him and rested it on the table while she said what was on her mind. 'I'd not be exaggerating at all if I said that Gertrude is a saint. She's about thirty years older than Dot, Betty and meself, but glory be to God, she can run rings around the lot of us, so she can. Nobody could have handled Mary better than she did, always so kind and gentle, and never once losing her patience. It's a saint she is, I'm telling yer.'

When the two men were alone again, John said, 'I don't know about you, Paddy, but I feel like the father of this baby. Shouldn't we have a drink to wet its head? And isn't it usual for cigars to be handed out?'

'It would be, if the baby had a normal father, John, but it grieves me to say that this one hasn't. Sure, isn't me heart full of pity for the poor wee child?'

'I'm going to insist on being its uncle,' John said. 'How about you, Paddy?'

The gentle giant of an Irishman beamed. 'I'd be as proud as a peacock, so I would.' He held out his hand. 'Shall we shake on it? Uncle John and Uncle Paddy.'

They broke their handshake when they heard Dot's voice on the stairs. 'Betty, I can't see the flamin' stairs with you in front of me. Ye're blocking out the daylight.'

'Stop yer ruddy moaning, girl! I'm walking in front of yer 'cos I'm frightened of yer falling and dropping the baby. This way yer'd have a nice soft landing if yer fell on me.' Betty came into the room shaking her head and her chins. 'I can't do right for doing wrong with Dot Baker. She's an ungrateful cow.' But the big woman's eyes were tender as she stepped aside to allow her friend to pass. 'Here's the little tinker what's had us all worried out of our mind. But she's a little love, worth every white hair she's put on me head.'

Dot held the precious bundle close. 'Only a little look, then

276

her mam wants her back.' She parted the white baby blanket just enough for the two men to see the scrap of humanity they'd been waiting for. Pale blue eyes stared at them out of a red, crinkled face. And a tiny rosebud mouth was opening and closing as though asking for a drink.

'Her eyes are open!' John said, in wonder. 'She's looking at me.'

'She can't see yer, yer daft thing.' Dot smiled up at him, her eyes brimming with tears of happiness. 'All new babies can open their eyes, but they can't see.'

'Will yer look at the tiny fingers?' Paddy marvelled. 'So tiny, yet so perfect. It's a miracle, so it is.'

'Can I hold her, Dot?' John's eyes were pleading. 'Just for a minute?'

When the bundle was carefully placed in his arms he was moved to tears. Stroking the tiny fingers, he said, 'I'm your Uncle John, darling, and you and me are going to be very good friends. And when you're older, I'll sit you on my knee and tell you what a beautiful baby you were.'

Dot felt a pang of sadness as she watched. He should have children of his own, he'd make a wonderful father. But if he didn't pull his socks up and find himself a wife soon, it would be too late.

'What about Uncle Paddy?' The Irishman's arms were ready to cradle the precious bundle. 'Sure, I'll not be left out, that I'll not.'

John looked awkward as he tried to hand the baby over, so Dot took it from him. 'Men! Yer haven't got a flamin' clue.'

'I know, I know!' John grinned at her. 'And I'm expecting to be told I'm stupid when I ask if Mary's got a name in mind for the baby?'

Betty was fed-up being left out of things, so she answered before Dot could open her mouth. 'She's posh, she's got two names. Gertrude, after the woman who worked so hard to bring her into the world, and Elizabeth, after Mary's mother. The nurse was delighted, I could tell, even though she said it was terrible to lumber a baby with the name Gertrude. So she'll be christened with the full titles, but called Trudy for short.'

277

'Now that's a nice name for a little girl.' Paddy was hooked, he couldn't take his eyes off the baby's face. 'She's perfect, isn't she?'

'Yes, she is,' Dot said. 'Perfect.'

'Now we don't know that for certain, girl, do we? Not until the doctor's seen her.' Betty saw Paddy about to open the blanket, curious to see the feet he could feel kicking out, and she quickly put a hand on his to stop him. 'Don't open that, Paddy, we don't want the baby to catch a cold.'

Dot laughed. 'Betty, it's the middle of summer!'

But Betty was unrepentant as she took the child from Paddy. 'There's draughts in all these houses and I'm not going to be responsible for her catching cold. Anyway, I'm taking her back up to her mother.'

'I'll carry her up for yer,' Dot offered. 'You can follow me.'

'You go and teach yer mother how to milk ducks, Dot Baker! Anyone would think I was helpless and bloody hopeless. I do know how to carry a baby, yer know. And so I should, having had plenty of practice with me own kids.'

Betty sighed as she slowly climbed the stairs. Why did she have to be the one to offer to wash the baby? If she hadn't been so quick to open her big mouth, she wouldn't have this terrible weight on her mind. She hadn't mentioned it because everyone was so happy and she didn't want to be the one to take the smile off Mary's face.

As Mary watched the baby suckling at her breast she could feel the love flowing between herself and her daughter. It was so strong, it caught the breath in her throat. She had never known that love could be so powerful. This tiny being was hers, her own flesh and blood. And she'd make sure she came to no harm; she'd give her enough love to make up for the man who had sired her. The father who didn't even know she'd been born.

There was a gentle tapping on the door and Mary quickly covered her breast as best as she could. 'Come in.'

Gertrude's head came around the door. 'I've just popped up to make sure you're managing all right. Is she taking the milk?'

278

Mary smiled and nodded. 'She took to it like a duck to water. She's a greedy little beggar but I love her so much I could eat her.'

'I'm going to take her off you now, my dear, so you can get some rest. You've had a long, hard labour, and you need to sleep.'

'She can sleep in here, with me.' Mary didn't want to be parted from her daughter and held the baby close. 'She'll be all right, I'll look after her.'

'I'm sorry, Mary, but I have to be strict with you over this. If you were in hospital the baby would be taken from you whether you liked it or not. Maggie has prepared a bed for her in the front bedroom, and she'll wake you when the baby's ready for another feed. But you need as much sleep as possible to get your strength back.'

Mary was reluctant to agree, but she owed this little woman too much to disobey her. 'Maggie will wake me, won't she?'

'If she doesn't, the baby will, so don't worry.' Gertrude took the child from her. 'Come along, Trudy, let Mammy have some rest.' She smiled at Mary. 'To think I've gone through life being called Gertrude, which I've always disliked, when I could so easily have shortened it to Trudy. Still, it's a bit late in life to fret about it now.'

Mary watched the bedroom door close. The nurse was right, she was very tired. And for the first time in months, she was in a bed, not on her lumpy living-room couch. And this bed was a hundred times more comfortable and welcoming than the one next door. The bedclothes were crisp and clean and the feather pillows lovely and soft. Within seconds she was drifting off to sleep, happier than she'd been since the day she got married. And her last conscious thought was that she would never allow Tom Campbell to take this happiness from her.

While Mary slept in the O'Connors' spare bedroom, Dr Gray was examining the baby in the next room. 'I'm sorry to call you out on a Saturday night,' Gertrude said, 'but I needed your opinion and your advice.'

The baby was fast asleep and didn't stir when the doctor

held an ankle in each hand and pulled gently on her legs to straighten them. 'You were right to call me, Gertrude. I would say the right leg is about three inches shorter than the left. That is not precise, of course, they would need to be measured properly. But there is a noticeable difference and I'm in no doubt the child will be somewhat lame.'

The nurse sighed. 'It'll break her heart. And mine, if I have to tell her.'

'Would you like me to tell her?'

'No, thank you all the same. She needs to be told by someone she's close to, someone who'll cry with her.' Gertrude very seldom lost her temper, and only swore in exceptional circumstances. 'It's that bloody husband of hers who should be here with her, to hold her hand and comfort her. What sort of a man is he, to treat his wife the way he does?'

'He's a rotter, Gertrude, an out-and-out rotter. She'd be better off without him, and so would this little mite.'

'Look, she's bound to ask questions, about whether the leg will grow to be the same size as the other as the child gets older, or whether it will even grow at all. What can I say to her?'

'No one could give her an answer to those questions, my dear. They'd only be hazarding a guess and that would be very wrong. My advice is to make little of it, leave her with some hope. I never give a new mother bad news unless I'm forced to. Far better for them to find out gradually than have it sprung on them. In my opinion, the legs will both grow at the same rate, so one will always be shorter than the other, leaving the child with a permanent limp. But that can be rectified to a small degree by having special shoes made.'

'I'll get Dot Baker to tell her, they're very close. And I know she'll find the right words to say so Mary doesn't get too upset.' Gertrude wrapped the blanket around the baby and settled her in the middle of Maggie's bed. 'Thank you for coming out, Doctor, I appreciate it.'

'There's something else she'll ask, too, Gertrude. She'll want to know if the beating her husband gave her is responsible for the handicap. The answer to that is "no". The trauma of the beating may have caused the baby to arrive a few weeks early, but this slight deformity has been present since the day of conception.'

'I'll explain all that to Dot and she can tell Mary in her own way. Now, I'll see you out and have a word with her friends before taking myself off home. I'm bone weary and don't know whether I've got feet on me or not.'

'Is it not time you retired, Gertrude?'

'There's days when I would agree with you, but not today. I'm glad I was here for Mary, she would have been lost and alone in hospital.' The little woman drew herself up to her full height. 'Did I tell you she's called the baby after me?'

'A well-deserved compliment, my dear.' Hunger pangs gripped the doctor as he walked downstairs with her. He'd barely eaten anything since breakfast and was more than ready for his dinner. And if he wasn't mistaken, the delicious smell coming from their kitchen when he left the house was roast pork, his favourite. With the crackling off the joint, crispy roast potatoes and his wife's apple sauce, you couldn't beat it.

'Tell Mary I'll call in tomorrow to see her.' Dr Gray righted his wayward spectacles as he stepped into the street. 'And give my regards to her friends.'

'I'm going to have a word with them now, before I leave. It's best they know what the situation is before they see Mary. The last thing she needs is shocked faces and words of sympathy.'

The nurse began to close the front door. 'Thanks again, Doctor, and good night.'

Dot waited until Colin was in bed before explaining to Katy. 'They've asked me to tell her, but I'm dreading it.'

There were tears in Katy's eyes. 'Ah, Mam, that's terrible! Fancy a little baby like that, it doesn't seem fair. And I'm awful sorry for Mrs Campbell. But perhaps the doctor's made a mistake, Mam, yer never know.'

'No, sunshine, because Gertrude knew before she sent for him. And Betty noticed when she was washing the baby, but she didn't have the heart to tell anyone.' Dot shook her head sadly. 'I wish to God they were mistaken.'

John drew in his legs and sat forward on the chair. 'Dot, a

few hours ago, Mary gave birth to a beautiful baby girl and we all laughed and cried with happiness. And our hearts were filled with love for her. Do you love her any the less, now?'

Dot looked horrified. 'Of course not! How can you even think such a thing?'

John clasped his hands between his knees. 'I was as devastated as everyone else when Gertrude told us. But she is still a beautiful baby, nothing has changed that. And she'll still be beautiful as she grows older. It is very sad if she has to go through life with a limp, but children are born every day with worse handicaps than that and still manage to enjoy a full life. And that's the line I think you should take with Mary. Don't go in there looking sad or hold her hand while you sympathise with her. Keep a smile on that pretty face of yours and tell her she has a beautiful baby, we all adore her, and it isn't the end of the world.'

Dot's eyes never left his face as she digested every word. Then she let out a deep sigh. 'I needed that lecture, John, to put things in perspective. Ye're right, of course, I would have gone in there and cried me eyes out while I was telling her. But your little speech has brought me to me senses. This is a day for rejoicing, not worrying about what might happen in the future.' She managed a smile. 'For being so clever, yer can come with me to see Mary.'

'Ooh, Mam, can I come as well?' Katy bounced on the chair with excitement. 'I'm dying to see the baby.'

'I don't think that would be a good idea, sunshine. Besides, I don't like leaving our Colin in the house on his own.'

'Colin's fast asleep, he won't come to any harm for ten minutes,' John said. 'And I think Katy would be good for Mary.'

'Why do I always end up giving in to you?' Dot narrowed her eyes. 'D'yer know, I give in to you more than I give in to meself? I must be losing me grip.' But her heart felt lighter as she stood up and pushed the chair under the table. 'Come on, let's go. Time is marching on and I'd like to be in me bed by midnight.'

'Shall I take the nappies I've bought for her?' Katy asked. 'And the little pair of bootees?'

'Yeah, that would be nice.' Dot picked the key off the sideboard. 'No noise on the way out, or me laddo will be down like a shot.'

Maggie opened the door to them. 'Go in the living room for a few minutes, Dot, while I see if Mary is respectable. She was feeding the baby a few minutes ago.'

Paddy nodded a welcome and folded the newspaper he'd been reading. 'Sit yerselves down and take the weight off yer feet. Sure, it's been a long day for all of us, so it has. Betty left about half an hour ago, swearing that if she hasn't lost a stone in weight after all the running around, then there isn't any justice.'

Dot grinned. 'I bet she said, "bleedin' justice", Paddy.'

The Irishman scratched his head, a smile on his face. 'Sure, she has a liking for the word, I'll grant yer that. But yer can't take exception to it because she's very funny. Tired as she was, she had me and Maggie in stitches, the things she comes out with. And her heart is certainly in the right place, that's for sure.'

Dot had been leaning on the sideboard, frightened to sit down in case she couldn't get up again. When she heard Maggie's footsteps on the stairs, she straightened up. 'Is she ready for visitors, Maggie?'

'Yes, the baby's been fed and is fast asleep.' Her eyes were troubled. 'Are you going to tell her?'

Dot nodded. 'I wasn't looking forward to it at all, 'cos I knew I'd end up crying with her. But I feel a lot better about it now, after John gave me a good talking to. No tears, no sympathy, just joy that the baby is healthy. So d'yer want to come up with us, Maggie, and perhaps we can take that troubled look off yer face?'

The baby was nestled in Mary's arms, and she smiled with pleasure at her visitors. 'I'm just making friends with me daughter. Come and say hello to her, Katy.'

'I've brought a present for her.' Katy laid the bag on the bed before looking down at the sleeping child. 'Oh, isn't she lovely! Ah, Mam, will yer just look at the size of her! She's like a little doll.'

'Would you like to hold her, Katy?'

The girl's eyes were like saucers. 'Could I, please? I'd love to. I've never held a newborn baby in me arms before.'

When Mary tried to raise herself, she winced with pain. 'Me back is still sore. Will you do it, Dot, please?'

Dot rounded the bed. 'Only for a minute, sunshine.' She picked the baby up and smiled at her daughter. 'Watch how I'm holding her. The head in the crook of yer right arm, and yer left arm goes across the body and under, to support her back. Babies like to feel secure, so don't be frightened to hold her tight.'

Katy's face was a picture of happiness. 'Mr Kershaw, I'm going to pinch one of your favourite words, if yer don't mind. She's adorable.'

'Oh, it's not one of my words, Katy, it's one of your mother's. When she's in one of her good moods, she uses it to describe me.'

Dot gasped. 'Well, you big-headed so-and-so, John Kershaw! I have never once said yer were adorable; yer must be dreaming.'

'So that's where I've heard it, in my dreams, eh?' John puckered his lips and nodded his head slowly. 'Yes, I remember now, D.D. That was the morning I woke up with a smile on my face and a song in my heart.'

'What would yer do with the man, Maggie? I never win with him, he's got an answer for everything.'

The Irishwoman smiled. 'Sure, it's pleasant dreams the man has, Dot, and I'd not begrudge him those.'

Mary took her watchful eyes from the baby to say, 'I think ye're adorable, John.'

Katy giggled. 'I think ye're adorable, too, Mr Kershaw. And all the other things, like kind, caring and generous. I think ye're all those.'

'Oh, my God!' Dot lifted her hands in mock horror. 'He's big-headed enough without all that flattery! I bet he won't be able to get his hat on after this. Probably won't even be able to get through the ruddy door.'

John chuckled. 'Am I as adorable as Trudy?'

Four voices answered as one. 'No!'

'Talking about Trudy,' Dot said, 'it's time she was back with her mother.' She was about to take the child from Katy when she said, 'Why don't yer try those bootees on her, sunshine, to see if they fit?'

Maggie held her breath, wishing she was downstairs with her Paddy. But it would be cowardly to walk out of the room now. It was something that had to be done and the sooner it was over the better. Then perhaps her heartbeats would stop racing and the headache she'd had for the last few hours would disappear.

Mary patted the side of the bed. 'Lay her down here, Katy.'

'You'd better do it, Mam, I'd be frightened of dropping her.'

'Give her here to me and you get the bootees out.' Dot placed the baby down on the bed, and as she opened the blanket she raised her eyes to meet John's. He nodded, and his smile seemed to tell her she was doing fine. 'You bought them, Katy, so you put them on her.'

Free from the restriction of the tightly-wrapped blanket, the baby's legs were kicking out like mad and Katy was terrified of holding one of the legs still in case she hurt her. So she appealed to her mother for help. 'Give us a hand, Mam.'

'Hey, young lady, who's handy with their feet, eh? It'll be footie with the lads for you, not playing with a doll and pram.' Dot laughed as she tied the satin ribbon on the white woollen bootee which was far too big for the tiny foot. 'Mary, have yer noticed that Trudy's right leg is a bit shorter than her left?'

Mary pushed herself up on her elbow, ignoring the pains shooting up her back. 'No! There's nothing wrong with her legs!'

'I know there's nothing wrong with her legs, look at the way she's kicking out.' Dot kept her tone light. 'I wouldn't have known, it's barely noticeable. But Gertrude's used to delivering babies and she mentioned it. She said it's nothing to worry about, so take her advice and don't worry. Ye're very lucky, Mary, yer've got a beautiful healthy baby, an' if yer don't want it yer can pass it over to me.'

'Ooh, yeah,' Katy said, following her mother's lead. 'It would be smashing to have a baby in the house.'

'No, no, no!' John said. 'If Trudy's being given away, I'm first in the queue. And I should be a firm favourite, with Mary thinking I'm adorable.'

'Only because she doesn't know yer, John Kershaw.' Dot's head fell to the side and her hands went to her hips. 'She doesn't know how stubborn and bloody-minded yer are. How yer'll keep on about something until yer get yer own way, like a big soft kid.'

'Excuse me,' Maggie interrupted, 'but isn't it *my* bed that Mary's in? So doesn't that give me priority over the lot of yer? Me and Paddy have already discussed it, so we have. And when Mary decides it's time to go home, sure she'll not be allowed to take the child with her.'

Dot kept on talking as she placed the baby in Mary's arms. 'Over my dead body, Maggie O'Connor! Blimey! They've only been in the street five minutes and already they're ruling the flippin' roost.'

Mary held her daughter close. She'd got a terrible shock when Dot had mentioned that about Trudy's legs, but she felt more at ease with herself now. If it was anything serious, her friends wouldn't be acting the goat the way they were.

'I'll go straight up, if yer don't mind, Mam,' Katy said when she closed the front door after them. 'I can't keep me eyes open.'

'You poppy off, sunshine, I won't be long behind yer. His nibs here is in for a disappointment if he thinks I'm making him a cup of tea, I'm too whacked. He can pick up his coat and then he's on his merry way.'

Katy leaned forward and kissed her mother's cheek. 'Yer did well tonight, Mam, I really was proud of yer.'

'Thanks, sunshine. It's a load off me mind, I can tell yer. And all the praise isn't down to me – you can take your share of it. A little brick, yer were.'

Katy smiled with pleasure. 'Good night and God bless, Mam, and you, Mr Kershaw.'

'Good night, Katy.'

As soon as they were in the living room, Dot shook a finger at him. 'I meant what I said, John Kershaw, no cup of tea tonight. I've been on me feet since half-six this morning, that's seventeen hours, and me legs are like jelly.'

'At least you can sit down for two minutes for a quiet chat. We haven't had any time to ourselves all day, and it'll do you good to unwind before you go to bed. Otherwise your head will be so full you'll never be able to sleep.'

'I've got news for you, sunshine, right now I could sleep on a flippin' clothes-line. And that's with the pegs still on it.'

'What about me? Don't you care whether I'll be able to sleep or not?'

'Oh, don't try and soft soap me, John Kershaw.' Without thinking, Dot sat down on the arm of the couch. 'Yer can stay here and talk to yerself all night, if yer wish, but I'm going up to bed to rest me weary head.'

Before she realised what his intentions were, Dot was picked up and put down on the couch with her legs outstretched. 'There you are, you can rest easy while we go over the events of the day.' John pulled the fireside chair nearer. 'I thought you were marvellous, the way you handled Mary. No one could have done it better.'

Dot's mouth had dropped open with shock, and she closed it now as she glared at him. 'I am going to bed whether you like it or not, yer cheeky so-and-so. Whatever yer want to talk about can wait until the next time yer come.'

'Tomorrow?'

'Yer can come tomorrow, I've promised to sit with Mary in the afternoon to give Maggie a break. I won't be able to do much to help through the week, with working, so I'll do me stint tomorrow.'

'I'll sit with you. That would please Mary because, as you know, she thinks I'm adorable. So does your Katy! You are the only one who doesn't think so.'

Despite herself, Dot grinned. 'Well, two out of three isn't bad going, yer can't complain about that.' She slipped her legs over the side of the couch and pushed herself up. 'And now, Mr John Kershaw, I'll bid you good night and sweet dreams.'

'OK, you win, this time. But before you go, will you tell me how much Mary needs to pay her rent? Plus a few shillings to give Maggie, so she doesn't feel she's accepting charity.'

'I suppose you're going to pay it yerself, are yer?'

John shook his head. 'No, I'm going to ask her husband for it.'

'Never! Ye're not, are yer?'

'I most certainly am! Mary and the baby are his responsibility and so far he's got off very lightly. I would willingly pay it, but why should I? If I don't take the rent-money off him it will be spent on ale, and Mary will find herself in arrears when she goes home. Arrears that she won't be able to pay off.'

'You're full of surprises, you are. For a man that's never been married and doesn't know what it's like to run a house and family, ye're very thoughtful. Yer should get married, John, 'cos yer'd make a damn good husband.'

'Oh, I have every intention of getting married, probably in the next year or so. But in the meantime, you haven't answered my question. How much am I to ask Mr Thomas Campbell for? The rent, plus a few shillings.'

'Yer can ask for ten bob, but whether yer'll get it or not is another thing.' Dot looked very thoughtful before asking. 'Yer've got someone in mind for yer wife, then?'

John nodded. 'Have done for a while now. It's just a case of getting the lady in question to see sense.'

Again Dot thought for a while before saying, 'I wish yer luck, John. Whoever she is, she's getting a good 'un, and yer can tell her I said so.'

'I wouldn't dare do that, she can be very awkward at times.'

'Put yer foot down with her and start as yer mean to go on.' Dot jerked a thumb towards the door. 'Go home now, please, I really need me bed.'

She held the door open and as he passed her, John kissed her cheek. 'Sleep well and have pleasant dreams. I'll be dreaming about the two out of three adorables, and wondering what they can see in me that the third one can't.'

'Get yer ladyfriend to be the third one, then yer'll be happy.'

'I can't do that, D.D. You see, she's not one for showing sentiment or affection.'

'Ye're an unlucky blighter, aren't yer? Still, I'm sure things

288

will look up for yer.' She began to close the door. 'Good night, John.'

'I'll see you tomorrow, after dinner.' His voice came through the closed door and Dot smiled as she climbed the stairs. He was a persistent beggar, wouldn't take 'no' for an answer.

She undressed quietly then slipped between the sheets. Katy was already fast asleep, her breathing gentle and even. Dot turned on her side, closed her eyes and waited to join her daughter in dreamland. But sleep didn't come right away because there was a niggle at the back of her mind. How could he have a ladyfriend when he was round at theirs practically every night? Perhaps it was someone he worked with, she thought. But it was a queer kind of courtship if they didn't meet outside of work. And she must be a cold fish if she never showed sentiment or affection. He deserved someone better than that.

Chapter Eighteen

It was hunger that took Tom Campbell downstairs at midday on Sunday. He'd been in bed since the doctor had called the day before, nursing his aches and pains, but his bruises weren't as sore now and he was starving with hunger. When he found the cupboards in the kitchen bare of food, he tried the sideboard, hoping to find something to satisfy his rumbling tummy. But that cupboard was also bare, apart from a half-tin of condensed milk. 'The bloody bitch!' he snarled, his top lip curling upwards. 'Not a bleedin' thing in the house. I'll have her for this, just wait until she comes home.'

Then he remembered he had his wage packet in his trouser pocket, still intact. That brought a smile to his face. She could whistle for it now; she wouldn't get a penny from him even if she crawled on all fours. He rubbed his hands in glee. The corner shop was open on a Sunday, he could get a loaf of bread and a quarter of brawn, that would see him through today and there'd be enough over for his breakfast and carry-out. The rest of his wages he could do what he liked with. And he knew exactly what he'd do. A whole night with Esmée cost four bob. He could afford that now, and still have his two bob's worth later in the week. He licked his lips in eager anticipation of the treat he was in for tomorrow night.

Tom rubbed his chin which was rough with stubble. He'd better have a shave before he went to the corner shop in case he bumped into anyone he knew. They'd be getting out of eleven o'clock Mass now, so there'd be plenty of people about. That set his mind thinking. It was probably all over the neighbourhood by now that he'd been beaten up by that fat cow from down the street, and he'd be a laughing stock. The best thing he could do was use the back jiggers and go to the small shop in Springwell Road, where he wasn't known.

He struck a match to warm some water for a shave but when he turned the knob on the stove there was no plop, which meant there was no gas. Once again he cursed his wife, forgetting he was the one who had taken the coppers she kept for the gas-meter. And he knew there was only silver in his wage packet, so he'd have to go out as he was and hope no one saw him. Anyway, to hell with everyone. If the men only knew where he went twice a week, and what the whores were prepared to do for their money, they wouldn't laugh at him, they'd envy him. He'd heard them talking in work about how their wives allowed them their conjugal rights once a week, and that under duress. One bloke even said his wife lay as stiff as a board, counting the cracks in the ceiling. Poor buggers, they didn't know what they were missing.

John walked past Dot's house and knocked on the next door. When there was no answer, he knocked harder, and was rewarded by the sound of the latch being turned before the door was opened a crack and a surly voice asked, 'What the hell do you want?'

'What I do not want, is to talk to a piece of wood.' John raised his foot and pushed the door wider. 'And unless you want the whole street to hear what I've got to say, you will have the good manners to invite me in.'

It was on the tip of Tom's tongue to tell him to go to hell, but he bit the words back. He'd learned the hard way that this bloke wasn't one to mess around with. 'Yer can come in, but just for a minute. I'm making meself something to eat.'

John stood in the middle of the dark, shabby room and mentally compared it with the O'Connors' bright and welcoming living room. To think Mary would have to leave that to come home to this. 'I'm here to get some money off you,' he said bluntly. 'The rent-man will want paying, and on top of that Mary needs a few shillings.'

'Some bleedin' hope you've got! If she wants money, let her come home for it. She should be here now, the bitch, cooking me Sunday dinner.' Tom's bubble had burst and with it his temper. He shook his head. 'No, ye're wasting yer time,

Mister Whatever-yer-name-is. I'm not forkin' out for a wife who's not doing her job.'

He doesn't know Mary's had the baby, John thought. And he doesn't even care enough to ask how she is. Well, I'm not going to enlighten him – let him stew in his own juice. 'You made rather a mess of Mary when you beat her up – she's had to stay in bed,' he said quietly. 'So as she's unable to come for herself, I volunteered to get the money off you. Personally, I think you're being let off lightly. I would ask for far more, but I've been told that ten shillings will suffice.'

His dreams of sexual fantasy shattering around him, Tom made one last act of bravado. He started for the kitchen, saying over his shoulder, 'I'm seein' to me dinner. Close the door on yer way out, Mister.'

He'd only taken a couple of steps when John collared him. Dragging him back into the centre of the living room, the big man sighed. 'You really are a glutton for punishment, aren't you? I'm beginning to think you like being beaten up.'

'Ye're nearly choking me, yer stupid bastard. Take yer bleedin' hands off me.'

'As soon as you hand the ten shillings over, I'll be glad to take my hands off you. It makes me feel quite sick, actually, just touching you.'

'I've told yer, ye're wasting yer time. I'm buggered if I'm handing money over for a wife what's not here.'

'Oh dear,' John sighed. 'This is becoming quite a ritual. Do you want me to fight you in this room, or would you prefer the street?'

'I don't get you, Mister.' Tom stopped struggling when he realised he wasn't getting anywhere, only making things worse for himself. 'What interest have you got in my wife, and why? She's none of your business.'

'Oh, I've made her my business. As, indeed, has Paddy next door. Neither of us like to see a nice woman being used as a punch-bag. If you would prefer to hand the money over to Paddy, I'll willingly stand aside. But you can rest assured that one way or another, we will get the money off you. So instead of tempers being frayed and punches thrown, why don't you save us all this bother and pay up quietly?'

Tom Campbell wasn't a small man by any means, but the six-inch difference between him and John meant his eyes were on a level with the big man's chin. 'Yer don't even know her! She's a lousy bleedin' wife, won't work for love nor money. Just look at the state of this place! How would you like it if yer were married to a lazy cow?'

'Don't say another word.' John's voice was low and threatening. 'Not one word, if you know what's good for you. Just hand over the ten shillings or be kicked from one end of Edith Road to the other. The choice is yours.'

There was no choice, and Tom knew it. He had no doubt the bloke would carry out his threat. 'Let go of me an' I'll give yer the bleedin' money.' He stepped back when John released his grip and pulled the wage packet from his pocket. 'Here's the ten bob, now hop it, out of my house.'

John folded the ten-shilling note and put it in his breast-pocket. 'The word for this place is not house, but hovel. And the reason it's a hovel is because you prefer to spend your money in the pub, instead of giving your wife sufficient housekeeping.' He waved his hand around the room. 'This seedy room, with its broken furniture and torn lino, is down to you, not Mary. Given a decent husband who cared and shared, she'd have this place like a little palace.' John eyed the man in front of him up and down, a look of contempt on his face. 'I'll call again next week for the same amount of money, so have it ready.'

'Ay, and she'd better be back here before next week. It's a wife's duty to have a meal ready for her husband, see to his carry-out and wash and iron his clothes. So you tell her from me that she'd better get back bleedin' sharpish.'

'Oh, I wouldn't bank on that, if I were you.' John walked into the hall and opened the front door. 'But you can bank on me coming back next week, that's a certainty.'

'Me mam's not in, Mr Kershaw, she's gone to sit with Mrs Campbell.' Colin's face, as always, lit up when he saw John. 'But yer can come in.'

It was very quiet in the living room; the only sound was the ticking of the clock on the mantelpiece. 'Isn't Katy in?'

'No, she said it was too nice to sit in the house, so she's gone for a walk to the park with Doreen.'

'It's a beautiful day, Katy's right,' John said. 'Why aren't you out playing with one of your friends?'

'I called for Danny, but his mam opened the door and chased me.' Colin pulled a face. 'She said he's not playing out because the Sabbath is a day of rest.'

John grinned. 'So you're all on your lonesome?'

'Yeah, I can't play ollies or footie on me own.'

John studied the lad's crestfallen face and took pity. 'Look, how would you like to come out with me? We could get a tram down to the Pier Head and watch the ferries coming and going. On a day like this they'll be very busy.'

The change in Colin's face was nothing short of miraculous. 'Ooh, yeah! That would be the gear, Mr Kershaw! I've never seen the ferries.'

John was about to voice his disbelief when he remembered the straitened circumstances in which the family had lived since the father died. A father this boy had never known. 'I'll have to ask your mother first, but I can't see her objecting.'

'Yer've no need to ask me mam, Mr Kershaw, she won't mind.'

'I wouldn't dream of taking you out without her permission, Colin – that would be very irresponsible of me. Besides,' John chuckled, 'she'd probably give me a clip around the ears if I did.'

'You like me mam, don't yer?'

'Yes, of course I do. She's a lovely lady and it would be hard not to like her.' John knew the boy was noted for repeating everything he heard, so he chose his words carefully. 'In fact, I like all the ladies I've met since I started coming here.'

That didn't satisfy Colin, it wasn't definite enough. 'But yer like me mam the best?'

'Is this a man-to-man talk, Colin, or are you just being nosy?'

Being treated like a grown-up caused the boy's chest to expand with pride. 'Man-to-man, of course, Mr Kershaw. I won't tell no one, honest.'

'In that case, yes, I do like your mother best. But if you tell her, she'll send me packing and you won't ever see me again. You don't want that to happen, do you?'

The very idea had Colin shaking his head vigorously. 'My lips are sealed, Mr Kershaw. It's our little secret, eh?'

'Yes, our little secret.' John smiled as he ruffled the mop of dark hair. 'And now I'll nip down to the O'Connors' to see how Mary and the baby are, and ask your mother's permission for our voyage into the unknown.'

'Yeah, like in the comics, where the hero slashes his way through the jungle to rescue the girl being held prisoner.' The boy's eyes were agog with excitement. 'And he fights with lions and tigers, and even crocodiles. And he always wins, doesn't he, Mr Kershaw?'

John's head fell back and he roared with laughter. 'Don't get carried away, son, I don't think we'll see any lions or tigers down at the Pier Head. Would you be satisfied with an ice-cream cornet?'

Colin's mind was too busy to speak, so he answered with a nod. Mr Kershaw had called him 'son', and it was the first time he'd ever done that. I wish I *was* his son, the boy thought wistfully. I'd be made-up to have him for me dad.

'You get yourself ready while I'm gone.' John turned to leave. 'I'll be about fifteen to twenty minutes.' He glanced at the clock. 'If I'm not back by half-past, give a knock on the O'Connors' door.'

Next door, Maggie greeted him with a smile. 'Mother and baby are doing well, John. I know you'll be glad to hear that.'

'Yes, I am. It's just what I wanted to hear. I'll say hello to your husband, then slip up and see them.' John popped his head around the living-room door. 'How is Uncle Paddy on this fine sunny day?'

'On top of the world, so I am. I've been nursing the baby while Mary was getting washed, and didn't the wee thing steal me heart? It's contented I'd be to sit with her in me arms all day, and that's the truth of it. And although my Maggie doesn't believe me, I'll swear she smiled at me.'

'Paddy, yer great daft thing, it was wind!' Maggie grinned at John. 'The next thing, he'll be saying she spoke to him.

And this time next week, won't she be having long conversations with him?'

'I can't have your husband taking advantage of the situation by worming his way into her affection, that wouldn't do at all,' John said. 'I'm going to cadge a five-minute cuddle to let her know she's got an Uncle John as well as an Uncle Paddy. And if he got a smile, I'm going to demand a bigger one.'

'Would yer be after taking yerself up there, John? I want to get me feet up for an hour, while I've got the chance. I didn't get much sleep last night with listening for the baby. Mary told me she could manage but the poor girl's in agony with her back, so she is. That wicked husband of hers nearly punched the life out of her. And God help the baby when she takes her home, it doesn't bear thinking about.'

'He'd be a very silly man to lay a finger on the child, Maggie, because I'd break every bone in his body if he did.' John remembered Colin would be knocking in fifteen minutes and he wanted to spend some time with Mary and the baby. And Dot. Oh yes, especially with Dot.

'I won't stay up there long because I've promised to take Colin out for a few hours, if his mother agrees. I'll give you a shout when I'm leaving.'

As John's long legs took the stairs three at a time, he could hear Dot laughing. She had an infectious laugh and it never failed to bring a smile to his face. He rapped lightly on the door and waited for an answer before opening it to see Mary propped up with pillows and looking comfortable and contented. 'You look very well, Mrs Campbell, I'm glad to say.'

'I feel a darn sight better than this time yesterday,' Mary told him, a look of embarrassment on her face at the memory. 'I made a right fool of meself.'

'Nonsense! I think yer were a ruddy hero.' Dot was sitting on the side of the bed with the baby cradled in her arms and she gave John a broad wink. 'Here's your Uncle John, sunshine, checking up on us to make sure we're looking after yer properly.'

'And to claim my right to a cuddle. Paddy is one ahead of me and I'm not having that, I'm claiming equal rights.'

'My God, ye're worse than a couple of kids.' Dot glanced at Mary. 'Is it all right if he has five minutes?'

'Of course it is, but I don't want her to get too used to being nursed, or she'll be spoilt and expect it all the time.'

As Dot made to stand up, John put a hand on her shoulder. 'Hang on a minute, D.D., I've got something for Mary.' He took the ten-shilling note from his pocket and handed it over. 'This is off your husband, for the rent and whatever.'

Mary gasped as she sat bolt upright. 'When did yer get that off him?'

'About twenty minutes ago.'

'It's not like Tom Campbell to hand money over just like that. Did he offer it, or did yer have to force it out of him?'

'I asked him for it and he gave it to me.' John believed if he told the truth it would take the contentment from Mary's face. 'No problem, really.'

Mary held the note between her two fingers. 'Does he know about the baby?'

'I don't think so. From the way he was talking I got the impression he had no idea. And I thought it best not to tell him in case he came barging in here. It wouldn't be fair on the O'Connors, you, or the baby. You are both being well looked after and if you can stay for the two weeks, you'll feel stronger and you'll also have a routine with Trudy.'

'There speaks a man after me own heart,' Dot said. 'Yer won't take any notice of me but perhaps yer'll listen to John.'

'I'm sure Mary is sensible enough to do what's best. And now, before I have my five minutes' cuddle, D.D., I've got something to ask you.'

'If it's a loan ye're after, ye're out of luck. I'm boracic lint, skint.'

'Nothing like that, my Delightful Dorothy, I just want to know if I can take Colin out for a couple of hours. He's sitting in the house on his own and it's such a shame on a beautiful day like this. I thought I'd take him down to the Pier Head to see the ferries.'

Dot's eyes were like saucers. 'He'll make a holy show of yer! He's not dressed for going anywhere on a Sunday.'

John tutted. 'Dot, don't be such a snob! The lad looks

perfectly respectable, and I've checked his ears are clean *and* his neck.'

Dot stood up and handed him the baby. 'He's not going anywhere until I'm satisfied he won't make a show of yer. I'm not having people wondering what sort of a mother he's got.' With a curt nod of her head she vacated the room at speed, leaving John holding the baby and Mary with a smile on her face.

'What a woman!' John smiled down at the sleeping child. 'A woman and a half, your Auntie Dorothy is.'

Mary settled back on the pillows, a glint of amusement in her eyes. 'Ye're right there, John. I'd say Dot had everything. She's got a heart of pure gold, a marvellous sense of humour that never fails to cheer me up, and on top of all that she really is a very pretty woman. Don't you agree with me?'

'Oh, most definitely! She's all of those things, and more. I find her most attractive when she's in a temper. She really is quite adorable then, and I could eat her.'

Mary knew she'd caught him offguard when he was wrapped up in the delight of holding the baby, but she was pleased with herself because she was convinced more than ever that she'd been right all along. He was head over heels in love with Dot. She won't have it, just laughs it off, but anyone with half an eye can see he's crazy about her, Mary thought to herself.

'She's smiling at me!' John bent so Mary could see the tiny face split in a smile. 'Paddy wasn't imagining it, he was right!'

Colin wanted to go on the top deck of the tram and laughed with glee as he gripped the hand-rail while the tram swayed from side to side. 'Can we sit on the front seat, Mr Kershaw? Yer can see more from the front.'

'Whatever you want, Colin.' John was deriving great pleasure from the boy's obvious excitement and enjoyment. 'This is your afternoon, so your wish is my command.'

'This is the gear.' A huge grin covered the boy's face as he sat down. 'Look, yer can see everything from here.' He shuffled forward in his seat to grab the safety bar that ran across the front window. 'I think I'll be a tram-driver when I leave school.'

'And when will that be?'

'Not this Christmas, but the one after. Then I'll be getting a wage and can give me mam some money, like our Katy does.' The boy's eyes were animated. 'Then we're going to get some new furniture and curtains for the living room, and new beds. Me mam said we won't know ourselves. She said there'll be no flies on us, we'll be proper posh.'

John grinned. They were Dot's expressions all right. He could almost hear her speaking them. 'Your mother confides in you and Katy, doesn't she? You're lucky, because not many mothers do that.'

'Me mam's great, Mr Kershaw, an' I don't half love her.' Colin's eyes went back to the window. 'Where are we now?'

'This is Scotland Road, not far to go now.'

When they stepped off the tram at the Pier Head and Colin saw the crowds of people, he was stunned into silence. His eyes were everywhere as he kept close to John's side. It would be easy to get split up in this crowd and he'd never find his way home. He had tuppence in his pocket that would pay his fare, but he wouldn't know what number tram to get. 'Can I hold on to yer coat, Mr Kershaw? I'd easy get lost in this lot.'

'Hold my hand, that's the best.' John could feel his own excitement growing. He had a surprise in store for the boy and couldn't wait to see his face. 'Just keep tight hold and we'll follow the crowd.'

Feeling safe now his hand was being tightly held, Colin began to show an interest in the people around, who were taking advantage of the beautiful sunny weather. There were young girls in bright summer dresses, men in open-necked short-sleeved shirts, and young children clutching buckets and spades and colourful beach balls. And everyone looked happy, except for some mothers who appeared hot and harassed as they tried to keep their over-excited children in check while carrying heavy bags filled with towels, sandwiches and bottles of home-made lemonade. It was all new to Colin, and he was enjoying every thrilling second. 'Are these people going to watch the ferries?'

'No, from the looks of them I'd say they're going to the

300

beach at New Brighton.' John looked down from his great height. 'The same as us.'

This was too much for Colin. He nearly pulled John's arm out of its socket as he jumped up and down with excitement. 'D'yer mean I'm goin' on a boat, Mr Kershaw?'

'It's the only way to get to New Brighton, son, unless you're a good swimmer.' They were now walking under cover and John guided the boy to one side so they could join a long queue of people outside the ticket office. 'We'll not make it in time for the ferry that's in now, but there's one every fifteen minutes.'

Colin lapsed into silence. Wait until he told their Katy, she'd be green with envy because she'd never been to New Brighton. Then he felt ashamed of himself. His sister could afford these luxuries if she didn't hand nearly all her wages over. If Mr Kershaw ever offered to bring him again, he'd ask if Katy could come with them.

The queue moved quickly and soon they were walking up the gangway of a rocking ferry boat. Colin made a bee-line for the rails and John hurried after him to put an arm across his shoulders as he leaned too far over. 'You won't see any crocodiles, Colin, but look at all the seagulls. They follow every boat, hoping for scraps of food.'

The boy looked up just as a bird swooped as low as his head. 'Did yer see that cheeky beggar, Mr Kershaw? I thought it was going to land on me flippin' head.'

'A word of warning, my lad. When you look up, make sure your mouth is closed. You see, birds don't use a toilet.'

'Ooh, er! The dirty things!' A mischievous gleam came in the boy's eyes. 'If they dirty on me best pullover they'll not get any scraps of food from me.'

'You haven't got any scraps of food, Colin.'

'I know that, Mr Kershaw, and you know that. But the blinkin' birds don't.'

They heard the gangway being raised, then the ferry stirred into motion. It moved slowly at first until it was clear of the quayside then gathered speed as it faced the open river. Colin was mesmerised by the white foam swirling around the boat as it ploughed its way through the water.

301

'What's all that white stuff, Mr Kershaw?'

John explained while keeping a tight grip on the boy who was balancing precariously over the rail. And with infinite patience answered all the questions thrown at him. Did anyone ever fall overboard? Were there any fish in the river? Would they see any sharks? What would happen if the boat had a hole in the bottom that nobody knew about, and sunk when they were in the middle of the river? He seemed quite disappointed when John told him he had never heard of a ferryboat sinking.

His curiosity satisfied, Colin turned to watch the noisy activities on deck. Dozens of children were running wild, shrieking with delight at the freedom. And behind them came panting fathers and worried mothers. One stout lady smiled at John as she hurried past. 'Flamin' kids! We want our bumps feelin' for havin' them.'

'She's right, yer know,' Colin said knowingly. 'Kids are a ruddy nuisance.'

'Do you include yourself in that remark?'

'I didn't mean all kids, just most of them.'

John grinned as he turned the boy towards the rails. 'There's New Brighton, we'll be there in five minutes.' He pointed a stiffened finger. 'Look, you can see the Tower. Have you ever heard of the famous New Brighton Tower ballroom?'

Colin shook his head. 'No, but I know there's a fair there, 'cos one of me mates told me.'

'Yes, there is, but we'll have to give it a miss, I'm afraid. I promised your mother I'd have you back for half-five. So we'll just have a short walk along the promenade today, then next time we come we'll set out earlier and I'll take you to the fair.'

Colin was quite happy just being in John's company. It would be nice to go to a big fairground because he'd never been to one. Sometimes a travelling fair came to the North Park, but his mate said it wasn't in the meg specks compared to New Brighton. Even so, if it came to a choice between a fair, or sitting on a bench in a park with the big man by his side, Colin knew which one he'd choose.

When the gangway was lowered there was a huge surge forward, and John held Colin back. 'Wait until the rush is over or we'll get trampled underfoot. Five minutes isn't going to make much difference.'

The boy grinned up into his face. 'Me tummy's rolling with the boat. It's a nice feeling, isn't it, Mr Kershaw?'

'It is if you don't suffer from seasickness.' John watched the crowds thinning out and reached for the boy's hand. 'Come on, it's safe to go now.'

When they reached the promenade, Colin's excitement reached fever pitch. He'd never seen anything like it. The beach was bustling and noisy. A lot of young people were wearing bathing costumes and lying on towels with their faces pointed to the sun in the hope of getting brown so they could swank in work the next day. Men were playing football and rounders with their trouser legs rolled up and knotted handkerchieves covering their heads. And down by the water's edge, Colin could see children sitting in the water, splashing and shouting with glee while their mothers paddled with their dresses tucked up in their bloomers. 'It's not half-busy, isn't it, Mr Kershaw?'

'It'll be worse still in a few weeks when the factories close down for the holidays. You won't be able to move, then.'

'The schools close down, too, yer know. Six weeks, we get.' The boy tugged on John's sleeve. 'Will you be on holiday?'

'All the factories close down for the last week in July and the first week in August. That's when I'll be having my holidays.' John could almost see the boy's mind ticking over. 'Perhaps we'll come over here for a full day, eh? We could bring a picnic with us. Would you like that?'

'What about me mam? She'll be off then, as well, and I wouldn't like to come and leave her behind, it wouldn't be fair.'

'I'd be delighted if your mother would come, but she wouldn't if I asked her. You'll have to try and persuade her.' I shouldn't be using him in this way, John thought. But as they say, all's fair in love and war. 'Anyway, there's an ice-cream cart just over the road; let's go and get ourselves a cornet.'

As they strolled along the promenade licking their cornets, they passed a couple of small kiosks selling rock and souvenirs. They caught Colin's eye. 'How much is the rock, Mr Kershaw?

303

I'd like to take a stick home for me mam if they're not more than tuppence.'

'There's some there for a penny a stick, and they've got "New Brighton" written right through them. I'm sure your mother would be pleased with one of those.' John took a hankie from his pocket and handed it over. 'You've got ice-cream on the end of your nose, and it's running down your chin. I'd get the blame if your mother saw you, so clean yourself up.'

Colin quickly demolished the cornet before dutifully wiping the offending spots. 'I could buy two of those sticks of rock, one for me mam and one for our Katy.'

'Then by all means, do so. And ask the lady nicely if she'll put them in a bag for you to keep them clean.' John looked at his wrist-watch. 'When you've been served we'll have to make our way back, otherwise I'll be in your mother's bad books.'

'Nah, me mam likes yer!'

'I'm taking no chances, Colin. Your tea will be on the table at half-five and I'll have you home for then if we have to run every foot of the way.'

'Are you having tea with us?'

'We'll have to wait and see. Now hurry up, there's a good lad.'

'Ah, the wanderers return.' Dot came through from the kitchen wiping her hands on her pinny. 'Did yer have a nice time, sunshine?'

'It was magic, Mam, really magic.' Colin handed her a white paper bag. 'I've brought yer some rock, one for you and one for our Katy.'

'Yer sister's upstairs, she'll be down in a minute.' As Dot took the bag she glanced in John's direction. 'I suppose it goes without saying that you paid for these?'

Before John had time to open his mouth, Colin chipped in. 'No, Mr Kershaw didn't buy them, so there!' The boy's face was a picture of injured pride. After all, he'd spent his last tuppence on that rock. 'I bought them meself with what I had left out of me pocket money.'

'All right, keep yer hair on, sunshine, I only asked.' Dot

slid a stick of the pink rock out of the bag. 'Ooh, I say, we've been to New Brighton.'

Katy came running into the room. 'Did I hear yer say they'd been to New Brighton? Ye're a lucky so-and-so, our Colin. I've never been and I'd love to go and see what it was like.'

'*You* mightn't have been, sunshine, but this rock has.' Dot passed one of the sticks over. 'Bought by yer brother out of his hard-earned pocket money. And now he's skint and not very happy.'

'Thanks, our kid, ye're a little love.' Katy planted a kiss on his cheek. 'I'll go there one of these days, but tell us what it's like.'

The words tumbling from his mouth, Colin gave her a condensed account of everything he'd seen. He even mentioned that seagulls don't have a toilet so if she ever went on the ferry she better keep her mouth shut. Then turning to his mother, he said, 'And d'yer know what, Mam? Some of the ladies had their dresses tucked inside their knickers and they didn't half look a sight. Fancy doing that, and all those people looking at them. I think it's rude, and they should know better at their age.'

'And what age would that be, sunshine?' Dot asked, tongue in cheek.

'They were as old as you.' Too late Colin realised his mistake and quickly tried to make amends. 'But you'd look all right, Mam, 'cos ye're nice and slim. Some of these women had big tummies and backsides, and great big fat legs.'

'Fat people feel the heat as well as young ones, sunshine, and they're entitled to cool off in the sea.' Dot couldn't contain her laughter, and when it erupted it filled the room. 'If I ever get to go to New Brighton, I'll borrow a pair of yer Auntie Betty's blue fleecy-lined bloomers – they should cover me embarrassment.'

John, laughing, said, 'They'd cover more than your embarrassment, Dot, you'd get lost in them.'

Colin was restored to good humour with this. 'We could all get in a pair of Auntie Betty's knickers, Mam.'

'I wouldn't let her hear you say that, sunshine, 'cos she'd kick yer into the middle of next week.' Dot waved a hand.

'You sit yerself down, John, and you, Katy, can give me a hand to set the table. Tea, such as it is, will be ready in five minutes.'

When his mother's back was turned, Colin, as happy as a sand boy, winked at John. 'See, I told yer me Mam would let yer stay to tea.'

When Billy Harlow called for Katy they decided to go out for a walk. And Colin, tired from the fresh sea air, went to bed early, leaving Dot and John on their own. 'Now yer can tell me how yer got that ten bob off Tom Campbell. I know he wouldn't part with money unless he was forced to.'

'I won't say I didn't lay a finger on him, because that wouldn't be true. But I certainly didn't have to resort to violence.' John crossed his long legs, at ease and feeling so contented he wished he could stay here forever. Everything he wanted from life was in this house. A woman he'd loved almost from the minute he set eyes on her, and two children he idolised. 'He's a nasty piece of work, though. I worry about Mary having to go back there with the baby because he'll lead her a dog's life.'

Dot sighed. 'Me and the O'Connors have been talking about the very same thing this afternoon. Paddy's in a real state about it; he wants Mary and Trudy to stay with them.'

'They'd never know a minute's peace living next door to him.' John jerked a thumb at the dividing wall. 'I get the feeling he's not all there in the head. I wouldn't put anything past the blighter.'

There was anxiety in Dot's hazel eyes as she ran her fingers through her thick auburn hair. 'There's something else to worry about, too.' She shook her head sadly. 'I washed the baby in the O'Connors' living room while Mary was having a snooze, and there's no doubt the child will have a limp. There's quite a difference in her legs; one is very much shorter than the other. Mary hasn't washed the baby herself yet, but it won't be long before she notices just how bad it is.

'She's certainly got her share of trouble, there's no doubt about that. But there's nothing we can do about it, except be there when she needs us,' John said. 'Unfortunately, we can't

306

be with her twenty-four hours a day.'

'I know, I've been going over it in me mind until me head's spinning. We'll just have to take it one day at a time, that's all we can do.' Dot's skirt was riding high up her thighs and she stood up to tug it down to cover her knees. 'Anyway, let's talk about something pleasant for a change. Did my son behave himself today?'

'He always behaves himself, he's a pleasure to take out. He gets so excited over things, I find myself getting excited with him, even though I've seen them hundreds of times. So you see, he's good for me.'

Dot was in her element talking about her children, the two people she loved most in the world. And John was happy to sit quietly and listen to the sound of her voice and watch her changing facial expressions – something of which he would never tire.

When the hands on the clock reached a quarter to ten, Dot uncurled her legs and got to her feet. 'Time yer were on yer way, John Kershaw. The neighbours will think there's something going on between us, the time yer spend here.'

'They wouldn't be right, though, would they?'

'No, they wouldn't ruddy-well be right! But you try telling them that; they're a bad-minded lot of beggars.'

'You wouldn't like to supply them with something to gossip about, and give me a kiss at the door, would you? That would keep them going for a week.'

'No, I wouldn't like to give yer a kiss at the front door. And anyway, yer ladyfriend wouldn't like it, would she? This elusive girlfriend that yer don't see much of.'

'Oh, I do see quite a lot of her, actually. Not as much as I'd like, I'll admit – but then we can't always have everything we want, can we?'

'It's a funny state of affairs, if yer ask me. Anyway, on yer way, sunshine.'

'I'll see you tomorrow night, if that's all right with you. Just to check on Mary's progress.'

Dot pushed him towards the door. 'Do I have a choice?'

'No, not really. Good night and sweet dreams, D.D.'

Chapter Nineteen

'Betty, will yer be a pal and come with us to look for a second-hand pram for Mary? This is the only chance I've got, with working all week, and she's taking the baby home next Saturday.' Dot handed her neighbour a cup of tea before sitting down. 'We've all tried to get her to change her mind and stay on another week or so, but she's determined.'

'She wants her bumps feeling, if yer ask me,' Betty said, the saucer balanced on her ample lap. 'She's getting well looked after at the O'Connors', they treat her like flippin' royalty. Another few weeks there and she'd have her strength back. She'll get no ruddy help, or rest, once she's back home. That bleedin' husband of hers will expect her to wait on him hand and foot, and she won't be up to it. Having a baby upsets yer whole system, girl, as yer well know, and it takes ages to get back to normal.'

'We've talked to her until we're blue in the face, Betty, but she's determined. She says she's got to go back sometime and the longer she leaves it, the worse it'll be. And she'll need a pram for the baby to sleep in.' Dot pursed her lips and shook her head. 'Can yer just imagine what it'll be like? Her sleeping on the couch with a pram at the side of her, and the queer feller coming in drunk from the pub, falling all over the place and ranting and raving? Oh no, it wouldn't do for me. I wouldn't swap places with her for all the tea in China.'

When there was a knock on the door, Betty grinned mischievously. 'This sounds like that lodger of yours.'

Dot bent down to put her cup on the floor at the side of her chair. 'Betty Mason, if you don't stop saying that, so help me I'll clock yer one. John is not me lodger, just a friend. The same as he's a friend to you, and Mary and the O'Connors.'

She turned at the door and wagged a finger in warning. 'So you just knock it off and behave yerself.'

John smiled as he stepped into the hall. 'I know it's not Colin you're talking to because he's playing ollies in the street, so who are you telling to behave themselves?'

'I'll give yer one guess,' Dot said, closing the door after him. 'Who is it that we both know who's always misbehaving and making a ruddy nuisance of herself?'

'There's only one person I know who fits that description,' John said as he entered the living room. 'Ah, yes, the redoubtable Mrs Mason.'

Betty's chubby face was set. 'Ay, you just watch it! A flamin' dictionary on legs, that's what you are.' She appealed to Dot. 'Did yer hear what he just called me?'

'I heard, sunshine, but don't ask me what it means because I haven't a clue. As thick as two short planks, I am. I can't even say the word, let alone know what it means.'

As Betty's head and chins shook, the tea was spilling over the rim of her cup and filling the saucer. 'Yer've got ten seconds to tell me what it means, Mr Clever Clogs. And if I don't like it, I'm going to stand on a chair and belt yer round the ears.'

John raised his arm as though defending himself against an onslaught. 'Oh, please don't hit me! It wasn't an insult, missus, honest!'

'Right, well let's be having yer.'

'Now let me see.' John stroked his chin. 'Redoubtable means, er, how can I put it? It can mean many things, really.'

When Betty's tummy started to shake, the tea slopped over the saucer on to her dress, making a dark stain. But she was laughing so much inwardly she didn't feel the dampness. 'Does it mean I'm so bloody gorgeous that ye're out of yer mind with burning desire for me beautiful, voluptuous body?'

'In the name of God, Betty Mason, have yer no shame?' Dot tutted. 'Talk about having a one-track mind isn't in it. There are times when I don't know where to put meself, when I wish the floor would open and swallow me up.'

'I keep forgetting that yer were brought up in a strict convent, girl, and that yer've got a sensitive soul. So rather than offend those delicate lugholes of yours, why don't yer go in the kitchen and pour John a nice cup of tea, while he tells me how he lies awake at night filled with longing for me. And take yer time pouring the tea out, girl, because that miserable gob yer've got on yer is enough to put him off his bleedin' stroke.'

John put his hands together as though in prayer. 'Don't leave me alone with her, Dot, I beg you. If she's determined to have her wicked way with me, I'd be putty in her hands.'

'Will you two grow up, please? I don't know which one's the worst, yer both as bad as one another.' Dot's hands went on her hips and her head dropped sideways. 'Just tell her what the flamin' word means and get it over with.'

John knew the signs by now. As far as Dot was concerned they'd gone far enough. So he made his answer short and simple. 'It means bold, or daring.'

'That's me, down to the ground.' Betty's smile had her cheeks moving upwards to cover her eyes. 'At least, I would be daring if I had someone willing to be daring with me.' She leaned forward so quickly the cup fell on its side and deposited the remainder of the tea on her lap. 'Oh, bloody hell, I've wet meself!'

'Serves yer right, I've no sympathy for yer.' Dot relieved her of the cup and saucer. 'Go and dry yerself off with the towel.'

'I'll have to go home and get changed, girl, I can't go out with me dress all wet. People will think I've wet me knickers.'

'Ye're not going home 'cos we'll never make it to the shops if yer do. Dry yerself as much as yer can and no one will notice.'

Muttering and groaning, Betty waddled to the kitchen. They grinned when they heard her saying, 'I bet she makes me walk six steps behind her, pretending she's not with me. The way she treats me it's a wonder I haven't got one of those . . .' Her head appeared around the door. 'Ay, John, what's the words I'm lookin' for, when someone's always pulling yer down, making little of yer?'

'Would it be inferiority complex, Betty?'

'That's it! That's what me best friend is giving me – an infroroty complex.'

'I'll give yer more than that, sunshine, if yer don't shift yerself. I'm not a lady of leisure with every day free to walk around the shops choosing what to buy for the day's dinner. I've got a couple of hours on a Saturday afternoon to do the lot. And on today's list, along with me groceries, potatoes, veg and meat, I've got a second-hand pram to get.'

'I've told you to get a new pram for Mary,' John said. 'I don't fancy putting Trudy in a pram that might have been used for half a dozen babies.'

'Well, that's just too bad, isn't it, John Kershaw? My children had second-hand prams and it hasn't done them any harm.'

Like a streak of greased lightning, Betty threw the towel back in the kitchen and took a seat. If there was going to be an argument she wanted to be in on it. To hell with the wet dress, the sun would dry it in no time. If anyone was bad-minded enough to think she'd wet herself, that was their look-out. She wouldn't lose any sleep over it. So folding her arms under her bosom, and with a look of innocence on her face, she asked, 'What's going on? Are you two going to have cross words?'

'No, we're not going to have cross words, because John's not getting his own way over this.' Her hands still on her hips, Dot sat on the arm of the couch. 'He wants to buy Mary a brand-new pram. And not just any new pram, but a Silver Cross one! I can't get it through his thick head what a stupid idea it is.'

Betty screwed her face up and pinched the end of her nose to keep the smile off her face. 'There's no one in this street ever had a Silver Cross pram, so they'd be coming from miles around to gawp at it. Apart from the fact that they're far too dear for anyone to buy, they're also too ruddy big! She'd never be able to get it through the living-room door and then through the front door – there's no room for manoeuvre. So she'd have to come in and out the back way all the time.'

John looked sheepish. 'I can see now that a Silver Cross wasn't a good idea, but I still think Mary should have a new pram. It's my present to her and I'd feel terrible giving her an old second-hand one.'

'Then yer'll have to go on feeling terrible because that's

what she's getting.' Dot's face was determined. 'Everyone in the street knows the state her house is in – they'd think she'd gone stark staring mad if they saw a new pram outside her door.'

'Yeah,' Betty nodded, 'it would be one thing laughing at the other. Like wearing a fur coat and having no knickers on. So I'm afraid I'm going to have to go against yer, John, because I think me mate is right.'

'It's not only me,' Dot said heatedly, 'it's Mary as well! I mean, how would she explain it away to the queer feller? As it is, he'll be wondering where she got the money from for any sort of pram. So to keep the peace, she's going to say it belonged to one of her brothers. Otherwise, she reckons, if he knew John had bought it he wouldn't think twice about taking a pick-axe to it.'

'It must be a barrel of laughs being married to a bloke like that, mustn't it? Never a dull moment, anyway.' Betty fingered the dimples in her elbow. 'The Silver Cross pram wasn't a bad idea, though, John. I mean, Mary could have sold tickets and made a few bob. A halfpenny for a peep and a penny for a little wheel.'

'Don't you be making yerself comfortable, sunshine, because I'm just going to get me basket and then we're off.' Dot put a hand on the damp stain on her neighbour's dress. 'You don't care how yer go out, do yer? Where's yer pride?'

'Can't afford to have none, girl. But if ye're ashamed of me, I can always stay in and keep John company.'

'Not on your life, yer can't. Besides, John is coming with us. He's paying for the pram so it's only right he should have some say in choosing it.'

John's face lit up. 'Do you mean that you're actually going to let me walk down the street with you? In full view of all the neighbours?'

Dot gave a throaty chuckle. 'No, I'm going to let yer walk six steps behind me, with Betty. That should confuse the nosy-parkers; they'll think yer've got two fancy women on the go.'

Smiling broadly, Betty pushed herself up. 'Suits me, girl. In fact, I'll even link him to make it look authentic.' She tucked her arm through John's, her eyes full of devilment. 'I always fancied being called a scarlet woman.'

John pleaded with Dot. 'Rescue me, please?'

'Just keep yer eyes straight ahead and let everything she says go in one ear and out the other.' Dot picked up her wicker basket and placed it in the crook of her arm. She was following them out when she heard Betty say, 'D'yer know before, when I said all that about fur coat and no knickers? Well, how do they know that everyone wearing a fur coat hasn't got no knickers on? I mean, they haven't got no dirty bugger going around lifting women's clothes up, have they?'

John grinned down at her. 'Do you know what I think? I think that if I said they *did* have a dirty bugger going around lifting women's clothes up, you would go out and buy yourself a fur coat.'

Dot giggled silently. If John was in her mate's company for long he'd be swearing like a trooper. 'What did I tell yer, John?' she called. 'Keep yer eyes straight ahead and yer ears closed. Otherwise she'll be corrupting yer.'

Hanging on to John's arm like grim death, Betty gave a beaming smile to a passing neighbour whose eyes were popping out of her head. 'Good afternoon, Mrs Munro. And what a beautiful day it is, don't you think?' The neighbour, weighed down with bags of shopping, fled without answering, causing the big woman to turn and wink at Dot. 'Well, that should give me reputation a kick up the backside. There'll be plenty of curtains twitching when we come back.'

'I should think there will be,' said John, 'especially as you'll be pushing a pram.'

'Don't you be encouraging her,' Dot said, prodding him in the back. 'She's bad enough without you egging her on.'

'Ay, girl, don't you be punching my escort. And don't be such a long string of misery, either! If yer don't behave yerself, me and John won't bring yer out with us next time.'

What am I going to do with her? Dot thought, walking a short distance behind. She'll never change, that's a dead cert. But do I really want her to change? The answer came quickly. No, she wouldn't want her friend any different. She was generous, always on hand when you needed help, and never failed to cheer you up when you were down. You couldn't ask for more from a friend than that.

The three of them stood at the junction of Stanley Road and Linacre Lane, hot and tired. They'd been in three second-hand shops and still hadn't come across a pram worth buying. The ones they'd seen had really only been fit for the scrapheap. The hoods were torn, the insides dirty and stained, the body paintwork peeling and the wheel-spokes broken. 'You look tired, Dot, so let's call it a day.' John was feeling fed-up himself. He thought of Trudy and couldn't imagine putting her in any of the dirty carriages they'd seen. 'I'll take a couple of hours off work one day and have a scout around.'

Dot sighed. 'I'd love to go home because me feet are killing me, but Mary needs a pram before next Saturday. Although God alone knows where we're going to get one from.'

'There's another shop in Marsh Lane,' Betty said. 'It's only two stops on the tram so we may as well try there while we're at it. And next to it is a sweetshop that has cards in the window that people pay to put in if they've got anything to sell. I've seen prams advertised in there so we might just be lucky.'

Tired and weary, the three stepped off the tram and followed Betty across the busy main road. They stopped outside a second-hand shop where the goods on display seemed of a better quality than the other shops they'd visited. 'You two look in here while I have a gander in the window next door.' Betty walked away, saying over her shoulder, 'If yer see anything worth having, give us a shout.'

John stood on the pavement with the basket and shopping bags at his feet. 'You go in, Dot, I'll stay here. It's no good carting this lot in there unless you see something worthwhile.'

But before Dot had time to walk through the shop door, Betty was calling and beckoning them over. She pointed to a small glass-fronted display case in which there were cards and bits of paper stuck on with drawing pins, all advertising various items for sale. 'See the white card halfway down? It says, *A small pram in excellent condition. Only ten months old. Bargain. £3.*' Reading the words aloud cheered Betty up no end and her round chubby face was beaming as she said, 'Doesn't that sound just the job?'

315

'It sounds ideal,' Dot said, 'but there's no address.'

'Yer have to ask inside for the address, but it can't be far away. Only local people put adverts in here because only those living around here would read them.'

'I'll keep me fingers crossed,' Dot said, 'but with our luck it'll be sold by now.'

'Oh, my God! Go on, girl, put the bleedin' mockers on it!' Betty rolled her eyes at John. 'While I go in for the address, will you tell her a dirty joke and see if yer can bring a smile to her face?'

'I don't know any dirty jokes, Mrs Mason.'

'My God, ye're a fine pair you are. D'yer know what? If you were her lodger, and I'm not saying yer are, mind, but if yer were yer'd get on like a ruddy house on fire.' Betty shook her head in mock disgust as she transferred her basket from one arm to the other. 'If yer don't know any dirty jokes, tell her a clean one but throw in plenty of dirty words.' With that she squared her shoulders and pushed the shop door open.

Dot and John looked at each other and burst out laughing. 'She didn't give me a chance to say I didn't know any dirty words,' John said. 'I know them, of course, because I work in a factory and would have to be deaf not to hear them. But I would never use them in front of a woman, especially you.'

'I'd crack yer one if yer did.' Dot was still chuckling. 'What would yer do with that friend of mine? She shames me to death sometimes, but I love the bones of her.'

Betty came out of the shop waving a piece of paper triumphantly. 'Here yer are, girl, not five minutes' walk away. And if this doesn't put a smile on yer bleedin' face then there's something wrong with yer and yer should go and see yer doctor.' Her bosom thrust out and her eyes shining with excitement, she told them, 'The card was only put in a couple of hours ago and the man behind the counter said it would be a miracle if it had been sold so quick.'

'Ye're a little love, that's what yer are.' Dot gave her friend a hug. 'Now, what's the name of the road?'

'Hornby Road, off Strand Road.' Betty put the piece of paper in her pocket. 'They're big houses down there, girl – some of them have six bedrooms.' She did a little jig. 'Aren't

I clever for bringing yer down here?'

'You certainly are, sunshine. I wouldn't have thought of it.' Dot linked her arm and they set off, John walking by Dot's side and carrying the bags. 'If we're lucky and we get the pram, I'll buy yer a nice cream slice to have with a cup of tea when we get home. Now, what d'yer say to that, eh?'

'What I say to that, girl, is that yer can sod off! This is worth a Victoria sponge sandwich at least.' Betty huffed and puffed as she tried to keep up with their pace. 'A cream slice me backside. I could devour one of them in one bite and wouldn't even know I'd had it.'

They stood outside the gate of the house in Hornby Road and their hopes were raised when they saw the neatly-kept garden, the white net curtains hanging behind the shining windows and the polished woodwork. 'I'll stay here,' John said. 'We can't all go in.'

'Of course we can!' Betty grinned. 'They'll think the pram is for you two, 'cos yer look like a married couple expecting a happy event.'

John roared with laughter as Dot went the colour of beetroot. 'I'd be more than prepared to go along with that, Betty, but I don't think D.D. appreciates your suggestion.'

'I'll wring your neck for you, Betty Mason,' Dot hissed. 'If you say that to whoever opens the door, so help me I'll walk away.'

'God, ye're a misery-guts, you are.' Betty had to bite hard on the inside of her cheek to stop the laughter. 'All right, I'll be the expectant mother if it makes yer feel better. They won't know that I always look ten months' pregnant.'

John stayed by the gate while the two women walked up the path and knocked on the door. It was opened by an attractive woman who looked to be in her late twenties. Her hair was nicely set, her face expertly made-up and her clothes were obviously expensive. What was also very obvious, was the fact she was very heavily pregnant. She looked down at the two surprised faces and smiled. 'Can I help you?'

'We've come about the advert you put in the sweetshop,' Dot said, thinking there must be some mistake. Why would a woman expecting a baby sell a pram?

'Ah, yes,' the door was opened wider, 'come in, please.'

Betty gazed at the beautifully decorated walls and then at the deep red carpet that was fitted from skirting board to skirting board, covering every inch of the large hall. She'd never seen anything like it in her life and she didn't think John should miss it. She waved her hand to where he was standing. 'Can my, er, can he come in, too?'

'Yes, of course he can. It's only natural the father would like to see it.'

'I'll go and give him a hand with the bags.' Betty fled before her face gave her away, leaving Dot looking everywhere but at the woman. 'Come on, John, but for heaven's sake keep yer trap shut or yer'll make a liar out of me.' She picked one of the bags up from the ground and smiled at him with mischief in her eyes. 'Just look at me with love in yer eyes and call me sweetheart.' She walked a few steps, then turned. 'Oh, by the way, we're hoping for a boy.'

John followed her up the path in a trance. What on earth was she up to? Surely she hadn't told the woman they were man and wife? He enjoyed a joke as well as the next man, but that would be going beyond a joke.

The woman welcomed him with a smile. 'You can leave the bags here, Mr . . .?'

'Kershaw – John Kershaw.'

'I'm Joyce Sinclair. If you and your wife and friend will follow me, the pram is in the front parlour.' As she led the way, Joyce Sinclair was thinking of the old adage that says opposites attract. It was certainly true in the case of this couple; they didn't seem at all suited. 'This is the pram I advertised.'

Three faces lit up at the sight of the small, navy-blue carriage. The chrome was gleaming, the bodywork didn't have a scratch or a mark on it, the hood and apron were perfect and the inside looked as though it had never been used. It seemed almost too good to be true. 'It's just what we've been looking for,' Dot said, before catching Mrs Sinclair eyeing her with a strange look on her face. 'Isn't it just what you want, Betty?'

'It's better than I expected to get, girl.' Then Betty got them out of an awkward situation with her usual bluntness.

'If yer don't mind me asking, Mrs Sinclair, why are yer selling it when yer'll soon be needing one yerself?'

Dot gasped. 'Betty, don't be so personal!'

'That's all right, it's a perfectly reasonable question.' Joyce showed a set of strong white teeth when she smiled. 'You see, I've got a ten-month-old baby who will only be twelve months when the new addition arrives. So my husband and I decided to go in for a bigger pram, one that will hold both children.'

'Ye're going to have yer hands full, girl,' Betty said, 'I had two . . .' Her words petered out when John touched her arm. 'What's up?' she asked.

'I think it's time we made our way home, sweetheart.' He slipped his hand in his trouser pocket and brought out his wallet. He took out three one-pound notes and offered them to Joyce. 'We'll take the pram if we may, Mrs Sinclair?'

She took the money and thanked him. 'Are you taking it now?'

'Yes, we'll take it with us. It will save me carrying all these bags – they can go inside.'

'Ah, ay, I thought yer could push me home in the pram,' Betty said, pulling a baby face. 'Me feet are dropping off.'

'I'm sure they'll last out until we get home, sweetheart.' John was already wheeling the pram towards the door. 'Thank you, Mrs Sinclair, we're very grateful to you.'

'You're welcome.' Joyce watched as they walked down the path and turned out of the gate and out of sight. Closing the door, she murmured, 'What an odd couple. I would never in a month of Sundays have taken them for man and wife. Still, it takes all sorts to make a world and it wouldn't do for us all to like the same thing.'

The trio waited until they were at the corner of Hornby Road before stopping to give vent to their feelings. Dot doubled up with laughter. 'John, in the last half-hour yer have committed bigamy with my mate here. Oh, if yer could have seen yer face,' she cried, 'it was a picture.'

'No, he wasn't very loving, was he, girl?' Betty was really enjoying herself. Her tummy was shaking, her bosom bouncing and her face creased with laughter. 'Did yer notice when he called me "sweetheart" how he gritted his teeth? I bet that woman thinks we'd had a lover's tiff 'cos we were barely on speaking terms.'

John, who had insisted on wheeling the pram, was still trying to make up his mind whether he thought the whole thing funny or not. In the end, his sense of humour won the day. 'If you'd given me some warning I would have been prepared and done the job properly. A hug, perhaps, and even a few kisses.' He chuckled. 'That would have turned the tables on you, Mrs Mason, if I'd given you a kiss. You'd have run a mile.'

'Would I hell! I'd have been the dutiful wife and puckered me lips for yer. I'd even have thrown in a "darling" or two, just for good measure.'

'Anyway, joking aside, we've done very well,' Dot said. 'It's a beautiful pram, well worth the money.'

John nodded. 'Yes, I'm delighted with it. And I think Mary will be pleased.'

'She'll be over the moon,' Betty said. 'It looks brand-new. We weren't half lucky, seeing that advert. And, ay, what about the house? There wasn't an inch of floor that wasn't carpeted, did yer notice? They're not short of a penny there, that's for sure. The wallpaper, the curtains and the furniture were all good quality, all expensive stuff. It makes yer wish, doesn't it, girl?'

Dot shook her head. 'It was a lovely house, and the woman was nice, but I'm quite happy with what I've got, sunshine. As long as I've enough money to scrape by on, and me two lovely children, I'm perfectly satisfied.'

Betty grinned. 'And yer've got yer lodger, yer mustn't forget him. He's at your place so often yer can count him as one of the family. Mind you, ye're not greedy with him, I'll say that for yer. After all, yer did let me borrow him to be me husband, back there, which goes to show that ye're very generous with him.'

'Excuse me, ladies, but I wish you wouldn't talk about me as though I'm not here,' John said. 'I am capable of thinking and speaking for myself.'

'Well, start speaking then, and tell her ye're not me ruddy lodger!'

'Oh, I don't mind Betty thinking I'm your lodger. In fact, I quite like it.'

'You might not mind, but I ruddy-well do!' Dot was too footsore and weary to argue further. 'Let's get going, we've wasted enough time. Our Colin will wonder where I've got to and our Katy will be in from work before I've had time to make the tea.'

'You and Betty get the tram home,' John said, seeing the tiredness in Dot's eyes. 'I'll wheel the pram to the O'Connors'.'

Both women looked at him as though he'd gone mad. Men didn't wheel prams, it wasn't the done thing. 'I'm not letting yer do that, everyone will laugh at yer.' Dot pushed him aside and took hold of the handlebar. 'If we cut up one of these streets it'll take us to Hawthorne Road and we'll be home quicker than going the way we came.'

'I'll agree on one condition,' John said. 'That you let me buy fish and chips for the tea, save you standing on your feet cooking something.'

Dot studied his face for a few seconds, then sighed. 'Any other time I'd tell yer to get lost, but right now all I want to do is put me feet up. The thought of standing in the kitchen peeling spuds doesn't appeal to me at all, so I'll take yer up on yer offer and thank yer kindly.'

'Ay, my feet are tired, too!' Betty said. 'Am I invited for fish and chips?'

'You certainly are not! You've got a family to see to, so it's straight home for you.' Dot began to push the pram with Betty holding on to the side. 'When we get to Monfa Road we'll use the entry and go in the O'Connors' back door. I don't want to bump into Tom Campbell.'

'Oh, it's beautiful.' The pram was standing in the living room and Mary had come downstairs to see it. 'I never expected anything as nice as this. It looks brand-new.'

'We got a bargain, girl, it was only—' Betty yelped when Dot gave her a sharp dig in the ribs. 'What was that for?'

'For not minding yer own business! When yer give anyone a present, yer don't tell them how much it was! Honest, ye're as bad as our Colin, yer can't keep a thing to yerself.'

321

Betty, looking suitably contrite, shrugged her shoulders at John. 'Me and my big mouth, it'll get me hung one of these days. I'm sorry about that, John, I wasn't thinking.' A grin came to her face. 'That's my trouble, yer know, me head and me mouth don't work together. Me mouth gets in before me head has a chance to think.'

'You're excused, Betty, on the grounds that we would never have got the pram without you,' John told her. 'Credit where it's due.'

'Credit to all of you,' Mary said, lowering the hood to inspect the inside of the carriage more closely. 'Especially you, John, for being so kind. I'm very grateful for me present, it's beautiful.' She turned to the O'Connors. 'Aren't I lucky?'

'You certainly are, me darlin'. It's as nice as any I've seen.'

Paddy stroked his chin. 'I'm happy to say it passes inspection, so I am. Only the best is good enough for Trudy and sure, isn't this the best? It's a proud man I'll be to wheel her to the park on a Sunday afternoon if I'm given permission.'

'And I'll be walking beside you,' John said, determined not to be left out. 'She has two uncles, don't forget.'

'I'm afraid you two are in for a big disappointment, because there's a long list,' Dot laughed. 'There's me and me mate here, and our Katy and Billy have been talking about taking the baby for a walk. So the park is going to be quite crowded.'

'Excuse me!' Mary said, as she ran her hands along the handlebar, delighted beyond words with her present. She wanted the best for her daughter, but because of who she was married to, she never expected to be able to give it to her. Now, through these wonderful friends, at least her child was starting life with the best. 'Don't I get a look in? After all, she is my baby.'

'We'll let yer come to the park with us, girl,' Betty said magnanimously. 'You can carry the bottle of home-made lemonade.' She gave Dot a dig. 'Ay, doesn't it take yer back? I remember me mam giving me a halfpenny for lemonade powder and a bottle of water, and strict instructions not to come back until tea-time.'

Dot grinned. 'Yer must have been as big a nuisance then as

yer are now and yer mam wanted yer out from under her feet.'

'That's charming, that is. And you me best mate.'

'Yer can be me best mate again when me feet are not so tired. Right now I'm going home to stretch out on the couch while the big feller here sees to the tea.' Dot gave Mary a hug and a kiss. 'Yer look marvellous, sunshine, the picture of health. I'll slip in tomorrow and sit with yer for an hour. I've got something funny to tell yer,' she looked across at Maggie and Paddy, 'and you two. Yer'll roar yer heads off when I tell yer what this mate of mine got up to this afternoon.'

Her nostrils flared and her arms folded across her tummy, Betty gave a good imitation of being angry. 'John, are yer going to stand there and let her insult yer wife?'

John sat on the arm of the couch. 'No, I'll sit down and let her insult you.'

Sobbing loudly, Betty cried, 'Me husband and me best mate have turned against me. Oh, woe is me.'

Paddy, his arm across his wife's shoulders, grinned. 'What has she been up to now? Is it fit for our ears?'

'Oh yes, it's hilarious,' Dot chuckled. 'But I'm not telling yer now because I'm too tired to do justice to the story. Yer know I like to do the actions as well, and I haven't got the energy. So we'll be on our way and leave you good people in peace.'

Maggie put a hand on her arm. 'Before yer go, me darlin', we've got something to tell yer. We had a visitor this afternoon – at least, not a visitor as such, because yer usually invite a visitor into your home and this one was left on the doorstep. It was Mary's husband, so it was.'

Dot's mouth gaped. 'Go 'way! What did he have to say?'

'Sure, wasn't it a stroke of luck that Paddy was home, and he answered the door? I'd have died on the spot if it had been me and I found him standing on me doorstep. But Paddy will tell yer himself what the man had to say.'

All eyes turned to the big Irishman. 'It wasn't a long conversation, I have to tell yer, because he got short shrift from me. He was arrogant at first, demanding that his wife get back home right that minute. I told him his wife would go

323

back home when she was fit and well, and not a day before.' When Paddy looked from Dot to John, there was a message in his eyes telling them not to question him further. 'That was it, really – short and sweet. Except that he went away with a flea in his ear.'

'There was more than that, me darlin',' Maggie said, 'Sure—'

Paddy interrupted his wife. 'I'm not like Betty, sweetheart, I can't think things up out of the top of me head, just to make them interesting. Mary will go home when she's good and ready, so she will, and her husband understands that now.'

Maggie closed her mouth. How stupid she'd been not to remember that Mary had only been given the brief version of the confrontation. Sure, wasn't her tongue as bad as Betty's for saying the wrong thing? 'Mary, it's back to bed with you, me darlin', it's time for Trudy's feed. I'll come up with yer while Paddy sees our friends out.'

'Yes, OK,' Mary smiled. 'She'll be wondering where I've got to.' She gave one last look at the pram then at the three people who had wheeled it up the yard half an hour before. 'I can't find the right words to tell you how I feel, how grateful I am for what yer've done for me, and for Trudy. And as for Maggie and Paddy, they've been wonderful, kindness itself. When I lie in bed thinking about having to go back to that shack next door, and to the man I was daft enough to marry, I worry about what's going to happen to me and the baby. Then I push the bad thoughts from me head and think of all the good friends I've got. You, all of you, have helped me realise that life is worth living after all.'

There was complete silence. Mary's words had filled them all with emotion. Then Maggie cleared her throat and took her arm. 'Before yer have us all in tears, me darlin', I'm taking you back to bed. But I think I speak for everyone when I say we care deeply for yer, that we do. And we'll always be there when yer need us.'

Mary allowed herself to be led away, leaving Dot and Betty with tears streaming down their faces and John and Paddy wishing that men weren't supposed to be too strong to cry.

John took a hankie from his pocket and passed it to Dot.

'Wipe your eyes and blow your nose. The hankie is clean.'

'I'll never moan again about little things that don't really matter.' Dot sniffed up. 'And I'll tell yer something else – if Tom Campbell ever hurts her or that tiny baby, I won't wait for Betty to thump him one, I'll do it meself.'

'I didn't want to say anything in front of Mary because I told her the same as I told you about her husband. But he came here in a terrible temper, so he did.' Paddy shook his head at the memory. 'Demanding, he was, that she get home right away or it would be the worse for her. I told him she'd be confined to bed for another week, and the wicked man just sneered. The words he used were, "She's had the brat, then, has she?" Only the good Lord knows how I kept me hands off him. Sure, I may be wrong, but I'd say the man isn't right in the head. He certainly isn't normal, and that's the truth of it. He didn't show any interest in the child, didn't even ask if it was a boy or a girl.'

John was banging a clenched fist into the palm of his other hand. 'Mary's a fool if she goes back to him. He'll beat her up on her first day home, just for the sheer hell of it.'

Dot picked up her basket and turned towards the door. 'I'll have to go. I can't bear to listen to any more – it's breaking my heart. All I know is, I won't have a minute's peace when that man is within striking distance of the baby. I hope he rots in hell.' She jerked her head at her friend. 'Come on, Betty, let's go home.'

Betty sighed. 'All right, girl, I'm coming.'

'I'll be on my way as well, Paddy, but I'll see you tomorrow.' John followed the women into the street. 'I'll go straight to the chip shop, Dot – you get in and put your feet up. I'll see to the tea when I get back.' He touched her arm as she was putting the key in the lock. 'And don't cry, please don't cry.'

Betty was walking with her head bent when John caught up with her. 'It's only a few steps, I know, but I can't let my wife walk home on her own, can I?'

Chapter Twenty

Colin came bounding into the room, his eyes bright with hope. 'Mam, will you and Mr Kershaw take me to the first-house pictures tonight? *Mutiny on the Bounty* is on, with Charles Laughton and Clark Gable. Danny's going with his mam and dad – he said his brother went to see it last night and it's dead exciting.'

'I'm sorry, sunshine, but I won't be able to afford it. I promised our Katy faithfully that I'd get that new dress I promised her weeks ago. And I need one meself.' Dot fingered the jumper her daughter had bought her for Christmas which was now looking so washed-out even the rag man would turn his nose up at it. 'The sun's cracking the flags and this is all I've got to me name to go out in. Perhaps I can take yer next week – how about that?'

'Ah, go on, Mam,' the boy pleaded. 'I could pay for meself out of me pocket money when yer give it to me.'

Dot could feel herself weakening and turned away. 'Go out and play with Danny while I make me shopping list and work me money out. If I can wangle it, I'll take yer.'

'And Mr Kershaw?'

'Ay, come off it! I'm not asking him, and you're not to, either. It always ends up with him paying, and it's not fair – makes me feel like a scrounger.' Dot sat at the table with a piece of paper and a stub of pencil. Life was a bit easier since Katy started work but they weren't well off by a long chalk; she still had to count the pennies. But she had sympathy for her son. With having no dad, he missed out on a lot of treats his mates got. 'I'll see what I can do, son, and I'll let yer know when I've sorted meself out.'

Colin had the sense not to push it. He had detected the

327

note of softness enter her voice and thought he was in with a good chance. So when he rejoined his friend he said, 'I'm probably going to the Broadway meself tonight, Danny, so I'll see yer there.' He knelt down in the gutter, his multi-coloured ollie ready to play. 'Ay, what d'yer think ye're doing? It's my turn!' The good-natured argument was nothing new to the two lads. That's what a game of ollies was all about, trying to cheat on your opponent without him noticing. Mind you, if you gave a good flick and knocked his ollie away, you got accused of cheating anyway.

'That's two games I've won,' Colin said, with the air of a victor, 'so by rights, you owe me an ollie.'

'You can go and jump in a lake, mate,' Danny told him, with the air of a bad loser. 'Yer only won both games because yer cheated.'

'I never did!' Colin saw a familiar figure walking up the street and quickly changed his tune. 'OK, we'll call it quits, eh? The two games were a draw.'

'I bet I win the next one.' Danny was being very optimistic because everyone knew Colin Baker was the best player in the street. 'I'll go first, this time.'

But Colin was already on his feet. 'No, I've got to go now, Danny, but I might see yer later in the pictures. Look out for us.' With that the boy crossed the cobbled street and ran towards the man who, next to his mam, Katy and his grandma, was his very favourite person. 'Hello, Mr Kershaw.' He fell into step beside the big man and lost no time in putting his plan into action. 'What d' yer think, Mr Kershaw, me mam said she might take me to the Broadway tonight, to see *Mutiny on the Bounty*.'

The piece of news had John slowing his pace. This sounded like a situation where he would probably need the boy's help. 'Did your mother mention me coming with you?'

'No, she just said if she had enough money she'd take me. She must have forgot about yer, Mr Kershaw, 'cos she wouldn't stop yer from coming with us, would she?'

'I find your mother a complex person, Colin. Very lovely and adorable, but complex. So I think you and I are going to have to play our cards right. What say I go in first, then after a few minutes you come in and ask if she's taking you to the pictures.' John looked down on the animated face, little knowing that the boy was way ahead of him. 'I'm not teaching you to be deceitful to your mother, because that would be wrong. But we're doing it in a good cause, helping two nice people,' he grinned, 'your mother and me. She doesn't get out very often, in fact hardly ever, so she deserves a treat. And for myself, I've heard such a lot about *Mutiny on the Bounty*, I'd really like to see it.'

And so it was that John went in first, to find Dot with her basket on her arm and a shopping list in her hand. 'You certainly pick a fine time to call,' she said. 'I'm just on me way out to the shops. I'm late getting out because I called into the O'Connors' when I was passing, to see what was happening with Mary.'

John sat down, ignoring the fact that she was ready to walk out of the door. He'd keep her there until Colin came in, even if he had to do a flying tackle at her legs. 'Oh, and what is happening with Mary? Has she gone home?'

Dot rested her hand on the table but remained standing. 'The O'Connors have talked her out of leaving today; she's going on Monday instead. The queer feller won't be there, so she'll have time to settle herself in without having him yelling and bawling his filthy language down her ears.' She fitted the basket into the crook of her arm, saying, 'I'll have to scoot, John, so why don't yer go and sit with Mary for an hour?'

Colin came bouncing in on cue, his timing perfect. Another minute and Dot would have been on her way down the street. 'Hello, Mr Kershaw, I saw yer passing when I was playing with Danny. Have yer heard, me mam might take me to the pictures tonight? That's what yer said, isn't it, Mam?'

'I'm sorry, son, but it's too much of a rush. By the time I get back from the shops, our Katy will be home and ready for her meal. After working all day she needs some food inside her.'

'Can I make a suggestion?' John asked. 'Why don't we *all* go to the pictures – we three and Katy and Billy? We haven't been for weeks, Dot, and I've heard it's a very good film.'

'Ooh, yeah, Mam, that would be the gear!' Colin's eyes lit up. 'Go on, say we can.'

John could see Dot was between the devil and the deep blue sea. The idea didn't appeal to her but she didn't want to disappoint her son. So John pressed while the iron was hot. 'You could buy a meat pie while you're at the shops – that would keep Katy going for a couple of hours. We'd be home about half-eight.'

Dot's eyes rolled from one to the other. 'You two have got me boxed in, haven't yer? If I refuse I'll be the worst misery-guts in the world.'

'I'll come to the shops with yer, Mam, and carry yer bags. Yer'll be round the shops in no time with me to help yer.'

John tried not to let his pleasure show. This courting business wasn't going at all to his liking. Dot treated him like a brother she was fond of, and she was at ease in his company. But he didn't want to be treated like a brother. He wanted her to look at him and see him as a man who had very strong feelings for her. He didn't mind the waiting, if only she would give some sign that perhaps in time she would return his feelings. 'I'll call into the sweetshop and see if Molly will let Katy finish a quarter of an hour early,' he said now. 'I'm sure she won't mind. And I'll give Billy a knock.'

'Yer've got it all worked out, haven't yer? The pair of yer have stitched me up good and proper. And I know there's no point in me wasting me breath arguing with yer, 'cos I don't stand a chance, not when there's two against one. But if it's all the same with you, John, I'd like to alter yer routine a little.' Dot's face was the picture of innocence as she bent to put the basket on the floor. 'If you're both so keen on going to the pictures, then yer won't mind doing all the running around, will yer? Our Colin knows which shops I go to, John, so he'll help yer out there. And as yer've got to pass Billy's house and the sweetshop on yer way, it won't be no trouble to stop off and give those little messages, will it?'

John gave a hearty chuckle. 'I might have known you wouldn't give in so easily. What you've done is lull me into a sense of false security, then you've hit hard. But shall I tell you something, D.D.? I'd much rather you got mad and were your usual, delectable self.'

Dot kept the smile off her face when she put her hands

on her hips and let her head drop sideways. 'If this is what yer want, Mr Kershaw, then I'm only too happy to oblige.' She leaned forward and stared into his face. 'Just because you and my son want to go to the flicks, and neither of yer like not getting yer own way, yer think I should run the feet off meself to please yer. Well, yer can just sod off, because the sooner yer both learn that when a woman comes home from the job she gets paid for, it's to start the job she *doesn't* get paid for, the better! And that's looking after a home and family.' She straightened up and nodded her head sharply. 'So now yer know, and yer can put that in yer pipe and smoke it.'

'Beautifully delivered, D.D.' John clapped his hands. 'No one has the knack of putting someone in their place like you do. And even if they did, they wouldn't look as pretty as you while they were doing it.'

'Well, now that's out of the way, I've got a couple of hours to meself this afternoon, something that has never happened before. So I'm going to get the tram into town and take me time buying new dresses for me and me daughter!'

Colin had been listening to all this in silence. Now he said, 'Get a blue one, Mam, 'cos yer don't half suit blue. Don't yer think so, Mr Kershaw?'

'Your mother looks pretty in whatever she wears, Colin. Even a coal sack would look good on her.'

'Even if it was still filled with coal?' Dot asked dryly. 'I wish yer wouldn't keep flattering me, Mr Kershaw, it's embarrassing.'

'There's a difference between flattering and paying a compliment, Mrs Baker. I do not flatter you, I pay you well-deserved compliments.'

Dot threw her hands in the air. 'I give up! There's no talking to you, ye're as stubborn as a ruddy mule. Anyway, I'm off to spend a couple of wonderful hours on me own. You two behave yerselves, d'yer hear? I'll see yer later, ta-ra, now.'

'Where does the sugar go, son?' John asked, looking around the tiny kitchen. 'In one of these cupboards?'

'No, the sugar and tea go in the sideboard cupboard, 'cos

it gets damp out here.' Colin was smiling to himself. Mr Kershaw had called him 'son' again, and it didn't half make him feel good. 'The potatoes and veg go in the pantry under the stairs and the bread goes in that bread bin.'

'Your mother was right when she said it's no joke going around the shops. And how she manages to carry such a heavy load I'll never know.'

'Me mam works hard, Mr Kershaw, always has done. But yer never hear her moaning and she never really gets in a temper. She's the best mam in the whole world.'

'I wonder where she's got to?' For John, there was something missing in the house when Dot wasn't there. 'I thought she'd be back by now. I hope she's found a dress she likes and is on her way home.'

'Have yer ever told me mam that yer like her?'

'No, I haven't, but she must be blind not to see it.' John lowered his head to look into the boy's face. 'And you mustn't tell her, either. When I talk to you, it's man-to-man talk and not to be repeated. Is that understood?'

'I won't tell no one what we talk about, Mr Kershaw. I'm nearly thirteen now, I'm not a kid any more.' Colin frowned. 'I wonder why me mam can't see that yer like her? I can see it, and so can our Katy. And I know me Auntie Betty and Mary can, 'cos I've heard them dropping hints.'

'Everything takes its course, son, so we'll just have to bide our time. Who knows, one day your mother might look at me and say, "I like you, John Kershaw".'

The boy's face creased in a broad smile. 'Yeah, that's what'll happen, I bet.'

John ruffled his hair. 'How about you and me making some sandwiches for when she comes home? It'll save her the trouble and be a nice surprise for her.'

The sandwiches were made and the table set when Dot came in. She took one look and grinned. 'I'll have to get in a paddy more often, won't I? The table looks good, thank you very much. Now I could murder a cup of tea.'

Man and boy stood by the table, reluctant to move. 'Did you manage to find a dress you liked, D.D.?'

Dot held a bag aloft and waved it in their faces. 'Success!

332

One for me and one for our Katy. I feel really pleased with meself.'

'Are yer going to put it on to go to the pictures, Mam?'

'Oh, I don't think so, sunshine. That would look as though I'm showing off.'

'Dot, you're the last person in the world anyone could accuse of showing off.' John couldn't understand why anyone with Dot's looks could be so modest. 'If you were to wear it tomorrow, would you still be showing off?'

'No, 'cos I'd be in me own house then, wouldn't I?'

'That's daft, that is.' Colin moved closer to John. They were going to fight this together, side by side. 'I want yer to wear it tonight, and so does Mr Kershaw.'

John nodded his head solemnly. 'Once again it's two against one, Dorothy, and the majority wins.'

'Yeah, that's right, Mam, it's two to one,' Colin said, looking all grown-up. 'We want yer looking nice to take out, don't we, Mr Kershaw?'

Dot smiled in spite of herself as she saw her son looking up at his hero. She had to admit that John had been good for Colin. The boy was better behaved and more sensible. 'If one of yer will put the kettle on, I'll go upstairs and get changed, just to please yer. And the dress is staying on whether yer like it or not, 'cos I ain't getting changed twice. You asked for it, so ye're stuck with it.'

Colin did a little dance as he followed John into the kitchen. 'We did good there, Mr Kershaw. And me mam must like yer or she'd have told yer to get lost.' His eyes narrowed in thought, his forefinger played with his bottom lip, pulling it forward and then letting it spring back to make a plopping sound. 'D'yer know me friend, Danny? Well, his brother's got his eye on a girl but she's giving him the runaround, and Danny said she's playing hard to get. D'yer think that's what me mam's doing with you? Playing hard to get?'

John roared with laughter as he poured the boiling water into the teapot. It wasn't so much what the boy said that made him laugh, but the fact that it was a schoolboy saying it to him. Here he was, forty years of age, being taught the wiles of women by a twelve-year-old. His mother had made sure he had a good education, and he was grateful to her for that because it meant he would never have to worry about money. But throughout his education there'd never been one lesson in how to deal with women who, to use Colin's words, were playing hard to get.

John put the lid on the teapot, a smile still on his face. 'Tell me, does Danny's brother have a way of dealing with this girl he's got his eye on? The one who's playing hard to get?'

'If he has, it's not working, is it?' Colin's chuckle joined John's laughter. 'Otherwise he wouldn't be getting the runaround, would he?'

'That's the logical assumption, I suppose. So really, there's no point in me going to him for advice, is there?'

'I didn't understand the first part of what yer said, Mr Kershaw, but ye're right about it being no good asking him for advice. Danny's brother is tuppence short of a shilling.'

'What's all the laughter about?' Dot stood framed in the doorway. 'I could hear yer from upstairs. Let me in on the joke.'

'Oh Mam, yer look lovely. The dress doesn't half suit yer. I bet that ye're the prettiest mother in the whole of Liverpool.'

'That's stretching the imagination a bit, sunshine, but thank you for the compliment.' Dot glanced at John. 'Does it meet with your approval, Mr Kershaw?'

The dress was in a pale blue cotton, with a buckled belt and a flared skirt. It had a shirt-like collar with three pearl buttons which Dot had left unfastened, showing off the smooth skin of her neck. 'You look as pretty as a picture, D.D. – a woman any man would be proud to have on his arm and in his heart.'

'Blimey!' Dot was pleased but embarrassed. 'All that for a cheap dress from TJs. I wonder what yer'd have come up with if I'd gone to Henderson's and paid a fortune for one?'

'If you'd paid a hundred pounds for a dress, Dot, it wouldn't look any nicer on you than that one. It's not the cost that makes the dress, it's the person wearing it.'

Colin eyed the big man with admiration. When he was older, he was going to learn to speak like Mr Kershaw. Not just speak nicely like him, but use all those big words he knew that suited every occasion. Then the boy had a brainwave, remembering something his hero had said last week. 'Those are my views entirely.'

The small kitchen nearly burst at the seams with laughter. Dot was bent double and John was holding his head in his hands. And as the boy looked on he wondered why his mam couldn't show she liked Mr Kershaw. Just look at them now, they got on really well together. What she needed was a little push in the right direction. The trouble was, if his mam knew she was being pushed, she'd dig her heels in. So he'd have to be sly so she wouldn't notice. And tonight would be a good chance to start, when they went to the pictures.

'On yer own today, Mrs Williams?' Katy asked. 'It's not often we see you without Mrs Armstrong.'

'I'm not on me own, queen, Dolly's gone next door for a reel of cotton.' Rita Williams turned when the shop bell tinkled. 'Here she is now.' She waited until her friend was standing beside her, then laid a hand on her arm. 'Yer see before yer the only woman I know who can tell one mutton chop from another.'

Molly, serving the other end of the counter, overheard the remark and called, 'Don't say another word until I get there.' She quickly counted her customer's change into her hand.

'There yer go, sweetheart, tuppence-halfpenny change. Don't go mad and spend it all in the one shop.' She waited until the woman reached the door before making her way to stand next to Katy. 'Go on, Rita, what were yer saying?'

Dolly Armstrong gave her friend a dig in the ribs and a dark look. 'She wasn't saying nothing, was yer, Rita?'

'I bloody-well was! You made a holy show of me in the butcher's, now it's my turn.' Hitching her bosom and striking a haughty pose, Rita said, 'She asked the butcher for two mutton chops, and when he was weighing them, soft girl here said, "I don't like the look of that one, will yer change it?" Now can yer imagine it, Molly, there's two chops on the scale, as alike as two peas in a pod, and my friend here takes a dislike to one of them.'

'Perhaps one had more fat on than the other?' Molly

suggested, hoping she was wrong because she could just do with a good laugh.

Rita shook her head while her friend gave her looks to kill. 'Spittin' image of each other, they were. I'd defy anyone to know one from the other. And everyone in the shop was of the same opinion, except for Tilly Mint, here. She insisted she didn't like the look of the flamin' chop and asked Bob to change it. By this time we were all feeling heartily sorry for the poor bleedin' chop – I mean, it had never done no one any harm.'

Katy's eyes were wide and shining. 'What happened? Did Bob change it?'

'Yer should have been there, queen, it was bloody hilarious. Bob was as red as a beetroot and spitting feathers. I thought he was going to have a heart attack right in front of us. And all over a ruddy chop!' Rita's bosom began to bounce. 'Can yer just see the headlines in the *Echo*, queen? BUTCHER KILLED BY MUTTON CHOP.'

The only one who didn't see the joke was Dolly Armstrong. While they were all laughing their heads off, she was thinking of ways to get even with her friend. She'd take her down a peg or two if it killed her.

Rita took a few deep breaths and then continued, 'How Bob kept his patience with her I'll never know. If it had been me I'd have hit her with the ruddy things. Anyway, Bob took the chops off the scale, walked to the window and picked out another one. He laid the three on the counter, moved them around until we were all dizzy, then asked Dolly to pick out the one she didn't like.'

Molly cupped her chin in her hand. Who'd have thought you could get such a laugh out of a mutton chop? Wait until Jim came back from his break and she told him. 'And was she able to pick it out?'

'Oh, wait until yer hear this, Molly, this is the funniest part of the lot.' Rita glanced at Dolly, who was looking down at her feet. At least she would have been looking down at her feet if her bust hadn't been so big and she could have seen them. 'My mate here pointed to the chop in the middle and said, "That's the one. It didn't come from the same sheep as the other two. If this lot weren't so ignorant they'd see that for themselves".'

'Fancy you knowing that, Mrs Armstrong,' Katy said. 'Aren't yer clever?'

'Clever be buggered!' Rita snorted. 'Even though he had a full shop, Bob said he didn't want to rush her, so to take her time and tell him which two she wanted. And when she'd finally made up her mind, he turned the two of them over. On the back of one of them was a bit of paper he'd stuck on. She'd only chosen the one that she'd caused all the fuss about. So in her shopping bag, right this minute, is a chop she'll be giving her feller for his dinner tomorrow, even though she thinks it might poison him.'

'I don't think it'll poison him!' Dolly had eventually come to life. 'I wouldn't give my Arthur anything that would make him ill.'

Rita raised her brows. 'So, you're going to eat it yerself, then?'

Dolly had the grace to blush. 'Well, no, I won't be doing that, I'd be retching with every mouthful. But if I think it's off when I smell it, I won't give it to Arthur – that wouldn't be fair.'

'By the way, did your Arthur ever get his new set of false teeth?' Molly asked. 'I keep meaning to ask yer, then I forget.'

'No, not yet. We've never had the money.'

'Well, if that flamin' chop *is* off, it'll be a ruddy slow death,' Rita sniggered. 'He'll be hours sucking the meat off the bleedin' bone.'

'How come ye're always making fun of my feller?' Dolly asked. Her temper had been simmering slowly, now it boiled over. 'Yer never hear me making fun of yours.'

'It's you what gives me the ammunition to make fun of your feller,' Rita retorted. 'If you didn't open yer mouth, I wouldn't know what he got up to.'

'Well, I'm bloody sure your feller isn't the ruddy saint yer make him out to be. If he was, he'd be wearing a flamin' halo.' Getting into her stride now, and nodding to emphasise the strength of her feelings, Dolly said, 'According to you, he never says a word out of place, never puts a foot wrong and waits on yer hand and foot. He's such a bloody goodie-goodie, he'd get on me bleedin' wick if I had to live with him. Dull as ditch-water, I'd say, wouldn't see a joke if it stopped him in the bleedin' street and asked him the time.'

Molly's and Katy's eyes were wide and their lips pursed as they waited for Rita's retaliation. It should be good when it came because she'd never let Dolly get away with that. But to their amazement Rita's head fell back and she roared with laughter. As she rocked back, she fell against the counter and her arm caught on a jar. If it hadn't been for the speed with which Katy moved, a whole jar of liquorice sticks would have fallen to the ground and smashed to smithereens. The incident sobered Molly up, but only for as long as it took Katy to move the jar to a place of safety on the back shelf.

Rita rubbed the back of her hand across her eyes as her laughter gave way to hiccups. 'Oh, Dolly, Dolly, Dolly! What would I do without me Saturday afternoon laughs? If it makes yer feel better, ye're right about my feller, he is as dull as ditch-water. He never says a word out of place because he seldom opens his mouth, and how can he put a foot wrong when he never gets off his bleedin' backside? And as for waiting on me hand and foot, he can't even wait on his bleedin' self! I won't say he never makes me laugh because he does, but not by telling me funny jokes. Some of the things he gets up to – well, if I didn't laugh I'd end up in the loony bin.'

Dolly didn't know how to take this confession and was suspicious. 'How can he make yer laugh if he doesn't do anything funny? I think this is another one of yer tricks, Rita Williams, and ye're having me on.'

'Yeah, I was thinking the same thing,' Molly said, wishing the two women who were now pushing the shop door open would do the rest of their shopping first and come back when she wasn't so involved. If she didn't hear the outcome of this tale she'd never get a wink of sleep tonight. 'What does he do that makes yer laugh but isn't funny?'

'Have yer got twenty-four hours, Molly? 'Cos that's how long it would take. For instance, last Sunday he was still in bed when I was going to Mass so I left an egg and some bread on a plate and shouted up to him to see to his own breakfast.'

Rita broke off as the memory brought forth more laughter. 'When I got back from church, d'yer know what the silly bugger had done? And his face was so serious when he was telling me, yer'd have thought there'd been a death in the family. He'd made himself a pot of tea and buttered the bread, then sat down to enjoy his breakfast. The trouble was, when he sliced the top off the egg it ran all over his hands and trousers because he hadn't boiled the bleedin' thing.'

The two new customers had been impatient at first, thinking it would do Molly more good to look after her customers than stand gabbing. But they couldn't help but overhear what was being said and they joined in the laughter. 'All men are bloody useless,' one cried. 'Mine can't boil an egg, either!'

'Ay, watch it, Mrs Jackson,' Molly laughed. 'I'll tell your feller what yer said when he comes in for his two ounces and the *Echo*.'

Rita wasn't to be outdone. After all, this was her show and she wasn't having anyone else getting in on the act. 'I bet your feller knows how to light a fire, though? Mine does it all the wrong way around. Puts the coal on first, each piece lovingly laid, with the tongs, mind you, in case he gets his lily-white hands dirty. Then comes the firewood, followed by screwed-up pieces of newspaper. He uses nearly a box of matches to set light to the paper, then gets all upset because the paper doesn't light the wood, and the coal is wondering why it was put in the grate in the first place when it was quite happy in the coal-scuttle. And after half an hour on his knees, willing the fire to light, my dearly beloved gets really upset and takes it as a personal insult.'

Dolly was as happy as could be, listening to someone else's husband getting pulled to pieces for a change. From the sound of things, her Arthur was a gift from God. When she got home she'd give him the best kiss he'd had since the day they got married. 'My husband was in the Scouts,' she boasted. 'He can make a fire by rubbing two twigs together.'

Rita turned away for a second to wipe the smile off her face. Then she faced her friend. 'Don't be taking advantage of me good nature, girl, or I'll clock yer one. My husband is every bit as good as yours, any day, and don't yer dare let me hear yer saying otherwise.'

Katy's laughter rang out. 'That's more like it! You two were getting so lovey-dovey yer had me worried. I thought I was going to have to change your nickname from the "terrible twins" to the "polite pair".'

The two friends looked at each other and pulled faces. Then Rita said, 'I know what we'll do, queen, seeing as we both like the girl and would want to make her happy. I'll give yer a black eye, eh?'

Dolly grinned. 'Yeah, after I've knocked a couple of yer front teeth out.'

'Oh Mam, yer look lovely!' Katy beamed as she closed the shop door behind her. 'Did yer manage to get me a new dress, as well?'

'I did, sunshine, and it's just as nice as this one. Yer don't think I'd get one for meself and leave you out, do yer?'

'No, I know yer wouldn't do that, Mam.' Katy gave her a big hug before smiling up at John. 'She looks great, doesn't she, Mr Kershaw?'

His eyes were smiling when he said, 'I've been told off half a dozen times for paying your mother compliments, Katy, so I'd better keep silent.'

'Well, I haven't been told off,' Billy said, 'so I'll say yer look nice, Mrs Baker. You and Katy look more like sisters.'

'Now, that *is* a compliment,' Dot laughed. 'Give this boy the best seat in the cinema for his chivalry.'

They began walking, Katy and Billy in front, Colin walking between his mother and John. 'I hope yer tell me I look nice in my new dress, Billy Harlow.' Katy looked sideways at him, a glint of mischief in her eyes. 'If yer know what's good for yer, yer'll tell me I look nice even if I look a sight.'

'Yer look nice in yer new dress, Katy.'

'Not now, soft lad, wait until yer've seen it.'

'Yer always look nice to me, a new dress won't make no difference.'

Colin pulled on his mother's dress. 'Ay, Mam, just listen to those two soppy beggars in front. Make yer sick, wouldn't it?'

'I'll remind yer of that in a couple of years, sunshine, when

340

yer find yerself a girlfriend. Yer'll have changed yer tune by then.'

I wish you'd change your tune about Mr Kershaw, the boy thought. He'd give anything for you to be his girlfriend if you'd only give him the chance. And if you did become his girlfriend, then you'd get married and he'd live with us all the time.

Colin's mind was still on the subject when they reached the picture house and he decided to give Mr Kershaw a helping hand. So when the usherette showed them to their seats he watched Billy go in first, followed by Katy, then he quickly ducked around his mother and was halfway along the row before she realised what was happening. It was too late to do anything about it then, without causing a fuss. So it was that John found himself sitting next to Dot and sharing an arm-rest with her.

'I'd like to call in and see Mary on our way home.'

'Hang on a minute, John, while I give this pic to Katy. She must be starving.' Dot leaned across her son and passed a white bag over. 'Here yer are, sunshine, it'll keep the hunger off till we get home.' Then she leaned back in her seat. 'What were yer saying about Mary?'

'I called in to see Tom Campbell before going to the shops. When you said Mary wasn't going home until Monday, I thought it best to get some money off him. He didn't want to part with any, but I got fifteen shillings off him. I wanted more, but he said that's all he ever gives her.'

'He wasn't lying, that's all she gets. It was good of yer to do that, John, because I know Mary's been worried sick.'

'How on earth does she manage on fifteen shillings a week? That wouldn't go anywhere near paying for rent, gas, coal, food and clothing. And now she's got a baby they'll never manage. They'll starve to death.'

'You've seen how she lives. She never buys clothes, is careful about using gas, never lights a fire unless the weather's really cold, and then she only lights it just before he comes in. She feeds him, but doesn't eat enough herself to keep a sparrow alive.' The lights began to dim and Dot put a finger to her lips. 'We'll talk later.' She felt his arm pressing against hers on the arm-rest and quickly decided it wasn't big enough for both of them, so she folded her hands on her lap.

The big picture was gripping. Charles Laughton's acting was magnificent. But the character he played, Captain Bligh, was hard and cruel. If a member of the crew dared to displease him he would have him flogged to within an inch of his life. And everytime the whip tore at the unfortunate seaman's bare back, Dot would close her eyes and Colin would sit on the edge of his seat, his eyes like saucers. To add to the excitement, the ship was rolling in heavy seas, storms raging and high waves coming over the side and sweeping men out to sea. But the captain had no sympathy for his crew, and anyone leaving their posts would be tied to the mast and left there until they died.

But no film could have a baddie without a goodie, and he came in the form of Clark Gable playing the part of Fletcher Christian. He was handsome, tough, and on the side of the crew. But even the film hero was no match for the wicked captain. And when the crew began to mutiny, the violence was all too much for Dot. She closed her eyes and was biting on her nails until John pulled her hand away and held it in his. And to his delight she let it stay there without a murmur.

Colin heard a low cry from his sister and took his eyes off the screen to glance to his right. There was Katy, eyes screwed up and gripping Billy's arm. That's just like a girl, the boy thought, they can't take any excitement. He turned to tell his mother that her daughter was a daft article, but the words never left his mouth. A grin came to his face and his heart soared when he saw Mr Kershaw was holding his mother's hand and getting away with it. He might get a thick ear off her later, when she came to her senses, but the look on the big man's face told Colin he would face the wrath of Captain Bligh just to savour these few moments of bliss.

Before getting wrapped up in the film again, Colin wondered if there were any other frightening films he could ask his mam to take him to. And Mr Kershaw, of course, because there'd be no point without him there, would there? I mean, if he wasn't there to hold his mother's hand they might as well go and see a Shirley Temple picture.

Chapter Twenty-One

They came out of the darkness of the Broadway picture house into dazzling sunlight, and grouped on the pavement until their eyes adjusted to the brightness. 'What a beautiful evening it is, D.D.'

Dot nodded in agreement but kept her eyes averted. She felt so embarrassed and ashamed, she didn't know where to put herself. Fancy a woman of thirty-seven years of age acting like a seventeen-year-old, letting a man hold her hand in the darkness of a cinema. Her Ted used to do it when they were courting, but she was a mere slip of a girl then. John must think she was a fine one, throwing herself at him like that.

'Wow! Ay, Mam, look at all these people waiting to get into the second house.' Colin gestured towards the queue of people which was so long it stretched past the picture house and disappeared down a side street. 'Some hopes they've got – they'll never all get in there, not in a million years.'

'Yer'd be surprised, sunshine, there's an awful lot of seats in there. I'd say they're all in with a good chance.'

'I don't half wish I was going in again; it was the best picture I've ever seen. It knocked Tom Mix and all the cowboys and Indians into a cocked hat.' Colin was skipping along beside his mother reliving the most exciting moments. 'I hated that Captain Bligh, he was horrible. He deserved to be put in that little boat after what he'd done. I wish the boat had toppled over in the storm and he got eaten by sharks.'

'You're bloodthirsty, you are, our Colin,' Katy said, walking a few steps behind with Billy, 'I couldn't even watch when those men were being whipped.'

'That's 'cos ye're a cissy. It was a waste of good money you going, 'cos yer had yer eyes closed most of the time and missed half the picture.' There was devilment in his eyes and smile. 'I saw yer hanging on to Billy for dear life. It's a wonder to me he's got any blinkin' arm left.'

'Me arm's still in one piece, Colin, so don't be worrying about me,' Billy said. 'It'll be black and blue by tomorrow and me mam will probably want to call the police to Katy for battering her lovely son, but I don't care 'cos I enjoyed gettin' battered.'

'You would, 'cos ye're as soppy as our Katy is.'

'All right, that's enough now.' Dot put her arm on his shoulders and turned him to face the front. If her son had seen John holding her hand, and he mentioned it, she'd skin him alive. She felt bad enough as it was without him making a joke about it. She couldn't look the man in the face she was that ashamed. What had come over her, or quite how it happened, she didn't know. But she'd make sure it didn't happen again. 'It was a good picture, no doubt about that. The acting was brilliant. But I've got to admit it wasn't my cup of tea. I'd rather have a comedy or a romance, something that puts a smile on me face, not one that puts the fear of God in me heart and gives me nightmares.'

'I thoroughly enjoyed the film, thought it was excellent,' John said, winking at Colin. 'And I enjoyed the company most of all.'

'Aye, well, ye're easily pleased, aren't yer!' Dot knew she had to look at him some time, she couldn't pretend he wasn't there. So she turned her head and asked, 'What about this ladyfriend of yours? Why don't yer ever take *her* to the pictures?'

Colin stopped dead in his tracks. 'What ladyfriend? Mr Kershaw hasn't got no ladyfriend, have yer, Mr Kershaw?'

'Yes, I suppose in a manner of speaking, I have, Colin.' The look he gave the boy was full of meaning and took away the frown from the young forehead. 'But like your mother she prefers weepy films. And anyway, she doesn't go out much in the evenings because she has two children and she won't leave them. Devoted mother, she is.'

Dot nearly tripped over herself. 'Yer don't mean to tell me that ye're marrying a widow, one with a family?'

'If all goes according to plan, yes, I am going to marry her.'

If Dot had glanced her son's way, she'd have seen him grinning like a Cheshire cat and he would have given the game away. But she stared straight ahead and increased her speed. 'All I can say is, yer want yer bumps feeling.'

'There are times I would agree with you, D.D., but at other times I think I'm doing the right thing. Right for me, and right for her.'

They turned into Province Road and automatically stopped outside Billy's house. 'Are yer leaving us here, Billy?' Dot asked.

'No, I'm walking Katy home. I always walk her home, wouldn't seem right if I didn't.' His boyish face split into a wide smile. 'Just like that song, you know – *Walking My Baby Back Home*. Except in the song it says "arm in arm" but Katy won't link arms with me 'cos she said we're too young and would look daft.'

Dot smiled at his honesty. 'She has a point, sunshine, but the time will come. Anyway, yer might as well have a cup of tea in ours.'

'Like Billy, I'll be a gentleman and walk you home,' John said, a smile playing around his mouth. 'Then I'll go to the chip shop and get us some supper.'

When Dot opened her bag to get the front door key, she also took out her purse. 'I'm paying for the chips, you paid for us all to get in the pictures.'

John shook his head. 'Billy seems to be well-versed on the behaviour of a gentleman, so I'm sure he'd tell you that a gentleman never takes money off a lady. Besides, I'll be eating the chips as well, don't forget. Plus, I'll be drinking your tea and eating your bread and butter. So I think that just about makes us quits.'

Dot put the purse back in her bag without a word. She wasn't going to stand and argue in the street, but she would later. And, she would tell him in no uncertain terms that she didn't make a habit of holding a man's hand in the pictures. The thought brought a smile to her face as she slipped the key in the lock. Since she'd never been out with a man since Ted died ten years ago, she could hardly call it a habit. Still, she would bring the subject up to clear the air and her conscience.

John waved away the plate Dot was holding out to him. 'I'll eat them out of the paper, they taste better. Besides, it saves having dirty dishes.'

'I think we're teaching you bad habits.' Dot spread the newspaper out on her lap and sniffed up in appreciation of the appetising smell of chips sprinkled liberally with salt and vinegar. 'I bet yer'd never eaten chips out of newspaper before yer started coming here, now had yer?'

'No, D.D., I hadn't. Just think of what I've been missing for forty years.'

'Is that how old you are, Mr Kershaw?' Colin spoke with his mouth half-full. 'It's me mam's birthday next week, did yer know? She'll be thirty-eight.'

Dot nearly choked on a chip. 'Gee, thanks, sunshine! I suppose everyone in the street will know how old I am.'

'No, they won't.' The boy looked hurt. 'I don't tell no one nothing any more. Only Mr Kershaw, and he doesn't count 'cos he's our friend.'

Billy sat on the couch shaking his head. 'I've told yer me dad always says it's not worth arguing with women 'cos yer don't stand a snowball's chance in hell of winning. Well, he also advises never to ask a woman her age because yer wouldn't get the truth anyway. He says one of our neighbours has been forty-five for as long as he can remember, even though she's got snow-white hair, no teeth, and hairs growing out of a wart on her chin. They always knock a few years off, according to me dad, so it's best to just smile and tell them they don't look anywhere near their age. That makes for an easier life, he reckons.' He turned to grin at Katy. 'So if you want to tell me ye're four years of age, I won't argue with yer.'

'I won't bother, thank you,' Katy giggled. 'And when I'm older I won't be walking around with no teeth in me head and a wart on me chin with hairs growing out of it.'

'I hope not, Katy Baker,' Billy put the last chip in his mouth, ''cos if yer do, yer won't see my heels for dust. I'll go away to sea and never come back.'

'Are you still hankering for the sea, sunshine?' Dot asked.

'I thought yer mam had put her foot down good and proper over that.'

Billy screwed the piece of newspaper up into a tight ball. 'I think she's weakening a bit, Mrs Baker. She said she might think about it when I'm fifteen, as long as it's only for a few trips and I don't want to make a career of it.'

'Wouldn't you be worried that Katy might find another boyfriend while you're away?' John asked. 'If I had a pretty girl like her, I wouldn't be going away and leaving her.'

Billy turned to Katy with surprise written all over his face. 'You wouldn't do that, would yer, Katy? Nah, yer wouldn't do that.'

'Don't you be too sure of yerself, Billy Harlow! You want to go away to sea, well you go. But while ye're away, I'll be doing what I want to do. That's fair, isn't it? What's good for the gander is good for the goose.'

Billy's grin was never far away and it surfaced now. 'Yer've got that the wrong way round, Katy. It should be, what's good for the goose is good for the gander.'

'No, I haven't so there!' Katy pulled tongues at him. 'You're the gander what's going away, and I'm the goose what's staying and doing what she wants.'

'That's given yer something to worry about, sunshine,' Dot said, thinking that Billy, like John, seemed to have become one of the family. She could understand the lad because he was, in his own young way, courting Katy. But why John spent most of his free time here was nothing short of a mystery to her. 'If I were you, I wouldn't go on a ship that's away for long. You might be better satisfying yer taste for the sea on the New Brighton ferry. Me daughter couldn't get up to much mischief in an hour.'

'Can we get back to the matter in hand, D.D.?' John asked. 'About this birthday of yours, when is it?'

When Dot didn't answer right away, Colin did it for her. 'It's next Saturday, isn't it, Mam?'

'Oh, that's the day we all break up for our holidays,' John said. 'Two whole weeks of not having to get up early in the morning. And two Saturdays when you can't use the excuse of having to do your shopping.'

'That's not an excuse, it's the truth! Yer don't think I walk around the shops for pleasure, do yer? With me feet tired after a morning's work, and me arms nearly pulled out of their sockets with lugging all the potatoes and stuff around. Yer must think I'm a ruddy glutton for punishment, John Kershaw.'

'Well, you are not doing it next week, I forbid it. It's your birthday and we, the five of us, are going to celebrate.'

'Ah, no!' Katy wailed. 'I have to work on a Saturday, and I can't ask for a day off because it's our busiest day.'

'I hadn't thought of that,' John admitted. 'What we could do, I suppose, is I take your mother and Colin to New Brighton or Southport for the day and get back in time for us all to go to the pictures.'

'Don't mind me, I'm only here to make the numbers up. Carry on, just pretend I'm not here,' Dot muttered. 'After all, it's got nothing to do with me, it's only my birthday.'

'Without wanting to sound rude, D.D., it really doesn't have anything to do with you. Apart, as you say, from it being your birthday, of course. But what we're talking about is your birthday present, and people don't usually tell their friends what they want, or do not want, as a present. So if it's all the same to you, your daughter and son, and Billy, will help me decide what we want to give you.'

'Excuse me, Mr John Kershaw, but I am going to have my say. I'm not letting you spend any more money on me, yer've spent enough. It must have cost yer a fortune to take us to the pictures tonight, and although I'm very grateful, I'll not take any more off yer.'

'Now you excuse me, Mrs Dorothy Baker,' John said, leaning forward with hands on his knees. 'If you want to tell me off, you will do it in the correct, and expected manner. You will get to your feet and put your hands on your hips, tilt your head and glare. If you don't do that, I won't think you're telling me off and my colleagues and I will continue our discussions on how best to celebrate your coming birthday.'

Billy was the first to start laughing, then Katy and Colin joined in. 'Oh Mam, yer've got to laugh at that,' Katy said. 'Mr Kershaw said it beautifully.'

'Yeah,' Billy agreed. 'It's the opposite to what me dad taught me, but then he's never heard anyone talking posh, like you do. I wouldn't mind getting told off like that. It beats "bugger off" any day of the week.'

Dot was bursting with laughter inside, but she kept it hidden as she jumped to her feet and stood in front of John. 'What did yer say, Mr Kershaw? Hands on hips – like this, yer mean? Head tilted – is that OK for yer? And what was the other? Oh yeah, I know.' She leaned forward and put her face close to his. 'Is this glare angry enough for yer?'

'Keep your face there, Dorothy, and you're asking to be kissed.'

'Kiss me, John, and ye're asking for a thick ear.'

'Nothing ventured, nothing gained, Mr Kershaw,' Billy said, daringly. 'I'd take a chance if I were you 'cos Mrs Baker doesn't half look pretty in that new dress.'

Katy's high squeal brought all eyes in her direction. 'Oh, me new dress, Mam, I'd forgotten all about it!' She jumped to her feet, her face alive with excitement. 'Where is it, Mam?'

'I'm sorry, sunshine, I forgot about it meself. It's in a bag in the sideboard cupboard.' Dot glared at John. 'It's all your fault, making me forget me own daughter's dress. Getting something new is a big thing in this house, definitely more of a cause for celebration than my ruddy birthday.'

Colin wasn't standing for his hero taking the blame. 'It wasn't Mr Kershaw's fault, it was me what mentioned yer birthday. If yer must shout at anyone, shout at me.'

He looked so grown-up at that moment, so like his dad, Dot would have forgiven him anything. 'I was only joking, sunshine, and John knows that.' She turned around to see her daughter holding the dress aloft, her mouth and eyes wide open. 'Do yer like it, sunshine?'

'Like it? It's beautiful!' The dress was in a paler blue than her mother's and had an all-over pattern of small pink and white flowers. It had a sweetheart neck, short puffed sleeves and a flared skirt. Katy held the dress to her and smiled. 'I can't wait to wear this – I won't half be a swank.'

John saw the pride in Dot's eyes and would have given anything to be able to put his arm across her shoulders and be allowed to share in that pride. Instead he contented himself with asking, 'Shall we call a truce, D.D., and ask Katy to let us see her in the dress?'

Dot nodded, 'Yeah, go on, Katy, put it on and give us all a treat.' She watched her daughter hurry from the room, the precious dress clutched to her breast. Then she wagged a finger at John. 'You keep yer eye off my Katy, Mr Kershaw, or yer'll have Billy after yer. And remember, yer've already got one ladyfriend.'

'Not for one second do I ever forget that, Mrs Baker.'

Colin was standing behind the couch, leaning on the back of it. In his mind he was talking to himself, asking why Mr Kershaw didn't take the bull by the horns and give his mother a kiss. After all, she could only clock him one.

When Katy made her grand entrance, she looked as pretty as a picture. She twirled around for them to see it from all angles, and the reception she received had her cup of happiness overflowing. 'Yer can take me for a walk tomorrow, Billy, so I can show me new dress off.'

'Yeah!' Billy showed his feelings openly. Katy was his girl and he adored her. 'If any bloke looks sideways at her, I'll thump him one.'

'Why don't we all go for a walk?' John asked. 'The weather is too nice to stay indoors, and your mother has a new dress to show off, too. And I might even follow Billy's instinct to thump any bloke that looks sideways at her. Another thing, we could ask Mary to come with the baby, she'd enjoy that.' When he saw the doubt on Dot's face, he added, 'It doesn't cost anything to go for a walk – even the fresh air is free. So you wouldn't be under any obligation to me.'

Katy added her plea. 'Yeah, go on, Mam. Yer can leave the housework until the following week, when ye're off work. And if Mary comes, I bags first wheel of the pram.'

Dot had learned that when her children sided with John, there was no point in arguing. And it would be nice for the whole family to go for a walk together. To refuse would be childish and spiteful. 'You've got money for Mary, haven't you, John?'

'Yes, but it'll have to wait until tomorrow now, I wouldn't

knock this time of night – it's nearly ten o'clock.'

Dot looked at the clock then at her son. 'You little tinker, no wonder yer've been quiet for a while. It's way past yer bedtime, so up the stairs yer go. And don't bother pretending yer've got a tummyache or a sore throat in the morning because ye're going to Mass if I have to carry yer.'

Colin went to bed as good as gold after saying good night. Tomorrow was another day out and he was looking forward to it. He wasn't half glad he'd run into Mr Kershaw's bike that night, because now he didn't feel left out when his mates were bragging about where they'd been and what they'd done. He was getting as many treats as them, if not more.

The boy folded the blankets back before he got into bed. It was so warm, all he needed was a sheet to cover him. He lay awake for a while wondering if Mr Kershaw was having any luck persuading his mam over her birthday outing. If he did, and they asked him where he'd like to go, he'd say Southport. A lot of his mates had been to New Brighton, some had even been as far as North Wales, but he'd never heard one say they'd been to Southport. So for once in his life he would be the first to have gone somewhere special.

When Katy stood on the front step saying good night to Billy, she was surprised when he said, in his usual forthright manner, 'Mr Kershaw hasn't half got a crush on your mam – it's sticking out a mile. It's a wonder yer haven't noticed.'

'Of course I've noticed, yer daft article, I'm not blind. Me and our Colin are doing everything we can to make her see how nice he is, and Mr Kershaw – well, he practically lets her walk all over him. If God loves a trier, then He must adore him.'

'I'm glad you don't give me the cold shoulder, like yer mam does.' Billy kicked the step before remembering he was wearing his best pair of shoes. Then he wished he'd kicked himself instead, because if his mam saw them scuffed she wouldn't be very happy and she was the best kicker of the lot. 'We've always known we liked each other, haven't we, Katy?'

'There's a big difference between me and me mam, Billy. Yer see, she often talks about me dad, and how much she loved him. Perhaps she'll never love anyone else, no matter how nice they are.'

'D'yer remember yer dad, Katy?'

She shook her head. 'Not really, 'cos I was less than four years old when he died. I can get images in me head of things, like being picked up by a man with a laughing face, and being tossed in the air. I can see meself lying on the floor, screaming with laughter as the man with the smiling face tickled me tummy. But the face isn't clear, it's just a blur. Me mam says our Colin is the spittin' image of me dad, but I honestly can't remember what he looked like. What I do remember of him was that he loved me very much, I could tell, even though I was so young. I also know there was a lot of laughter in the house and I was a happy child.'

'Yer mam does laugh a lot, I really like her. She's too nice to spend the rest of her life on her own being lonely. Even if she can't love another man like she loved yer dad, she could be happy with someone who was good to her, like Mr Kershaw.'

'Me mam will never be lonely while me and our Colin are around, we'll make sure of that. But I understand what yer mean, Billy. It would be lovely if she had someone of her own – especially someone as nice as Mr Kershaw, because I know he'd be good to her. She wouldn't have to work herself to death, like she does now. That would be a blessing. And it would be nice for me and our kid to have a man in the house, like having a dad. But for heaven's sake don't breathe a word of that to anyone, in case it gets back to me mam. She loved me real dad so much, she might be very hurt if she thought we were wanting someone to take his place.'

Katy gave a deep sigh. She felt better now she'd confided in someone and Billy was a good listener. 'That was a long speech for me, wasn't it?'

'It needed saying, and yer said it.' Billy chuckled, 'But I hope when we get married yer don't talk the ear off me every night.'

'You cheeky begger! I don't talk a lot, and anyway, what gave yer the idea that I'd marry yer? I've never said I would.'

'Of course yer will! I've known since I was about twelve

352

that you were the girl for me. If yer don't feel the same, then ye're mean for letting me go on thinking me life was all planned out and we were going to live happy ever after.'

Katy giggled softly. 'Billy Harlow, ye're passed the post, yer know that, don't yer?'

'Well, seeing as yer've almost agreed to marry me, d'yer think yer could give me a little kiss? Just to give me a taste of things to come.'

While Katy was getting her first real kiss, John was broaching the prickly subject of Dot's birthday. 'Let me take you and Colin out as my present to you. I know it's not just a present for you because Colin and I would be sharing it. But it would give me so much pleasure to repay, in a small way, the friendliness and hospitality you've shown me over the last six or seven months. You have given me so much but are loath to take anything in return.'

Dot studied his face before answering. 'I'm not used to being given things, John. I've had to struggle so hard over the years with no one to help me, and now I've got into the habit of living within me means, being independent.'

'It was your independence that drew me to you in the first place, D.D. I admired you so much for it and for being so honest about it. But there has to be a happy medium in everything in life. With you it's learning to give and take in equal measures.'

'If I'd had the same education as you, I might have had a chance of winning this argument. But as it is, I don't stand an earthly. If I refuse what ye're asking, yer'll get our Colin to have a go at me. And if that fails, ye're not beyond bringing Katy into it.' Dot put a finger to her mouth and cocked an ear. 'There's Katy going up to bed. It's time you were on yer way, John Kershaw, so I can get me beauty sleep. I'll give Mary a knock in the morning to see if she'd like to come for a walk with us. But I don't want to see yer before two o'clock; give me a chance to get the dinner over.'

'And what about next Saturday? Are we celebrating your birthday?'

'I'll think about it and let yer know tomorrow.'

John hid his smile as he stood up. That was good enough

for him. 'I'll see you tomorrow, then, Dear, Delightful Dorothy.'

He was walking towards the door when Dot put a hand on his arm. 'Before yer go, John, I want to get something off me chest. It's about me holding yer hand in the pictures. I don't know what came over me, and I apologise.'

'You didn't hold my hand, Dot, I held yours. And I was delighted to do so.'

'Well that's another thing I'd like to get off me chest. You're not expecting anything from this – er – this friendship, are yer?'

'I expect only what you want to give.' John walked towards the door. 'Now come and throw me out before we get into a heated discussion.'

'I don't want yer to think I'm big-headed, hinting that yer've got yer eye on me. But I've got to say I haven't for one minute believed this cock-and-bull story about you having a ladyfriend. It's a load of eye-wash.'

John chuckled as he stepped into the street. 'As I said, Dot, I only expect from our friendship what you want to give. And right now I expect you want me to kiss you so I will happily oblige.'

He'd disappeared before Dot had time to gather her brains together. 'The cheeky, cheeky devil! Two kisses he pinched tonight, the hard-faced thing.' She closed the door and turned towards the stairs. 'The trouble is, I'm so out of practice I wouldn't know whether they were the kisses of a friend, or not. I could make a fool of meself if I tackle him over it, so as there's no harm been done, I'd best leave it be.'

The man Dot was having a conversation with herself about, was covering the ground quickly with his long strides. He was asking himself if he were a betting man, would he place a bet on himself to win the hand of the fair Dorothy. After thoughtful deliberation, he decided he would. He'd stick with it until he won her round because she was worth fighting for. The more he saw of her, and the children, the more he knew how much he wanted to be part of them. They'd brought into his life something he didn't even know was missing. Fun, laughter, and a love so open and natural, they demonstrated it in every way. He'd been loved by his mother and had loved her in return, but it was a gentle, undemonstrative love. A love taken for granted rather than shown. There'd never been any impulsive show of affection, the hugging and kissing that he witnessed every time he went to the Bakers' house. Their love for each other showed in their looks, their smiles, their actions and their sense of fun.

Yes, if I were a betting man I'd bet on myself. John was determined as he pushed the gate open and walked up the path to the house that he knew would be as spick and span as ever – his cleaner would have made sure of that. But it was a house that had never rung with the sound of laughter. He hoped one day to change that.

'Listen, Dot, I won't be able to stay out for long, because of feeding the baby. But I don't want to say that in front of the others, I'd be too embarrassed. So if I say I'm feeling tired, you'll know what I mean, won't yer?'

'Yeah, of course I will.' Dot smiled into Mary's anxious face. 'Anyway, sunshine, it's yer first time out, so yer will get tired quickly. It takes a while after yer've had a baby to get yer strength back, so don't overdo it. When yer give me the eye, I'll come home with yer and get our tea ready.' She opened the yard door and wheeled the pram into the entry. 'The others are waiting for us at the top. Our Katy can't wait to wheel the pram, she's been talking about it all morning.'

John smiled when he saw them coming up the entry. 'The pram suits you, Dorothy.'

The words were hardly out of his mouth before Katy dodged past him and took over from her mother. 'Can I have a peep at Trudy, Auntie Mary?'

'And me,' Billy said, having followed hot on Katy's heels. 'But I've got to warn yer that I seem to have a bad effect on babies; they usually bawl their heads off when they see me.'

'This one won't,' Mary smiled, 'she's fast asleep.'

'Oh look, she must have heard yer, she's opened her eyes.' Katy was beside herself with excitement. 'Aren't you a beautiful little girl for yer mammy, eh? Just like a little doll, yes, you are. And here's yer Uncle Billy to say hello to yer.'

Colin, standing next to John, pulled a face when he heard all the cooing and baby talk. 'Why do women always make stupid noises when they talk to a baby?'

'Maternal instincts, son, all females have them. And even some men go dotty over a baby. I have to confess that when I was holding Trudy, I too made those noises, and she seemed to like them.' John glanced down at the boy. 'Have you seen her yet?'

Colin shook his head. 'No, me mama wouldn't let me go into the O'Connors', she said they had enough to do. I wasn't that fussy, anyway, 'cos what's so special about a baby? They all look alike and all they do is whinge.'

'I bet your mother thought you were special, son. And if we asked her, I'm sure she'd say you didn't whinge all the time.'

The boy grinned. 'She would, yer know. She'd tell yer our Katy was as good as gold, but I cried day and night. She said she seriously thought of putting me in the Cottage Homes.'

'Who looked after you and Katy when your father died and your mother had to go out to work? You were both only babies, too young to be left.'

'A woman in the next street, Chrissie Brady, looked after us. She minded us up until I started school and our Katy was old enough to look after me until me mam got in.'

Katy was wheeling the pram past them, with Billy in tow, when John put his hand out and brought them to a halt. 'Hang on, Katy, your brother hasn't been introduced yet. Come on, Colin, say hello to Trudy.'

Shrugging his shoulders as though to say he found the whole thing boring, the boy sidled up to the pram. He only intended to take one quick peek, just to please John. But at that precise moment, a spasm of wind brought a smile to the baby's face and Colin was hooked. 'Ay, she looked right at me and smiled!' He turned to his mother and Mary. 'Did yer see that, Mam? She likes me!'

'And why wouldn't she like a handsome lad like you?' There was love and pride in Dot's smile. 'But don't yer think she's just a wee bit too young to be weighing yer up as a future boyfriend?'

Mary happened to glance at John and saw the look in his eyes as he watched mother and son sharing the joke. His feelings were there for the whole world to see. All except Dot, the one person who mattered. Either she doesn't want to see, her neighbour thought, or she's as blind as a bat.

With Colin walking ahead, chattering away to Billy and Katy, the three grown-ups were free to talk. Mary had been given the fifteen shillings John had got from her husband, and at first she was lost for words. To say 'thank you' seemed so inadequate for all the love, kindness and consideration she'd been shown by her neighbours, but they were the only words she knew. 'I've been spoilt rotten over the last two weeks by all of you. I've wanted for nothing, even a pram and baby clothes, thanks to you. It's going to be a big come-down when I go home tomorrow, but like it or not, it is still my home.'

'If things get rough, sunshine, just put the baby in her pram and walk out. The O'Connors would welcome yer back with open arms until something could be sorted out.'

'I agree with Dot,' John said. 'She's right, as usual. If your husband starts his shenanigans, walk out without a backward glance.' He paused before asking, 'Why do you have to sleep on the couch? Don't you have a spare bedroom?'

Mary's laugh was hollow. 'Oh yeah, we've got another bedroom same as all the houses. But the only thing in that room is the wallpaper on the walls, and that is falling off with the damp, so I couldn't put the baby in there even if we had furniture for it.'

'I don't envy yer, sunshine, because the place will be a damn sight worse than when yer left. The queer feller won't have done a hand's turn.'

'That goes without saying, Dot, it's what I'm expecting. But Maggie and Betty are coming in with me to help. They said they'll do the cleaning for me. At least we'll have the place to ourselves until Tom gets in from work. And I know ye're all worried about him touching the baby, but ye're not to worry, I won't let him near her. I know I've been a coward and let him get away with murder in the past, but those days are gone. Tom Campbell is in for a rude awakening, believe me.'

'Don't let him keep you away from your friends, Mary,

because you need them, and so does Trudy,' John said. 'Visit your friends, have a life of your own, and that way you might hold on to your sanity.'

'Oh, I intend to, John, you can rely on that. The days are gone when I sit in every night, looking at the four walls of a house that's as dark as a dungeon, while he's propping a bar counter up. With the fine weather, I'll be walking up to me mam's to let the family see the baby.' She turned to grin at Dot. 'Or I'll be calling in to one of me neighbours for afternoon tea.'

'My café only opens on a Saturday and Sunday, sunshine, but yer'll be very welcome. In fact, if yer don't come, I'll be hammering yer door down.'

John had a thought. 'You could come out with us next Saturday. We're going out for the day to celebrate Dot's birthday.'

'Oh, aye!' Dot was wide-eyed. 'Who said so?'

'I just said so.'

'Oh well, I suppose because you said so, that makes it all right, eh? There's just one little thing yer haven't thought of, clever clogs. The baby needs to be fed every couple of hours.'

'Mary could bring the baby food and bottle with her – it would go in the pram.'

'Oh, yer think Mary would fit in the pram, do yer?' When Dot saw Mary blush and hang her head, she glared at John. 'For a man of forty, who knows the meaning of every ruddy word in the dictionary, and who is manager of a factory, yer haven't a bloody clue what real life is all about, have yer, John Kershaw?'

'What have I said wrong, D.D.?'

'Mary feeds the baby herself, yer great big daft nit!'

In the seven months Dot had known John, she had never seen him blush. But right now he was the colour of beetroot and looking as though he was wishing the ground would open up. And she felt a surge of pity for him. How was he expected to know? He'd never had any experience.

'I don't know, what am I going to do with yer?' she tutted loudly. 'Go and catch our Katy up and bring the pram back. Mary's beginning to look tired.'

When he'd gone, she shook her head at Mary. 'He's never been married or had children, Mary, so yer'll have to excuse him for embarrassing yer. Yer know he wouldn't do it on purpose, he's too much of a gentleman.'

'He's not the only one without experience, Dot.'

'How d'yer mean, sunshine?'

'Ye're not very clever yerself. Everyone else can see the man is deeply in love with yer, but you seem to be blind to it.'

'Go 'way! Ye're imagining things, Mary – we're just friends He's lonely, that's why he's always round at our house. That's all there is to it.'

'I'll tell that to all the other people who are imagining things, shall I? Like Maggie and Paddy, Betty and Alec, and your own Katy and Colin. Let's see if they believe yer any more than I do.'

Chapter Twenty-Two

Mary held the baby while Betty and Maggie manoeuvred the pram up the front step. It was tricky, because the hall was so small they had to angle it so that it went straight from the front door into the living room. 'Yer'll never manage this on yer own, sweetheart, indeed yer won't. Sure, it's taken two of us all our time and we only just made it with about an inch to spare either side.'

Betty sniffed and pulled a face. 'My God, it stinks to high heaven in here, girl! That lazy bugger hasn't done a tap since the day yer left.'

Mary held the baby's face close to her body, trying to shield her from the horrible smell of dirt, sweat and other unpleasant odours. 'That's nothing unusual, Betty, he never does a tap in the house. As he would say, that's what a wife's for. Or, another expression he's fond of is: "why keep a dog and bark yerself?".'

'It's stupid we've been, so it is.' Maggie wagged her head, a look of disgust on her face. 'Why didn't we put the child in the pram and leave her outside in the fresh air?'

'And why didn't yer have that bright idea before we pulled a gut getting the bleedin' pram in here?' Betty wrinkled her nose; the smell was making her feel sick. 'We're not going through that palaver again, it can go in the yard. The fresh air out there is just the same as the air in the street.'

Mary turned the apron of the pram back and laid the sleeping baby inside. 'I'll wheel it out there, but we'll have to keep our eye open for that cat of Mrs Steel's. It's always coming in our yard, and it sits on the window-ledge as though it's got every right to. If it jumped on Trudy it could suffocate her.'

'While ye're doing that, me darlin', I'll slip home and get me mop and bucket and a bottle of Parr's Aunt Sally. If we

361

get this place mopped out it will get rid of some of the smell.'
When Maggie got outside she stood for a moment gulping in
the fresh air. My God, fancy a newborn baby having to live in
such squalor. And there was no chance of it improving when
Mary was only given fifteen shillings a week to pay the rent
and keep the house on. With the best will in the world, no one
could buy cleaning materials out of that.

Betty fished in the pocket of her wrap-around pinny. 'I've
brought a handful of pennies for the gas, girl, so can I put
some pans of water on to boil?'

'Of course yer can, there's no need to ask.' Mary was
standing looking out of the back window. 'If that cat comes in
I'll throw a bucket of water over it.'

'I'll do it for yer, girl, I've got a good aim. If yer ask my
Alec he'll tell yer I never fail to hit the target.' Betty waddled
out to the kitchen but was back within seconds. 'No wonder
the bleedin' place stinks – have yer seen all these dirty clothes
on the floor? The filthy swine has left yer his dirty underpants
that pong, his shirts and sweaty socks. With no disrespect to
you, girl, I ain't touching them. Me inside's turning over as it
is.'

Mary sighed. She was home again, all right. 'I wouldn't
expect yer to touch them, Betty. I'll see to them.'

'Not bleedin' likely, yer won't! I'll pull the dolly tub out
and fill it with hot water when the pans boil. I've got some
powder at home that we can throw in, it's guaranteed to get
the dirt out. It'll probably take the colour out too, and there's
a good chance they might fall to pieces, but that's not our
worry. If your feller has anything to say, send the dirty bugger
down to our house and I'll sort him out.'

Mary wasn't allowed to do anything. They put a chair in
the yard for her and she sat near the pram in the sunshine.
She was filled with shame at first, that her neighbours were
having to clean the filth left by her husband. But gradually
her nerves calmed down as she listened to Betty telling Maggie
one of her outrageous tales, and heard the resulting laughter.
With the sun beating down on her face, her beloved baby at
hand, she felt relaxed. If only things could stay like this, how
happy life would be. If only her husband wouldn't be walking

through the door at six o'clock. If only she never had to set eyes on him again. If only—

'Come on, me darlin'.' Maggie's voice brought Mary down to earth. 'It's twelve o'clock and time for a bite to eat. Betty's tummy is rumbling so loud didn't I think we were having a thunderstorm?'

Betty appeared at the kitchen door, her chubby face streaked with dirt, but beaming. 'I'm packing this job in, me bleedin' boss is a real slave-driver. No eleven o'clock sit-down with a cup of tea and a ginger snap to dunk in it. Yer can sod that for a lark, girl!'

'Wheel the pram through to the entry, sweetheart, and I'll run and open our backyard door for yer. We'll have a bite to eat, and then it's time for Trudy's feed. While you're busy doing that, me and Betty will come back and get stuck in again. Another hour or so should have the place looking a damn sight better than when we came. Isn't that right now, Betty, me darlin'?'

'I'll tell yer what, Maggie, we'd be hard pushed to make it any worse than it was. It's a wonder the queer feller didn't poison himself with all the pots and pans in the house used and left to go green-mouldy.' Betty gave a cheeky grin. 'Pity he didn't bleedin' poison himself, that's what I say. It would have been good riddance to bad rubbish.'

'May the good Lord have mercy on yer, Betty Mason.' Maggie kept her face straight but couldn't hide the smile in her eyes. 'It's some explaining yer'll have to do when yer get to the Pearly Gates.'

Betty's bosom bounced. 'Maggie, if I ever got to the Pearly Gates I don't know who'd be the more surprised, me or Saint Peter.'

'I think yer good points outweigh yer bad ones, me darlin'. But just to be on the safe side, I'll say an extra prayer for yer tonight.' When Maggie turned to Mary, she was pleased to see a smile on her face. 'You go out the back with Betty and I'll open our entry door for yer.'

Maggie had mopped the floor in the living room twice, and although there was a strong smell of Aunty Sally, she was

363

satisfied it was clean. Then she washed the woodwork, cleaned the windows and dusted the furniture. Standing back she looked around with satisfaction. 'I've finished in here, Betty. Will yer come and see what yer think?'

A head appeared around the door. 'Bloody marvellous, girl, but I ain't got time to give it me full attention 'cos I'm up to me neck in water.'

Maggie went into the kitchen to find Betty plunging the dolly peg up and down on the clothes in the tub. The sweat was pouring off the big woman as she pressed with all her might. 'They'll not be as clean as I'd like, but they were too dirty to begin with.' She stopped for a moment and ran the back of her hand across her forehead. 'He's a filthy swine, Maggie, and that's putting it mild. Wouldn't yer think he'd have rinsed his things through every night, save Mary coming back to a muck midden? Anyway, that's me lot, I'll start rinsing them in the sink and put them on the line. They should dry in no time in this weather.'

Maggie pushed her aside. 'I'll do that, you take a breather. Mary hasn't got a mangle, so I'll wring as much water out of them as I can get, then take them home and run them through our mangle.' She put the plug in the sink and turned the tap on. 'I'll hang them out on our line and iron them tomorrow for her. She's not fit yet to be standing for long; she needs to take things easy for a few more weeks.'

'And do yer really think, Maggie, that she's going to be given the chance to take things easy? Not on yer bleedin' life, she isn't. Mr Tom Campbell will be delighted to have his skivvy back, he'll have her run off her feet. In fact, she's started to worry about him already.' Betty's face and neck were running with sweat and she wiped them over with the corner of her pinny. 'Yer heard her asking me if I'd get a few things for her when I go to the shops? Well, she hasn't asked for one thing for herself. Half a pound of sausages and two eggs – she said that'll do him tonight and tomorrow night. She hasn't got one item of food in this house yet all she's asked for is two ounces of tea, a loaf, margarine and a tin of conny-onny. Oh, and some corned beef for the queer feller's carry-out. What's she going to live on – fresh air? She needs nourishment if she's feeding the baby or they'll both be ill.'

Maggie turned the tap off and lifted a pair of trousers from the tub. She squeezed the excess water from them before plunging them in the sink. 'Sure, didn't me and Dot talk about this very thing last night? So, to make sure Mary gets enough of the right food down her, we're going back to the arrangement we had before. Dot will see to her breakfast, and I'll make her a hot dinner every day. And I'll give her a hand with her housework for a few weeks.'

'I'll do my whack, as well,' Betty said. 'But I've got to say it goes against the grain when I see that bloody husband of hers passing our window every night to go to the pub. He's got money for that, and to have his bets on the gee-gees, while his wife starves! It makes me blood boil, I feel like wringing his ruddy neck. Still, I'll not see Mary suffer so I'll muck in with yer, like I did before, and make sure she gets a hot dinner every day.'

Mary heard the key turn in the lock and her heart lurched. 'Now for it,' she said under her breath. 'Remember what yer've been telling yerself all afternoon. Start as yer mean to go on or yer life will be hell.'

Tom Campbell knew she was home as soon as he opened the door and was greeted by the smell of disinfectant and sausages frying. He sauntered into the room with a sneer on his face. 'So yer've decided to come back, have yer?' His lip curled as he eyed the pram. 'And yer've brought the brat with yer.'

'This is my home, I don't have to ask your permission when I come and go.' Mary's eyes locked with his and she forced herself to stare him out. 'And it's Trudy's home, too.'

'Trudy! What sort of a bleedin' name is that?'

'I think Trudy is a lovely name. It's just a pity she has to have Campbell stuck after it, but that can't be helped. I'll explain to her when she's old enough to understand, that her mother had lousy taste in men.'

Tom's eyes narrowed. He'd never seen his wife like this before; she'd changed. The bloody neighbours were the cause of it, filling her head with big ideas. Well, he'd soon bring her down to earth with a jolt, but not tonight, he had better things to do. 'Where's me bleedin' dinner? I'm going out at seven.'

'Well, thank heaven for small mercies,' Mary drawled as she made for the kitchen. She was even surprising herself for standing up to him. How long he'd let her get away with it was another thing, but right now she felt good. She turned at the door, saying, 'Don't you go near that pram.'

'I told yer I didn't want the bleedin' brat, and I still don't. Just keep her well away from me, that's all.'

Mary had fried the sausages and egg in margarine and they didn't look very appetising on the plate. Still, she had no dripping in so it was a case of like it or lump it. She was carrying the plate through but stopped dead at the sight that met her eyes. Her husband was standing in front of the fireplace, his fly buttons undone and his hand moving around inside his trousers. 'What the hell d'yer think you're doing? You dirty bugger!'

'I'm itchy and I'm scratching meself, so what?'

Mary dropped his plate on the table. 'You disgust me with yer filthy habits.' She couldn't bear to be in the same room as him, so she picked the baby out of the pram. 'I'm going next door for an hour or two. I'll take the key so bang the door after yer.'

It wouldn't occur to Tom Campbell to wash his hands. He sat down at the table and picked up his knife and fork. He'd had this itch for weeks now, only it wasn't just an ordinary itch, it was tender and sore. Like when you had a gum-boil, and you wanted to touch it with your tongue all the time. It was that Esmée, she was being too rough with him. Not that he didn't enjoy it, she took him to heaven and back. But he'd tell her to take it easy tonight, just until this rash went away.

John was waiting for Dot when she got home from work on the Saturday. She threw her bag and overall on the table and grinned. 'Two whole weeks off! Oh, what a wonderful feeling it is.'

'You're not the only one, D.D., I've got two weeks off as well.'

'I'm better off than any of yer, I've got six weeks,' Colin said, looking clean and neat in his best shirt and trousers. 'We can have a lie-in every morning, Mam. There's only our Kate got to get up, and she sees to herself.'

'I know. It's the gear, isn't it, sunshine?' Dot picked her overall up from the table. 'I'll stick this in the tub ready for washing, then I'll get meself ready.'

'Just hang on a minute, D.D., I haven't wished you a Happy Birthday yet.' John had been holding his hand behind his back, hiding the card and parcel he now handed to her. 'Have a lovely day.'

'Ay, I'm here as well, yer know.' Colin was brimming with excitement at having a present to give his mother. And of course, the prospect of going to Southport. 'Here's a card and a pressie for yer, Mam.'

Dot took the small square parcel off her son but looked at John's with suspicion. 'I was under the impression yer were taking me to Southport for me birthday. I don't want two presents off yer.'

'We're all going to Southport – you, me, Colin and Betty. I wanted to give you something just for yourself.'

Dot could see the hope in his eyes and didn't have the heart to disappoint him. 'Oh, all right, but I'll open me son's first.' As she was ripping the paper from the small square box, she added, 'Yer don't half spoil me, John Kershaw. I don't know what I'm going to do when yer marry this mysterious ladyfriend of yours.'

'Marrying her won't stop me spoiling you, my Delightful Dorothy.'

Dot was staring down at the small black box when she answered. 'Ay, I'm not going to be the other woman. I'm not a marriage wrecker.' Then she lifted the lid of the box and gasped. 'You never bought this, Colin, yer'd never have had enough money.' The link of pearls were coiled on a layer of cotton wool and she thought they were beautiful. But she was suspicious of who paid for them. 'You didn't pay for them, did yer?'

'Ah, ay, Mam, I did!' The boy was cut to the quick. 'I saved all me pocket money last week, I didn't spend a penny of it!

367

And Mr Kershaw lent me sixpence until I get this week's pocket money off yer. I went to Woolworth's this morning for them, they cost elevenpence halfpenny.'

Dot threw her arms around him and hugged him tight. 'You are one little love, you are, I could eat yer. It's the best present I've ever had in all me life.'

Tears were glistening in her eyes when she looked over his shoulder at John. 'He's the best son in the whole world and I love the bones of him.'

John was wishing he was in the boy's shoes when he said, 'Do I get the same treatment if you like my present?'

'Not on yer blinkin' life, yer don't.' Dot released her son and took the parcel John was holding out to her. It was about eighteen inches square and was soft to the touch. She grinned at him as she carefully unwrapped the paper. 'At least it's not a tiara.'

She stared down at the folded garment she could tell was a dress. 'You shouldn't have done this, John. A little gift is one thing, this is another. I can't accept it.'

'Can't, or won't, Dorothy?'

'Ay, ay, Mam, don't be so mean! Our Katy went all the way into town on Wednesday afternoon to get that.' Colin was beside himself. 'She was dead excited about going on her own into one of the big shops to buy something, and she can't wait to see if yer like it. And now ye're goin to spoil it for her and for Mr Kershaw. That's not half mean, that is.'

Dot's eyes rolled. 'Our Katy went for it?'

'Well, I'm not very knowledgeable about what women like, or what the fashions are. So I asked your daughter to suggest something and then asked her to choose it.'

Dot turned her head away from two pairs of anxious eyes. 'It's not that I'm not grateful, John, or that I want to be contrary. But you spend a fortune on us and I can't let yer carry on doing it. Last Saturday yer paid for all of us to go to the pictures, now ye're taking four of us to Southport for the day and then to the pictures again tonight. It's got to stop somewhere, ye're not made of money.'

'Neither am I stupid, Dorothy. What I couldn't afford, I wouldn't buy. Your daughter asked me to tell you to wear it today and call in the shop on our way out so she can see what you look like in it. Now I've given you the present, and the message, so I'll leave you to make up your own mind.' With that, John sat down and folded his arms.

Dot laid the parcel on the table and lifted the dress from the paper. It was a straight, figure-hugging dress in pale green. It had a white belt, a low-cut round neck trimmed with white binding, and short cap sleeves also trimmed with white. It was a very smart dress, ideal for a lovely summer day. 'Our Katy's got good taste, it's lovely.' She glanced at her son and smiled. 'The pearls will just set it off.'

John jumped up from his chair. His face, like Colin's, was beaming. 'Now that's sorted out we can give you your cards.' He handed a large envelope over. 'Happy Birthday, Dorothy, and may you enjoy many more.'

'And here's mine, Mam.' Colin's envelope had fingermarks all over it, but Dot was too full up to see them. 'There's four more for yer, and they're from me grandma, Auntie Betty, Mary and the O'Connors.'

'How d'er know that, sunshine?'

"Cos I opened them, of course.'

'Well, yer can help me open them again, and then I'll stand them on the sideboard.'

When all the cards had been read and admired, Dot gave her son the job of arranging them on top of the sideboard. Then she looked at John. 'Thank you, I love the dress. I'll wear it today and we'll call in and let Katy see it. Are yer quite satisfied now?'

'No. I want a birthday kiss.'

'It's not your birthday!'

'That's true, it's your birthday so it's my place to give you a kiss.'

Dot held her head sideways and pointed to her cheek. 'Right there.'

But John wasn't having any of that. He tilted his head to match hers and kissed her lightly on the lips. All to the amusement of Colin, who looked as though he'd lost sixpence and found half-a-crown. As long as his mam took it in good humour and didn't clock Mr Kershaw this would be the

369

highlight of the boy's day. When his mother stood still, looking bewildered, Colin silently urged his hero to pinch another kiss and make it last longer this time. But the spell was broken by Betty's loud ran-tan on the knocker.

Dot patted her hair even though no one had touched it. It was as if she believed Betty would know that John Kershaw had just kissed her. The cheeky devil. In front of her son, too!

'Open the door for Auntie Betty, sunshine, while I get a swill in the sink. Then I'll get changed, it won't take me long.'

When Dot came downstairs looking like a million dollars in her new dress, and the pearls adding attraction to her whole appearance, Betty whistled. 'My God, girl, there's no flies on you today. Anyone would think it was yer birthday, the state of yer.'

'My lovely son bought me the pearls, aren't they nice?'

Colin's foot was always ready to plunge into trouble. 'And Mr Kershaw bought her the dress. That's nice as well, isn't it?'

Betty's eyes disappeared when she grinned. 'It's no good, I'm going to have to get meself a lodger. I'm not half missing out on the good things in life. Yer don't happen to have a friend looking for digs, have yer, John? Someone like yerself, with a few bob in their pocket? It's no good if they're skint, I may as well stick to my feller.'

'I'm sorry, Betty, but most of the men I know are married. However, I'll put the feelers out for you, and who knows? There could be a millionaire somewhere out there searching for someone with the very qualities you possess.'

'Another thing, he's got to speak posh, like what you do. I don't want no one who uses bad language – like bleedin' this, and sod that. No, I only want the best, like what I'm used to. It's no use bringing me no one as common as muck, 'cos I'll chase them. Only the best is good enough for Betty Mason.'

'I've got some very clever, well-to-do friends, John, as yer can see,' Dot said, her eyes brimming with laughter and a feeling of well-being. 'Now take Betty here. She went to college and passed all her exams to become a teacher. And when she got married, it was in a big church and she wore a white dress with a big long train and six bridesmaids.'

Betty raised her brow scornfully as she corrected her friend. 'No girl, yer telling a fib there. I had seven bridesmaids, not six. Oh, it was a big posh wedding, the talk of the neighbourhood for weeks, it was.' The chair began to creak in protest and Dot waited for the laughter that wasn't long in coming. 'There was only one little drawback, and the neighbours were arguing for months about whether me dress was white or not. Yer see, I went to the church on the back of Billy McCardle's coal-cart.'

John and Colin were doubled up. 'Oh dear, oh dear, oh dear.' John wiped the tears from his eyes. 'I don't know why we bother going to the pictures, not when we could be entertained in the comfort of our own home.'

'Oh, I'm a good all-round entertainer, John, even if I do say so meself. The only thing I can't do is dance. And for the life of me I can't understand why, 'cos I used to be able to tap-dance when I was little. Me dad used to play the spoons and I used to dance the feet off meself. I wonder why I can't do that no more?'

'Perhaps it's because yer've grown a bit since then,' Dot suggested, her imagination running riot as in her mind's eye she pictured the big woman trying to tap-dance. 'That could have something to do with it.'

'Yeah, yer could be right, girl, 'cos I have put a bit of weight on. Not that much, mind yer, not so yer'd notice. Only about ten stone, give or take a pound or two either way.' Betty screwed up her face, folded her arms and tried to cross her legs. But no matter how hard she tried she couldn't get her right leg over her left. To the amusement of the onlookers, every time she managed, with a lot of exertion and determination, to get it almost over, it just slid off. In the end, with a grunt of disgust, she gave it up as a bad job, saying, 'All right, if that's what yer want, sod yer.'

John had his eye on the clock. 'Dot, we're not going to make it to Southport. It's nearly two o'clock now – by the time we got there, it would be time to come home.'

'It's me mate's fault, keeping us talking. Perhaps we'd better skip Southport for today.' Dot noticed the smile leave her son's face and felt sorry for him. He'd really been looking

371

forward to it, counting off the days. 'We can go another day, sunshine, we've got two whole weeks off.'

'We could go tomorrow and spend the whole day there,' John said, hoping to ease the disappointment. He didn't care where they went as long as he was with Dot, but he didn't want to let the boy down. 'We wouldn't have to rush back, and Katy and Billy could come with us.'

'I know this is going to break yer hearts,' Betty said, 'but I wouldn't be able to come with yer tomorrow because me family like their Sunday dinner.'

'Well, seeing as you and Dot are all dressed up, we'll have to go somewhere. How about going into town and getting on one of the ferries?'

Colin grinned. 'Oh, yeah! But we will go to Southport tomorrow, won't we?'

'Scout's honour,' John promised, pushing himself up from the chair. 'Let's be on our way and call into the sweetshop so Katy can see how lovely her mother looks.'

'Ay, what about her mother's friend?' Betty was putting her poor chair through torture as she made several attempts to part it from her backside. 'Here's me, all glamorous in me French navy with a white spot, and I don't get a look in!'

'Betty, you look adorable.'

The big woman preened herself. 'I knew yer thought that, but were too shy to say it. That's why I gave yer a gentle hint. I've got a feeling that, deep down, yer fancy me. And I wouldn't be the least bit surprised if I opened me door one night to see yer standing there with a pleading look in yer eye, asking, "Do yer take lodgers in, Missus?".'

'Oh, Mam, yer look lovely.' Katy's face glowed with pride. 'Mrs Edwards, come and see me mam's dress.'

Molly came to stand beside her young assistant. 'She's been on pins waiting for yer to come in. I've been hearing nothing but this dress since Thursday, but now I know why. It's real bonny, Dot, and it doesn't half suit yer.'

The arms were folded and the bosom hitched up as Betty glared at the woman behind the counter. 'Ay, missus, how about telling me *I* look nice? Me what buys me regular quarter of walnut toffee and helps to keep a roof over yer head.'

'You always look the picture of elegance, Betty, so I suppose we take yer for granted. I've never see yer look anything short of perfection, from yer head to yer toes.'

The doorbell tinkled and Katy smiled when she saw who the customer was. 'Hello, Mrs Fitzsimmons, ye're early today. But I'm glad yer are 'cos now yer can meet me mam.'

The little old lady smiled to reveal her toothless gums. 'I don't need to be told that, queen, 'cos ye're the spittin' image of each other. Now I know where yer get yer good looks from.' She shuffled across the shop floor to where Dot was standing with a smile of welcome on her face. 'Yeah, alike as two peas in a pod. And I bet yer've always got a smile on yer face like yer daughter has. She brightens my day, does young Katy, she's a little cracker and I bet ye're proud of her.'

Dot couldn't resist bending to kiss the wrinkled face. 'I am proud of her, sunshine, and of me son. I've been blessed with two good'uns.'

The shop door tinkled again and all eyes turned to see Rita Williams and Dolly Armstrong struggling to get through the narrow entrance with their arms linked. 'Yer'll break that ruddy door one of these days,' Molly called. 'And if yer do, I'll send yer the repair bill.'

Rita had an answer on her lips, but the sight of Dot struck her dumb. And as John, standing on the side-lines with Colin, was to say later, he'd never seen anything so funny. She squeezed her friend's arm, and when Dolly looked at her to see what she wanted, Rita rolled her eyes several times towards where Dot was standing. Then both women stood and gawped.

It was Katy who broke the silence. 'And here's the terrible twins. Good afternoon to you, ladies.'

Rita shook herself free of Dolly's arm and drew herself to her full height. 'Hello, queen, I see yer've got all yer family here today.'

'Yeah, it's me mam's birthday. Doesn't she look marvellous?'

'Oh, Happy Birthday, Dot.' Rita's eyes lighted on John and she asked herself, who do they think they're kidding? There's definitely something fishy going on between these two, it's sticking out a mile. The trouble was, Dot Baker never stood gossiping in the street like normal neighbours did, so they couldn't get to the bottom of her. 'Ye're all dressed up like a dog's dinner.'

Katy was ready for her. 'Ye're only jealous, Mrs Williams. Anyway, I bet your dog doesn't get a dinner what looks as good as me mam does.'

Dolly Armstrong found her voice. 'No, it doesn't, queen, 'cos she hasn't got a bleedin' dog. She can't stand them, won't have one near her. I have to lock our Rover in the kitchen when she comes to our house.' Delighted that for once she wasn't the butt of everyone's laughter, she went on: 'I'll let yer into a secret, queen – our Rover's terrified of her. I don't have to lock him out, he scarpers as soon as he hears her voice.'

Oh, she's not getting away with that, Rita thought, winking at Dot. 'I take that back. Yer don't look like a dog's dinner, yer look like the cat's whiskers.' She turned and gave a sharp nod of her head to Dolly. 'There yer are, yer can't crack any jokes about that because yer've not got no bleedin' cat.'

Dolly was congratulating herself on her sharp wit when she said, 'No, it's sad, that is. We used to have a cat, Tiddles, but we haven't seen hide nor hair of her since the first day you came to our house. She took one look at yer and ran hell for leather out of the back door, never to be seen again.' Then, to add to her delight, she remembered a word she'd heard once and thought how clever it was. But she'd never had the occasion to use it, until now. 'Yer seem to have a profound effect on animals, girl.'

The loudest laughter came from Rita. 'Is that why yer tortoise has been in hibernation for the last four years? Oh dear, oh dear. I'm going to have to buy a collar and lead for yer, so I can keep yer in check.'

'No need to do that, girl, I'll save yer the money,' said a straight-faced but exhilarated Dolly. 'Yer can borrow our Rover's.'

Two more customers came into the shop and Molly moved with reluctance to the other end of the counter. 'Come on, Mrs Fitzsimmons, let's get you done and dusted.'

The old lady's smile covered everyone. 'Thank yer for

cheering me up. I'll be laughing at that until it's time for bed.'
She shuffled to where Molly was waiting. 'Just a pennyworth
of snuff, queen.'

'We'll have to go, too,' Dot said, before smiling at the two
neighbours she usually avoided like the plague because they
were the worst gossip-mongers in the neighbourhood. But
she could see now why her daughter thought they were
hilarious. 'Mind you, I could listen to you two all day, you're
so funny. It's no wonder our Katy looks forward to yer coming
in the shop.'

The two women grew six inches upwards and outwards.
'She's a good girl, is your Katy,' Dolly said. 'We're very fond
of her, aren't we, Rita?'

'Yeah,' Rita agreed. 'There's only one thing wrong with
her, she won't let us fight in the shop. She makes us wait until
we're outside, and by that time we've forgotten what we were
arguing about in the first place.'

'Well, it's been a pleasure.' Dot turned to Betty and frowned.
'I've never known you so quiet, sunshine, yer haven't opened
yer mouth. That's not a bit like you.'

'I know me limits, girl.' Her friend grinned. 'I'm not daft
enough to try and compete with a double act. Unfair
competition, that would be.'

Katy saw John leading Colin to the door and called, 'Which
picture house are we going to, Mr Kershaw?'

'It's your mother's birthday, Katy, we go where she wants
to go.'

'We're going to see something that will make me laugh,
not frighten the life out of me,' Dot said. 'William Powell in
The Thin Man, that's just up my street.'

Rita and Dolly exchanged glances that said this might be
the time to glean a juicy tit-bit. 'Are yer all going to the pictures,
then?' Rita asked hopefully.

Old crafty boots, Dot thought, always fishing for gossip.
She smiled sweetly. 'Yeah, and John's bringing his ladyfriend.'

John pulled Colin through the door and passed the window
of the shop before letting his laughter rip. 'Your mother had
the last laugh, there, Colin. I think she's adorable.'

'And lovable, Mr Kershaw. Yer do think she's lovable, as well, don't yer?'

'Man-to-man, son, yes, I do think she's lovable.'

Colin made up his mind then that he would try and arrange things so his hero and his mam were thrown together more. But he was thwarted that afternoon as his mother stuck to Betty's side like glue. She made sure she sat in the same seat as her on the tram, and on the ferry the two women leaned against the rails nattering while John and the boy walked the decks.

He had a bit more luck in the pictures, pushing himself in the row after Billy and Katy, but he might as well not have bothered for all the good it did him. It was a comedy film, and nobody wants their hands holding when they're splitting their sides laughing at the antics of a dog that was cleverer than its owners. He sighed when they came out of the cinema, consoling himself that he might have more luck tomorrow, when they went to Southport. And there were still two weeks' holiday ahead of them; anything could happen in two weeks.

'It's been donkey's ages since I came to Southport. Well, yer can tell how long, I was only courting Ted at the time,' Dot said, her tongue licking the side of the ice-cream cornet where the melting ice was running. She was wearing her new dress again and she'd have a fit if she got a stain on it. The children were walking ahead as she strolled down the pier with John.

'Once we got married we could never afford to come. There were too many things we needed to buy for the house.' She glanced sideways. 'He was very houseproud, was my Ted, and the house was like a little palace with all brand-new furniture.'

'Your house is nice as it is, Dot.' John sighed inwardly. Was this her way of warning him off? Or did she really not know how he felt about her? 'As soon as you walk through the door you can feel its warmth and comfort, and the love there is in it.'

'Ye're very poetic, John, yer know all the right words to say.'

'Not true, Dorothy. There are some very easy words I have great difficulty getting out.'

'I don't believe that. What sort of words?'

'For instance, "I like you, do you like me"?'

'Are you pulling my leg, John Kershaw? Yer say there's some words yer can't get out, and then yer go and say them!'

'But you didn't answer them, did you?'

'I didn't know I was supposed to! Say them again.'

'I like you, do you like me?'

'Of course I like yer, yer big daft nit! I wouldn't be here now if I didn't like yer.' Dot popped the end of the cornet in her mouth and quickened her pace. 'Come on, let's catch up with the children.'

If I didn't know her better, I'd think she was teasing me, John thought as he hurried after her. But I'm not going to give up. I'll stay around until the day she tells me straight out that she doesn't want to see me any more. He crossed his fingers, hoping that day would never come.

But six months later, John was no further advanced and his fingers were still crossed.

Chapter Twenty-Three

The glowing coals and the dancing flames in the O'Connors' grate had baby Trudy chuckling and clapping her tiny hands. 'She only sees a proper fire when she comes in here,' Mary said, bouncing the child up and down on her knee. 'We're lucky if we get a flicker out of the few coals we have on, and with this cold weather it's freezing in our living room.'

'I've told yer, sweetheart, there's no need for you and the baby to sit in the cold. It's more than welcome yer are in here, and isn't it true that the fire eats no more coal whether there's two or ten people sitting in front of it.' Maggie held her arms wide as she crossed the room. 'Come to yer auntie, me darlin', and let me have a cuddle.'

Trudy's arms and legs were waving excitedly. She was a pleasant child, always smiling and contented. Only Mary knew that in her own home, when her father was in, there were no smiles on her pretty face. Young as she was, she had learned that any noise she made would bring forth loud, angry shouting which frightened her.

'Yer get more like yer mammy every day, me darlin', so yer do.' Maggie held the child out and pretended to waltz with her. Faster and faster she twirled, much to the delight of the baby who was chuckling loudly. 'It's bonny yer are, too, me darlin' – sure, can't I feel yer getting heavier every day?'

'Her legs are strong,' Mary said, a proud, loving smile on her face. 'Sit her on yer knee, Maggie, facing her, and see how she tries to stand up.'

Maggie sat down and put a hand under each of Trudy's arms to stop her from falling backwards, and gasped in surprise when she felt two tiny feet digging into her tummy as the baby tried to stand up. 'Well, I never! Will yer look at that, now? Won't yer Uncle Paddy get a surprise when he knows? The day's not far off when he'll be holding yer little hand and walking yer down the street, and won't he be the proudest man in Liverpool?'

'She's advanced for her age, isn't she?' Mary sat back, basking in the warmth, comfort and love she could feel all around her. She felt more at home in this house than she ever had in her own. The daily visits here, and to Dot's, were the highlight of her days. Even at the weekend she never missed. Tom had tried to stop her in the beginning, threatening to do all sorts to her. But she'd ignored his threats and walked out with the baby. He still snarled and made sarcastic remarks, but he'd never lifted a hand to her. 'Remember, she's not six months old until next week.'

Maggie was holding on tight as Trudy bounced up and down on her lap. She loved the child as if she were her own, and it showed in the delight on her face. 'Will yer be getting a Christmas tree for her? Sure, her eyes would pop out of her head, so they would, if she saw a tree all decorated with tinsel and coloured balls. She'd not understand the meaning of it, but she's all there in the head, she doesn't miss anything.'

'There'll be no tree, Maggie, I'm afraid. My husband thinks that Christmas was invented for men to get drunk, not to give their wives extra money for food or presents.'

'Then yer must bring her in here on Christmas Day, spend the day with us.' Maggie hugged the child and rained kisses on her. 'We'll have a grand tree, so we will. And wouldn't it make my Paddy's day to have yer both here?'

'I wouldn't impose on yer on Christmas Day, yer have us every other day of the year. But thanks for asking, Maggie.'

'Impose? It's a favour yer'd be doing us, me darlin', and that's the truth of it. Since we came to England, me and Paddy have spent the day on our own. We've neither kith nor kin, so having you and Trudy would be like having a family. It would make all the difference, give us a reason to decorate the room and have a tree. It's a big favour yer'd be doing us, Mary, and I'm saying that from the bottom of my heart. But I know things aren't easy for yer, and I wouldn't want to cause trouble between you and yer husband.'

Thinking of the cheerless room, with a tiny fire burning in the grate, no food to put on the table and not a sign or a word to make it a special day, different from any other, Mary decided quickly. 'We'd love to come, if you're sure yer want us.'

Maggie's face lit up, then she looked anxious. 'Would yer not get in trouble with yer husband? Sure, I'm selfish enough to want yer, and so would Paddy be, but not if it means yer suffering for it.'

'I'll probably be cursed from here to hell and back, Maggie, but I can stand verbal abuse, it just rolls off my back now. He won't lift his hand to me, hasn't done since I had the baby. And it's her I've got to think of; she's the most important thing in my life. Her first Christmas should be spent with people she loves and who love her. I've put up with years of squalor, poverty and a loveless marriage, but that was my own doing, it's what I chose. But Trudy didn't choose Tom Campbell for a father, so I don't see why she should suffer for my mistakes. She'll have enough to put up with when she's old enough to walk. I can't be with her every minute of her life to stop those who will skit and make fun of her. So while she can, I want her to have as much happiness that life can give her.'

Maggie sighed. 'Does Tom know about her leg?'

'I haven't told him; we don't even pass each other the time of day. I haven't even told me mam, yet, because we don't know how bad the limp is going to be and I don't want her to worry any more than she has to. But as to my husband, yer can rest assured that he'll be the first to poke fun at her.'

'He'd better not let Paddy hear him, or John. Not unless he wants to end up in hospital with two broken legs.' Maggie noticed the baby had stopped bouncing and was looking at her questioningly. 'Will yer look at this one? She wants to know why I'm not smiling, don't yer, sweetheart? Sure, she's quick to sense things, right enough, so I'll put the smile back.' She gazed across at Mary. 'I've never been a violent person in me life, with me fists or with me tongue, and that's the God's honest truth. But if it came to Tom Campbell getting a hiding for hurting you or the baby, I'd not shed a tear for the man.'

* * *

'In two days, it will be exactly one year since I first came in this house.' John had his long legs stretched out and Dot had to step over them. 'I can remember it clearly, can you?'

Dot looked at him with surprise. 'What made yer think of that?'

'Because it was the day that changed my life. I came in here carrying Colin, expecting to put him down, explain what had happened, and be on my way. Instead I've been here nearly every day since.'

'Are yer bragging or complaining, John? Or did yer think it was a bit of useless information I should know?' Dot lifted his feet to straighten the rug in front of the hearth, then she let them drop, 'Anyway, how d'yer mean, it was the day that changed yer life?'

'You've changed my life. You and the children. Before I met you, I used to spend every night in the house on my own.'

'Oh dear, shall I get the violin out, John Kershaw, so yer can go all dramatic on me? It does help to have violin music in the background.'

Colin looked up from the comic he was reading. Why couldn't his mam make an effort to be nice to Mr Kershaw? He'd done all he could to help his hero but none of it had worked. Twelve months now, and they were still just friends. In that time, he'd had a birthday and so had Katy. They'd both got good presents, better than other years, but the present they would both have liked was his mam realising she was fond enough of the big man to let him court her. 'I wouldn't have thought of it, Mr Kershaw, but I'm glad yer reminded me. The day I ran into your bike was a good day for all of us, wasn't it, Mam?'

Dot was about to make a joke of it, but changed her mind. She made jokes of a lot of things these days, then regretted it afterwards. 'Of course it was, sunshine. It brought a new friend into our house, didn't it?'

Man and boy looked at each other and shrugged. No matter what they said, they couldn't break down the barrier that Dot had built around herself where John was concerned. 'Would you allow your new friend to make a suggestion, then?'

Dot was immediately suspicious. 'Oh, aye, what is it now?'

'Let me give a party in my house on Christmas Day. You could all come, and we could ask the Masons, the O'Connors and Billy. And Mary, of course, if she could make it. I'd like to have a party to pay everyone back for the hospitality they've shown me over the year.'

'Oh John, I've already asked the Masons down for a drink on Christmas Day, and Mary's going to the O'Connors'.' Dot saw the disappointment on his face and felt as though she'd kicked a man while he was down. 'I took it for granted you'd be coming here – we all did, didn't we, Colin? Anyway, all those people, it would be a lot of work for yer.'

'I was going to ask you to help me.'

'Oh, yer make me feel like a right heel, now. But Mary and the O'Connors had already made their plans before I knew anything about it.' Dot groaned inwardly. Why was it she always seemed to put a damper on anything he suggested? He was a real gentleman, so kind and generous, yet she treated him like a child. 'I'll tell you what we can do, John, if it's OK with you. Let's have your party in this house, eh? Yer can have yer Christmas dinner with us, then the rest of the day will be yours. I'll help yer, we all will, but you say what yer want, who yer want, and yer can pay for all the food and stuff.' When he didn't answer, she went on, 'The O'Connors would come, and Mary. She'd have to leave early because of the baby, but she'd come for an hour or so.' When there was still no response, she put her hands on her hips and tilted her head. 'John Kershaw, will yer open yer ruddy mouth?'

John was smiling when he looked up. Was this a step forward? 'You mean you will actually let me pay for all the food, and the drink? We'll have to have a few bottles in, otherwise it wouldn't be a party.'

'It'll be your party, yer can be in total control.'

He jumped from the chair. 'Right now you are at your most Delightful, Dorothy. So much so I have this urge to kiss you.' He did so quickly, before she could move out of his way. 'That has quite made up for the disappointment I felt.'

'Ay, you!' Dot wagged a finger under his nose. 'Have yer forgotten that my son is watching?'

'Oh yes, I had forgotten, I'm sorry.' John winked at the boy who had suddenly let hope into his heart. 'Colin, do I have your permission to kiss your mother?'

'Yer certainly do, Mr Kershaw!'

'Right, thank you.' As he turned, Dot was backing away from him. When her legs struck the edge of the couch she fell backwards and her hands flayed the air trying to balance herself. John reached out to try and save her, and when Dot fell back on to the couch he couldn't right himself and fell on top of her. It happened so quickly Colin was dumbstruck for a few seconds, then, roaring with laughter he made a giant leap and landed on top of both of them.

'Get off, both of yer.' Dot's muffled voice was a mixture of laughter and embarrassment. She could feel her skirt riding up her thighs and couldn't get to it. 'Me blinkin dress is around me neck, now get off.'

'Shall we keep her there, son, to teach her a lesson?'

'Is she laughing?'

'I think so.'

'As long as she's laughing, we're all right. But as soon as she stops, get as far away from her as yer can 'cos she'll murder us.'

Tom Campbell was passing the Bakers' window and heard the laughter. 'Silly cow,' he muttered to himself. 'All these years without a man, she can't be made right.'

His hands deep in his pockets and head bent against the cold wind, he quickened his pace. He'd fancied Dot Baker himself at one time, but not now. Oh, not now. She'd probably be a cold fish in bed, like his wife. There's no way they could satisfy his needs as Esmée did. They'd die rather than do some of the things she got up to.

It was a long walk to Seaforth from Edith Road, but he couldn't afford to get a tram or bus, not if he was to keep up with his twice-weekly visits. Anyway, the walk did him good, whetted his appetite for the pleasures to come. He was very sore between his legs though, and it didn't seem to be getting any better. Esmée had told him it was nothing to worry about, he should ask the chemist for some cream. But he didn't have the nerve to do that, wouldn't know what to say. He'd look a right nit walking into a shop and saying, 'I've got a sore on my thingy.'

The pub was crowded and a waft of warm, smoky air hit him when he pushed the door open. He elbowed his way to the bar, ordered a pint of bitter and let his eyes roam the room in search of Esmée. She'd be expecting him, this was one of his regular nights. There was no sign of her however, so he leaned on the counter and slowly sipped his beer. She'd come breezing in any minute and would seek him out. She didn't waste any time, because time was money for her.

Tom looked at the clock on the wall behind the bar. It was nearly nine o'clock; she'd never kept him waiting this long before. Then he saw Elsie coming through the door with a foreign sailor on her arm. It was she who'd introduced him to this life, and to Esmée. He beckoned her over and she pushed her companion towards an empty seat before joining him at the bar.

Her voice was abrupt. 'What d'yer want? I'm a working girl, I've got no time to spare.'

'Esmée's late tonight. D'yer know where she is?'

Elsie, whose real name was Alice, stared at him hard for a few seconds, then jerked her head towards the door. 'Come outside for a minute. What I've got to say is for your ears only.'

Tom hunched his shoulders when the cold air hit him. 'What's up? Is she sick?'

The prostitute looked right and left before answering. 'Oh, she's sick, all right. Only got the bleedin' clap, hasn't she? Syphilis, no less.'

The implication took a while to sink in, then the sensation between his legs seemed to magnify. 'Oh no, don't tell me that.'

'Oh, bleedin' yes, I will tell yer that! And she's probably passed it on to all her punters – you included.'

'But how d'yer know?' Tom's heartbeat was racing and he began to break out in a cold sweat. 'Are yer sure?'

'Of course I'm bleedin' sure, yer stupid bastard! D'yer think I'd make something like that up? The stupid cow must have known for months that she's got it, but she carried on without saying a word. Now all the poor buggers she went with will have it, and they'll pass it on to their wives and girlfriends.'

'How did yer find out?'

'One of her regulars came lookin' for her, and she scarpered as soon as she saw him. Bloody good job she did, he'd have strangled her. The poor sod went to see his doctor, not knowing what was wrong with him, and was told he had a venereal disease that there was no cure for. The bloke was out of his mind and came looking for her. She'd better not show herself around here 'cos the women will lynch her. It's not goin' to do our business any good if it gets about, so keep yer trap shut.'

'Are any of the other women free for twenty minutes?'

'Listen, lover boy, none of us would touch yer with a barge-pole now. Yer must be riddled with the clap – it stands to sense, yer were one of her best punters.' She pushed him in the chest and spoke through gritted teeth. 'D'yer think we're all bloody nut-cases, eh?' Again she pushed him. 'Yer'd better go home and tell yer wife yer've been a naughty boy, hadn't yer? That's if yer've got the bleedin' guts.'

Tom hung his head, and when he spoke he kept his voice quiet to hide the anger building up inside him. He needed the help of this woman. 'Can yer buy anything to get rid of it?'

'Go and see yer doctor, that's my advice. And I'll give yer another bit of advice – don't show yer face in these parts again.' Alice wrapped her coat more closely around her voluptuous body. She'd never liked this man, his eyes were too close together for her liking, but she couldn't help feeling a flicker of sympathy. 'I don't know nothing about it, thank Christ, and I don't want to. Yer'd be best seeing yer doctor. And I wouldn't leave it too long, either.' With that she spun on her heels and left him.

Tom let out a cry of rage and punched the brick wall with his curled fist. He didn't feel the pain or the skin bursting on his knuckles, he was too full of anger against everyone but himself. If his wife hadn't been such a prude, he wouldn't be in this fix. And that cow, Elsie, she was the one who'd picked him up that night in the pub, and she'd told him about this place. As for Esmée, that bleeding scheming bitch must have known she'd passed it on to him. She kept on taking his money even though she knew it wasn't just a rash he had. The crafty cow had seen the hard, round flat sores, she must have known what they were because she probably had them herself.

He let out another cry of rage as he pictured her in his mind's eye. She was looking at him with such an innocent expression on her face, saying, 'It's only a rash, lover boy. Go to the chemist and get some cream to rub on it.' And he'd fallen for it. Like a fool he'd believed her, as he'd believed all the flattery she dished out about him being the best lover out of all her customers. She'd certainly taken him for a ride, as she had many others from the sound of things. He'd been a fool, and now he was in a right mess. Elsie said there was no cure for it, but the bitch would say that just to put the fear of God into him. She'd get a kick out of it because she made no bones about the fact that she didn't like him.

Tom put his hands in his pockets and began the long walk home. He wasn't a happy, satisfied man tonight, though, he was a man with fear in his heart. What if there was no cure for it? *Of course there's a cure for it*, a little voice in his head said. *Don't take any notice of that tart, she was just trying to frighten you*. And because that was what he wanted to hear, Tom believed that small voice. 'Yeah, that's right,' he muttered to himself. 'I'll put a clean pair of underpants on in the morning and call to the doctor's on me way home from work. He won't tell no one, 'cos doctors have to swear on oath that they won't tell.'

A look of distaste came over Dr Gray's face when he called for the next patient and Tom Campbell walked in. The last time he'd seen this rotter was when he'd been called out to see his wife when she was in labour. He remembered the bruising on her and the pain she was in. He also remembered being ordered out of the bedroom and Mrs Campbell being told to get downstairs and see to this man's dinner. So his voice was cold when he asked, 'What do you want?'

Tom Campbell was shaking with fear, but he wasn't going to let this feller see it. After all, this visit was going to cost him one and sixpence and he wanted his money's worth. 'Ye're not allowed to tell anyone what we say in this room, are yer?'

'Are you trying to teach me my job, Mr Campbell?'

There was steel in the voice and Tom told himself he'd better tread carefully or he'd be thrown out. 'No, I didn't mean nothing like that, Doctor. But yer see, it's very personal and I wouldn't want no one to find out.'

'Out with it, man, and don't be wasting my time. I've got a surgery full of people waiting to see me.'

'Well, it's like this, Doctor. I got drunk one night and I went with this prostitute. It was when me wife was due to have the baby and she wouldn't let me have me marital rights. I wouldn't have done it if I hadn't been drunk, mind, but I was badly in need of a woman's company. D'yer follow me meaning?'

'You've been with prostitutes, Mr Campbell, and you now fear you have venereal disease. Is that what you're telling me?' When Tom nodded, the doctor pointed to a screen. 'Go behind there, take off your trousers and lie on the couch. I'll be with you in a minute.'

Five minutes later the doctor came from behind the screen pulling off a pair of rubber gloves. 'Get dressed, Mr Campbell.' He went to a sink in the corner of the room and while he was washing his hands, he was thinking that this was a day of judgement for the arrogant Mr Campbell. He felt no pity for the man, but he was concerned for his wife.

The doctor was sitting back at his desk when Tom came from behind the screen, buttoning up his trousers. 'It's only a rash, isn't it, Doctor?'

'No, I'm afraid it isn't. The disease is called syphilis and it is in an advanced state, which means you were infected several months ago. You are paying for your sins now, Mr Campbell, because your version of a one-night stand is a pack of lies. You would have to be the unluckiest man alive to have picked up a prostitute carrying the disease in what you say was just the one night of debauchery.'

Him and his big words, Tom Campbell thought, they're not going to help me. 'Can yer give me anything for it?'

The doctor shook his head. 'There is no cure for it and I

know of nothing that would halt the process. You will experience other symptoms in the near future, like headaches, feverishness and sickness. I can give you something to help with those, so I suggest you come to see me again when you feel it necessary.'

'It won't kill me, will it?'

'I can't tell you when you're going to die, Mr Campbell, no more than I can tell you when I'm going to die, or any of the people sitting in the surgery. I could tell you you were going to die, then you could live to be a hundred. On the other hand, I could say you weren't, and you could go outside and be run over by a bus.' The doctor pushed his chair back and stood up. 'I have a lot of patients waiting to see me. But before you go I must warn you, under no circumstances are you to have intercourse with your wife. Do I make myself perfectly clear?'

Tom nodded and shuffled towards the door. He didn't see why he should tell the quack he hadn't been near his wife for six months and didn't intend to. Why should he when he was better pleasured elsewhere?

On Christmas Eve, John came in laden with parcels wrapped in colourful Christmassy paper. He laid them out under the tree and stood back to admire the effect. 'That just adds the finishing touch, don't you think, D.D.?'

Dot looked at the number of neatly wrapped, labelled parcels. 'I hope yer haven't been splashing out, John Kershaw, 'cos we've only got little presents for you.'

'It's not the gift, it's the thought that counts.' He gazed around the room which was festooned with balloons and coloured streamers. And the big silver star hanging from the gas light was turning around with the draught coming through from the kitchen. 'The room looks lovely and cosy, doesn't it?'

'Yeah,' Colin said, coming through with a shovelful of coal. 'Yer did a good job on it, Mr Kershaw, it looks brilliant.'

Dot tutted. 'I wish yer'd close the kitchen door when yer go out for coal, sunshine. Yer let all the warmth out.'

'Sorry, Mam, I keep forgetting.' Colin threw the coal on the fire and as he turned he spotted the presents. 'Wow! Just look at them, Mam!'

'You keep yer fingers off them, sunshine, they're not to be touched until the morning. And I don't want yer getting me up at six o'clock, either. Ye're almost thirteen years of age now, not a blinking baby.'

'What time will the presents be getting opened, Dorothy? I'd like to be here for that. It's the highlight of Christmas Day, isn't it?' John smiled down into her face. 'I don't want to miss the excitement.'

Dot rolled her eyes to the ceiling. 'Ye're worse than our Colin, you are. But ye're not coming here at seven in the morning, not to see me looking like something the cat dragged in.'

'We've no need to open them at seven, Mam,' Colin said. 'We could leave it until about nine o'clock. That's not too early, is it?'

'What! You, leave yer presents until nine o'clock?'

'For Mr Kershaw I would, yeah.'

'Wonders will never cease.' Dot didn't know what else to say. She couldn't tell him they didn't get dressed until after they'd opened their presents, and that she'd be in her old nightdress with her hair all skew-whiff. But she was being selfish. It wouldn't hurt her to get up a bit earlier and get dressed properly. Better for her to do that than have John sitting alone at home while they were laughing and whooping it up as they opened their presents. 'Nine o'clock, then, and not a minute before.'

'Nine o'clock it shall be, Dorothy, your word is my command.' John looked through to the kitchen. 'Where's Katy, is she out with Billy?'

'No, she's working late. She should be in any minute now, though.' Dot stretched her arms over her head and yawned. 'Christmas Day is the nicest day of the year, but the week leading up to it is a nightmare for mothers. Thank goodness I've prepared the dinner, that's a load off me mind. Oh, and by the way, we only have toast for breakfast, so don't say yer haven't been warned.'

'That will suit me fine.' John stifled a yawn and grinned. 'You've got me at it now.'

'It's funny that, isn't it, Mr Kershaw?' Colin ran a hand

across his face leaving a streak of coal dust. 'When one yawns, everybody yawns. I wonder why that is?'

'One of the mysteries of the world, son. Like young Billy wanting to go away to sea. I never thought he was serious when he used to talk about it, but here he is, ready for the off.'

'He's had it in his mind for years,' Dot said, 'so it's best he gets it out of his system before he settles down. He'll only be away about three weeks, but what a time to go, four days after Christmas. Lousy timing.'

'He won't like it, yer know, Mam.' Colin nodded his head knowingly. 'I bet he's as sick as a pig all the time. Remember that ship in *Mutiny on the Bounty*? It bobbed up and down like a cork. Billy won't like that.'

'That's for him to find out for himself, sunshine. All I know is, our Katy will miss him. And if it comes to that, I'll miss him as well.'

'And he'll miss her,' John said. 'They were made for each other.'

When there was a knock on the door, Colin answered it and Katy came in, her face wreathed in smiles. 'Mam, yer'll never guess, I've got a shilling a week rise in me wages. Isn't that the gear?'

'Oh, I'm made up for yer, sunshine, 'cos yer deserve it. Ye're a cracking little worker and Molly and Jim are showing their appreciation.'

'Nice work, our Katy.' Colin grinned. 'I wish someone would show me some appreciation 'cos I work hard.'

'This time next year you'll be looking for a job,' John reminded him. 'Work hard for your boss and you'll be rewarded accordingly.'

Dot dug her fists into the couch and pushed herself up. 'I'll see to yer tea, sunshine. Oh, yer'll be glad to know that John will be here at nine o'clock in the morning for the opening of the presents ceremony. So it's up and dressed by half-eight.'

'I don't mind that, Mam. I'm glad Mr Kershaw will be here.'

Her smile of pleasure was so genuine it touched John's heart. He got up from his chair to hug her. 'Thank you, Katy.'

Dot put the light out under the pan keeping her daughter's dinner warm, then turned to go back into the living room to set the table for her. She stopped on the threshold when she saw John with a hand on each of Katy's shoulders, smiling down at her. And her daughter's smile was one of such obvious affection, it turned Dot around and she retreated to the kitchen. There she stood with her hands gripping the edge of the sink. The two kids were getting too fond of him, he was almost like a father to them.

Tears came to Dot's eyes. But he wasn't their father, he wasn't, he wasn't, he wasn't!

John insisted on pouring a glass of sherry for Dot and himself, and a glass of lemonade for the children. 'We may as well enjoy ourselves whilst opening our presents.' This was all very new and exciting to him and he was enjoying every minute of it. His mother had never made a big fuss over Christmas, she wasn't that type of person. Oh, she bought him presents and they always had a tree, but it was a quiet affair. There was never an air of festivity as there was here in the Bakers' house. They'd pulled crackers as soon as he'd arrived, laughed themselves silly over the mottos inside and were now wearing the paper hats.

'Shall I give the presents out, Mam?' Katy asked, rubbing her hands in excitement. 'Or do you want to do it?'

'You do it, sunshine, but give our Colin his first before he has a heart attack. We'll open them one at a time and he can be the first.'

Colin downed his lemonade in one go and waited expectantly. His eyes grew wider and his shoulders jiggled as Katy put parcel after parcel on his knees. 'That's right, our kid, you just keep them coming.'

'That's yer lot, greedy guts.'

'I've got six, Mam, six presents! I've never had that many before.'

'Are yer going to open them, sunshine, or just sit and look at them all day?'

The first parcel he opened contained a pair of bedroom slippers from John. He put them on his feet right away and danced up and down the room. 'Oh, they're dead comfortable. Thank you, Mr Kershaw.' Next came a pair of grey trousers from his mother, and this brought a cheeky grin to his face. 'I won't try these on for size because I'd have to go upstairs and I don't want to miss anything.' Then came a Christmas stocking that his grandma had brought down and which had been hidden away until now. He was all for eating one of the chocolate bars until his mother put her foot down saying it would put him off his dinner.

There were two presents from Katy – a pale blue shirt and a matching tie. He'd never possessed a tie before and his shout was so loud the people living next door either side must have heard him. 'Ay, look at this! Won't I look dead grown-up, eh? I'll wear it for the party tonight, and there'll be no flies on me.'

'Colin, will yer put a move on? It'll be bedtime before we get to open ours.'

'Okay, Sis, keep her hair on, I've only got one more to open.' The last parcel turned out to be the latest *Beano Annual* from his mother, and after one loud shriek of delight, the boy buried his head in it and lost interest in the proceedings.

Katy was next, and she quickly opened her parcels. A pair of bedroom slippers from John, a box of hankies from her grandma, a blouse and underskirt from her mother and a handbag from Molly and Jim. 'Ooh, they're all lovely, I've done really well.' She laid the gifts on the couch before kissing her mother and John. 'Thank you, I'm a lucky girl.'

Dot's brow creased in a frown. 'Ay, Colin, where's yer sister's present?'

He looked up from his book and frowned back at her. 'What present, Mam?'

'Stop acting the goat, sunshine, 'cos I don't want to have to give yer a clout on Christmas Day. Now let's be having yer.'

'It's hanging on the tree, Katy. Look, just under the fairy. Shall I get it for yer?'

But Katy was already reaching for it. And her face split into a wide smile when she found the pair of stockings. 'Oh, they're just what I wanted!' Colin was hugged and kissed.

'All me others have got ladders in.'

Stepping over the discarded wrapping paper, she made for the tree. 'I feel sorry for you poor things, yer've only got two each, I'm afraid, the rest are all for Trudy. Still, let's hope they're good ones.'

John spread out his hands. 'Ladies first, Dorothy.'

Dot drained her glass and passed it to him before taking her parcels. Both of them bore the names of Katy, Colin and John. 'We all clubbed together to buy yer something decent, Mam,' Katy explained. 'We thought it was better than buying a lot of little fiddling things.'

'Hang on a second while I refill your glass.' John poured the sherry then watched anxiously as Dot fingered the large bulky parcel. He would have liked to have bought her something really nice, just from himself, but wasn't sure she'd accept it. So he'd done the next best thing and involved the children. 'Before you open them, Dorothy, and I get the length of your tongue, I want you to know that we three have been putting a certain amount away each week since September. Your daughter and son have handed the money over religiously every Saturday and I put it away. So they really are from the three of us.'

Dot took a drink before putting the glass down at the side of her chair. She was feeling warm inside and happy. 'This feller's got me half-drunk, I'll be seeing two of everything if I have any more.' She was grinning when she ripped the paper off the larger parcel. 'These should be good if yer all bought them.' But she gasped at the sight of the cherry-red, warm dressing gown. 'I don't know what to say. It's beautiful! I haven't had a dressing gown since – er – since Adam was a lad.'

Colin had come to join them, leaving his beloved *Beano* open at page ten. 'Yer've got another one, Mam, see what's in that.'

Dot looked at the three happy faces, all waiting for her reaction. So when she pulled a pair of cherry-red slippers from the paper, she didn't let them down. And her delight was genuine, she didn't have to pretend. 'I've done better than any of yer.' She held the soft fleecy dressing gown to her cheek and sighed happily. 'I'll be better dressed going to bed than I am on a Sunday morning going to church. And I'll swank to the neighbours if it kills me.' She chuckled. 'I know, I'll stand on the step on Tuesday morning and pretend I'm waiting for the postman. That should open a few eyes and set tongues wagging.'

Colin, too young to be tactful, had no qualms about telling his mother how he'd deprived himself over the last few months. 'Fourpence a week I've been saving, Mam. Haven't I been good?'

'Yer've been a treasure, sunshine, so has Katy and John. And while we're speaking of him, don't yer think Mr Kershaw would like to see what Father Christmas has brought him?'

It was Dot's turn to watch anxiously as John opened his presents. The dark brown pure wool cardigan had cost more than she'd ever paid for anything. She'd had to dip into the money they were saving to buy new furniture, but it couldn't be helped. All his clothes were of the best quality so there was no way she was going to let the side down by giving him something cheap.

'It's a very fine cardi, Dorothy, but you shouldn't have spent so much money on me.'

'I know I shouldn't, John Kershaw, but ye're getting a taste of yer own medicine now.'

John's pleasure came from knowing she'd taken the time to choose something she knew he would like. So she must think of him sometimes. 'I love it, and am delighted.'

And the two children were delighted when he kissed and hugged their mother. 'I shall wear it tonight for the party.'

'Ay, what about the present me and our Katy bought yer?'

John grinned and chucked the boy under the chin. 'I hadn't forgotten it, Colin, I'm very eager to see what it is.'

The tie had been chosen by Dot and was the same colour as the cardigan. And the two white handkerchiefs had his initial in the corner. The gifts had been chosen with care and he was very touched. 'I can honestly say, with my hand on my heart, this is the best Christmas I've ever had, thanks to the Baker family. And I'm going to be the best dressed at the party tonight, again thanks to the Baker family.'

'If I don't get a move on and see to the dinner, there won't *be* a party. I want the meal over and dishes washed by two o'clock, so I can start on the sandwiches. And while I'm busy in the kitchen, you lot can clear this mess.'

'Finish your drink off first, Dorothy.'

Dot made a great play of lumbering to her feet, where she stood swaying. 'Will yer stand still – hic – John Kershaw – hic – and stop moving around?' She narrowed her eyes. 'Is that yer brother with yer? Well, tell him – hic – to keep still as well. Between the pair of yer yer've got me dizzy.'

Katy and Colin saw the bemused expression on John's face and put their hands over their mouths to keep the laughter at bay. Mr Kershaw thought their mam was drunk!

'Dorothy, I'm not moving.'

The pose was dropped, the hands went on the hips and the head tilted. 'No, ye're not ruddy-well moving, are yer? Well, we'll soon alter that! Get this lot cleared away and be quick about it.'

John joined in the laughter before standing to attention, clicking his heels and giving a smart salute. 'Aye, aye, sir! On the double, *sir*!'

Chapter Twenty-Four

'It's been a marvellous day, and I want to thank you both for being so kind to Trudy and me.' Mary smiled from Maggie to Paddy. 'It reminded me of the happy Christmases I used to have when I was young and living with me mam and dad. If my daughter was old enough to be spoilt, then she certainly would be, with all the presents you bought her and the ones Dot and Betty brought down. She's got enough toys to last her for years. But will yer do us a favour and let me leave them here for now? If my husband's in a bad mood, which he probably will be, then I wouldn't put it past him to throw them on the fire.'

'Of course yer can leave them here, sweetheart, but why go home at all? You could come straight to Dot's, with me and Paddy.'

'No, I'll show me face. Besides, I want to get changed. I've still got a dress that John gave me and I haven't worn.' Mary smiled. 'I may as well show off and be as posh as everybody else.'

Paddy looked anxious. 'If yer husband starts his funny business, Mary, then just yell out. Sure, won't I be having me ear to the wall?'

'I'll scream the place down, Paddy, have no fear.' Mary wrapped the heavy shawl tightly around her daughter, leaving just her smiling face showing. 'Say ta-ta to Auntie Maggie and Uncle Paddy, and thank them for everything.'

Maggie stroked the smooth, silky cheek. 'Sure, this time next year yer'll be doing just that, won't yer, me darlin? It's all over the place yer'll be, gabbing yer little head off.'

'Please God.' Mary's eyes were tender as she held the baby close. 'It's what I pray for every night.' She gazed at the two people who had been so kind to them. 'I'll see you later, in Dot's. If I'm a bit late, don't worry because I'll feed Trudy before I come and she'll be ready for a nap. Dot said I can put her on the bed and with a bit of luck she'll sleep for a few hours.'

Maggie walked to the door with her. 'Are yer sure yer'll be all right, me darlin'?'

'I'll be fine.' Mary had the front door key ready in her hand. 'I'll see yer later.' She walked the few yards to her house, then turned to wave to Maggie before opening the door.

Tom Campbell was slouched in the chair and didn't even turn his head. Mary could see by his face he was in a foul temper, so she turned on her heels and made for the stairs. There was no way she'd leave the baby in the pram while her husband was in the room. She'd caught him pinching the child once, while she was in the kitchen seeing to his dinner. It was the child's crying that had brought her running, to find him leaning over the pram with an evil smile on his face. The next day she'd found a bruise on Trudy's arm. She swore then she'd never leave them alone together.

Mary went into the spare bedroom where she kept a kitchen chair to sit on while she was feeding the baby when Tom was home. It was the only item of furniture in the cold, cheerless room. On the floor, just inside the door, was a candle set in a saucer with a box of matches beside it, and hanging on a nail behind the door was the dress Mary was wearing for the party. She held the child tight in one arm while she reached down for the saucer which she set on the chair before striking a match. The flame flickered for a few seconds, then the wick caught and shed an eerie light on the walls and ceiling. It was like something you'd see in a horror movie, Mary thought, only this was for real.

'We'll have to make do as best we can, I'm afraid, darling. I'll feed you first then lay yer on the floor with my coat under yer, while I get changed.' Mary slipped one arm out of a sleeve, then changed the baby over to her other side while she slid the coat off and laid it as best she could on the floor.

Downstairs, Tom's mind was in turmoil. He needed a woman badly. He could go without food or drink, but not

398

without a woman. He'd thought about going down to Lime Street and picking up a prostitute, but he was afraid of prostitutes now, after Esmée. You couldn't tell by looking at them whether they had the disease or not, and he might be buying himself a load of trouble. He wouldn't let himself believe the doctor was right. He and that bitch Elsie didn't like him and were only saying there was no cure to frighten him. Of course there was a cure for it. He had a few sores, that was all, and they'd probably disappear of their own accord any day now. It was that Esmée, she was cause of it, far too rough she was. So he'd be doing himself a favour if he kept away from whores in future.

He beat his clenched fist on the arm of the couch. When he came to think about it, that doctor had a bloody cheek telling him to keep away from his wife. What he did in his own home, with his wife, was his business, it had nothing to do with anyone. That bloody quack must think he was a monk! To hell with that! He wanted a woman, he had one upstairs, and nobody would know the difference because Mary wouldn't tell anyone, she'd be too ashamed. And if he did have the clap, and he passed it on to her, so what?

Tom slipped off his shoes before creeping up the stairs. The door of the spare bedroom was slightly ajar and he could see Mary sitting on the chair feeding the baby. When he saw the full, ripe breast, he ran his tongue over lips dry with excitement. She'd filled out since she'd had the baby and what he saw he wanted. But he'd wait until she'd finished feeding the brat before pouncing. Just then he heard someone knocking at the Bakers' door, followed by the sound of voices and laughter. Mary had heard, too, and she raised her head. He moved back quickly, knowing that if she saw him she'd scream the place down. She'd fight him tooth and nail if he tried to take her, and then all hell would be let loose. Her friends would boot the door down and think nothing of it, he was sure of that.

As he crept down the dark staircase, he cursed everyone to high heaven. But there'd be other times, he vowed, when there'd be no one around to keep an eye on their precious Mary. Then he would get what he wanted, and more.

After three bottles of milk stout, Betty was in fine form. Standing in the middle of the room she had given her impersonation of Gracie Fields, Tessie O'Shea and George Formby. Not that she could sing like any of them, it was only the songs that gave her noisy, appreciative audience a clue as to who she was supposed to be. Now she was thinking who she could impersonate next. 'I know, I'll do the Street Singer, singing *Marta*, yer all know that.'

'Ah, no!' Alec groaned. 'Don't murder poor Arthur, he's me favourite.'

Betty glared at her husband. 'I don't see you getting off yer backside to entertain us. If we were all as miserable as you it would be a fine party. Mind you, yer haven't got a good voice, have yer, my love? More like a ruddy foghorn.'

Alec grinned. 'You haven't got a good voice, either, my sweet.'

'No, but I've got a bleedin' loud one.' And to prove it, Betty opened her mouth and let it rip, to much laughter and cheers. While she was belting out the words, beginning, 'Oh, we ain't got a barrel of money . . .' Betty was shaking her shoulders and hips in rhythm. And when she lifted her skirt to show off her nifty footwork, she also showed a large expanse of pale pink fleecy-lined bloomers above the knotted pieces of elastic keeping her stockings up.

The room rang with laughter, the stamping of feet and the clapping of hands. But the loudest laughter came from her husband, Alec, who adored every ounce of her eighteen-stone body. He'd loved her since the minute he'd clapped eyes on her at the local dance hall, with her long shiny hair bouncing on her shoulders, lovely slim figure and a smile that melted his heart. He envied the bloke who was twirling her around the dance floor and couldn't wait for the dance to finish to see if they were together. But to Alec's relief she gave her partner a smile then walked to the side of the hall where her girlfriend was standing. He beat off several rivals to claim the next dance and they'd been together ever since. His love for her had never dimmed over the years and he loved her as much now as he had then. She never complained, even when the children came along and money was tight with only his wage coming in. There was always a smile on her face and a joke on her lips. He'd got a good one when he got Betty, she was the perfect wife.

The only person in the room who didn't find it amusing was Doreen, whose nose was wrinkled in disgust. Why did her mother have to make a show of herself like this? She wasn't a bit funny, she looked ridiculous. 'Shall we go in the kitchen where we can talk, Katy? Yer can't hear yerself think with all this noise.'

Katy was enjoying herself and didn't want to miss any of the fun, but she couldn't help feeling sorry for her friend. Doreen didn't seem to be able to let herself go and have a good time. 'Me and Doreen are going in the kitchen for a few minutes, Billy,' she told him, 'but you don't have to come. You stay here and enjoy yerself.'

Billy turned to her, his face red where he'd been wiping away the tears of laughter with the back of his hand. 'Yer'll miss all the fun out there.'

'I know,' Katy whispered, 'but Doreen said it's too noisy in here for her.'

'Wouldn't yer know she'd have something to complain about? She's as miserable as a wet week, is Doreen Mason. She certainly doesn't take after her mother, more's the pity.'

'You stay in here, then.'

'Not likely, I'm coming with you.' He put his arm across her shoulders and whispered in her ear, 'We might as well give her the opportunity of boring us both to death.' He looked back from the kitchen door and laughed at the antics of Betty, who was swaggering around the room with her thumbs hooked in an imaginary pair of braces, and singing, 'My old man said follow the van,' in a Cockney accent.

'She doesn't half liven the party up, she's a real case.'

'Oh, she's a case all right,' Doreen said, a sour expression on her face. 'A head case.'

Billy groaned. He wouldn't mind being in the kitchen and missing the fun if he was alone with Katy. He could claim his Christmas kiss then. But because of Misery-Guts, he was missing out on the fun in both rooms. 'Personally, I think yer

401

mam's a cracker. It's a pity ye're not more like her.'

Katy stepped in to smooth things over. 'Yer know Billy's going away on Wednesday, don't yer, Doreen? He's going to Rotterdam.'

'So yer won't be seeing each other for a while, then?' Doreen seemed to have cheered up at the news. 'How long are yer away for, Billy?'

'Only for a couple of weeks, three at the most. But me uncle said I might not get any leave this trip because he thinks the ship will be coming back empty and they'll just load up again and sail the next day.' He squeezed Katy's shoulder. 'He did say I'll get a couple of hours off, though, just long enough to nip home and see me family and me girlfriend.'

'I'll keep Katy company while ye're away,' Doreen said. 'Perhaps she'll come to a dance with me one night, now. I've asked her loads of times, but she always says she's seeing you. She won't have that excuse now.'

'Maybe not, but she'll have another one. Yer see, I don't want her to go dancing unless it's me what takes her.'

'Oh, fancy that now!' Doreen pulled a face. 'Are yer expecting her to stay in every night while you're playing sailor boy?'

'Excuse me, both of yer,' Katy said hotly. 'I don't need either of yer to tell me what I can do or what I can't do. I'm quite capable of thinking for meself and pleasing meself.'

'D'yer see what yer've done now, Doreen Mason?' Billy was livid. 'Yer'd cause trouble in an empty bloody house, you would.'

'Billy! There's no need to use bad language,' Katy said. 'I've never heard yer swear before, in all the time I've known yer.'

'Your mate would make a saint swear.'

John walked into the kitchen at that moment to pick up a bottle to replenish the drinks, and he could feel the tension in the air. One look at Billy's face told him all was not well.

'What have we here?' he asked, his tone breezy. 'A mothers' meeting for fathers only?'

'We're going in now, Mr Kershaw.' Katy was relieved at his timely appearance. 'We were just talking about Billy going away.'

'Yeah.' Billy put on a bright smile. 'Only two more nights to walk me girl home from work, then I'm off to sail the seven seas. D'yer think she'll miss me, Mr Kershaw? D'yer think her heart might break?'

'I'm sure she'll miss you, Billy. As to her heart breaking, I don't know about that. From what I've heard you're only doing a couple of trips, so I think Katy's heart will stand that.' John picked up a bottle from the draining board. 'Come in and join the party.'

Betty was urging each one of the guests to stand up and give a song, but was having no success. Then she had an idea. Punching the air, she said, 'I've got it! Just the thing to liven you lot up. We'll have a game of Pass the Parcel, and the one left holding the parcel has to stand up and give a turn. It doesn't matter whether yer sing, dance, recite a poem or stand on yer bleedin' heads.'

'But we've got no music, Betty,' Dot objected. 'How will we know when to stop?'

'Easy, peasy, girl.' Betty tapped her forehead. 'Use yer nous! One of us will stand in the kitchen and yell "stop" every so often. And the one left holding the parcel has to pay a forfeit. If they don't, we'll brand them on the forehead with the poker.'

That sounded good to Colin, who bounced up and down on the arm of John's chair. 'I'll go in the kitchen, Auntie Betty. And I won't peek, honest I won't.'

'That's a good lad.' Betty gave him one of her beaming smiles. 'Now, while we get all the chairs in a circle, you go and wrap something up, there's a good boy. But make sure it's not something breakable, or yer mam will have me guts for garters.'

They made a circle of sorts, but there weren't enough seats for everyone so Katy and Billy sat next to each other on the floor. And when they were all settled, Colin came in with a pan lid wrapped in newspaper. 'It's the best I can do, Auntie Betty, but the paper's going to come off.'

'Leave the paper off, then, and we'll make do with the pan lid. And no cheating, mind, Colin, there's no favourites in this game.'

Much to Billy's delight, Doreen was the first one to be

403

caught out. She flatly refused to make an exhibition of herself and sat with her face set, until she saw her mother reaching for the poker. That brought her to her feet to recite *Old Mother Hubbard*. And the enthusiastic clapping and cheering from the slightly inebriated audience put a seldom-seen smile on her face. She was allowed to sit out after that and the circle moved closer. Then came Paddy's turn and he sang a song called *Smiling Through*, which Maggie made him stop after the first verse because it was a sad song and not at all suitable for a party.

Betty was the next to be caught out by Colin's shout, and her song, *Nellie Dean*, had the whole room joining in. They enjoyed it so much, they sang it several times over, making the rafters ring. Then Mary was the recipient of the pan lid and she shook her head, partly with shyness and partly because she couldn't think of anything to do. 'It'll have to be *Jack and Jill*, I'm afraid.'

'On yer feet, girl,' Betty shouted. 'No one sits down at this party.'

Then there were only four left – Dot, John, Katy and Billy. The two youngsters had been whispering in each other's ear, now they smiled broadly. 'Me and Katy are going to sing together,' Billy said, 'when it's our turn.'

'Can I sing with yer?' Dot asked, having taken a dislike to the pan lid she'd been using for the last twelve years. She'd never feel the same about that pan lid again.

'And me.' John had never sung in front of anyone in his life, or recited a poem, and the idea didn't appeal one little bit. 'You are not leaving me out.'

'Bloody hell!' Betty gave her husband a dig in the ribs that nearly knocked him off his chair. 'What d'yer think of that, eh? We can't say anything to them 'cos it's their ruddy house! Just wait until next time I give a party, then I'll pull rank on them.'

'Seeing as yer've never given a party, my love, yer can't have a next time until yer've had the first one.'

'Don't change the subject, and don't be so bleedin' clever.' Betty gave her husband a broad wink. 'I suppose we'd better let them have their own way, eh? Otherwise they won't invite us again.'

'Right, let's get it over with.' Dot stood up. 'What are we singing?'

'Me and Katy will start it off 'cos it's our signature tune. You and Mr Kershaw can join in when yer like.' Billy pulled Katy into the middle of the room and put his arm across her shoulders. There was a look of pure bliss on his face when he asked, 'Are yer ready?'

Betty interrupted the proceedings. 'Hey, hold on a minute.' She pointed to John, standing next to Dot, both with their arms hanging by their sides and a space between them. 'You look like two stuffed dummies! Put yer arm around her, John, and put a bit of bleedin' life into it, for heaven's sake. Yer remind me of two strangers waiting at a bus stop!'

John laughed and put his arm around Dot's waist. 'Is that better, Mrs Mason?'

'It sure is, kiddo. Now let's be having yer, Billy.'

After a few nervous coughs, the young couple began. 'Gee, but it's great . . .' ending with a resounding: 'Walking my baby back home!'

The youngsters harmonised well together, their bodies swaying to the tune. And John squeezed Dot's waist, saying, 'Come on, my Delightful Dorothy, we can't let the young ones beat us.' So they joined in the lovely tune with gusto. The tune was too catchy for the others to just listen to, so soon everyone was singing at the top of their voices. And when Betty dragged Alec to his feet to dance, Maggie did the same with Paddy. Even Doreen joined in, singing and swaying. And Colin, not to be left out, ran to stand beside his mother, his young face aglow.

Mary was smiling and humming as she crept from the room to check on her daughter. She stood at the bottom of the stairs and when she heard a faint cry, she took the stairs two at a time. The baby had been very good, there hadn't been a peep from her in three hours. But she was ready for a feed now, and letting it be known. 'Come on, my lovely.' Mary pulled the blanket back and swept the baby into her arms. 'Yer've been a very good girl for yer mammy, haven't yer? But yer must be hungry now, and yer need yer nappy changing.' As she was talking, Mary was rocking from side to side and the crying stopped. 'We'll go down and yer can say good night to all yer aunties and uncles before we go home.'

The room fell silent when Mary entered, then there was a surge forward with everyone wanting a peek at the baby. 'Sure, she's been goodness itself, so she has,' Maggie said, 'sleeping through enough noise to waken the dead.'

When Dot noticed the tiny rosebud lips quiver, she pushed back those who were standing too close. 'Move away, ye're frightening the life out of the poor thing. We probably look like huge giants to her, and drunken ones, into the bargain.'

'I'm sorry to break the party up, Dot, but I'll have to take Trudy home,' Mary said. 'She's hungry and very, very wet.'

'Ye're not breaking the party up, sunshine, they're all getting thrown out now. It's eleven o'clock and it'll take me an hour to clear this mess up. I couldn't bear to come down tomorrow morning to this lot.' Dot smiled. 'Especially that ruddy pan lid. I'll be viewing it in a different light from now on.'

'I'll stay and give her a hand, girl,' Betty offered. 'We can't go and leave it all to you.'

'No, it's all right, sunshine, we'll manage. John and Billy can stay and help, so between us we'll have it done in no time.'

'We'll go with Mary, then, me darlin'.' Maggie gave Dot a knowing look. 'Make sure she gets in all right.'

'We may as well all go out together, seeing as we're not wanted.' Betty jerked her head at Colin. 'Be a good lad and get our coats.' She noticed Doreen sit back and cross her legs. 'Don't be making yerself comfortable, young lady, ye're coming home with us. And don't bother arguing because yer Auntie Dot's had enough of us for one night.'

It was a happy, noisy group standing on the pavement saying their goodbyes and stating unanimously that it had been a terrific party. There was feeling of well-being and smiles of affection and happiness on their faces. They were not to know that in the very near future something would happen to turn those smiles to tears.

Dot was on her way out one Saturday morning when she found a letter lying on the hall floor addressed to Katy. She knew right away who it was from and hurried through to the kitchen where her daughter was getting washed. Billy had been away ten days and this was the first they'd heard from him. And for those ten days Katy had been very quiet, missing him badly. 'This should put a smile on yer face, sunshine! I can't stay to hear what he's got to say, or I'll be late for work. But I'll call in the shop on me way home and yer can give me his news then.' She grinned. 'Yer needn't tell me how many kisses he's put on.'

'As if I would.' Katy dried her hands before taking the letter. 'I hope it's to say when he'll be home.' She waited until she heard the front door bang before ripping the envelope open. It was only a one-page letter telling her he was all right, but that he hadn't yet got the hang of walking with the roll of the ship. The blokes he worked with were great and always telling jokes that were funny but not suitable for the ears of a lady.

The rest of the letter was what Katy wanted to hear. He missed her like mad and couldn't wait to see her again. He wasn't sure of the date the ship would be docking, but it couldn't come fast enough for him. He'd let her know as soon as he found out. Was she missing him? She better had be or she'd have some explaining to do. Then he sent her lots of love and had put a line of kisses on the bottom which he said he'd trade for the real thing when he got home.

Katy read the letter through again before putting it back in the envelope. She would never have dreamed of telling him so, but she'd been praying he wouldn't like going away to sea. He'd given no indication whether he liked it or not, so she'd have to wait until he came home to find out. She'd stayed in every night since he'd gone away, and life was pretty miserable. Doreen had tried to coax her to go dancing but she wouldn't be talked into it. She'd seen Billy every day since she was twelve, that was three years, and she wasn't interested in meeting anyone new, she was happy with what she had. Mind you, if he decided to make the sea his career, she'd soon have something to say. A couple of trips was one thing, a lifetime was another.

Chapter Twenty-Five

Dot waved when she saw Betty standing on her step with her arms folded across her tummy. 'What are yer standing there for? Yer'll get yer death of cold.'

'I don't feel the cold, girl, that's one good thing about being fat. But I wasn't standing here for the good of me health, I've been watching out for yer. I'm feeling a bit fed-up with meself and need to have a good gab. Yer know I'm only happy when I'm pulling someone to pieces. Have yer got time for a cuppa? In your house, of course, 'cos these two lads of mine are noisy beggars, we'd have no privacy.'

'Oh, come one, then! But I've got to do me shopping, so I'm afraid yer'll have to talk quick to get all the gossip out in half an hour.'

Betty stuck her head around the living-room door and bawled, 'I'm going to Dot's for half an hour if anyone wants me.' Then she banged the door after herself and swayed her way up to her friend's. 'Ye're late today, I've been watching for ages.'

'I called into the shop to see Katy.' Dot stepped into the hall and stood aside for Betty to pass. 'She had a letter from Billy this morning and I was dying to hear what the lad had to say.'

Betty settled herself on a dining chair and rested her chubby elbows on the table. 'God, but ye're not half a nosy beggar, Dot Baker. Fancy wanting to know what was in yer daughter's love letter.' Her cheeks moved upwards in a cheeky smile. 'What did he have to say?'

Dot threw her bag on the couch before hanging up her coat. 'Not much from the sound of things. He didn't say when he'd be home, but Katy seemed happy enough so he must have said something that pleased her.' She glanced in the kitchen. 'Have yer seen our Colin, by any chance? I want him to come to the shops with me to help carry the bags.'

'He was playing out when Danny's mam wanted a message running so Colin went with him. They've only gone to the Maypole in Hawthorne Road so they won't be long. You go and put the kettle on, girl, or yer'll be chasing me out before a get a chance to bring yer up-to-date with all the goings-on.' Betty rubbed a finger round and round in the dimples in her elbows then swivelled her bottom so she was facing the kitchen. 'Ay, girl, the queer feller next door passed me when I was standing at the door. He's an evil bugger, that one. If looks could kill, I'd be a dead bleedin' duck right now.'

Dot came to lean on the jamb of the door while she waited for the kettle to boil. 'Mary doesn't have much to say about him, these days, but I don't think he knocks her around like he used to.'

'If I was her I'd be making plans for the future, when the baby's older. She wants to get out of that bleedin' house and make a new life for herself.' Betty jerked her head. 'There's the kettle boiling, girl.'

Dot brought the brown earthenware teapot back and plonked it in the middle of the table. 'I may as well leave it here. Ye're never satisfied with one cup of tea and it'll save me getting up and down like a flippin' yo-yo.'

'Ay, what d'yer think, girl? Our Freddie's got himself a girlfriend.'

'Go 'way!' Dot was suitably impressed. Betty had two sons, Freddie eighteen and Stan, seventeen, and neither of them had ever shown any interest in girls. 'What's she like? Have yer seen her?'

'Not yet.' Betty gave the teapot a shake before pouring the tea into the two cups. 'He must be keen though, 'cos he's asked if he can bring her for tea tomorrow. Our Stan says she's a bit of a drip, but then he would, wouldn't he? He's probably jealous because, as yer know, him and Freddie have always gone everywhere together.'

'Your Stan won't be long getting himself a girl. Him and Freddie are both nice-looking lads and I'm surprised they haven't been snapped up before now.'

Betty preened herself. 'Yeah, they are nice-looking, aren't they? Have yer ever noticed how like their mother they are?'

Dot smiled and sat back, her hands curled around the cup. It was nice to relax and have a chat, and if she was a bit late getting to the shops, so what? She'd have to run, that's all.

Mary had fed the baby and was making her comfortable on the couch when her husband came in. 'I'll get yer dinner.'

Tom's response was a grunt as he flopped in the armchair. He didn't even look at the baby, she was just another irritation to him. Something else to fuel his bad temper. He hadn't been feeling well all week, what with headaches and a sickly feeling in his tummy. And he kept getting spells where he was sweating, even though the weather was bitter. He put it down to a cold coming on, that's all it was. The little voice in his head which kept reminding him that the doctor had warned of these symptoms, was always quickly silenced. The doctor was a bloody fool and didn't know what he was talking about.

Tom ate the sausage and mash Mary set before him, even though he had no appetite. Not for food, anyway. He had an appetite for something else, and that he intended to get off his wife today. She'd had it easy for too long; it was now time for her to pay for her keep. He pushed the plate away, undid the top button on his trousers and belched loudly. He saw Mary wince, and hid his evil smile behind his hand. He'd give her something to pull a face about, any minute now; just let his dinner settle.

Mary felt uneasy. She couldn't put a finger on it, but there was something different about her husband today. It wasn't that he was quiet, for they never spoke to each other at any time and that suited her fine. But she had this premonition and it frightened her. Perhaps she was being stupid, imagining things, but she couldn't shake it off. The best thing she could do, to be on the safe side, was put Trudy in the pram and take her for a walk.

Having made up her mind, Mary stood up at the same time as Tom pushed his chair back and got to his feet. They stared at each other, and Mary watched with mounting horror as he rounded the table and came to stand in front of her.

'Put her in the pram and get up those stairs.'

'Oh no, not on your life! If you think I'm going up those stairs with you, then ye're sadly mistaken. Move out of the way, I'm taking the baby for a walk.'

'Yer'll do as ye're bleedin' well told.' Tom put the palm of his hand on her chest and pushed her away from the couch and into a corner. 'What d'er think I keep yer for, eh? I want something back for me money and I intend getting it. Ye're me wife and I'm entitled to me marital rights, yer can't refuse.'

'I'll not let yer lay one of yer dirty hands on me, Tom Campbell. Go and get what yer want off one of yer floosies.'

He grabbed her by the front of her dress and pressed his face close to hers. 'I said get up the stairs and give me what I want.'

'I am not going up those stairs with you, get that through yer head.'

'Suits me, I can take what I want right here.' He moved his hand to the neck of Mary's dress and gave one sharp pull, ripping the dress from top to bottom. Then he stepped back a pace to gaze leeringly at her full breasts. 'Get on the floor.'

Mary moved so quickly she took him offguard. She picked up the poker and waved it at him. 'Touch me, and yer'll feel this.'

But Tom was one step ahead of her. Before she knew what he intended, he had picked the baby up by an arm and a leg and dangled the whimpering child in front of her. 'Go on, hit me now.' His laugh was that of a maniac, his smile that of the devil. 'Go on, see if yer can miss the brat and hit me.'

Mary froze. If she lifted the poker, he'd shield himself with his daughter, she knew that. Her silence brought forth more laughter and he began to swing the baby around by an arm and a leg, missing the table and fireplace by inches. Faster and faster he went and Mary knew he didn't care if he killed the child. She started swinging the poker at his legs, and the blows must have hurt, but he gave no sign. Round and round he went, with the baby screaming. *He's mad, he doesn't care if he kills her. He's going to kill my beautiful baby.*

412

Mary opened her mouth and desperate, tortured screams filled the air.

'Here's our Colin coming up the yard now, sunshine, so I'd better make an effort. Much as I enjoy hearing about Mrs Cousins being a brazen hussy for hanging her fancy rayon knickers on the line, I've got to get some food in for the weekend.'

'Haven't yer been to the shops, yet, Mam?' Colin's face had been whipped a bright red by the brisk wind. 'I thought yer'd be well gone.'

'Blame yer Auntie Betty, sunshine, yer know what she's like for talking. Once she starts there's no stopping her until she needs winding up again.'

'Ay, missus, you've done yer share as well. Anyone hearing yer would think yer'd just sat there like a dummy and I've done all the yapping.'

'I was only kidding, can't yer take a joke? Anyway, I'm—'

The screams turned Dot's blood to ice. 'In the name of God, he must be killing her!' She jumped to her feet, the screams ringing in her ears. 'Come on, Betty.'

She made a dash for the companion set and grabbed the poker and tongs. 'We'll have to go the back way, the front door won't be open.' As they ran down the yard, she passed the tongs to Betty. 'If he's giving her a hammering, or the baby, I'll give him a taste of this.' She brandished the poker. 'He's a bad bastard.'

'I'll be right beside yer, girl, yer can count on me.'

They met a worried-looking Maggie in the entry and without exchanging a word she joined them in running up the Campbells' yard. The screams were louder and more chilling as they passed the window, and the women feared what they would see inside. Dot didn't bother knocking, she threw the kitchen door open and made straight for the living room, Betty and Maggie at her heels. The sight that met their eyes was one that would stay with them forever. Tom Campbell had the look of a madman as he swung the baby around as though she was a rag doll. It was a miracle he hadn't bashed her head against the furniture or fireplace. Mary was raining blows on his legs while screaming her head off. '*He's going to kill my baby!*'

Dot pulled the table back and raised the poker, intending to strike Tom when he had his back to them and the baby wouldn't be in danger of being hit. Beside her stood Betty, who had discarded the tongs, believing her fists would serve her better. Behind them, Maggie was wringing her hands and crying.

While she was waiting for just the right moment, Dot happened to glance at Mary and saw her raising the poker until it was on a level with her chin before swinging out wildly. She heard it connect with Tom's head, and in that split second it flashed through her mind that they hang people in this country for murder. So she let fly with the poker on his back just as he began to totter and followed it quickly with another blow as he was hitting the floor.

The screaming stopped and Mary ran forward to pick up Trudy and hold her close. 'He was going to kill her.'

Dot took a deep breath. Her head was fuddled, she couldn't think straight, only that they were in trouble and she didn't know how to handle it. She called to Colin, her voice urgent. 'Go to John's, sunshine, then run to the doctor's. Tell them both it's an emergency and to hurry. Run all the way, please, love, faster than yer've ever run before. And not a word to anyone except the two men.'

'Is he dead?' Mary's whole body was shaking as she gazed down at the still form lying on the floor. 'I don't care if he is, he doesn't deserve to live.'

For the first time the women saw the state of Mary's dress and knew right away what had caused the trouble. It was ripped from top to bottom and that hadn't happened by accident. Nor had the deep scratch on her neck come by accident. He must have dug his nail in while pulling at the dress. Dot sighed. He didn't deserve to live, Mary was right. She must have refused to give him what he wanted and he was taking his revenge on the one thing she loved, the baby.

'I'm not touching him, we'll wait until the doctor gets here.' Dot met Betty's eyes and they silently agreed it was best to say nothing to the woman who had suffered enough already.

'I think you should take the baby into Maggie's and get a cup of tea down yer to calm yer nerves. Me and Betty will wait for the doctor.'

'I've killed him, haven't I?'

'Listen, sunshine, I'm not very good at things like this. He could be unconscious for all I know. Anyway, yer weren't the only one to hit him, I gave him a few belts.'

'And me,' Betty lied. 'I hit him, too.'

Maggie dried her eyes with the corner of her pinny, then, skirting the body on the floor she held out her arms to Mary. 'Come on, me darlin', let's get you and the baby out of here. Sure, it's a terrible shock yer've both had.'

As they were leaving, Dot whispered in Maggie's ear, 'Go out the back way, Maggie, there's a crowd outside. And leave her dress the way it is, for the doctor to see. It might not be important, but yer never know.'

When they were alone, Betty said, 'He's dead, yer know. His chest isn't going up and down so he's not breathing.'

'I know that, Betty, but I wanted to get Mary out of here so I can sort me thoughts out.' Then Dot told her friend about the to-do over the poker last year, and what John had said. 'But if three of us say we hit him, they can't hang three of us, can they?'

'I bloody-well hope not, girl, I quite enjoy living.'

The shock that had numbed Dot's senses was wearing off and the enormity of what had happened began to sink in. She could hear the babble of voices, loud knocking at the door and there were faces at the window, trying to peer through the net curtains. 'I'd better go and shift them, they must be wondering what's going on. They're not being nosy, they probably came to see if they could help.'

Dot told the neighbours gathered outside that Mr Campbell had fallen and banged his head, and they were waiting for the doctor. 'So will yer go home now, please, and we'll let yer know later what's happening.'

She returned to her friend with her shoulders slumped. 'Let's stand in the kitchen, Betty, this room's giving me the creeps. Me flippin' nerves are shot to pieces.'

'Ye're not the only one, girl, my heart's in me mouth. But

if it's bad for us, what's it like for Mary? We saw a bit of what was going on, but God knows what she had gone through before we came.'

'Through hell, that's what she'd gone through. She's been living a life of hell since she married Tom Campbell. It's terrible to speak ill of the dead, but he was a rotter. She's well rid of him, so is the baby.'

'It's to be hoped she doesn't get into trouble, girl. If that man's dead, and we both know he is, then there'll be questions asked.'

'It was self-defence, Betty! Mary is a mother who was protecting her baby. We all saw what he was doing to her! Surely to God, no one would expect her to stand by and do nothing. Anyway, I hit him twice so they can do what they like about it.'

'No, girl, you hit him once and I hit him once. That's our story, we'll stick to it and won't let anybody budge us.'

They heard the entry door close, then footsteps hurrying up the yard. And when John entered the kitchen, the anxiety and concern on his face was all Dot needed to let her tears flow. Her face crumpled, she sobbed, 'Yer should have seen what he was doing to Trudy, John, I'll never forget it as long as I live.'

Betty took up the story. 'He had hold of one of her little ankles and a wrist, and he was turning around, like this.' She closed her eyes and couldn't go on, the lump in her throat was like a hard rock.

John stretched his arms wide and drew them to him. He held them close as they sobbed their hearts out. And as he listened, he wondered what on earth the outcome of this would be. He waited until their crying eased, then asked, 'Is he dead?'

Dot lifted tear-stained eyes and nodded. 'We haven't touched him, we were too afraid. But we both think he's dead.'

There came a loud knocking on the front door and John dropped his arms. 'This will be the doctor, I'll let him in.' As he passed through the living room and saw the lifeless form of Tom Campbell, he asked himself again what the outcome would be.

Dot and Betty clung to each other as they heard the doctor

ask what had happened. And they heard John say he'd only just got here and didn't know the details, but Mrs Baker and Mrs Mason were in the kitchen and could perhaps tell him more. 'I'd better have a look at Mr Campbell first.' The doctor's words had the two women covering their ears. Neither of them wanted to hear what they knew already.

'Dot, Dr Gray would like a word with you and Betty.'

'I'm not going back in that room, John, I couldn't.'

'It's all right, Mrs Baker, we can talk out here.' The doctor's voice was sympathetic. 'Where are Mrs Campbell and the baby?'

'I sent them next door, Doctor, they were both in a terrible state. Me and Betty can tell yer what we saw, and Mrs O'Connor was with us, yer can ask her. And we can also tell yer what we think started it off.' Slowly, and with a catch in her voice, Dot told him everything from beginning to end. 'How he didn't kill that baby I'll never know. I couldn't believe me eyes when I saw what he was doing to it. And he had this look on his face, like a madman.'

'Mr Campbell was a scoundrel, Mrs Baker, but he'll never hurt them again – he's dead.' Dr Gray turned to John. 'I'll have to see Mrs Campbell to get the facts right before I can issue a death certificate. I would like you to stay with me, John, until all the arrangements are made. There's a lot to do and I would like to take as much of the burden from Mrs Campbell's shoulders as possible.'

'Of course I'll come with you, anything to help,' John put his hands on Dot's shoulders and bent to kiss her cheek. 'You and Betty go home, I'll be with you as soon as I can be.'

'But what about—' Dot pointed to the living room. 'We can't leave Mary on her own to face that.'

It was Dr Gray who answered. 'I'm sure Mrs O'Connor will allow Mrs Campbell to stay there for a few days. And as soon as I've had a word with her, to establish the cause of death, I shall ring an undertakers and have the body removed.'

Establish the cause of death! Oh, my God! 'We all hit him, yer know, Dr Gray,' Dot blurted out. 'It wasn't only Mary.'

'So you said, Mrs Baker. However, I need a statement from Mrs Campbell. So I suggest you do as John says, and go home.

It's been a nasty experience and I'm sure you and Mrs Mason are upset. Try not to worry, though, I'm sure there's no need.'

John took her elbow as he lifted the latch on the kitchen door. 'Send Colin for the messages, don't you go out yourself. I'll be in to see you as soon as I can.'

Betty slipped home to tell her family what had happened and asked them to see to their own meals as she wanted to stay with Dot. 'Is there anything I can do?' Alec asked.

'No, love, we've just got to wait. But me and Dot are in this together and I want to stay with her.'

Colin was sent to the shops with a hastily written list, and the two friends sat at the table drinking cup after cup of tea. 'Dr Gray said not to worry, but how can we not flaming-well worry?' Dot kept glancing at the clock. 'A man's dead, and he didn't die through natural causes, so someone, somewhere, is bound to want to know how he *did* die.'

'D'yer know, girl, this is one time I wished I smoked. They say it calms yer nerves and I could do with puffing me bleedin' head off right now.' Betty couldn't settle and was fidgeting on the chair. 'To think we were laughing about Mrs Cousins' fancy knickers just a minute before all this started. It just goes to show that yer never know from one minute to the next what's going to happen.'

'If you hadn't wanted to come for a natter, sunshine, I'd have been at the shops. And where would Mary have been without us? It was fate, that's what it was.'

The hands on the clock turned and an hour passed, with still no sign of John. Colin came back with the shopping and Dot busied herself putting the groceries away while her son went out to play before it got too dark. 'I wonder if I should nip up to the O'Connors' and see what's happening?'

'I wouldn't if I were you, girl, I'd wait for John. For all you know, yer could be walking into a bundle of trouble.'

It was turned five o'clock when John finally arrived to be greeted by a barrage of questions. He held his hand up. 'Calm down and I'll tell you what's happened so far. It's not a very pleasant story, but I'll tell it quickly to put your minds as rest. Firstly, the undertakers have been and taken the body of Mr

Campbell away. They're going to ring me in work on Monday to give me the date of the funeral.'

Dot couldn't wait. 'What did the doctor say he died of?'

'Bear with me, will you, Dot? There are some unpleasant surprises in store. Apparently Tom Campbell went to see Dr Gray some weeks ago and was told he had a venereal disease called syphilis. He'd caught it from prostitutes and it was quite advanced. There is no cure for it, and in some cases it affects the brain, among other things.'

'Oh, my God!' Dot looked horrified. 'Could he have passed it on to Mary?'

'He could have, but Mary didn't give him the chance. She had guessed he was going with what she called floosies, because she could smell their cheap perfume on him. But she didn't know he had the disease. And today was the first time in about eight months that he tried to force her into having intercourse with him. She threatened him with the poker and that's when he grabbed the baby. The rest you know.'

'My God, he was a bigger swine than I thought he was.' Betty's nostrils were flared in anger. He knew what he had was catching and yet he'd have passed it on to Mary. 'I'm glad he's dead, the bugger.'

'But what is going on the death certificate as the cause of death?' Dot still wasn't easy in her mind. 'Mary's not in trouble, is she?'

'No.' John looked from one to the other. 'What I'm going to tell you isn't to go any further than these four walls. I can't tell you what Dr Gray will write on the certificate, but from what he said, Tom Campbell could have had a dizzy spell while trying to abuse his wife, fallen over and hit his head on the fender. Under the circumstances, he's quite satisfied that the man brought about his own death. So as far as anyone else is concerned, all they need to be told is that he had an unlucky fall.'

'Does Mary know all this?'

'Yes, Dot, she knows it all. She's taking it quite well, thanks to the O'Connors. They are going to be her lifeline.'

'I'll go up and see her after we've had our tea. I want to see for meself that she's all right, and the baby.'

John grinned. 'What is for tea, Dorothy?'

'Bacon, egg and tomato.'

'Good, I'm famished.'

Betty sighed as she pushed herself up. 'I suppose I'd better show me face and feed the gang. But I'm coming up to see Mary with yer, otherwise I won't get any sleep for worrying.'

Mary seemed calm and composed as she sat on the O'Connors' couch dressed in one of Maggie's warm dressing gowns. The baby was upstairs in bed, and although she'd cried for a while, Mary said her daughter was cute enough to know she was back in the house she was born in, with people who loved her. 'Maggie and Paddy are spoiling her, and they're spoiling me. I don't know what I'm going to do now. I don't ever fancy going back to that house because it holds so many bad memories.'

'It wouldn't if it was decorated from top to bottom,' John said. 'It would look a different house altogether.'

'Sure, John and me could have it like a little palace for yer in no time at all, so we could.' Paddy reached for his wife's hand. 'Me and my Maggie don't want yer to move away from us, and that's the truth of it.'

'But how am I going to live? I'll have no money, I couldn't even pay the rent.' There was no self-pity in Mary's voice, she was just stating facts. 'Today's been a bad day for me. I can't seem to think clearly. John's brought me the wages he found in Tom's pocket, and I can claim his week in hand. That will keep me going for a few weeks, but after that I've no idea.'

'Listen to me, me darlin'.' Maggie sat forward, her elbows resting on her knees. 'While yer were upstairs with the baby, me and Paddy had a good talk. We'd not like yer to think we want to run yer life for yer, but sure, at a time like this, yer need help. So why don't yer bury yer pride and let all yer friends muck in together to decorate yer house? We all want to help yer, so we do, and what's a few rolls of wallpaper and a few tins of paint?'

'We'll decorate it whether yer like it or not, Mary,' Dot said. 'We'll be doing it for ourselves as much as you, because when we come for a cuppa we want to sit somewhere cheerful, not in a ruddy mausoleum.'

Betty gave her a dig in the ribs. 'What's a mausoleum, girl?'

'I don't really know, sunshine, except it sounds a miserable place.'

Mary smiled briefly. 'Dot, I know ye're all trying to do yer best for me, but I have to be realistic. I don't want to move away from you, any of you – it'll break my heart. Don't yer think I know that Trudy's going to need all the love she can get when she starts walking and playing out? I think about nothing else! But how do I pay the rent and other bills, and keep meself and the baby?'

'You could get a job, me darlin',' Maggie said in her soft Irish brogue, 'and I'll mind the baby. That way we all get what we want. We'll still have you and Trudy amongst us, and you'll have a wage coming in and keep yer pride and independence.'

'Brilliant!' Like everyone else, John's eyes had lit up at Maggie's words. 'There you have the perfect solution, Mary.'

'Oh, sunshine, wouldn't that be marvellous?'

'What more d'yer want, girl? Handed to yer on a bleedin' plate, it is.'

They talked until nearly midnight, and when Mary went to bed she felt as though her life was just beginning. Her friends had filled her heart with hope of a bright future ahead for her and Trudy. What she would have done without those friends she couldn't imagine. They'd shown her a love and generosity that went beyond mere friendship. They'd help her put the darkness behind her, and her beloved baby would grow up surrounded by love and laughter. She would never know the evil that was her father.

Dot sighed as she slipped into her coat on the Monday morning. It had been the most miserable weekend she'd ever known and she found herself wishing the week away. After the funeral perhaps they could get back to normal instead of creeping around the house, afraid to smile. 'I'm off, sunshine!' she shouted through to Katy who was getting washed in the kitchen. 'I'll see yer tonight.'

'OK, Mam.'

When Dot saw the letter lying on the floor in the hall, she

421

felt like kissing it. At last, something to be happy about. She hurried back to the kitchen. 'Ye're doing well, sunshine – here's another letter from Billy.'

Katy's face lit up. 'Ooh, I hope he tells me when he's coming home.'

'I hope so, too, sunshine, Anyway, ta-ra for now.'

It was a one-page letter again, but Katy didn't mind because, as her eyes scanned the lines, it told her what she wanted to know. Billy would be home on Thursday night. He couldn't tell her the exact time, and it would only be for a few hours, but it might be long enough for them to go to the pictures. He told her to be ready about half-six and he'd be there as near that time as possible. There was a long line of kisses, then he'd written a PS which had Katy laughing out loud. They'd be going on the back row of the pictures and she wasn't to wear lipstick because he intended to make up for lost time.

She hugged the letter to her chest. She was going to have a serious talk with him in between kisses on that back row. She'd allow him one more trip to sea and that was all. Life wasn't the same without him; she felt as though part of her was missing. And that part was Billy Harlow.

'The funeral is on Thursday morning at ten o'clock,' John said, when he called that night. 'I've just been along to tell Mary and ask what arrangements she'd like making.'

'I can't go, John, because I can't afford to lose a day's pay. But Betty said she'll go with the O'Connors, so at least someone will be there.' Dot narrowed her eyes. 'Who's paying for all this? I know Mary can't afford it.'

John gave a quick, knowing glance to where Colin was sitting. 'Dr Gray managed to get some money from a welfare fund, and that's taking care of the funeral arrangements – nothing elaborate, but better than a pauper's burial. I'm paying for the hire of a car and some flowers, and I'm taking a couple of hours off, so I'll be on hand if Mary needs help. She doesn't want the hearse coming here, it's to go straight to the cemetery. So it'll just be the one car going from here.'

'I'll come with yer, Mr Kershaw.' Colin was looking very serious. He hadn't seen what was happening next door, he'd

422

never got further than the back door, but the urgency in the voices had affected him. And then Mr Campbell dying, it was all very serious stuff to a thirteen-year-old lad. 'I can take a day off school.'

'Yer will not!' Dot was adamant. 'A funeral is no place for a youngster, only if it's someone in the family.' She turned her eyes on John. 'At least our Katy's got something to be happy about – Billy's coming home on Thursday.'

'Yes, I know. She'd been up to tell the O'Connors and Mary, just before I got there. They said she looks as happy as Larry.'

'God love her, she's over the moon. She'll be in Doreen's now, telling her the good news. If Billy's missing her as much as she's missing him, I think his life at sea will be a very short and miserable one.'

Chapter Twenty-Six

It was a bitterly cold night and Dot was glad to close the door behind her. As soon as the dinner was over she was going to put her feet up in front of the fire and to hell with everything. The world wouldn't stop turning if she didn't change the beds tonight – it wasn't as though they were dirty. She was dropping the key in her bag when she cocked an ear. That sounded like Katy's laugh, but it was too early for her to be home.

Dot pushed the living-room door open and her eyes widened in surprise when she saw her daughter sitting next to Colin at the table, while John was reclining in front of the fire with his hands laced behind his head and his long legs stretched out. 'Well, I'll be blowed!' Dot closed the door quickly to keep out the draught. 'Am I the only worker in this house?'

'Mrs Edwards let me off early, Mam, so I could doll meself up for Billy coming.' Katy's face was glowing. 'She said he might just come early and I wouldn't want to miss spending as much time with him as possible.'

'That was thoughtful of her.' Dot smiled, happy for her daughter. It was nice to have something pleasant happen after the horror of last Saturday. She didn't think she'd ever get that out of her mind. 'You look very nice, too, sunshine.' Her eyes were on John as she was hanging her coat up. 'And what, pray, are you doing here so early?'

'I didn't go back to work after the funeral. Mary looked dreadful – white as a sheet and shaking like a leaf. So Betty and I decided to have a bite to eat with the O'Connors and it ended up with us staying a couple of hours. I'm pleased to say Mary was looking better by the time we left.'

'How did the funeral go?'

'No funeral is ever a happy occasion. We tried to persuade Mary not to go because she is obviously still in shock, but she wouldn't hear of it. She said no matter what he was, what he'd put her through, he was still her husband and she'd never forgive herself if she didn't go to his funeral.'

Dot was eyeing the couch. Should she sit down for five minutes or see to the dinner? The trouble was, if she sat down she'd never get up again. John saw the expression on her face and knew what she was thinking. He lowered his arms, drew in his legs, and smiled. 'Sit down, my Delectable Dorothy, the dinner will be served in about five minutes.'

When the children's faces gave nothing away, Dot rounded on John. Hands on hips and head tilted, she demanded: 'Have you been and bought fish and chips? I'll crown yer, if yer have.'

'Does your delicate nose not detect a smell?'

The children were giggling now as Dot sniffed up. 'I thought I could smell baking when I came in, but it can't be 'cos there's no one here to bake.' Then she grinned down at him. 'Go on, clever clogs, tell me yer as good as baking as yer are at everything else.'

John got to his feet. 'Sit down, Dorothy, and get waited on for a change.' He pressed her down on to the couch and patted her cheek. 'Behave yourself and do as you're told.' He slipped off his suit jacket and hung it over the back of a chair. 'Set the table, Katy, please, while I prepare dinner.'

As soon as he opened the kitchen door the most delicious smell wafted in and Dot sniffed in appreciation. 'That smells absolutely bloody marvellous! What have yer been up to, John Kershaw? Not that I mind. If it tastes as good as it smells, I don't give a monkey's who, why, when or where.'

John appeared in the doorway. 'Will you take your seats at the table, please, dinner is about to be served.' He disappeared briefly then returned carrying a huge brown earthenware dish. The steam was rising from it, and he had a cloth around his hands to protect them from the heat. He set the basin in the middle of the table and stood back with a pleased expression on his face. 'Your dinner, my Delightful, Delectable Dorothy.'

Dot's jaw dropped. The dish was covered with a golden-brown pastry, and from the three slits in the centre of it came the most delicious aroma. 'I don't know whether to eat first and ask questions later, or ask questions first. The trouble is, if I didn't like yer answer I'd feel obligated not to eat any of that delicious pie which is making me mouth water and me tummy rumble. So I'll ask questions later and box yer ears if I don't like yer answer.'

John passed her a plate and a large spoon. 'You be mother.'

'I need a knife to cut the pastry, soft lad.' Dot rubbed her hand in circles on her tummy before taking the knife from him. 'I haven't had a proper steak and kidney pie for years. I used to be a dab hand at pastry, but I'm out of practice now.' She cut a large portion of the shortcrust pastry and put it on the plate, then spooned on steak and kidney, carrots, onions and potatoes, all in a rich dark gravy. 'Here yer are, Katy, you have yours first in case Billy comes.' As she was serving Colin, she said, 'It's no good, me curiosity is getting the better of me and I can't wait. Who's our guardian angel?'

'Maggie made it.'

'Maggie?' Dot's voice was high with surprise. 'Why would Maggie make a pie for us? Didn't she have enough on today, what with looking after Mary, and the funeral and all?'

'Would you like me to take it back and tell her you don't want it?'

'Not yet, yer can take it back after we've eaten it.' She passed the plate to her son. 'I might be pig-headed, John, but not that pig-headed. I'm delighted, I really am, it's very good of her. But how did it come about? She's never done it before, and I bet she didn't just say, right out of the blue, "Oh, I think I'll make a pie for the Bakers".'

'It was just one of those things. I happened to pass comment on the delicious smell coming from the kitchen and Maggie said she was cooking the steak and kidney to put in a pie she was making for their dinner. Then she said she'd done far too much, and did I think you'd be insulted if she made you one. It was as easy as that, Dorothy, nothing sinister.'

Katy gave a high-pitched shriek when a knock came on the door, and she was in such a hurry to stand up she sent her chair flying back to bang against the sideboard. 'It's Billy!'

'All right, sunshine, calm down, will yer? There's no need to knock the happy home around. I know the sideboard's as old as the hills, but it's all we've got.'

But Katy was in the hall by this time and they heard the happy sound of two young people meeting after a spell apart. When they came into the room, hand-in-hand, their faces were pink with happiness and traces of stolen kisses. 'Hi-ya, everyone.' Billy's grin covered them all. 'I bet ye're all glad to have me back, aren't yer? I hope yer answer's better than the one I got off me mam, when I asked if she'd missed me. "I missed yer like a pain in the backside, son," that's what she said. Mind you, she was hugging the life out of me when she said it.'

'It's lovely to see yer, son, and I've missed yer.' The joy of the two youngsters rubbed off on Dot and she felt part of their happiness. 'I don't know about Katy, but I certainly missed yer smiling face.'

'Does being a seafarer come up to your expectations, Billy?' John was filled with envy. This young lad, fifteen years of age, had found the girl he wanted to spend his life with and wasn't afraid to show his feelings. 'Do you fancy a life on the briny?'

'I enjoyed it, Mr Kershaw, it's a good life. I would have enjoyed it more if Katy had been with me.' He turned sideways to grin at the pretty girl hanging on to him like grim death. 'I'm too used to seeing her every day, and I didn't half miss her.'

'Who's going to win then, sunshine? Our Katy or the sea?'

'No competition there, Mrs Baker. One more trip and then I'm home for good.'

Katy couldn't have looked happier. 'That's my boy.'

'And this is your dinner, come and get it down yer.' Dot pointed to the half-empty plate. 'Billy, would yer like some steak and kidney pie? There's plenty here.'

'Mrs Baker, I'm full to the brim, I couldn't eat another mouthful.' Billy sat on the arm of the couch when Katy returned to her chair. 'Me mam had a big fry-up waiting for me, and she said if I didn't eat every scrap she'd give me a clip round the ears. She's of the opinion that her lovely son hasn't been getting fed properly. But we get plenty of grub, and it's good. I didn't tell me mam that though, or I'd definitely have got a clip around the ears for practically saying her cooking was no good.' He winked at John. 'Like me dad says, Mr Kershaw, yer can't win with women. It's best to just sit back and agree with everything they say.'

Katy pushed her plate away. 'Mam, is it all right if I leave you or Colin to wash the dishes? Billy hasn't got long and we want to go to the pictures.'

'You run along, sunshine, don't worry about the dishes.' Dot swivelled in her chair. 'Will we see yer again before yer go, Billy?'

He shook his head. 'I've got to be back on the ship for eleven o'clock, we're sailing with the first tide. But I'll walk Katy home first, so yer don't have to worry about her. I'd never leave her to walk home on her own, ever.'

Colin had been busy eating until now, but he had to air his complaint. 'Ah, ay, Billy! Haven't yer got time to tell us where yer've been, or what it's like when the wind's strong and the ship rolls around?'

'No, he hasn't!' Katy had her coat on and was pulling on Billy's arm. 'He'll tell yer all about it next time he's home.'

'I've got loads to tell yer, Colin, about what the crew get up to, but it'll have to wait for now.' He held Katy's hand while he bent to kiss Dot. 'Ta-ra, Mrs Baker, look after yerself. And you, Mr Kershaw, I'll see yer soon.'

Dot sighed when the front door banged behind them. 'There goes true love. And I've got to say I'll be very happy to have Billy for a son-in-law.' She began to collect the plates. 'Ah, well, back to the grind. But once these dishes are done I'm putting me feet up and to hell with everything.'

Billy had no intention of following the torch being shone by the usherette. He'd spied two seats on the back row and he made a dive for them. He sighed with contentment as he slipped his arm across Katy's shoulders. 'I haven't half missed yer. Give us a kiss and we'll make up for lost time.'

'I'm glad yer not staying at sea, Billy. I wouldn't have liked that. Not that I would have said anything to try and stop yer, but I'd have been miserable.'

'Yer haven't been going to any dances with Doreen, have yer?'

'Have I heck!' Katy giggled. 'I've stayed in every night and made everybody else as miserable as meself.'

'I've made friends with a lad on the ship, his name's Sully, and he's a good mate. I'll ask him down to meet yer when we get back. Perhaps we can make a foursome up with Doreen and go to the flicks one night.'

Katy pulled a face. 'Ooh, yer know what Doreen's like, she'd probably give him a hard time. Anyway, isn't Sully a funny name?'

'It's a nickname, Katy. His real name's Tony Sullivan. He lives down the Dingle and is the funniest thing on two legs. If Doreen doesn't get on with him then there's no hope for her.'

'Excuse me, Billy, but would yer leave Sully and Doreen to their own devices and give me a kiss? I reckon yer owe me a hundred and we'll never get them all in by the end of the big picture.'

'Taking the advice of me father, I'll give in. You just pucker yer lips and start counting.'

Dot was curled up on the couch, her feet tucked under her, and John was in the fireside chair, leafing through the *Echo*. Colin had gone to bed so Dot could ask the questions she wouldn't ask in front of her son. 'Did Maggie mention whether any of the neighbours have asked what happened to Tom Campbell? Yer know how some of them love to gossip. I wonder what story's going the rounds.'

John lowered the paper. 'Actually, Maggie said they've been kindness itself. Several of them have called to see how Mary is and offer their sympathy. The little lady who lives opposite, Miss Amelia Green, she called with a bunch of flowers and I believe Mary was so touched she gave the woman a kiss and asked if she'd like to hold the baby.'

'She's a little love, that Miss Green. Living right opposite, I think she saw a lot of what went on next door. Mary never made friends with the neighbours, because of Tom. But they'll all rally around her now and the days of her walking with her head bent are gone.' Dot shifted her position because she was getting cramp in her legs. 'Has any more been said about her going out to work?'

John folded the paper and laid it on the floor at his side. 'Yes, we talked about it this afternoon. Now the funeral is over, she can get her life sorted out. She's starting Trudy on the bottle from tomorrow – that's a must if Maggie is going to mind her. And there's a job going in the canteen where I work, as soon as she feels well enough.'

'I'm glad for her, she deserves some happiness. She's only young, and I hope she meets a nice bloke who'll be good to her.'

John lowered his head, thinking, I'm not a bad bloke and I'd be very good to you. But you don't see me in that light. Oh Billy, if only I had half your confidence. You wouldn't be sitting here like a stuffed dummy, you'd be right out with it.

'A penny for yer thoughts?' Dot smiled at him. 'Yer were miles away.'

John shrugged his shoulders. 'I was just hoping and wishing.'

'Hoping and wishing for what?'

'Let me sit next to you, I want to talk to you.'

Dot uncurled her legs and pulled her skirt down over her knees. 'We're very serious all of a sudden, aren't we?'

John sat down beside her and reached for her hand. 'My Dear Delightful Dorothy, have you any idea of how I feel about you?'

'Same as I feel about you, I suppose. We're good friends.'

'That's not how I feel about you, Dorothy, and I can't go on any longer pretending that it is. From the first night I walked in here, although I didn't know it then, I've been in love with you. I've been hoping for a sign that you felt the same.'

She snatched her hand away. 'No, yer can't love me! I don't love you – I still love my husband.'

'Dot, your husband was probably a far better man than I'll ever be. He must have been for you to have loved him so much. And I'm not asking you to push him out of your heart, I'm just asking that you give me a little of it.'

Dot jumped to her feet, her hazel eyes troubled. 'Yer

431

shouldn't be saying these things. I don't want to hear any more. And I think you should leave now.'

His sigh was deep. 'And never come back, Dorothy? Is that what you want?'

She hesitated, then turned her head away. 'Now I know how yer feel, I wouldn't be comfortable in yer company, so I think it would be best if yer didn't come again. But I want yer to know I'm sorry it's turned out like this, John, because yer've been a good friend and I think a lot of yer. But I can't change the way I am.'

John reached for his coat and left the room without saying a word. And when Dot heard the front door close she dropped her head in her hands and cried. She didn't want to hurt him, but she had to be straight with him, it was only fair. How long she stood in the middle of the room she didn't know, but when she heard Katy's key in the lock, she moved fast. The last thing she wanted was for her daughter to find her crying.

'I was just on me way up to bed, sunshine, I'm dead beat. Put the light out after yer, there's a good girl.'

Katy was disappointed as she watched her mother climb the stairs. They always had a last cup of tea and a natter before they went to bed, exchanging bits of news. And Katy had so much to talk about tonight, she was looking forward to passing on some of Billy's exploits. Still, there's always tomorrow, she thought, as she got undressed in front of the hearth. The fire was on its last legs, but the room was still warm and it was better than standing with your teeth chattering in the freezing bedroom. After folding her clothes neatly on a chair, ready for work the next day, Katy put the guard in front of the fire. There was hardly any life in the coals, but it was better to be sure than sorry.

Katy crept up the stairs and felt her way across the bedroom to the bed. She slipped in beside her mother and put an arm around her waist to cuddle up, as they always did. It was a few seconds before she felt her mother's body tremble. 'Mam, are yer crying?'

'I'm all right, sunshine, no need to worry. It's just that the last week has been a nightmare and I thought if I had a good cry I might cry it out of me system.'

'Yeah, it'll do yer good, Mam.' Katy was satisfied and gave her mother a squeeze before closing her eyes, eager to dream about how wonderful life would be when her Billy was back home to stay.

Colin looked at the clock for the umpteenth time. 'Mr Kershaw's not half late tonight, Mam. He's usually here well before now.'

'He's not coming, sunshine.'

'Oh, is he going somewhere?'

Dot had been expecting this, and she knew what she had to say wouldn't be very well received. 'No, he's not coming any more. I thought it best if he stayed away because I don't want him wasting his life coming here every night.'

Katy came in from the kitchen where she'd been polishing her shoes. 'Yer didn't tell Mr Kershaw not to come any more, did yer, Mam?'

'It was for the best, sunshine, because he'll never meet a girl if he spends all his spare time here.'

Katy pulled a chair out and sat next to Colin. There was disbelief on both their faces. 'That was a mean thing to do, Mam, 'cos he's a nice man and he's been so good to us.'

Colin was nearly in tears. 'It was dead mean, and yer had no right. I like Mr Kershaw, he's me mate, and now I won't see him no more.' The full implication hit him. 'Does that mean I won't be able to go to the match tomorrow? And we won't be going to the pictures with him no more?'

Dot looked into the accusing eyes of her children. 'He'll be visiting Mary and the O'Connors, I'm sure, so ye're bound to see him again. But it's – er – it's just that John told me he likes me, and I don't like him the same way. I know he's a nice man, a good man, and I'd like to be friends with him, but that's all. I couldn't love anyone else, not after yer dad. I'd feel as though I was betraying him.'

Colin's eyes were glistening with tears. 'Mam, I didn't know me dad. Mr Kershaw's been like a dad to me, and now yer've sent him away.'

Katy could see the hurt in her mother's eyes and it grieved her. But this once she had to say what she thought was right.

'I'm sorry for what yer've done, Mam, because he's been kinder to us than anyone in our whole lives. I don't know how anyone could know him and not love him. I love him, and I love Billy. So yer see, yer can love two people at the same time. Love them differently, perhaps, but love them just the same.' With that, Katy got to her feet and went back to the kitchen. Her heart was filled with sadness for the man who had been the nearest thing to a father that she and Colin had ever known. She knew he loved them, her mother in particular, and she could imagine how unhappy he was now.

The atmosphere in the house was heavy that night, with no one even looking at each other, never mind talking. So Colin took himself off to bed at nine o'clock, there to cry himself to sleep. And Dot followed him at ten o'clock when she could no longer stand the silence. She lay in bed in the darkness, staring at the ceiling. She had expected the children to be upset, but certainly hadn't anticipated the strength of their feelings for John. As she stared into the darkness she conjured up Ted's face. She often did this and she'd see him as the young man she'd known and loved, and he was always smiling. But tonight he looked sad, as though he too was disappointed in her.

'Hello, Colin.' John had expected the knock on the door to be a neighbour and was surprised to see the boy standing there, shuffling his feet in embarrassment. 'Is there something wrong at home?'

'No, I just wanted to see yer.'

'You'd better come in, then, it's too cold to stand at the door.'

When the boy was seated, John asked, 'Would you like a cup of tea, or hot chocolate?'

Colin shook his head, thinking, Mr Kershaw's house is not half posh. But even if he lived in a shack, I'd still like him. 'Me mam thinks I'm playing out with Danny, so I can't stay long.' He clasped and unclasped his hands nervously, then blurted out, 'Why don't yer come to our house no more, Mr Kershaw? Me and Katy don't half miss yer.'

'And I miss you, too. But I'm sure your mother told you

why I stopped coming. She didn't want to be friends with me any more.'

'But she will be friends with yer, Mr Kershaw, she said she would.'

'The trouble is, I want to be more than friends, son, and that is something your mother doesn't want. I've seen her a few times over the last three weeks, in Mary's and the O'Connors', and we are on speaking terms, but that's about it.'

'Then why does me mam cry herself to sleep every night? She does, yer know, Mr Kershaw, 'cos our Katy tells me. Me sister said she thinks it's because she's missing you.'

'I don't think so, Colin. If that was the case she's had plenty of opportunities to show she's had a change of heart. I think we can safely say that anything that was ever there between your mother and I is now dead.'

'But me mam's stubborn, yer know she is! Me Auntie Betty and me Auntie Mary, and Mrs O'Connor, they're all upset that yer've fallen out. But me mam's too stubborn to be the one to give in. Perhaps if yer called at our house she'd welcome yer with open arms. Why don't yer give it a try, Mr Kershaw? Yer still like me mam, don't yer?'

'Of course I still like your mother, but I am not going to chance another rejection. You and Katy are welcome to visit me here at any time, I would be very happy to see you, as long as you ask permission from your mother.'

Colin stood up, his shoulders slumped and his face unhappy. 'She cries herself to sleep every night, Mr Kershaw, and it can only be because of you.'

John ruffled his hair. 'What will be, will be, son, I can't change things. Give my love to Katy, and tell her I often think of her.'

'I'll come and see yer again next week, Mr Kershaw, I won't ever forget yer.'

Something in the boy's voice alarmed John. 'Colin, you're not giving your mother a hard time over this, are you?'

'Well, she had no right, it was mean.'

'She had every right, son. Only she knows how she feels. It's not for others to criticise. So go home and give her

435

an extra big hug. She deserves it.'

Katy lifted her eyes from her plate to gaze across the table at her mother. She looked awfully pale, there were dark rings under her eyes and she'd lost her sparkle. 'Would yer like to come to the pictures with me, Mam? Keep me company?'

Dot seemed to shake herself, as though trying to rid herself of something unpleasant. 'Yeah, if yer want. It'll make a change to get out. But will you be all right on yer own, Colin? We won't be in until after ten.'

'I'll be all right. I can put meself to bed when I'm tired.'

When they were walking down the street, Katy linked arms with her mother. 'What's the matter, Mam? Yer've been down in the dumps for weeks now.'

'Oh, it's that Tom Campbell affair, it really got to me. But it'll wear off soon and I'll be back to being me bright and cheerful self.'

Katy felt like stopping and giving her mother a good shake. Why didn't she give in and admit she was wrong? Was she going to let her pig-headedness spoil her life? Was she prepared to go on crying herself to sleep every night? She might be fooling herself, but not her children who knew her every mood.

John threw the evening paper down in disgust. He couldn't concentrate, he'd read the same line over a dozen times. And he hadn't been able to get to sleep last night, either. All because Colin had told him that Dot cried herself to sleep every night. Was the boy right, that his mother *was* missing him – but was too stubborn to admit it? She was stubborn, all right, the most stubborn person John had ever known. He'd be round at the house in Edith Road like a shot if he thought that was the case, but he couldn't bear the idea of her rejecting him again.

Giving a deep sigh, John pushed himself up from the chair and went to the kitchen to make himself a cup of tea. He filled the kettle and put it on the stove, then struck a match. He stared at the flame for a while, until it was almost burning his fingers, then blew it out. Would she reject him again? Or would she welcome him with open arms, as Colin had said?

He had to know, and there was only one way to find out.

As John was walking down Edith Road, young Billy was walking up, and they met outside the Bakers' house. 'I didn't know you were home, Billy, this is a surprise.'

'Got home half an hour ago, Mr Kershaw, and it's for good this time. Katy doesn't know I'm home yet, so she'll get a surprise as well.'

Colin opened the door and his mouth gaped. His eyes lit up briefly at the sight of John, then clouded when he remembered his mam wasn't in. If the big man went away he might not come back again. 'Me mam's gone to the pictures with our Katy. Do yer want to come in and wait for them? They won't be long.'

John was about to decline, when Billy spoke. 'Nah, we'll go and meet them coming out of the pictures, and we'll walk them home. That's what we'll do, isn't it, Mr Kershaw?'

'Yes, that's fine by me,' John said, thinking it was coming to something when a fifteen-year-old boy had more control over his life than he himself had. 'The walk will do me good.' He gave Colin a knowing look. 'I might see you later, Colin. It all depends.'

'I'll wait up for yer, Mr Kershaw.' The boy wanted to say so much more but didn't know the right words. So he put his heart and his hope into the look he gave his hero. 'They've gone to the Carlton and I hope they're glad to see yer.'

Billy, happy in his ignorance of the situation, chatted as they walked. 'They'll get a surprise, won't they?'

'I think you could safely say that they'll be *very* surprised, Billy.'

They leaned against the wall of the Carlton picture house, and Billy talked of his life at sea, as though he was a seasoned sailor. Little did he know the torment John was going through. If it weren't for the young lad he'd have turned tail and run.

'Here they are!' Billy said, his voice high with excitement, happiness and mischief. 'Don't let them see us, Mr Kershaw. We'll walk behind them and give them a fright.'

It was all right for the young lad – he knew he'd get a rapturous welcome. John was apprehensive about his.

They followed mother and daughter for about twenty yards,

then Billy called, 'Can I walk yer home, Katy Baker?'

The couple turned, startled at first, then Katy's feet seemed to leave the ground as she flung herself at Billy. In their delight at being together they were oblivious to the older couple who stood staring at each other. It seemed an eternity before John could get the words out. 'Can I walk you home, Dorothy?'

Dot stared across the yards that separated them. Oh, how she'd missed this man. How empty the evenings had been, and how lonely the fireside chair looked without him in it. She put her hands on her hips and tilted her head. 'I've a good mind to clock you one, John Kershaw, making me wait all this time. Where've yer been for the last three blinkin' weeks?' She held out her hand and he walked towards her.

'I'm not letting a fifteen-year-old boy get the better of me this time, my Delectable, Delightful, Darling Dorothy. I'm going to kiss you right now, even if we are in the middle of Moss Lane.'

Katy looked over Billy's shoulder to see her mother wrapped in John's arms and being kissed. Not a friendly kiss, like he used to give her, but a real lovers' kiss. 'Come on, Billy, let's go. I want to get home before our Colin goes to bed, 'cos me mam's got a surprise present for him.'

Last Tram to Lime Street

Joan Jonker

Molly Bennett and Nellie McDonough were newly-weds when they became neighbours in a Liverpool street of two-up two-down terraced houses. Over the years their friendship has helped them through lean times when their kids were little and money was scarce. They've shared tears, heartache and laughter – and often their last ha'penny.

When Nellie's son, Steve, proposes to Molly's daughter, Jill, their happiness knows no bounds. The pair soon have their heads together planning a knees-up, jars-out party to celebrate.

But a cloud hangs over their plans when unsettling events in the community are brought to their notice. A new family, the Bradleys, have moved in up the street and they're a bad lot. Things start to go missing – toys, milk money, washing off the line – then an elderly widow is robbed of her purse, and Molly and Nellie decide enough is enough . . .

0 7472 5131 2

HEADLINE

Sweet Rosie O'Grady

Joan Jonker

Neighbours Molly Bennett and Nellie McDonough are thrilled to see their children settling down. Doreen waits patiently at home for Phil's next leave, accosting the postman every day in the hope of another letter, and Jill and Steve are saving up the pennies for their wedding. But the horrors of the Second World War threaten to separate loved ones forever and, with rationing and air raids on everyone's minds, the future looks bleak . . .

Then Rosie O'Grady arrives in Liverpool from Ireland to stay with Molly's parents, Bridie and Bob. With her sparkling blue eyes, childlike honesty and heart of gold, sweet Rosie O'Grady is like a breath of fresh air. A smile forever lights up her face and a joke is never far from her lips and Rosie soon has everyone crying with laughter – particularly when she makes no bones about setting her cap at Molly's unsuspecting son Tommy. Tommy Bennett thinks girls are nothing but a nuisance but he's in for a big surprise!

0 7472 5374 9

HEADLINE

If you enjoyed this book here is a selection of other bestselling titles from Headline